Broken Beyond
Healing

A Novel by

RICHARD MOSELEY

WESTBOW®
PRESS
A DIVISION OF THOMAS NELSON
& ZONDERVAN

WestBow Press books may be ordered through booksellers or by contacting:

WestBow Press
A Division of Thomas Nelson & Zondervan
1663 Liberty Drive
Bloomington, IN 47403
www.westbowpress.com
1 (866) 928-1240

ISBN: 978-1-4908-7500-2 (sc)
ISBN: 978-1-4908-7501-9 (hc)
ISBN: 978-1-4908-7502-6 (e)

Library of Congress Control Number: 2015908631

Print information available on the last page.

WestBow Press rev. date: 05/22/2015

One who is often reproved, yet remains stubborn,
will suddenly be broken beyond healing.
When the righteous are in authority,
The people rejoice;
But when the wicked rule, the people groan.
(Proverbs 29:1-2)

Homage to Faulkner

Nobody understood the American South better than William Faulkner. An image from the second work of his trilogy, *The Town*, illustrates one of our greatest failings: the lack of ability to face a problem, deal with it squarely, and find a solution. He expressed it vividly in the image of a nail driven into a tree, which no one would pull out so the tree could have healthy and normal growth. Many of us have known the pain and anguish of that tree:

> It was like we had had something in Jefferson for eighteen years and whether it had been right or wrong to begin with didn't matter any more now because it was ours we had lived with it and now it didn't even show a scar, like the nail driven into the tree three years ago that violated and outraged and anguished that tree. Except that the tree hasn't got much choice either: either to put principle above sap and refuse the outrage and next year's sap both, or accept the outrage and the sap for the privilege of going on being a tree as long as it can, until in time the nail disappears ...[or] until one day the saw or the axe goes into it and hits that old nail....
>
> No: not buried not healed or annealed into the tree but just cysted into it, alien and poison; not healed over but scabbed over with a scab which merely renewed itself, incapable of healing, like a signpost....

And now, after eighteen years, the saw of retribution, which we of course called that of righteousness and simple justice, was about to touch that secret hidden unhealed nail buried in the moral tree of our community—that nail not only corrupted and unhealed but unhealable because it was not just a sin but mortal sin—a thing which should not exist at all, whose very conception should be self annihilative, yet a sin which people seemed constantly and almost universally to commit with complete impunity....

(William Faulkner, *The Town*, New York, 1957, pp. 303, 305-307)

The Church Related College

Bishop G. Bromley Oxnam gave the following definition of what it means to be a Methodist church-related college or university at a meeting of school executives:

> The Church desires that the actual contribution of the campus in terms of religion shall be more than chapel, more or less successful, and a few courses in Bible or religion; it shall be of such a nature religiously as to justify support. I am frank to say that very few schools have realized in practice that being a first-rate educational institution is not enough. The question of the religious life of the student is not faced with the same concern with which the educational life of the student is faced. The Church must be convinced that we stand deliberately for something in the field of religion and in practices that religion demands. There is a Christian world-view, a Christian way of life, a Christian commitment to the Christian leader. One is your leader, even Christ. The effort of our colleges must be, in addition to educational service, evangelistic in the proper sense of that term....
>
> Our schools must be Christian without apology, and Methodist with pride. Our faculties must be. Our efforts should be to make the student Christian just as truly as we teach him to think. We must seek to graduate

Christians as certainly as we graduate doctors, lawyers, and musicians.

Board of Education of the Methodist Church, *Second Annual Report* (John O. Gross, secretary), 20-22 May 1942, 49-53.

This book is dedicated to my
students and parishoners
over the years.

Chapter 1

A CROOKED MAN

The Rev. Dr. Albert L. Morton, President of Worthington College for twenty-five years, stood looking out of the large window of his office on the first floor of Stephens Hall. His critical glance analyzed the huge oaks on undulating hills and the aging Victorian Gothic buildings on the old campus. At the beginning of the twentieth century, the Methodists moved their college to the site of an old plantation in Harrison, the state capitol. The Administration Building replaced the plantation home, and the students replaced the many slaves. Now Morton, like the lord of the manor of old, was the master of all he surveyed.

On this hot August afternoon, the campus was empty. The second summer session was over and the fall semester had not yet begun. Morton watched the eccentric old librarian carefully locking up the large front doors of the library. Nearly all of his books were back in their places on the shelves and he was satisfied. He shuffled off to the front parking lot, got into his old Chevy, and drove away. Now there was nobody in the landscape to mar Morton's view of his little empire.

Morton's secretary of almost seven years, Audrey Reich, watched him as she lay on the large couch in his office. His small but muscular body was silhouetted against the outside brilliance of a late summer day. The sunlight was defused and absorbed by the trees and grass of

1

the palatial old campus. The intensity of the light was strong enough, however, to give Morton's body a pale, intense, unreal, and ethereal bluish glow. Audrey shuddered and drew her dress, which was loosely draped over her body, tighter around her. She thought she knew him pretty well, yet there was something alien and frightening about him.

She still could not believe she had just been intimate with this man. For years she had hated and feared him. She considered taking the secretarial job a mistake. She wanted to complete her education, which was not easy for a woman in her fifties. She enjoyed the attention and respect she received from professors, students, and other staff persons. She could have found a job with better salary and benefits, but the prospect of a free education was enticing.

The statue-like image of Morton changed as he turned around to face Audrey. She was a little startled as his eyes met hers. His look seemed to question what she was thinking and what right she had to do so. She had always had trouble looking him directly in the eyes. His hypnotic and demanding gaze controlled and possessed her. She immediately lowered her eyes to the floor.

Morton was proudly looking at the new landscape painting, which was placed in a prominent place above the couch upon which Audrey was lying. It appeared to be an impressionistic view of a Mediterranean beach, styled in pastel shades. Morton loved to brag about how many thousand dollars the college paid for the work of this special artist to brighten his office. The black and white architect's drawing of campus buildings—which had hung there as long as anyone could remember—were now stored in the deep recesses of the basement. Morton was proud of his taste in matters of art and fashion. This was one of the many aspects of his character that made him consider himself better than others.

Looking up again, she surveyed his body, which no longer shone with an otherworldly glow. It seemed to remember all of the physical insults of almost sixty years. His left knee showed the results of a skiing accident in Colorado several years before. There were little scars on his face and upper body, which came from his high school and college years when he was a boxer. He had a well-earned reputation as a fighter with a proclivity for low blows. A pair of boxing gloves hung on a hook inside his office door.

Audrey's analytical gaze surveyed Morton's body from his balding head through his twisted facial features, down his torso to his scarred and twisted left knee and lower leg. She realized how vulnerable and even comical he appeared. He looked like a baby bird before its first feathers emerged. In this unguarded moment she was able to confirm what she had suspected for years: Morton's body actually listed to the left.

"He is crooked all over!" she thought. She had to catch herself and put her hand over her mouth to keep from bursting out laughing. "This is so ridiculous."

She turned her head so he could not read her thoughts. Why in the world had she given up husband and family for this strange little man? She looked at this unattractive body so near to her, yet still so remote, and totally unappealing. Why had she been involved with him a few minutes before, rolling on the plush carpet of his inter sanctum? There was never any consideration in Audrey's mind of love for him.

Her relation with him was clearly based on his needs and wants. She never flattered herself, thinking he might love her. That did not matter to her. Their relationship was merely a matter of convenience. She had never been involved in a relationship with a man for whom she cared not a whit. This gave her the luxury of an objectivity she was not used to. The whole thing was repugnant to her, but necessary.

She enjoyed the privileged status that being Morton's secretary and mistress afforded her. She was afraid of him, and knew that after she gave into him the first time there was no going back. So why not enjoy it while it lasted?

"What are you thinking about?" he asked in his silky pseudo-charming voice.

He was teasing her, testing her, demanding to own even her thoughts.

3

"Oh nothing, I was just remembering how wonderful it was to be with you," she purred.

She matched his mocking insincerity with her own. He obviously had paid her little heed, because, before she could respond, he had already turned and was walking toward the broad expanse of his well-ordered desk. He sat down in a chair large enough to make him appear quite small.

Turning once again inward, she asked herself, "How did all of this ever come about?"

She was not sure she knew, but she was sure the coincidence of many variables played in Morton's favor. He was able to manipulate any situation to his own devious purposes. That was perhaps wherein his genius lay. Would she have ever given in to him if it had not been for the Rotary money? Morton had worked for years to be elected District Governor, and had finally succeeded. The position involved a lot of travel, meeting with the clubs in the district. It got him in touch with the power structure of nearly every significant community in the area.

There was a two thousand dollar allocation for a secretary included with the Rotary expenses. This he used as bait to lure Audrey into traveling with him as his secretary as he went around speaking to clubs all over the district. Her former husband, Thomas Reich, had been doubtful when she first presented him with Morton's proposal that she travel with him, first for Rotary functions, and then when he spoke to college alumni chapters. Tom was no fool and immediately told her not to go with Morton. This was enough to call forth the rebel in her. The extra money sweetened the deal. Morton promised to buy her a new wardrobe, out of his expense account from the college, of course. The secretary of the president of Worthington College and the Rotary District Governor had to be well-dressed.

Morton was absorbed in going over some papers on his desk and continued to read and reflect on them for about ten minutes. Audrey remained stretched out on the large over-stuffed couch reflecting on what had just happened. She knew better than to ask

Morton what he was doing. If he wanted her to know, he would tell her. If not, he would scowl at her and let her know it was none of her business. Why had she been willing to defy her husband and give him cause for divorce? She saw the gulf widening between them. Tom had been a good husband, provider, and father to their crippled daughter and her two sons from a first marriage. He was nine years older than she, and she was tired of him, but not ready to be finished with him.

A great deal of Tom's attraction for Audrey was the fact that he was a banker. When the savings and loan institution (of which he was vice president) began to fail, he lost most his appeal for her. He retired before the federal government took over the failed bank, but he still lost most of his pension. She saw him as a broken old man.

"Tom's problem was that he was too honest for his own good," she thought. "Honesty was okay, but it was a second-rate virtue." First of all, one had to survive, and even thrive. She admired Morton's sixth sense of how to turn every situation to his advantage, no matter how badly he had blundered.

When Morton began to pressure her to go with him on his trips, she was highly annoyed. She was even more offended when he came on to her. Slowly, almost imperceptibly, her resistance began to wear away. Fatigue, uncertainty, boredom, and unhappiness combined to make her vulnerable. Morton was, if anything, persistent. One minute, he was flattering, solicitous, and terribly nice. The next, he was cruel, demanding, and cold. She never knew what to expect. This unnerved her. She became more and more willing to do anything to please him and keep in his good graces. She now realized he had played her like a virtuoso with a first-class violin.

She was flattered that Morton had been forced to use many of his techniques on her, from the crassest to the most sophisticated. Some of it was possibly unintentional or just second nature to Morton. Other aspects of his two-year campaign to master her, however, were deliberate and rather diabolical. He had plied her with quantities of liquor and drugs to weaken her resolve.

There were other things she did not understand about Morton. He was a clergyman, but he dabbled in aspects of religion that would have shocked members of the many churches which supported the college. In his academic work, he majored in Psychology and Sociology, with a PhD in the latter. From many other overt and covert sources, he had collected the elements of control and seduction he employed so effectively. Whatever all this meant, she knew she had not, did not now, and never would, love Morton. That perhaps made the relationship even more interesting. There were no intense feelings to complicate things. She was able to look at their affair objectively, as if she were another person.

But still, she was forced to ask, "Why me?" Was it just that she was there, in close enough proximity to be attainable and finally conquered? She knew he had had several previous affairs. She had arranged Morton's trips to Atlanta to visit Martha Welsh, one of his former secretaries. She had lied to Rebecca, Morton's wife, when she asked about her husband's trips. She had been called upon to cancel the airline tickets when Rebecca wanted to go with him on a trip that was supposed to be about business.

Morton corrupted her by making her do his dirty work. He had ruined the lives of so many, and she had assisted him. In carrying out his orders she had come under his spell. It was amazing how simply and easily he could force an apparently respectable person to do the most absurd things for him. He had taken over her will before he came to own her body. She visibly nodded her head to affirm her agreement with this important truth.

Morton looked up at her, peering over his half glasses, but said nothing. For years such insights had been painfully distasteful to Audrey. She had discussed all of Morton's little games with her husband before the affair began. She recognized his blatant dishonesty and double-dealing, and asked Tom to confirm her perceptions. Then she became one of his trophies and had to endure Tom's dumping on her all of the garbage she had given him. It was all quite curious.

Why had she been taken in by him? Had she simply gotten too close to the flame not to get burned?

Audrey deeply resented the looks people gave her on campus. She knew when heads turned what they probably were thinking or saying. They could not know what she had been through. Nobody understood. Why did they matter anyway?

She became more and more resentful, and felt more and more guilty. She learned from Morton to look down on almost everyone. She wore the new and elegant clothes he bought her. She walked with her back straight, her head up, and her feet pointed in the direction she was going and did not look back. As she became more and more hardened, she also was more and more alone.

The only way to deal with her loneliness was to spend more time with Morton. The problem was that when she was with him, she was even more alone. He never shared much of himself with her, although they were intimate more and more frequently.

Her reverie as she sat half-covered in his office was interrupted by Morton's rather stern voice, "Get dressed. It is getting late. Rebecca will be wondering where I am."

She sat up, stretched leisurely like a large tabby cat, and dutifully began to put back on her clothes.

"If the people out there only knew what goes on in this office!" she thought, shaking her head. Morton must have noticed the expression on her face, because he gave her a disapproving look.

Chapter 2

What Did I Know?

People on campus had begun to suspect something was going on between Morton and his secretary. It wasn't my business, so I was not interested in discussing it. Generally speaking, "stay out of it" was conventional wisdom on campus. I was driving across campus after having gone to my office on a brilliant Saturday afternoon in the late summer. I had picked up my mail at the Student Center and was driving home.

Then I spotted Morton, walking between Stephens Hall and the student center along the roadway that bridged the ravine. Dressed to the nines, but informally, in sport shirt and slacks, both carefully coordinated. Audrey, his secretary, was walking slowly some ten steps behind him. They were a study in contrast. He was almost dancing along the sidewalk, with his crooked gait, but this time he had a sheepish look on his face. For once, Audrey did not maintain her usual rigid posture and dour expression. She looked embarrassed and withdrawn.

Morton skipped over to my car, and hailed me by my full, proper name. No one on campus addressed me that way. I rolled down the window and greeted him. I could see the twisted smile plastered on his face.

"Good afternoon, Dr. Morton. How are you today?"

He was meaner than a snake, and yet I bowed to him, doing obeisance, as we all did. I spoke with him cautiously as my grip on the steering wheel tightened. I ended the conversation as soon as I could and drove away. My eyes were opened wide and my mouth agape.

How did I know? How does a man know when another man has just scored? I have reflected on that moment many times over the years. I can sincerely say that at the precise moment I shook his hand and saw the looks on their faces, I knew. This was dangerous knowledge, and I would pay dearly for it. Knowledge is responsibility. My life would never be the same because of that knowledge. How could I know what I knew and what would come of it? Therein hangs a tale.

In my mind's eye, I could see Morton standing at the large windows of his office surveying his plantation after he had sex with his secretary. He was a brooding presence controlling everything on that campus; I turned around and looked up at the dark, cold windows of that office. I could almost make out his snake eyes behind the windowpanes. I have never met another person whose gaze could paralyze me with fear. There was something hypnotic about the eyes unevenly set in his mask-like face. Looking into them was like starring at a standing cobra—rigid, weaving back and forth, ready to strike. He was the serpent in this beautiful Eden in which we lived and worked.

What would become of this old campus with its massive trees, expansive greens, and towering pseudo-Gothic buildings? The new buildings, which Morton had built with such fanfare, never seemed to be part of the landscape. His campaign to revive the campus was deceptive, like everything he did. Was it not simply a way of letting the old buildings rot while attention was focused elsewhere? The huge amounts borrowed for the construction of these monuments to the glory of Morton proved difficult to repay with the changing economy and decreasing student enrollment.

The new buildings were supposed to herald a new era. They clashed creatively with the old structures, however, not just because of their style of architecture, but also because of their very existence in this place. The same was true of so many of us who came there with our holy innocence. We sincerely thought we would change this campus, make it be what it claimed to be, and foster the excellence we so often spoke about. How naïve we were! Our despair was part of the sadness that hung over the campus like dark storm clouds.

Anything that remained on this campus long was forced to conform and become part of the somber landscape. Tall and noble structures were supposed to challenge young minds while they housed them for four years and offered places for growth and study. Academic improvements were intended to strengthen existing programs. But the additions to the curriculum were manipulated and robbed of their significance. A constant parade of new and able administrative, staff, and faculty personnel should have enriched our community with talent and energy. Many of us thought we would leave some accomplishments to accumulate and energize this place. After we left, however, it was as if we had passed through some Dead Sea of the spirit, which absorbed vast amounts of life and gave back nothing, a black hole of the soul, which took vast amounts of energy in and never released it.

The new monumental red brick gateway through which I drove as I left the campus that day was built in Morton's honor by one of the many rich old ladies whose money he courted. It felt strange and rather disgusting driving through it, especially after what I had just witnessed. What had he ever done that was worthy of such an honor? What about all of us who lived, taught, and worked there over the years? Where was our monument? We were turned away with nothing to remember us except the memory of the students we taught.

Chapter 3

THE HOLINESS OF THIS PLACE

Several months following my encounter with Morton and his secretary, I came back to the campus early on a Saturday morning. I really did not want to see anyone—just to be there. I needed time to digest what I had seen and what it meant to my life and career. Without another living soul around, the old campus was majestically quiet and filled with its own powerful memories. I meditated on the profound beauty and peacefulness of the green. There was a gentle breeze blowing through the trees. The tall oaks and pines seemed alerted to the profound change in the weather that was coming. For the moment, however, everything was hushed and lulled into the somnambulant late southern summer.

I walked across the roadway, which formed a land bridge blocking off the ravine in the middle of the campus. I looked down into the amphitheater where we had homecomings, graduations, concerts, and other important events. When I walked down into the ravine, it was as if I had entered another dimension. The amoral and confused world I had left on the upper level of the campus was transcended by the spiritual and mystical beauty of a grove of trees with the stream running through it.

I was greeted by a large red Irish Setter, which galloped up to me as I walked the pathway. He must have overheard me mumbling to myself and wondered what was wrong with this crazy person. I wanted to apologize for interrupting his joyous romp, but thought the better of it, and reached over to pet him instead. He was quite friendly, and became a good therapist for me with my troubled thoughts.

On this beautiful campus, I felt I came to understand God's purposes in creation. There was a sense of peace and serenity that was deeply meaningful to me. It was one of those places in this country that was sacred to Native Americans for centuries before Europeans came to desacralize them.

One can tell such places, without any knowledge of the past, from a profound sense of a spiritual presence. It was something I found during my childhood in the bottomland near my home in Louisiana. I remember walking down a hillside to a giant magnolia tree beside a meandering stream. In the late spring, the giant white flowers perfumed the entire area with a heavenly fragrance. I felt a gentle breeze on the back of my neck, as if a divine being had passed by. There was a sense of holiness and wholeness that made me want to stop and pray.

I sat down and looked around at the beauty of this place and felt I was worshipping the God who created it. My attention returned to the old dog. Why couldn't I do what he was doing: simply roam and amble about the green and soak up the beauty and tranquility? I looked for his master or mistress, with whom I assumed he was out walking, but found no one. He had on a collar with a current vaccination tag, so I figured he lived nearby and would find his way back home. Meanwhile, I was thankful for his visit. What he needed was a romp through the lush hills and valleys of this old campus. He would return home the better for his explorations.

There was an early mist rising from the low areas following last night's shower. Years ago we laughingly called these vapors the campus "miasma." Being from Louisiana, I well knew the miasmatic theory that disease, contagion, and bad karma were all caused by "bad air" (as in mal-aria). My great-grandfather was a doctor in New Orleans who labored through the epidemics of yellow fever and malaria. He lived at a time when the germ theory was beginning to cause a revolution that enabled the advances we take for granted. Dirty hands were more dangerous than foul air.

Previously, miasma, the poisonous vapors or mist filled with particles of decomposed matter (*miasmata*), were seen as the cause of illness and death. For the ancient Greeks, the miasma had a contagious power with an independent life of its own. Society was chronically infected until it was purged of the evil perpetrated by wrongdoers. Miasma contaminated the entire family of Atreus, where one violent crime led to another. Cleansing the atmosphere and restoring society required the sacrificial action of heroic individuals. However, attempts to cleanse a city or a society from miasma might also have the opposite effect—reinforcing the miasma, or significantly increasing its effect.

Our campus desperately needed to be cleaned from the pollution Morton and his gang represented. This was especially significant because of the cultures and societies that lived on the land before the moving of the college from Cochetta to Harrison. The plantation on the new site had slave quarters up on the hillside where the women's dormitories were later located. Individuals who lived there honored the old African gods from beyond the sea. At the same time they sang spiritual songs and prayed to the Christian God. They longed for cleansing divine power to free them from the contagion of the miasma of slavery. I could hear the woeful and yet hopeful melody of the spiritual, "My Lord, What a Morning," echoing through the hills and valleys of the campus.

Long before the plantation culture settled on this land, it was the site of a Creek Indian village. The village was located on the high ground above the confluence of two streams. The Administration Building was later built on that hill. In the midst of the village was a large public square where important gatherings and events took place, including the annual Green Corn ceremony. It was the equivalent of the biblical celebration of the first fruits, essentially a harvest festival, celebrating the gathering of the new crop of corn.

The men of the tribe sat around a large ceremonial bonfire, "the Grandfather Fire." It was the focus of the songs and prayers of the people. During the festival, the great fire was considered to be a living sacred being, transmitting prayers upward in the smoke to the gods. This was a new year's celebration and a ceremony of renewal. One of the central aspects of the festival was the annual trial of pending violations of the laws and customs of the tribe. The gathered leaders served as a tribunal, which granted forgiveness for those judged to be guilty of venial crimes, such as theft or disrespect. For those convicted of rape, murder, and other capitol offenses, the sentence was either execution or banishment.

Down in the ravine, there was a large grove with a stream running through it. The stream was often shrouded in mist. During the festival, the people avoided it until the festival was finished. It was thought that the accumulated evils of the year's pollution settled there. The acts of bringing in the harvest, kindling a large fire, and administering justice brought about the lifting of the heavy mists of ambiguity, guilt, and contagion from the people.

Following the harvest festivals, the elders of the tribe gathered in the grove beside the stream. They prayed for cleansing, healing, and renewal in the coming year.

During normal times, individuals would make pilgrimage to this grove to pray, engage in contemplation, make important decisions, celebrate victories, or mourn loved ones. This grove beside the living stream of water was regarded as magical, possessing powerful medicine. Gods dwelt in these woods. The spirits of the dead ancestors hovered near. The magic here was usually beneficial, but also at times it could be malevolent, capricious, and even comical. One must be careful, and especially discerning, of the nature and mood of the spirits.

The power of the magic of this beautiful area touched the lives of human beings and changed things. Prayers were answered. Wishes granted. Curses overcome. Revenge carried out. Visitors from beyond transcended the limitations set on human existence and made life better. There was a redeeming quality about this place, which helped lift the miasma and restore the balance of good and evil.

I looked down at this area and inhaled the humid heavy air. I lived and worked for some of the best years of my life under the curse of an oppressive cloud that hung over the land. We all did. There could be healing after the Green Corn was harvested, the purifying Grandfather Fire enkindled, and justice administered; then the bright harvest sun would break through the clouds and the spirits of redemption, reconciliation, and renewal would begin to move about the land.

I heard the red Setter's mistress call and whistle for him.

"Brad-ley," she shouted.

What a terrible name for a dog! No wonder he needed to get out here where he could be a regular dog. He probably had a pedigree with papers to prove his noble lineage. Poor dog! As he bounded off, I realized it was time for me to leave too.

Chapter 4

A Momentous Choice

My association with Worthington College began several years earlier. It was the spring of 1974. I had finished my course work for my doctorate and completed my dissertation. I was waiting for my committee to meet and evaluate my work. Meanwhile, I was serving the mandatory year under appointment for ordination.

My wife, Julie, and I were sitting in the living room of the second parsonage of the church in the Texas city where I was serving as associate pastor. While we were talking, the telephone rang. It was Dean William Van Dale calling to ask me to come for an interview at Worthington College. I had sent out my curriculum vitae to over one hundred colleges and universities. I was not sure how effective these letters would be. I had received some responses, but nothing that was really interesting.

Then out of the blue, at the last minute, Van Dale called. I told him I would need some time to think about it and discuss it with my wife. I promised to call him back the next day.

I had already been invited to interview for a position at a large church in southwest Texas. The pastor invited me to come to San Antonio and meet with his staff and his lay leaders. He was intense, and definitely interested in my becoming his associate. His lay leaders were cordial. I knew the interview went well. The salary was excellent, and I could expect a raise the first of the year.

The Worthington interview also went well. I already knew a lot about the situation and about President Albert L. Morton. I had a friend from graduate school, Blair Smith, who had studied under the same advisor. Blair had been fired several years earlier from the position for which I was being interviewed. The young professor who had been there in the intervening two years had left suddenly. Dr. Ellen Patillo retired after being at the college for a number of years. They were asking me to replace two people! Something about all of this did not smell good.

The college had 430 students, down from double that number when Morton became president, and one quarter the size from the period following World War II. There had been nothing but conflict since the Morton era began. His first academic dean was a terrible mistake. Morton was able to place all the blame on him for the state of affairs at the college. Six young Turks from the faculty had gone to the trustees to demand that both the president and the dean resign. It took Morton a while to get rid of them. Three of them were heads of departents, including the Religiion Department.

Meanwhile, Morton was able to bring in Van Dale as the new dean. Van Dale had been a professor in the education department of the college in Iowa where he and Morton had worked. Morton served as chaplain and then academic dean. We could not find any record of his having ever taught, except as a graduate assistant while he was working on his PhD.

Van Dale had little administrative experience, but might have been a good dean at Worthington, if Morton had left him alone. I was anxious to meet Morton and see what kind of person he was. Blair would not tell me much about him, only that I could not trust him. In our first conversation, I verified that by asking him about the attempted coup and Blair's involvement in it. He lied to me about it and I let him know I knew he was lying.

There went that job, I thought. I kept on playing the game, however, and rather enjoyed it, knowing it would not lead anywhere. I tried to find out how many others were being interviewed for the position. I never got a straight answer. The main reason was because I was the only one. I found out later that Morton never brought in more than two candidates to interview for a position if he could help it. I had conversations with the head of the department, Van Dale, and a committee of students selected to meet with me. These were pleasant enough and informative. Blair suggested I get in touch with the pastor of a local church, Mark Austin, who was a member of the board of trustees of the college. When I told Mark who I was and why I was in town, he was cordial and supportive. He asked if he could come over that night and talk with me at the local motel where I was staying.

When I met Mark and shook his hand, I immediately liked and trusted him. He sat down, put his feet on the little coffee table, and sipped a beer while we talked for several hours that night. He frankly and openly told me the college had many problems and Morton was the source of most of them. He acknowledged Morton's representatives were forcing him off the board of trustees.

After we had discussed the college from every angle, he said the magic words: "Come anyway, we need you!" I do not know that anything else he might have said would have had the same effect on me.

Before I left to travel home, Morton offered me the job, to begin in the summer semester. I told him I would have to think about it and discuss it with my wife. I never expected to receive an offer. I knew too much. Even if things had been different, nobody ever offers you a job right off the bat. But Morton did. What did it mean?

I shared all I knew with Julie. I waited. Van Dale called several times before I gave him an answer. The church in Texas offered an ideal situation with a parsonage and a good salary. Worthington, on the other hand, was rather iffy, with a poor salary and no housing.

I was sure Morton was not trustworthy and that the college was in trouble. It was hard calling the pastor in San Antonio. I did not realize it, but he had gone all out for me. My turning him down did not help his position in the church. I tried to reassure him how much

I respected him and appreciated his confidence in me. I wrote a long letter to him and to the church. I asked myself whether I was a fool. How could I turn down the church job in Texas for the situation at Worthington? The answer was simple: I wanted to teach. I had spent most of my life preparing for this career and did not want to change course.

During our time in Texas, Julie became pregnant with our second child. She was due the end of September, near her own birthday. We knew wherever we moved would be the birthplace of our new baby. The pregnancy went well. We went to the Annual Conference in Amarillo, where I was ordained a permanent elder in the United Methodist Church. This is what we had come for, and I was pleased to have completed my requirements for full conference membership. Almost as soon as I became a member of the Northwest Texas Annual Conference, I applied to change conferences.

Chapter 5

HE'S MY FATHER

In addition to my appointment to teach at Worthington, I requested the bishop assign me to a small charge in the country. The salary at the college was not large. I also wanted to keep up my skills as a pastor. I was assigned a two-church charge, with both churches being about twenty miles from Harrison, and ten miles apart. It was not a parish pastors were lining up to serve. It was nowhere politically. I liked that a lot. There were good people in both churches. They were conservative in politics and fanatics in football, like most southerners. It was a decidedly Baptist area, and the Methodist churches were strongly tinged with Baptist theology. I soon learned the difference between denominations when I was asked how I felt about mixed marriages. This did not refer to atheist-religious, Jewish-Christian, or Protestant-Catholic unions. It was Methodist-Baptist!

Moving was not complicated. We did not have a lot of furniture. The parsonage we had lived in was furnished. We got our treasured possessions packed together and loaded together on a moving truck, and said goodbye to Texas. Since the college paid our moving expenses, we were not worried about the cost. There was a rather ancient parsonage at one of the churches. No one had lived in it for a while, and there was a reason.

The churches had used student pastors from the college who were planning to go on to seminary. This was not a good arrangement for pastors or churches. It was necessary, however, because there were not enough pastors, and because the churches could not pay for a full-time ordained minister. When we saw the parsonage we were almost ill, but we were determined to tough it out, at least for the summer. The fact that we could see light through the floorboards told us it would not be a good place to live in the winter.

Our son Stephen was a precocious three-year-old. He crawled around the floor and found dead roaches. We realized a thorough cleaning was essential. There was an old, rather pitiful piano in the living room. Steve would climb up, sit on the bench, and bang on the keys. It was the summer of Nixon's discontent, and we did not realize how much Steve had learned about it from watching television. He began a life long preoccupation with current affairs. As he accompanied himself on the piano, he sang, "President Nixon talked to some of his friends, if he told the truth, if he told the truth." This little song could go on and on indefinitely. We were shocked by how much our little man understood about the world of politics.

The chair of the Department of Religion and Philosophy was Dr. Phillip Maddox. He was supportive and warmly welcomed us. He had been a missionary and seminary professor in the Philippines for a number of years. He and his family returned to the United States because his oldest son had serious psychological problems, which could not be treated abroad. He invited Julie to teach classes in Christian Education. We were then a four-person department: Two of us full-time. Our part-time colleagues included Julie, who taught a Christian Education course each semester; and a local rabbi, who taught a History of Judaism course in the fall and a course in the Old Testament Prophets in the spring.

Phil and I divided up the course offerings according to our experience and preference: We both taught sections of Old and New Testament. Phil taught a Jesus course and I taught a course on St. Paul's career and theology. He taught Logic and I taught Ethics. I alternated a two-semester course in the History of Western Philosophy with a similar two-semester course in Church History.

Phil taught a course in Eastern Religions. We team-taught a two-semester philosophy course in Contemporary Issues.

We were busy and performed an essential function within the college. Back in the 1950s, the president of Coca Cola in the southern part of the state set up a trust fund that provided an annual grant to three different church-related colleges: Baptist, Presbyterian, and Methodist. The trustees of the soft drink company administered the trust. The donor wrote a document setting out his reasons for the endowment and the restrictions he placed on it. It was, in many ways, dated to the post-war Eisenhower era, but also expressive of what the message and mission of the church-related college should be. The amount given to the college was different each year, depending on the interest earned on the principle amount held in trust. It could be as much as a million dollars in a good year.

The document was patriotic and expressive of what this country meant to this successful corporate executive. It also was a confession of faith in which he detailed his dedication to the church, to the biblical faith, and to Christian ethics. He required the three colleges in question to teach the Old and New Testaments to every entering student. He also required two additional advanced courses before graduation which were related to the Bible and the Christian tradition.

We determined that most of the courses taught in our department were eligible to fulfill the upper level requirements. While they might not all be directly related to the Bible, they were based on biblical teachings and ethical principles. We clearly stretched the original intention of the donor to fit out curriculum. Of the three schools, however, we were closest to the intentions of the donor.

The first classes I taught at Worthington were during the summer semester of 1974. I had an Old Testament class, and a Contemporary Issues class (which was not team-taught in the summer). I worked constantly in my office and at the parsonage getting my class notes ready, especially for the Bible courses. I received the list of students from the registrar the first day of classes. As I called the roll in the philosophy course, I noticed a Robert George Walker, Jr. at the end of the list.

I read the name and tried to be funny, asking, "No kin to the governor?"

His response was immediate, "That's my father."

That left me with my mouth wide open. His father was the multi-term governor of the state, and one of the primary exponents of segregation in the country. After his father could not be elected for another consecutive term, his mother served as governor. Walker, Sr. then ran for president and was seriously wounded in an assassination attempt.

Little Bob, or Rob, was less powerfully built than his father. Many said he was more his mother's son than his father's. The father was bellicose and the mother gracious and compassionate. She died of cancer, and Robert, Sr. remarried. Junior had already attended two other institutions of higher learning, both state schools. He had not done well and lost interest. He was basically a C student, who would, nevertheless, eventually serve a term as State Treasurer.

Rob was quite honest with us. The class attempted to study relevant positions in the history of philosophy and relate them to issues in the society of the day, such as violence, racism, feminism, homelessness, poverty, etc.

Rob entered readily into our discussions. He was generally quiet and reserved, but he had a lot of ideas and was articulate in expressing them. He told us one day early in the class that he had tried "drugs, sex, and rock and roll" in an attempt to find himself. This was not meant to be amusing. He had really done those things. He wanted most of all to find out who he was, other than the son of the governor. It was hard not to give him special consideration, but he asked me to treat him like any other member of the class.

Chapter 6

THE BIRTH OF OUR DAUGHTER

After the summer semesters were over, we searched for a home in Harrison close to the college and to the hospital where our daughter would be born. It also needed to be on the southern side of the city, well on the way to one of my churches. We were satisfied with a second story apartment where the movers could get our possessions up the winding stairway. Our years there were some of the happiest of our lives, with our family and our new vocations.

We began the fall semester and nervously anticipated the birth of our child. Her due date was at the end of September. We were stretched between the conference health insurance back in Texas and our new conference insurance. If we did nothing, the old insurance would expire at the end of September and we would enter the new program with a real pre-existing condition. Since we did not know the date the stork was coming, we had to renew the Texas insurance for another quarter, so we were paying premiums in both conferences. Catherine, never to be rushed, came early morning on the second of October.

Our students were well aware the birth was immanent and were looking forward to a day off. Two students were preachers' daughters and roommates. One of them, Sara Richards, was our regular babysitter. She had agreed to be on call to stay with Steve when we went to the hospital. Her roommate was ready to come if she was not able to get there. They both said they would refuse any pay that night. Julie's water broke at the dinner hour. I was so calm, cool, and collected that Julie worried she would go into hard labor before we got to the hospital. I was an expert. It was our *second* child. I called Sarah for backup and she came as fast as she could. I took Julie to the hospital and we began preparations for the delivery. We took breast-feeding and natural childbirth classes. Dr. Kavenaugh was a real character, but we had confidence in him.

I was not allowed to be at the hospital at all for Stephen's birth in Germany, and Julie had no success in nursing him. Dr. Kavenaugh had recently had a change of heart. I was one of the first fathers he allowed to be present for the great event. He let me know he had birthed 10,000 babies without my help. He was paternal, calling mothers "honey," "sweetheart," and "baby." He was humorous, and he was known as the best doctor in the area.

I was with Julie in the delivery area while she was in labor. We were a team. When things got tough, I was there massaging, counting, and helping her to weather the waves. Unfortunately, there was an older nurse who kicked me out when the doctor came to check Julie. This, of course, interrupted the rhythm and caused Julie needless pain and worry. When they took her to delivery, I was invited to join the doctor to scrub and get suited up. He gave me directions and we went in. He carefully studied her progress and then informed me of a complication: The umbilical chord was twisted around our baby's neck. He calmly told me he was going to watch the heart rate and then take the baby when it got too fast. Meanwhile, the doctor prepared Julie with an epidural and an episiotomy. We stood beside Julie just watching and waiting. Then Dr. Kavenaugh told me that since Julie could not feel the contractions, I was responsible for letting him know when she had one.

He immediately unnerved me by shouting, "You just missed one!" After quietly waiting about ten minutes, he read the heart rate and then proceeded at warp speed, reaching in, removing the chord from around Catherine's neck and pulling her out, all nine pounds of her.

Once they got her cleaned up, she gave that first courageous cry, complaining about being forced from her really nice digs. She colored up and looked absolutely beautiful. I was very proud of both her and her mother. I got home about 2:00 a.m. and took Sarah back to her dorm. I got up at my regular time and was at my 8:00 a.m. Religion 101 class on time. They students had gotten word and were excited about the birth of our daughter, but terribly disappointed they did not get a free cut that day.

Dr. Kavenaugh said he was pleased everything had gone well with the birth. He also told us, however, that after the birth of such a large baby, Julie should not try to have another child. He recommended she have her tubes tied. I wanted to reserve the option of another child. Julie told me I was free to give birth any time, but she was done. Her wish, and the fact that we were doubled up on insurance, made the decision rather easy. Steve was proud of his new little sister and became a dedicated big brother.

Chapter 7

RELIGION 101

I taught two sections of the Bible courses every Monday, Wednesday, and Friday in the fall and spring semesters and one session of each every summer for eighteen years. Even when I was chair of the department, I did not try to farm them out to other faculty. I enjoyed them and considered each class a challenge. The students were primarily freshmen, and these were large classes for our school. Since everyone had to have six hours of Bible, we got all kinds of students. I tried to make clear the first day of class that there were different ways of studying the Bible: They included historical, cultural, sociological, devotional, and confessional. I told them our study was part of a liberal arts program, and that we would not approach the devotional and confessional dimensions. I assured them, although I was an ordained minister, I would teach objectively and not subjectively. I would not grade them on their faith, or lack thereof.

I knew there would be students who were quite religious and did not want to have anything taken away from them. Others did not want to have religion inflicted on them. In addition to a majority of Christian students, there were Jews, Muslims, and members of other religions. There were agnostics and atheists as well. I looked forward to the multiplicity of viewpoints. You would scarcely get that in any other discipline. I tried to reassure everyone.

Conventional wisdom is that you teach to the middle. I purposely taught to the extremes. I asked non-Christians and non-believers not to try to impress me by writing essays in which they expressed a belief stance that was not authentic. I wanted to know what they really thought, and not what they thought I wanted them to say. I encouraged any and all questions. When I became confident enough, I told them I did not know everything about the Bible and would not be able to answer all their questions. I used the example of Cain's wife. I told them I did not know where she came from.

One semester, in my lecture on the patriarchs, I stressed that they were more than just members of an ancient family. They were epic heroes and, as such, exemplified the character traits most admired by the Israelite culture. Abraham was the classic grandfather. He was quiet, wise, and righteous. Paul said he lived "by faith." Isaac, was blind, but had spiritual insight, and was a strong judge of character. Jacob was initially a trickster, who, like Prince Hal, later became a serious leader. He was the father of the twelve sons who became the twelve tribes. Joseph was a person of strong moral conviction who was able to resist temptation and make the best of bad situations.

These characterizations were meant to be suggestive rather than definitive. I made clear that the brief description of Isaac was because there is so little information in the text. He is at the end of the Abraham narrative and at the beginning of the Jacob stories. I believe I had a feel for him and tremendous admiration, but I was clearly reading into the story.

I used this method to humanize these major figures. I was not prepared for one student's reaction. Her name was Rebecca, or Becky, as she was known. "You're not being fair to Isaac," she avowed. I told her it was not my intention to discriminate against this worthy figure, but I could only express what I honestly knew.

She became indignant when I told her we needed to move on. She turned her desk around and gave me her back the rest of the hour. After class, she picked up her things and quickly marched out. I asked her if she would come to my office to discuss her displeasure with me, but she did not respond. I never saw her again. Since that time, I have always been careful in talking about Isaac, but I really have no more clues to his personality.

The most humorous thing that ever happened to me during the eighteen years in which I taught at Worthington was on an October morning in my 9:00 a.m. Old Testament class. I was illustrating the importance of studying the map of the little country of Israel. I told the students that God gave them two eyes: One to read the timeline I had given them, and the other to study the map at the rear of their biblical text. I had several large maps mounted at the front of the classroom. I was talking about the fifty by one hundred fifty mile area from Dan to Beersheba. I referred to the mountains in the north and the valleys in the south with Jerusalem in the middle. I had practiced this many times, so I could pull down the old roller shade maps with my right hand without looking and point at Jerusalem while continuing my lecture. This time there was an explosion of hysterical laughter. I looked at the map and burst out laughing too.

My right index finger was touching the navel of Miss October. When things calmed down, I was foolish enough to try to conduct the rest of my lecture.

Several years later, a young man confessed to me he had sacrificed the centerfold of the October issue of *Playboy* in order to tape it to my map. He was a tennis pro who was hired by the school to teach tennis in exchange for allowing him to pursue his education at Worthington. He was in his mid-twenties, and older than most of the others in the class. He had a wicked sense of humor. He was afraid to tell me he was the perpetrator, but finally did so because of our friendship. I told him I thought it was hilarious and I was not mad at him. I assured him I never pulled down my map without first looking at it.

It was just as well, because I had a repeat performance. Later that year, I started to pull down a map and caught a glimpse of a centerfold from *Hustler*. I let the map go immediately and it clattered as it rolled back up. I stuttered and stumbled before I regained my composure and continued with my lecture. The *Hustler* centerfold was a real shock and entirely inappropriate. I do not think anyone else knew it was there (except the person who taped it up there, of course).

After that, the idea of taping up centerfolds seemed passé, except for one other incident in a seminar my colleague Phil Maddox was leading in the large meeting room in the Student Center. It was an adult group of non-students who had come to the college for a special lecture on the Bible. Phil told them about what had happened to me with my map and then pulled down a map he had installed for his lecture. As he did so, the picture of another playmate appeared. He had no idea it was there and was doubly embarrassed because it seemed like he had set things up by mentioning what happened to me.

I had all sorts of other bizarre happenings during my years of teaching. The second floor classroom in Stephens Hall where I taught the Bible classes was subject to critter invasions. I had sparrows make love on the fire escape outside the windows at the front of the room while I was trying to lecture.

Wasps came indoors as it began to get cold in the fall. I never understood why my classroom was so popular for insects, but we sure got more than our share. Students were understandably frightened. I had people jump up and run out of the room in horror. My advice was to sit still and not to swat them. I occasionally modeled this when they lighted on me as I was teaching. During class one day, I had one crawl across the bridge of my glasses. I never flinched.

One of my bravest students was a wonderful young lady who was intelligent, funny, talented, and extremely dedicated. She was one of our department majors and planned a career in church music. She had a beautiful voice and was a talented pianist. She was also an albino. The most obvious handicap was her sight. It was difficult for her to take tests because she had difficulty in reading. It took her longer to complete her work. She and I were the only ones remaining in the classroom as she finished her final in an upper level course. A wasp landed on her cheek. She took my advice and kept on with her work. The wasp stung her and she cried in pain. She would not leave her seat until she finished the test, however. I will never forget her courage and perseverance. She wanted most of all to be treated as a regular student, with no attention paid to her handicap. She was a good sport and a fun person.

I had an unexpectedly large counseling load. Morton manipulated the office of chaplain, like every other position on campus. There were long periods when there was no chaplain. At other times the position was filled by persons who could not relate to the students. Perhaps the best and most devoted chaplain we had during my tenure was a former student who had gone to seminary and came back to his alma mater to work with students. He had been quite active as a student with a musical group that played at a Methodist beach ministry on the coast during the summer. He sang with the group and was generally its leader. They also played at numerous events on campus and in churches around the conference during the school year. He was handsome and musically gifted. The girls went crazy over him.

When he returned, his music was still an important part of his ministry. He was close enough in age to the students to relate to them. He was married when he went off to seminary. I was honored to baptize their son. Unfortunately, the marriage failed. We were a bit scandalized when he began dating a student while serving as chaplain. It was all out in the open, however. She was an outstanding student who also performed with his little band. She had a wonderful personality and was one of my favorite people. They asked me to officiate at their wedding on campus in the Chapel. It was a show-biz wedding where they sang their vows to each other and the band played the music for the ceremony. It was a beautiful wedding and the students thought it was cool.

Another chaplain was a pastor in the conference who was the parent of two students whom Julie and I had taught at the college. He was taking some time out of the parish because of burnout and some bad habits. He had one of the best collections of empty Old

Turkey whiskey bottles I have ever seen. They were attractively displayed in his office. One might ask how appropriate they were, however. He had been active in the Civil Rights struggle and was a strong partisan on the liberal side of the conference (which meant the anti-segregation party). One year he was a counter of ballots for General Conference delegates. He was caught stuffing the ballot box to prevent conservative delegates from being elected. He would literally do anything for a cause in which he believed. He was not a chaplain to whom the students could relate.

The last chaplain while I was at the school was a retired Air Force colonel, Steve Brunner, who was chosen because he was "a good soldier." He was pleasant enough, but a yes man to Morton who could not be trusted. Steve referred to Morton as "the Boss," and never questioned anything he said. The students generally related to him as a part of the administration, but not as someone who would minister to their needs or with whom they could have confidential conversations. I tried to fill this as best as I could.

Chapter 8

FACULTY MEETINGS

Our faculty meetings were truly depressing events. They lacked purpose and direction. We were all going through the motions and pretending to be a faculty. Meetings were set for the third Friday of each month, in the late afternoon. This was a terrible time for everyone, and, we were sure, intentionally so. We were tired and wanted to go home to begin the weekend. If one could possibly find an excuse to be absent, they used it. Some faculty members never attended, for example Manfred Schulz. He had been through his battle with Morton. He knew he would never get any rewards for his efforts. There was little that could be done to him, however, as long as he knew how to lay low and just teach his students, with little recognition, encouragement, or personal advancement. It was a shame because he had so much to offer.

We met in the Private Dining Room in the Cafeteria. This room was not used during the regular schedule of student meals. If we ran late, however, the activity in the dining hall began to get loud. We were all tired, hungry, and ready to go home. The smell of the food and the activity in the next room caused us to try to keep it short. In this kind of atmosphere, it was highly unlikely anything creative would happen. Van Dale presided and Registrar Sarah Robinson acted as secretary, keeping the minutes of our meetings. The two of them ran the academic program of the college.

Morton provided a kind of sideshow. He was almost always at faculty meetings, sitting silently and often taking notes. Most of us dared not question or challenge him. He basically was there to keep the faculty in line, but it was Van Dale's fault if things ever got out of hand. Morton's main job was fund-raising, or as Adam crudely expressed it, the "wooing of rich little old ladies."

At the beginning of each semester, Morton would give the faculty a speech, supposedly on the state of the college. He also would speak several times a year at convocations, at graduation, or on other special occasions. He was obviously pleased with his speeches. We were a captive audience and usually lapsed into a state of embarrassed somnolence. He assembled a boring collection of quotes he had gleaned from his readings concerning politics, current events, popular culture, and numerous other matters. They were like a bad collage by an artist with no talent. The individual pieces did not seem to fit or lead up to any real point, in a series of senseless non-sequiturs. I do not remember carrying away a single original thought or line worth remembering or quoting from these events.

He presented us with his "Smiling Al" personality and his energetic style, punching each point, whether it was important or not. Basically, we could not figure out what they had to do with us or with anything else. This, after all, was a group of rather capable people, individuals who were highly educated with years of academic work and experience in teaching. As I looked around the room at the detached intelligence and insulted passions of our members, I thought of Katherine Ann Taylor's great novel, *Ship of Fools*.

I can remember only two causes Morton vigorously supported before the faculty. We opposed both of them, in part or wholly. When he injected himself into the academic program of the school, it usually was disastrous, either on the merit of his proposals, or because there was so much resentment beneath the surface.

The first proposal was that we have a Caribbean cruise as a unified January Term offering. One of the few academic innovations Van Dale took credit for was the Jan Term. That seemed a bit ironic, since year after year he seemed ready to junk the whole program. Jan Term was really a gimmick from the 1970s to try and make the students think they were getting more for their money in a private school. There were good things about the Jan Term offerings, however.

Morton, who had never cared about the Jan Term, tried to hijack the entire school and take it on a Caribbean cruise. We struggled to see the point of it all. We were to submit proposals that would involve trips south. This was right down Andrew McNeill's alley, as he had taken groups to explore the jungles of Central and South America for years.

Mark Springer and Mitch Barnett proposed an interesting tour of South American cities for some thinly contrived cultural and political goals. The prize should have gone to Meredith Phillips and one of the physical education instructors, who organized a splendidly hedonistic tour of Caribbean ports. The original proposal had some obscure justification for the choice of ports of call and the wonderful educational benefits of the tour, but no one ever took that seriously. It was clear this was an opportunity for party animals with enough money to pay for a two-week long party at sea.

Morton was obviously pleased with the Phillips proposal because he wanted to take a group of alums on the cruise. He did renege, however, on his original promise that he would raise $50,000 to support an all-school Caribbean Jan Term. In my department we tried to come up with a proposal to study Liberation Theology and other church issues in Central and South America. It was a stretch, however, and we were not able to come up with a feasible proposal. Many others on the faculty did not have a clue as to what the benefits of a Caribbean setting would be for anything they might do.

Only six, therefore, of the list of some 30 proposals for January Term that year had anything to do with the Caribbean. Morton seemed annoyed and frustrated by our lack of ability to catch his drift. Soon he got over it, and only came through with funds to support some of the costs for taking alums and benefactors on a boat trip. Characteristically, he blamed the failure of the idea to catch fire on those of us who had no real desire to travel to the Caribbean, and on Van Dale. He made it seem like the whole bizarre thing was our fault, and he, of course, had nothing to do with it.

Another incredible episode involved Morton's wild idea concerning the proposed library annex. The Southern Association mandated we add to the holdings of our badly outdated library. This meant building additional space for books and for study areas. Morton had drained money from library funds for years. The school was badly in debt and had to do something about the library or face the threat of losing accreditation.

Convinced necessity is the mother of invention, Morton hatched the scheme of devoting one wing of a new library annex to honoring former governor, Robert George Walker and his wife. There would be a collection of books, newspapers, and magazines from the period in which they controlled state government. There would be a theatre showing movies and videos, including some lauding the governor for his stand against integration. Never mind the fact that Walker's actions had almost caused a race war. Morton envisioned buses loaded with school children making daily pilgrimages to the campus to worship at the shrine of the governor.

Morton was trying to use the governor's son, Rob, whom I had taught, and the rest of the family, to get money from Walker's supporters. Rob had become a state official on the basis of his name and the efforts of his father's cronies. He went with Morton and other family members and politicians on a tour of the Carter Library in Atlanta. Morton bragged a lot about his plans for the library. He told the faculty the governor's family, headed by Jr., was going to start a drive in which millions of dollars would be donated. In response to questions, especially those of Ralph Stevenson, an older professor in the Business Department, Morton alleged that the governor was old and infirm and couldn't count.

"I am sure," he said, "that we will get a million or two to put on the wing where all the books will be." The ethics of such an enterprise was suspect at every level.

Perhaps the only thing that saved us was Morton's preoccupation with touring all the Rotary Clubs in the District with his secretary. His year as Rotary District Governor was good for us, because it kept him away from the campus for weeks. Meanwhile, there was a courageous effort made by Ralph Stevenson and others to stop the absurd plan for the library annex.

"I don't care if it is a Washington Library, or a Lincoln Library with daily films on the lives of our greatest presidents, it has no place here," Ralph commented at a crucial faculty meeting, which was presided over by Van Dale, but without Morton present. Ralph used his connections with the local newspaper to get an article printed on the proposed library addition. This came out the same day as our faculty meeting, and Ralph predicted the results of the faculty vote even before it was taken. We voted down the concept overwhelmingly. It was our greatest hour!

Morton was furious at the outcome. He blamed Ralph and began efforts to force him out. He also held Van Dale responsible. As dean and head of the faculty, Van Dale was technically in charge, but he had given no support to efforts to dump the plan. He was firm in his usual neutrality. Indeed, there was little he could do to stop the negative vote. We thought Van Dale's head would roll, but somehow Morton sensed his value to him and kept him on. After that time, I do not remember that Morton ever missed another faculty meeting.

There were times when Ralph Stevenson stood up in these dismal meetings and spoke directly to Morton. He had come to a place where he had nothing to lose, and calling a spade a spade came naturally to him. I have never seen more courage or anyone better able to think on their feet.

Chapter 9

ADAM JOHNSON

"Have you ever noticed how he walks?" Adam Johnson asked me. "It reminds me of the way a rattlesnake moves across the sand. Have you ever watched them crawl to the side? He walks just like that. He is a sidewinder!" Adam gave that quick, infectious giggle which showed he really thought something was funny. "He is a snake, isn't he? A crooked snake," Adam said, hissing the word "snake." He then began chanting an off-key rendition of a nursery rhyme, "There was a crooked man, who had a crooked wife, and lived in a crooked house. He was a crooked president of a crooked college."

Adam was a friend and a comrade in arms in the struggle at Worthington. It was rather amazing how close we became and how much we worked together. Adam had only been at the college for two years when things began to disintegrate. He was head of the department and the holder of the Bennett Chair in Business. He was paid more than any other faculty member at the college, yet he was profoundly dissatisfied, and had been almost from the first day he set foot on campus.

Adam and I had a lot in common. He had graduated from an institution similar to Worthington. He had been a Religion and Philosophy major and had even had a year in seminary. He had decided at the end of that time, however, to transfer to the graduate school for a master's degree and then a PhD in Business. He had worked at several institutions, including his last position at one of the state's best-known universities. He had grown weary of all of the in-fighting and professional nonsense in the state system. He even had to sue the university to get a fair shake. Adam's record of teaching and his list of publications were impressive. When he saw the listing in *The Chronicle of Higher Education*, for the chair in a small church-related liberal arts college, he was drawn to apply. It was like returning to his roots.

Coming back to the state capital was also good for him and his family. He had grown up only an hour's drive away. He had a brother who was seriously ill who lived nearby and had other family in the area. He also knew a number of figures in the business community, having gone to school with some of them. This was a decided plus for his department and for him personally.

For all of his good qualities and generosity to anyone in need, Adam could be ruthless in his appraisal of people. Morton never fooled him, as he had so many of us. Perhaps it was because of Adam's struggles before coming to Worthington. It may also have been because of his uncanny and intuitive abilities at judging the territory and finding out where the landmines were. In any case, Adam got Morton's number early, and never wavered from his critical appraisal.

The response from the other side was equally prompt and drastic, even for Morton. Only months after Adam had come to Worthington, Morton called him into his office and read him the law and the prophets. He had Dean Van Dale in his office with him, as he always did when any dirty work was afoot. Van Dale was quiet as usual, expected only to say an amen or two in the course of the conversation to make Morton happy. All of us who were at the college any length of time inevitably had one of these hide and tallow meetings. It took me sixteen years. Adam's encounter took place after only three months. He never knew exactly what it was that caused Morton to pursue him. Was it his contacts within the business community, with sometime frank and candied comments being shared in an unguarded moment? Had a version of these comments gotten back to Morton? Or was it just Morton's read of him? Was it a combination of things? He never knew.

Adam was untenured at Worthington, and once he got on Morton's bad side, he was put on a thirty-day contract. He could be fired or could quit with thirty day's notice. This was just another example of the bizarre arrangements Morton could come up with. He had also just come away from a battle with Harold Manowski, the former head of the Business Department, who turned the school into the Division II Athletic Association. A local business magnet, Jack Taylor, had given $50,000 to start the golf team. Once the team got organized, he flew them to matches in his private jet and gave them championship rings when they were divisional champions. Everyone wondered how much money he lavished on the team. In any case, Manowski blew the whistle on Jack Taylor giving money to the athletes. He got fired for his trouble. As Manowski's successor, Adam felt that he and the Business Department were on a short leash.

Adam was a generous and good-hearted person. He also could cuss and drink with a passion. He could not refer to Morton or to the denomination that supposedly had control over the college without using his most choice four-letter words. After a while he developed certain formulas for referring to each. His references to Morton were especially colorful and had the ring of his own unique and creative composition.

He was below average height and had become paunchy in middle age. He moved fast and was rather frenetic in his actions. This was true in his work as well. He did a lot of things and did all of them well. When it was time to move from one thing to another, Adam was ready to go. At night, however, after he had eaten a late dinner with his wife and two children, he mellowed out and often drank too much. He generally either prepared the gourmet meal, or had a part in preparing it. His wife was lovely and gracious. She also knew when to get out of the way. It was generally after he had time to get mellow, then drunk, and then bitter that he would call me. We talked for hours, as often as every day.

Adam helped me tremendously in understanding what made Morton tick.

"All he understands is money, sex, and control over others," he said more than once. I kept mentioning Morton's connections with the church, the academic community, and other aspects of his position.

Adam told me abruptly, "All of that stuff doesn't mean anything to him. Can't you see, it's all just a cover?"

Even though I agreed, I still did not understand. It was too much of a jump for me. Through our discussions, I began to see how a devious mind works. It was through his manipulation of the local power structure that Morton was able to hold his position. He came into a southern city that was essentially closed to outsiders, especially people from the north. He was just a preacher with a PhD in Sociology and the position as president of a two bit little college. He had a distinct nose for where the power was, however. Once he sniffed it out, he broke into the system and became one of the good old boys. How did he do it? We were never able to answer that question. It was impossible, but he had done it and with aplomb.

"That Morton is a carpetbagger," Adam said. I never lost the ability to be shocked and profoundly amused at the outrageous descriptions he came up with.

"What do you mean?" I asked.

"I mean just what I said: A carpetbagger! He came down here to the Worthington plantation and took it over. You know that old McTaggart ruled this place from Stephens Hall for twenty-five years like a plantation owner. He became a letch, a drunkard, and an agnostic. After he was forced out, that silly bunch of bishops went north to find someone as different as possible from McTaggart, and I'll be darned if they didn't get a carpetbagger! We followed twenty-five years of slavery with a quarter century of reconstruction. All we are is a bunch of frigging academic sharecroppers. How much more can we stand?"

Although Morton was regarded as a Yankee, according to Adam, he was able to become part of the power structure and "adopt the standards of a decadent, debauched, and in-bread old pseudo-aristocracy with sex, money, and control as prime goals." It was bad enough for the men who controlled Harrison to run their businesses and the state government the way they did, but Morton did them one better. He ran a church-related liberal arts college the same way, and even did things no business or state institution could get away with. He was fond of styling himself the "CEO" of Worthington. His cronies called him "the Boss." We almost gagged on that one! Adam's acute insight allowed him to cut through the nonsense and evaluate the college by business standards. He called Worthington "a dismal swamp." We had one of the worst employment records for any institution in Harrison, and Morton and his cronies were running us into the ground financially.

In truth, we on the faculty did not discuss Morton a great deal, except with those whom we trusted, and then off campus. Generally most of us despised him, but we knew he had spies among us, particularly the men he brought with him. There also were more and more people whom he hired with a questionable past. He knew they would keep their mouths shut because he had something on them. It was good for me to able to talk with Adam openly and honestly. As rank as our discussions sometimes got, especially after Adam was sufficiently drunk to begin cussing with creative abandon, our intent was ultimately positive. What could be done to restore something we both valued highly? Adam would never have spoken about Morton, Worthington, and the church in such pejorative terms had he not expected, desired, and demanded something infinitely better.

Chapter 10

ALLEN VAN DALE

Allen Van Dale was a part of Morton's "Yankee Mafia," as we called it. It was interesting how Morton ran a well-oiled machine, involving white, male, middle-aged northerners. There was a second tier of people who were loyal to him, mostly southerners; they were kept out of the loop, however, and never treated as equals. Morton chose the persons in his inner circle carefully. They were transplants from their native soil into a region they did not know well and for which they had some degree of contempt.

Adam asked a telling and provocative question about them, with affected redneck rhetoric, "Why couldn't they make it where they came from? We need to send all of that, no-good, carpet-bagging trash back where it come from!"

I have always found Van Dale to be a curious bedfellow for Morton and his crowd. In truth, Van Dale must have loathed him more than any of us. If so, he never let it show. Van Dale was ten times the man Morton was. His worst mistake was coming to Worthington under Morton. He and Mark Springer had been on the same faculty with him at Winterset College in Iowa, where Morton came as chaplain and then became dean of students. Van Dale and Springer were professors in the Education and Chemistry departments. How could the promise of a deanship and a departmental chair be enough to lure anyone in their right mind into this tortured situation?

Morton probably promised him the moon, but the reality was that Van Dale remained as academic dean at Worthington for twenty-five years with nothing more than a thirty-day contract. It is the height of absurdity, but I heard Van Dale say it himself. It was at a search committee meeting for the Jenkins-Pittman Chair. We were at the end of our meeting and begin to chat before leaving. We discussed the question of tenure for a person coming to fill the chair.

Van Dale then referred to his own retirement, "Well, I hope that whomever they bring in as dean will insist on tenure."

I turned to him in disbelief. "You're tenured, aren't you?"

"No, I never have been," he replied.

"What kind of contract do you have then?" Roger Wilson (head of the History department) asked.

"Thirty-day," Van Dale answered.

"You mean . . .?" Wilson starred at him in disbelief, unable to finish his sentence.

"Yes," Van Dale replied. "I can quit or be fired on one month's notice."

"And you have remained on that basis . . .?" Wilson again stopped.

"For nearly twenty-five years," Van Dale finished Wilson's sentence again.

"No wonder Morton is able to control him," I thought. His quarter of a century at Worthington must have been sheer agony.

Van Dale was a complicated man and a person of ability. He had served as superintendent of schools in two different areas of his native state of Michigan before coming to Winterset College. He had infinitely more experience and ability in administration than Morton, and yet he was not in charge. He knew far better than the rest of us how childish Morton's whims were. If Van Dale had been the president of Worthington instead of Morton, would the place have been different? This was a useless question, of course, because it was not the case. Indeed, with the elements so mixed in Van Dale's character, his weaknesses might have made him a terrible president.

Van Dale had made the obligatory move when he came to Harrison and joined First United Methodist Church, where Morton and his family attended. His background, however, was the Reformed Church. I often wondered how his Dutch Calvinist conscience fared when he watched Morton lie, cheat, steal, have affairs, and ruin the lives of others. How could he be a part, even tacitly, in the attacks Morton mounted against those of us in the faculty, administration, staff, and student body who opposed him? The only explanation I ever heard came from my lawyer, Richard McArthur, who was the advocate of choice for anyone challenging the college. He responded with familiarity born of having dealt with this man many times before.

He cited a quote from Dante's Inferno: "The hottest places in hell are reserved for those who in time of great moral crisis maintain their neutrality." Whoever Van Dale really was, this fit him perfectly.

Von Dale never complained or gave us a hint about what he thought of the man who controlled him. Morton made it clear: He controlled Van Dale and enjoyed making him do his dirty work. Hours of hard administrative work could be overturned on a whim from Morton. Von Dale probably told his first lies for Morton and covered for him in some unseemly enterprise soon after he came to Worthington. After that, each successive encounter took him deeper into the vortex. He could not stop, even when he considered the implications of what he was doing.

He simply echoed Morton's absurd assertions, adding some unique comments of his own which were ambiguous enough to satisfy his boss. He also gave us tangible evidence that he was not our friend, would not stand with us, and would save his own skin at all costs. He had no stomach for the cruelty involved, but he would not defend his fellow administrators or protect his faculty. He knew right from wrong. Unlike Morton, he was not a sociopath. He was worse— he was an enabler. He understood the blatantly absurd nature of his situation, and maintained the status quo and perpetuated the lie.

It was pathetic the way he sacrificed principle in order to preserve his position. Morton would have fired him in a New York minute if he had ever stood up to him. What did he gain by staying there all those years? By letting Morton manipulate him he lost any semblance of integrity and authenticity. It was interesting to hear Mitch Barnett, Drew McNeill, and Mark Springer go on about how Van Dale was the good guy in all of this. They lauded him for keeping Worthington together during Morton's machinations.

What Barnett said about him sounded almost like an epitaph: "Dean Van Dale is responsible for whatever is honorable on this campus."

Adam was fond of reminding me of the delicious irony in that statement. "The word 'whatever' does not mean a lot. There was no honor on the Worthington campus that he could be responsible for."

Ruth Dalbert was a drama student who came from England. She performed in many campus productions. She also had a good analytical mind. I had her in several Philosophy classes and found her observations to be refreshingly accurate. She made a classic comment about Van Dale. He was walking across the campus to his car after a long tiring day late during a spring semester. She was standing on the sidewalk as Von Dale passed by. Although they were near each other, he did not look up or acknowledge her presence. Instead, he walked along staring at his feet.

Ruth told me, affecting a cockney accent, "He looked down at his shoe, and said, 'You're untied, aren't ya? We'll have to take care of you later, won't we?' He was talking to his shoe, his bloody shoe! He's as daft as a door mouse!"

Chapter 11

Mark Springer

Mark Springer came to Worthington from a church-related college in Iowa where he had been an assistant professor of Chemistry. He was appointed associate professor and then became department head following the retirement of one of truly great figures on campus. Dr. Lou Ann Danvers had taught at the college most of her career. She was known all over the region. She was a hard act to follow, and Mark did not try. Morton did not know much about teaching and couldn't have cared less. He did not want great teachers at Worthington. He wanted individuals whom he could control, and who could help him control

Mark was not a talented teacher or administrator, but he was known as Morton's buddy and that was enough. He was personable and had a dry Hoosier humor that was engaging. He was well liked by other faculty and staff members, but he was not trusted. We had ample evidence he carried messages to and from Morton.

It was interesting how Morton was able to place his people in strategic places. Most of his cronies were in the administration. Mark, however, was his man on the faculty. Mitch Barnett and Drew McNeill could be controlled, but Mark was one of Morton's cronies. He periodically joined Morton, Steve Brunner, Jack Taylor, and several wealthy businessmen whom Morton was courting in a golf outing. Mark had to be careful because he was a much better

47

golfer than the group with whom he was playing. He would have to let Morton, and possibly his business friends, win without giving the appearance he was not playing to the best of his ability. Anyone who knew Morton knew you never beat him.

Morton left nothing to chance in his little world. We wondered how he spent his time. He took little interest in academic matters—Allen Van Dale and Sarah Robinson took care of that. It was better when Morton stayed out of it. He enjoyed the tea parties, which were held periodically to court the rich. His amusements were skirt chasing and golf. But what was he doing the rest of the time? It took me years to confirm my suspicions that he was an academic Wizard of Oz, sitting behind the scenes manipulating almost every aspect of our lives. It was uncanny how good he was at it!

Two colleagues and invaluable aides in our struggle against Morton and company were junior members of the science faculties that Mark headed. They were Brian Washington and Kathleen Krantz. They were both good teachers and significant scholars who took their work seriously. They were the kind of people who made college life interesting.

When Brian first came to Worthington, I was not sure I liked him. He seemed to be another of Mitch Barnett's cultured despisers. I eventually found out I was wrong about Brian. Childhood scoliosis had shortened his statue and caused him to stand with one shoulder considerably lower than the other. Like many handicapped persons, I came to see Brian was more complicated than I at first had guessed. He was intelligent and genuinely interested in areas outside his field. He was an avid fan of old movies and sponsored an on-campus film festival. He was deeply concerned about issues such as birth control, abortion, and AIDS. This caused him to launch his annual campaign to provide free condoms to students. He appealed to the administration, but soon learned they would ignore him forever, so he kept a box of condoms outside his office.

Brian proudly labeled himself an agnostic, if not an atheist, but he was a person with values. He despised Morton, and defied him as often and as visibly as he could get away with. For example, every time we put on our academic dress, Brian would wear a large medallion on a chain around his neck. The medallion meant nothing that anyone could figure out. Brian had found it at a Goodwill store. His purpose in wearing it was to mock Morton. Morton's arrogance was never clearer than when he strutted out at graduation and other formal occasions. His crooked gait was exaggerated by a heavy copy of the great seal of the college suspended from his neck.

Kathleen Krantz was as different from Brian as one could imagine. Brian was a southerner and Kathleen was from Chicago. She was a devout Catholic and a violinist with the Harrison Symphony. She had a brisk, even abrupt manner, and generally scared the students to death (almost literally!). I was told once by a group of worried fraternity brothers that one of them, a bright young man who was determined to go to medical school, was considering suicide.

He was sure he was going to fail a senior level course with Kathleen, which would keep him from graduating and prevent him from ever going to med school. I talked with both Kathleen and the student. At the last minute she agreed to offer him a possible alternative to sure failure. If he passed the final examination, she would give him the grade he made on it. He had a D average in the course, passed the final, and got a B in the course. Only later did I learn she regularly plotted these scenarios to test the metal of these future healers. The young man in question made an excellent physician. He once told me he knew he could endure anything med school had to offer after Dr. Krantz finished with him.

She was deeply committed to her students, but had a curious way of showing it. She could get the most out of them, while never letting on how much she cared about them. She represented the best aspects of the Catholic Church coming out of Vatican II. She was liberal on many issues in theology, but she had a conservative streak on social issues and could be dogmatic and uncompromising. Her son, who was a student at Worthington, dated a little Baptist girl. He called me one evening and asked me to perform their marriage ceremony. It was a rush job. I met with the couple and begged for more time. The young woman blurted out between sobs, "We have to get married—I am pregnant!" I made a deal with them that I would perform the ceremony if she agreed never to say that again. The baby would have a difficult time at best, without being blamed for their marriage (in case things did not work out). Kathleen understood, but refused to come to the wedding.

Brian and Kathleen did not see Mark as a low-key, humorous, affable guy who happened to be friends with "the Boss." They saw him as inept, lazy, and calculating. They mistrusted and resented the way he used his position as the head of both the department and the division. They said he was jealous of their abilities and that he often conspired to sabotage their work and discredit them with students. He played his role so well I thought them jealous and petty at first. Later I learned to respect their judgment and to avoid Mark like the plague.

Mark's interest in sports became increasingly important to Morton. Before golf became big on campus, Mark was the golf coach. After Tommy Parnell took over and began winning championships in golf, Mark became the head of the faculty's academic affairs committee. This was crucial to Morton's plans after Tommy convinced him our salvation lay in recruiting athletes. We were suddenly involved in a situation where over 20 percent of the student body was involved in one or more sports. Most of them were promised some kind of scholarship. This was clearly a case of bait and switch; after a semester, many of them were cut either from the list of scholarship recipients or from the team altogether. There was a vast difference between a good soccer player who deserved a scholarship because of his or her value to the team, and one of the many who were promised aid but did not deserve it. It was a cruel and deceptive practice, and one that forced many students to go home, or trapped them on campus because it was too late to go somewhere else.

There were also large sums of money funneled into athletic programs, some from the college, and some from alumni and other contributors. Mark and Tommy had overall responsibility for scholarship aid and the use of funding. We tried to find out how much money came through these channels and was used in ways most of us would have found objectionable. Since Mark chaired the committee and presided over its meetings, he was able to steer proceedings largely as Morton desired. It was interesting that when the national accrediting association put Worthington on probation for clear and consistent violations, Mark took none of the heat for what had been done.

Chapter 12

MITCHELL BARNETT

Every time I thought I was beginning to understand Mitch Barnett, I found I was wrong. He came about the same time Mark Springer and I did. He spoke rapidly and with a slight stutter. He generally did not have a lot to say, but this did not keep him from saying it again and again. In one of our terribly boring Friday afternoon faculty meetings, Ron Trimble, an assistant professor in Math, and I tried to compute how many hours we had wasted over a ten-year period listening to Mitch running his mouth about nothing.

It was these Friday afternoon disasters that finally made me sure we were all on a ship of fools going nowhere. The real irony of it was that after so many years, almost all of us—faculty, staff, administrators—had been handpicked and hired by Morton. We were all losers and all doomed as long as Morton was captain of our little ship.

I wondered how Mitch ever became head of the English Department. His predecessor was Milton Butts, a large, pleasant man with a heavy Southern drawl. Milton was a good teacher and a member of the old guard. He had a wonderful and occasionally caustic sense of humor. The students loved him and seemed to learn a lot from him. He was a person I always wanted to get to know better. Milton suddenly quit one summer and we never saw him again. It was said he had gone home to Georgia to take care of his ailing mother. Does someone who is a full professor, a department head, and a campus leader suddenly quit? I have always been sorry I did not know what happened to Milton. We did not share each other's burdens and stand up for each other. That was why Morton was able to pick us off, one by one.

The English Department was composed of a curious and diverse group of people. Neal James was our resident Shakespeare expert, and also himself a character out of one of the plays. Estelle Cartwright went through several husbands before declaring herself bisexual. This was a polite way of saying our fire-breathing feminist was really a lesbian all the time. She was able to use men to hide her true preference until she realized it was safer to have an unusual sexual appetite in Morton's perverted little world. His chauvinistic mind could write off her feminism if he could explain it as the product of a devious mind.

Mitch suddenly was elevated out of the pack to the chairmanship. There were others who were, in my opinion, more gifted, but he got the job, and I was never sure why. His enigmatic nature made him a pain—for the administration as well as for the rest of us on the faculty. He had his causes and would ride off like Don Quixote to tilt at windmills. It was curious that, even though he was critical of the administration, he could nevertheless be counted on to support their positions when the chips were down. He often appeared to be a loose cannon, but he always fired in the direction Morton pointed him.

According to the grapevine he did not like Morton, but thought Van Dale was a good guy and wanted to support him. I have never been sure how much truth there was in this. In any case, we knew we could not trust him. He was one of the few individuals who remained long years at Worthington under Morton and was not broken. Mitch seemed to be a survivor, and to march to the tune of his own one-armed drummer. He seemed to enjoy switching positions at will and confusing both sides. Maybe that was what it took to survive around there. What was Mitch's game and how would he know if he won? I could never figure him out.

Diane Jackson was the most normal person in the department. She was a wife and mother and had no apparent unusual or perverse tendencies. She was attractive, bright, and fiercely independent. She was a faithful Catholic, but in her own way. She learned to take what the Church said with a grain of salt, especially if it dealt with women or sexuality.

"What did priests know about sex, anyway?" she was fond of asking. Each time she had another baby, she became a little larger until her obesity began to obscure her good looks. She was valuable to Morton because of her ability to balance her common sense with the self-centered egoism of some of the other faculty members.

I did not envy Mitch having to get this crowd together once a month for a departmental meeting. He seemed to enjoy it, however. He was able to keep them in check by telling them one thing and the administration something quite different. He became more and more eccentric in his interests and dogmatic in his assertions. He and I worked through the ranks from assistant, to associate, to full professor, and then to chair of our respective departments. We both operated on the belief that if we became chairpersons in our areas, we would have the power and influence to make our departments deserve the term "excellent."

Mitch took great pleasure in manipulating people for his own purposes. He became quite useful to Morton and Van Dale in controlling the faculty. He was not one of Morton's men, but he was willing to be used by him if it suited his own interest. After all, where else could he have become the head of an English Department? He seemed to feel quite differently about Van Dale, whom he really admired and respected. This was closeness at a distance, however, since they did not seem to be more than superficial friends. So far as we could tell, Von Dale had no close friends. He could not afford the distraction.

One of the most difficult aspects for me of having to deal with Mitch was trying to ascertain what motivated him. His wife was also an English professor, but at a local branch of a state university. They were an unusual couple. They (probably wisely) decided not to have children. It was hard to imagine him as a marriage partner. He was wed to his own image reflected in the waters of time like a pudgy, middle-aged Narcissus. There was little room for her or anybody else in his world.

Mitch's father-in-law had been a minister. Mitch could never quite get over the hard time this rather sanctimonious fellow had given him when he asked for the hand of his daughter in marriage. He quickly learned he was going to have to be nice to "the old fool," as he called him (but not to his face), if he was going to marry his daughter.

Mitch was critical of the church and of religion in general. He was continually saying tacky things about us in the Religion area. When I brought a petition with nearly one hundred names on it from the students requesting we have Good Friday off so they could go home for Easter, he was one of the strongest opponents of my motion. Van Dale was furious I had brought the petition without telling him I was going to do so. Morton laughed and joked about the whole thing. Walking back into Stephens Hall, with Susan Peterson beside him, he wished me "Happy Easter" and gave one of his deceitful smiles. She chuckled nervously. I wondered, for the first and only time, if she had been converted to the other side.

When I finally stood up against Morton, Mitch said behind my back that I had either gone crazy or became a religious fanatic. He did not do his most destructive fighting with blows to the face, but with knives in the back. Mitch treated those of us who were in what he called the "affective" disciplines as if we were inferior to the "real" college courses in the rigorous and respectable areas of study. This was perhaps most clearly true of Religion, which had no real part to play in the concert of the faculties.

In discussions of our situation, he was one of the faculty members who would resolutely defend Morton. He did this supposedly based on the fact that he thought if Morton were fired we would get a fundamentalist preacher as president. I told him the trustees had not done this when they hired Morton. What would make him think they would do it next time? But he would not listen to me. This gave him the justification he seemed to need to defend a man in authority whose own anti-church views (even though Morton was a minister) came close to agreeing with his own. Furthermore, Mitch brought up Morton's dalliances with his secretaries as typical of what happened with clergy in the church. This was what it was like and he had no use for it. This was typical of Mitch's ability to play off both ends against the middle.

Chapter 13

ANDREW MCNEILL

Morton did not allow anyone to have power on campus, least of all department heads. He understood power and its allure and used it to entrap us. He was able to find our breaking points and then destroy us—one way or another. This was certainly the case with Andrew McNeill. He and I both had the "Southern curse" of respecting authority almost to the level of idolatry. We desired to please everyone, especially those who had authority over us. We reacted in opposite ways to Morton, however. Andrew remained in his position, even though he knew the authority he obeyed did not deserve his respect.

I will never forget Bishop Noland Arthur's comment that I made two mistakes with regard to my relationship with Morton: "You tried to build a department, and you knew too much about Morton's private life." Andrew's disappointment over the former did not include the latter. He hated Morton, but learned not to see what was going on and to keep his mouth shut. When we first came to Worthington, Andrew was a nice guy. Later on, I was not always sure of his motives for some of the things he did. Had Andrew decided to sell out to Morton after he was broken by him? Morton knew how to pick up someone he had knocked down. If he could not do that, then he would jump on with both feet and try to destroy anyone whom he considered to be his adversary.

Margaret Simpson was a wealthy widow who had extensive land holdings in the county near Harrison. She was a loyal graduate of the college and wanted to benefit it in some way. She made provisions in her will to give a large tract of land to the college. It was to be a nature retreat used for the education of Worthington students, maintained in a pristine state for all to enjoy. She drew up the provisions of the grant and its protective trust carefully. Andrew was allowed to be part of the final discussions. He was extraordinarily pleased and worked long hours planning what would be done with the land. He even began (with Mrs. Simpson's permission and encouragement) to take students out to the area for classes.

He drove for miles inspecting the side roads into the property and cleaning up garbage. He undertook measures to stop erosion in areas that had been plowed by long-departed farmers, or cleared for roads and other projects. He gloried in the beauty of the forests, some of which almost approached the virgin state that preceded the invasion of European settlers. He spent all his free time walking long distances across the land, studying every aspect of its beauty and profundity. He became one in harmony with the land. His descriptions of it had religious overtones.

Mrs. Simpson died in the third week of the third month of her 91st year. By the end of that year the provisions of her will had been carried out, over some protests from distant cousins. Even before the college received control of its part of the land, Morton was negotiating with the help of some of his powerful friends on the trustee board to sell off parts of the land to a paper company. The money obtained from the sale of the land, and the rich stand of timber on it, helped ease an embarrassing shortfall in the budget that year. Morton considered it to be a real coup.

A tiny portion of the original property donated was to be designated the "Worthington Nature Reserve."

"Students and teachers would have a wonderful learning experience out there in the natural environment," Morton told Andrew. It was as if he had become an advocate for all Andrew stood for. Andrew could hardly believe it. He must have been wrong about Morton. The man was concerned about the environment and had provided him with the best possible resource for his students.

The first free Saturday Andrew could get away, he packed up his gear in his old pick-up. He and his son, Sean, went out at daybreak to the property. His dreams were coming true: He had become department chair and the college had a superior natural habitat to study the region. He could envision the eventual development of a program that would rival the best of the state schools. As he drove near the property, he began to see new fences with "No Trespassing" signs.

He thought there must have been some terrible mistake. Surely he had made a wrong turn and was passing through someone else's property. Or maybe the paper companies had made a mistake and fenced the wrong land. Then, as he traveled farther along the road to the land given to the college by the Simpson estate, he began to see the horrible toll taken by the saws and bulldozers of the clear cutters. He raced back to town and called Morton. A meeting with Morton and Van Dale was set up for Monday morning. Those who saw him that day as he came out of the meeting say he was white as a sheet.

For months Andrew looked straight ahead with a blank stare. Students began complaining about his classes. He seemed so depressed they thought he must have lost a loved one, or that he had some serious disease. We had no idea what happened until much latter. He never talked much about it.

Finally, he told Morton he intended to file suit against the college for violating the terms of the grant, which it clearly had done. Morton responded cynically, however, that his lawyers had found loopholes in the will and that the college was perfectly justified in what it had done.

The college did not need all that land anyway for students to play around in.

"How many majors do you have anyway?" Morton asked accusingly.

Andrew had to respond that there were only two dozen in the several fields covered by his department. He could not comment in that setting on how many students were influenced by the faculty in his area. The core exposed most of the students to the different disciplines included under Biology. Pre-med students, of course, spent much of their college career in classes or labs. He could not convince Morton and Van Dale that the land had infinitely greater worth as a habitat and natural environment than the dollars gained from its sale. He was bribed with talk of a raise and new equipment for the department. He withdrew the suit and shut his mouth.

Andrew became a shadow of the man he used to be. Morton appointed him to a special committee to talk with the trustees about long-range planning. This was the first of many such appointments involving busy work which had little meaning to Andrew. Morton destroyed the real Andrew by trashing what was of greatest value to him. He replaced him with a zombie that looked and talked like Andrew.

Andrew became a member of an unholy triumvirate with Mark. Springer and Mitch Barnett. He was chair of Biology, Mark was chair of Chemistry, and Mitch was of chair of English. The three of them could be seen going to Frank's Bar for a beer after faculty meetings. I wonder what they discussed. Andrew was, of course, not really in their league. His reputation for being tough and individualistic was earned by his stand on various issues.

This was allowed by the administration because Andrew was under their control. He could spout off all he wanted about things that did not concern them. His talk about ecological disaster in the rain forests of Central and South America was extreme. His avowal of vegetarianism, and his trips to Costa Rica with students to trek through the jungles were obsessive. The administration knew that when the chips were down, however, he could be counted on to support them.

I still could occasionally sense some of the fire in Andrew, but he essentially was a hollow man. No matter how he tried to recapture his earlier zeal, I found it usually misfired. From time to time he would speak in chapel about his concern for ecology. It was generally the gospel according to Lynn White. He agreed with her that "Christian anthropocentrism was the root cause of the environmental crisis." He delighted in describing the changes that resulted from the attitudinal shift against Nature and from Christian victories over the religions of animism and pantheism.

He quoted White as saying this was, "the greatest psychic revolution in the history of our culture." All of this did not bother me a great deal because I understood the problems in her logic and the bizarre historical nature of her charges. Andrew no more wanted the restoration of animism and paganism than he wanted to take on the Christian establishment. His speeches made him seem radical, however, and allowed him to present his ecological alternatives to "Christianity's desacralization of Western man's world." The loss of the sacred in Western culture was much more the product of antichristian forces than the abandonment of paganism.

Andrew had long since registered his complaint with Christendom. At first he shifted churches from Methodist to Unitarian, but later he left the church altogether. I often wondered whether it was really the Christian faith to which he objected. Or was it the fact that a Christian denomination could ordain a man like Morton, place him as president of one of its colleges, and allow him to destroy everything reasonable, moral, and holy? This meant for Andrew, of course, the great old trees and the habitat for hundreds of birds and animals on the Simpson property. Was it Christianity's God, or the mammon of Morton, which comprised the unholy trinity of power, control, and greed? In a sense, Andrew's twisted and peculiar protest may have been quite similar to mine. They represented similar, if nevertheless, different responses to the same perverted situation.

Chapter 14

TOMMY PARNELL

Thomas Parnell came originally from Boston and had worked as a coach in a small junior college in the southern part of Massachusetts. We called him "Morton, Jr." behind his back. He came to the college in the post-Flowers era as one of the new coaches. He somehow convinced Morton athletics would be our salvation. No one on the faculty associated with him except Mark Springer, who remained chairman of the Athletics Committee all of the time he was at Worthington.

I was on campus rather late one night for a study session with students for finals. As I was walking across campus, I met the head of security.

He was unusually cheerful in his greeting, "Good evening, Doc. What are you doing here so late at night?"

I told him about our session and carried on some superficial comments about issues on campus. He was a good man, and I knew I could talk freely with him.

"That your car over there?" he asked, pointing to a little sedan parked in the special place reserved for Morton's Buick. I was quite sure he knew every car regularly on campus and most of the first and last names of the drivers. I realized he must have been trying to make a point.

I responded, "Not hardly, I am not crazy!"

"Naw, that's not your car," he responded with a teasing inflection to his voice. He knew and I knew it was Parnell's car.

I cut to the chase and asked him, "What is Morton, Jr. doing parking in his daddy's place?"

"Don't know," he responded. "But I am sure he is up to no good."

Following the demise of basketball on campus, Morton went into a frenzy of activity, bringing in soccer and revamping the tennis, golf, and baseball programs. The most popular sport on campus, basketball, was almost eliminated and there was a flood of new sports and activities. This was the period when government requirements mandated elevation of women's athletics under Title 9.

It was said we had been spending too much on basketball, but it was all right only a year or two after closing it down to spend a small fortune transforming the campus into a locker room. Tommy certainly played a part in this process. He was a golf coach and promised Morton a national championship team. This was one of the few promises he ever kept. In fact, we won the national championship in our division three times during Tommy's stay at the college and once thereafter. Tommy was a kind of pitchman for college athletics. He could have sold beer coolers by the boxcar to the Eskimos.

Morton was a master liar, but he certainly met his match in Tommy. A joke sweeping the campus at that time asked: "How do know Morton and Jr. are lying?" The answer was, of course: "When you see their lips move." Like all real humor, this joke was built upon a foundation of truth. As much as Morton lied to us, we always thought he at least knew he was lying. We were not sure this was true of Tommy, however.

Jack Taylor was a successful local builder of shopping malls. He seeded the area with new malls rising out of cow pastures. He was one of the bullyboys whom Morton recruited for his board of trustees. According to the official rules mandated by the Methodist Church, trustee boards traditionally consisted of one half clergy and one half Methodist laypersons carefully chosen by local ministers and appointed by annual conferences. Morton could not get rid of the clergy or the church participation entirely. He was able to flatter clergy members, however, by awarding them honorary doctorates of divinity (which we called "donated dignity"). He was able to do away with the requirements for laypersons. Then he appointed a rather amoral crowd of millionaires who would rubber-stamp his requests. These individuals were affluent and active and did not know a lot about higher education. They did not watch the campus closely and relied on Morton for information on what was happening.

Taylor was a large, egoistic, self-made man, who was born into a wealthy family. He had gone to a state university, where he specialized in fraternity life and partying. He majored in business and took over the family construction business when his father retired. He met his future wife through the firm. They had several children. He was flattered to become a member of the board of an institution of higher education and responded favorably to the titles and accolades regularly given him.

I will never forget his speech one year at Founders' Day. After the dedication of a new building for the Business Department, given by the Taylor's family in honor of his father, he was given an honorary doctorate. When he took the podium to make his acceptance speech, he was plain spoken and crude. He evidently had cleaned up his manner of speaking considerably, but could not hide his contempt for intellectuals and theoreticians. For him, athletics should be the core of college life.

That year we were kicking off a school season labeled "The Year of the Arts."

By the time he finished, I whispered to Adam, "This must be 'the Year of the Jocks.'"

He began with a football story, the perennial mark of a real he-man in the South. Then he ended his rant with the announcement that he was sponsoring the new golf team under Tommy Parnell and giving $50,000 to establish a soccer team. This was amazing to us, because we knew that this man ate, slept, and breathed football. Who in the world had talked him into supporting two "sissy" sports like golf and soccer? The answer came to us immediately, of course: "Tommy and Smilin' Albert." For six years Worthington ran on Jack Taylor's testosterone level, which was very high.

Tommy recruited golfers from all over the country. I had one student whose father was one of the top pros in the country. I liked the kid, but found him to be spoiled and rather stifled by his famous father. He did not even stay the full semester. Many of them came with unrealistic expectations, due to Tommy's promises. But generally, once they settled down, they became valuable members of the campus community. Golfers were considered the aristocrats of athletes. This was certainly true after they began winning championships. Jack Taylor gave them large, expensive championship rings. He flew them all over the country in his private plane for games and gave them expensive parties. Tommy was able to get them almost anything they wanted, including apartments off campus, where they had all the liquor, spending money, cars, and girls they wanted..

Tommy created a group called the "Diamond Girls," which was the successor to the "Worthington Darlings" during the heyday of basketball. These girls led cheers at games, but they also had entertainment responsibilities. This meant being nice to prospective students, and making the boys on the team feel good if they won or console them if they lost. Nowhere was it specified that these girls were to get drunk with the jocks or sleep with them, but the expectation was there.. When Morton first came, he, his cronies, the coaches, and some of the faculty participated in the athletes' parties. Tommy revived this practice and had some of his parties on campus.

This would never have happened while David Flowers was a coach or the Athletic Director. Several years after David resigned as AD, Thomas Parnell succeeded him. Tommy seemed to soak up titles. He was not only in charge of the athletic program, but was made "Dean of Recruitment" and began calling himself Vice President. He even had stationary made up. Morton never gave anyone that title, however. At the pinnacle of his power, Tommy controlled just about every area of campus life outside the purely academic. He convinced Morton he would fill the campus with athletes. At one time, one student out of every five participated in one or more intercollegiate sports.

The recruiters were trained to turn over the records of anyone who had participated successfully in high school or college athletics to the coaches. They were to make immediate contact with the prospect and to promise the student a scholarship. They kept on calling and promising until the student came to visit the campus. The baseball team wound up each year with over sixty scholarship students, half of whom the coach had to wash out immediately or before spring practice began. The idea was that the thirty students with real ability would stay because they really did have scholarships. The other thirty would have to find the money somewhere else after their scholarship was taken away because they did not make the team. Both the baseball coach and the girls' softball coach came to me for counseling concerning their feelings of revulsion at being part of such a deceptive system.

Other recruitment practices represented major violations of regulations in the small college division. I had a Dutch student in class one semester who did well on his first two tests in Religion 101. I appreciated his ability and his studious and polite manner. All of a sudden he stopped coming to class. I sent word to him that I was concerned about him and wanted to know what was wrong. He contacted me to say he had already earned a degree in Holland, and was returning home within a few weeks. I told the dean's office I was concerned about him and did not understand the situation. Then I learned from Harold Manowski that the young man was recruited to play soccer all year.

He did not realize we only had games during a limited season, which lasted only part of the year. He had already graduated from a university program in his home country, which was equal, if not superior, to our college. Recruiting and playing a graduate was a violation of regulations. Manowski was busy collecting records about violations that would eventually unravel Tommy's little empire and put the entire program on probation. Manowski was forced out by Morton. He paid a high price for exposing this ugly situation, but so did all of us who stood up to Morton.

Tommy was married and the father of several children. There were rumors about his stormy relationship with his wife. I was shopping in a department store in a local mall one Christmas season when I saw a former student who worked there over the holidays. We discussed her marriage and family, her graduate work, and her goals.

She then asked me a strange question: "Do you know much about Coach Parnell?" I feigned innocence and told her I knew him, but was not close to him. I then asked why she asked.

She said, "Well, he and his family live in the house next to us. You would not believe how much they drink and the fights they get into. We can hear the shouting and the cursing. I am embarrassed for our children to hear them. What kind of people are they?" I worked hard to end the conversation without breaking out laughing or telling her what I really thought.

Besides bringing back the "Darlings" as the "Diamond Girls," Tommy had his own escapades with the girls and women on campus. He obviously learned a lot from Morton, and often called him a role model. For example, Morton was known to have a love nest in a locked room in the basement of Stephens Hall where he went with his mistresses over the years. Tommy found his own place where he met the woman who was the Dean of Women. They carried on an affair for the better part of a year. Tommy found an empty room on an unused floor of an old dorm and fitted it out for his purposes.

He did not realize the woman who was in charge of residential housekeeping and maintenance, Mabel Smith, had keys to all of these rooms. She was well-known at Worthington. She was tough and took no prisoners. She worked her way up from being a part of the custodial staff to being in charge of housekeeping for twenty years. She had enough on Morton to hang him, but never had enough reason to use it. She and I talked periodically.

After finding evidence that one of her rooms was a secret meeting place, Mable made periodic trips to the room until she caught Tommy and the dean in bed. Previous to her discovery, Tommy had treated her with contempt and disdain. He was constantly bringing students to campus to stay overnight and complaining that he never found the accommodations to be to his liking. She stood for several minutes with her arms folded over her chest glowering at them and then turned and left the room. Things changed after she caught the couple red-handed. Tommy never gave her any more trouble.

Mable had an extremely tough skin, but was fond of students. She knew their excessive behavior, and often had to clean up after them. She had plenty of stories about beer and whisky bottles, condoms, dope stashes, stolen TV sets and stereos, and other sorts of adolescent misbehavior. She had it in her heart not to hold it against them, but she could not forgive or forget the excesses of grown men and women.

She told me about the maid in Stephens Hall who kept Morton's lair in the basement in good order, and about catching Tommy and the dean in the midst of lovemaking. She shared a lot with me that she said she never told anyone. I had visited her and her husband in the hospital when he was dying of cancer. No one else from campus came, including Morton's handpicked chaplain.

Chapter 15

NEAL JAMES

The English Department at Worthington was peopled by a strange array of characters, which is probably true of any English Department. One of the most interesting was Neal James. Neal was brilliant, but had a difficult personality. He had keen insights and significant causes. He rather enjoyed being enigmatic and unpredictable, while giving the appearance of profound sincerity.

He was born in Kansas to a young woman out of wedlock. She tried to raise him, but finally admitted she was not able to do so when he was three years old. She wanted to give him up for adoption, but did not know how. She drove all one night from the little town where they lived, and left him at the front door of a police station in downtown Kansas City. He was a smart child, but could not give the police enough information to find his mother. He was placed in an orphanage where he remained through high school. He excelled in his schoolwork, but, like many orphans, was unsure of how to get along with people.

He was rather striking in his appearance, which was carefully and consciously studied and periodically changed drastically. He would let his hair and his beard grow long, and then show up one day clean shaven and with short hair. He would generally dress nicely without over-dressing. Sometimes, however, he would appear immaculately dressed for no apparent reason except that he needed a change. At other times he would dress down in blue jeans, sport shirt, and tennis shoes. He was always neat and clean and modest in his appearance and manner. He usually seemed to be considering some matter of great concern. At times he appeared downright depressed. Generally he was a screen upon which one could project all sorts of motives and characteristics. He could be moderately cordial, but I never saw him openly friendly with anyone. Most of the time he appeared to be on some important mission, but I had seen him in an unguarded moment looking like a lost child.

Neal's Shakespeare course was well-known, if not entirely popular, among the students. I often thought he would make a great actor, and would play the role of Hamlet especially well. I had been told by students he would often lose himself in reading a soliloquy. He could be extremely eloquent and inspiring in class. If a student came in late or was unprepared, however, he could be savage. He was known upon occasion to walk out of class abruptly, leaving the students in shock.

Faculty meetings were never interesting or especially helpful. Van Dale would preside and Morton would sit at the head of one of the tables looking out over the assembly in a threatening manner. There is almost nothing of value I remember coming out of those meetings. I do remember some of Neal's arguments for or against some issue or cause, however. I did not always agree with him, and sometimes did not even know what he was talking about, but when he directed himself against the administration, he could score verbal points. He was just as likely to stake out a position on some moral high ground and try to defend it against those who were fighting the administration. He would never fight fire with fire, even when this meant ultimately losing the battle.

Neal was one of the persons on the faculty who believed our struggle could be won through exhaustive and effective committee work. He spent long hours developing standards, additions to the Faculty Manual, lists of ways students could be retained, and scores of other important matters. These procedures would never mean anything as long as Morton and Van Dale were in charge. They could wipe out years of work with one sweep of the hand. Often they did what they pleased and let faculty committee work lay on the table, no matter what it said.

I think deep down, Neal knew all this. He could be amazingly perceptive. Where he seemed almost dense, however, was in terms of his refusal to do things any other way. By insisting on going through the channels set up by the administration and faculty, he set himself up for failure. He was determined to do things the only way he knew, simply because it was right. This had moral overtones, of course, and Neal could be one of the most ethical persons I have ever known. But most of the time it meant he was not going to paint outside the lines. It was as simple as that. What he considered to be right was right because it was right. Sometimes his axiological determinations seemed rather self-serving, however. Paradoxically, this made it easy for the administration to control him. All they had to do was pretend to play by the rules, and do what was right, and then ignore the outcome. I never could convince Neal the administration did not care what we thought or did.

We had a number of long conversations during the time my situation was coming to a head. He had studied Morton well and was able to intuit things I had not considered. I did not know how much he knew about psychology in any formal sense, but he seemed to be able to psych a person or figure a situation with natural and uncalculating ease. It was a pleasure to observe his keen and perceptive mind. He was able to analyze a situation and see where a set of circumstances would lead given the players and the time involved. He seldom was wrong. All of this insight seemed wasted when he tried to deal effectively with the actual situation. He seemed to be intellectually muscle-bound. I thought I could rely on him, but was disappointed. I had no doubt he understood what I was doing and why, but he could not travel with me.

His relationship with Bonnie Smith compromised his position. Bonnie was a beautiful young woman whom I had taught as a freshman. She was able to move freely between different groups within our little society, which gave her increasing attention. She had the maturity of a person a decade older than she was. She changed her major from Elementary Education to English in her junior year. This meant a heavy schedule and an extra semester. She took every upper-level course Neal offered. Students began to gossip as they saw the two of them leave class together. They were also seen together in other settings outside the confines of the college. Neal frequently called on her in class and often seemed to be talking directly to her in his lectures. When she was in his class, he appeared to be more animated and demonstrative in his lectures. They shared certain insights, secrets, and common tastes.

Neal's wife, Mary, worked in the library and took courses on campus and at the local branch of a state university. She suddenly separated from Neal and later divorced him. She maintained her position in the library until the end of that semester and then left to work in a local firm. After that, gossip had it that Bonnie was living with Neal. This became official when they moved together into a new apartment after she graduated.

One would have thought this kind of situation would have been cause for Neal's dismissal, especially on a church-related campus. Indeed, standards on state school campuses specifically forbid such relationships. At Worthington, this kind of behavior was not only tolerated, but also implicitly encouraged. Morton enjoyed such situations for a number of reasons, not the least of which was the fact that it seemed to tickle his libido. It also meant he had something that could be used against the persons involved if he ever needed it. I looked around me and realized how many people were sleeping around. Morton had sponsored an atmosphere in our little world in which it was all right to do just about anything you wanted. The thing one did not do, however, was blow the whistle or challenge what was going on in the administration of the college.

Neal was not religious and made a point of asserting his distaste for the church. For this, and other reasons, his humanistic standards lacked focus and depth. They were like a large tree with wide-spreading roots that were shallow and vulnerable in a storm.

I have no doubt about his sincerity, but in many situations, sincerity is a second-rate virtue. The crisis in which we eventually found ourselves seemed to confuse Neal. He wanted to do the right thing, but found himself to be hopelessly compromised. Since his concept of right was not necessarily informed by absolutes, he seemed to blow in the winds of relativism. He seemed, like many of the existential heroes in the literature he taught, deeply to desire anchors for his convictions, but to be chronically unable to find them.

After a detailed discussion of what was wrong with Morton, he told me he appreciated what I was doing. He was unusually charitable in his appraisal of my efforts. He told me, however, that he could not help me. He said he was obviously in no position to do so.

He then asked me an interesting and alarming question regarding my position concerning Morton's indiscretions: "Is this cheap moralizing?"

I interpreted his question to be whether I was judging him and his affair. I assured him I was not and went on to say I had not criticized the morality of his living with Bonnie. I told him I did not understand it. I did not think it appropriate for anyone of his standing in the community to do something like that, but my quarrel with Morton was different. I assured him it was not based on "cheap moralizing." I was not so much concerned with his affair with his secretary, as disgusting as that was. I was deeply troubled by how this affected the morale, and morality of everyone on the campus and the future of the institution.

Chapter 16

IRENE SANDERS AND
CHARLES ARNSDORF

Irene Sanders came to Worthington, as chair of the Music Department, several years after Julie and I moved to Harrison. Her predecessor was energetic and talented. He had a large ego and seemed solidly in control of the department and of his choirs. I did not realize it, but some of his students commented to me on how he suddenly became uncertain and then caustic in his remarks about the school and the administration. They said it was as if he had been poisoned. He left Harrison rather hurriedly for a new position elsewhere. We wondered at the time about his sudden departure, but had no idea why it had come about.

When Irene came in, she quickly began reorganizing her department. The critical Germanic presence of Manfred Schulz was an impediment. He was never fond of her. Given the situation, however, this was to be expected. Manfred was so extraordinary in his talent and so perceptive in his judgment that it would have been hard for anyone to come into the situation.

Irene was beautiful and had a wonderful soprano voice. She had sung as a young woman with one of the top swing bands in the country. She was versatile, with a range from opera to popular music. She was middle-aged and carried many scars, including two unsuccessful marriages. The first ended when she came home to find her husband hanging from a rope secured to exposed beams in their family room. The second ended when her husband came out of the closet. Both relationships had been devastating to her and her two daughters from her first marriage. She was able to project an effervescent charm, while simultaneously protecting a stoic inner citadel in which she really lived.

The politics of Irene's department were rather Machiavellian. There was a tone set by the others in the department, including Manfred Schulz, and a husband and wife who taught piano. They seemed to assume every student who majored in music would one day be a world-renowned soloist or a concert pianist. Churches often complained that they would rather have someone who could play "The Old Rugged Cross" than a snob who could only relate to long and boring offertories featuring Bach, Beethoven, or Brahms. Irene could understand both sides of this argument, so she did not take sides. She preferred to step back and let others in the department squabble

An important part of her agenda revolved around Colonel Charles Arnsdorf. Charles was in charge of the Department of Speech and Drama, and directed the Catacombs Theatre in the bowels of the old building that housed my office. He was born in Switzerland, but came to this country as a teenager and had a successful career in the Air Force. Swiss German was his first language. Since I had studied in Switzerland, he and I had fun talking to each other while others around us were trying to figure out what language we were speaking and why.

He played many roles in his life, and most of them well. Nothing about him reflected his foreign origins or his military background. He usually wore a large curled moustache and a jaunty black beret. Some of my Religion students would occasionally wander unsuspectingly into one of his classes or get involved in a play. They would come to me concerned about his use of four-letter words and other inappropriate terms. I tried to reassure them, not always successfully, that this was just his way and that he had a lot to offer.

I found Charles to be refreshingly honest and unpretentious. He also enjoyed making the right people angry. He worked on a play about the intimate life of our governor and his second wife. The governor's belligerent brother came to him and threatened to break both of his legs and harm his family. That project was deepsixed!

He also wrote a historical musical titled, *The Soul of the South*." It was difficult to get black students to play the role of slaves in the play, but once they opted in things went well. The play unfortunately never caught on as the epic Charles hoped it would be. He wrote and produced another play about the local aristocrats. It portrayed the social season and the grand fêtes, which absorbed the attention of the hopelessly rich and privileged. The title, *Mystic Balls*, was a bit too provocative for some of our provincial audience.

Charles got away with a lot because he was independently wealthy. He put a lot of his own money into the Catacombs. All he ever got from Morton was promises, which were almost never honored. He bought lights, set materials, sound equipment, costumes, etc. He loved what he was doing, and it showed. The students who knew him loved him, in spite of his chauvinism, his bawdy language, and the advances he occasionally made on some of the women. There was no hypocrisy in Charles, and he refused to play the games everyone else seemed to be involved in around Worthington.

At first, the departments of Music and Drama had little more to do with each other than the fact that both were in the Division of Visual Arts. As division chair, Irene was Charles's superior. She got involved with many of his productions. This included the musicals he produced and directed. They also began to stage operas together featuring her voice students. This helped her get away from the infighting of the Music Department. She simply did her own thing with Charles and ignored the others. They also produced a real potboiler she wrote about the suffragette movement. The music was wonderful, but the plot and the dialogue left a lot to be desired. Irene and Charles were creative and productive persons. They enjoyed collaborating, and gradually developed their skills together—both on the stage and off.

It was a public secret around campus that Irene and Charles were more involved with each more than just professionally. Their on-going relationship was a kind of soap opera that most of us knew about, but chose to ignore. We overlooked what we saw because of our high regard for these two remarkable and talented people. With no guidance from the leadership of the college, we really did not know how to deal with this situation. We were willing to let this be their business. Morton, of course, would not do anything about it because he found it to be interesting and amusing. He also knew he had some measure of control of these two middle-aged bohemians because of their relationship.

Charles had been married for some 30 years. He and his wife had three grown children. Marie Arnsdorf was a proud and talented person. She was suspicious of Charles and jealous of his contact with women in his productions. When she began to hear gossip about the time he was spending with Irene, she was deeply hurt and offended. This was the last straw for their relationship. She and Charles were persons of means with contacts in the community. She began to use these contacts to bring pressure on Morton.

At first she had assumed the administration would discover what was going on and do something about it. She knew well that Morton was amoral, but she assumed he would have to deal with the relationship between two prominent members of his faculty. When appeals to morality failed, she turned to monetary matters, in effect demanding action based on her ability to stop the flow of essential funds from individuals in the community. This got Morton's attention.

This began one of the many bizarre chapters in the long book of abusive actions against the Worthington faculty by Morton. Mary worked through the hapless and spineless Van Dale, who called Irene to meet with him and Morton in his office. She was informed she would no longer be chair of the Music Department for the corning year. In order to salve her pride, he further suggested she could go ahead and retire early.

She immediately contacted her lawyer, Richard McArthur, and asked him to represent her in this matter. In the meanwhile, Morton contacted Ralph Woods and offered him the chair of the Music Department. It is difficult to describe what an unreal move this was. Morton had the reputation of always doing what was least expected. Ralph was a tall, raw-boned country boy whom you could not help but like. He had an overwhelming bass voice. He was talented and could train and successfully conduct good choirs. He was more at home in a Baptist church, however, than in a college classroom. Van Dale gave him an early contract making him full-time and head of the department.

This was all exceeding strange, because Ralph had taught at Worthington for only two years as a part-time instructor in choral music. Irene had a doctorate from a nationally recognized program. Ralph had a master's degree, which he had struggled to finish at a local state college branch. Ralph was overwhelmed and deeply suspicious; He had not been born yesterday. He asked for time to consider the offer. Morton and Van Dale insisted they had to have his signature within twenty-four hours. They told him he must sign it. It was his duty to the college and his colleagues to take hold of the department and to bring it out of the chaos Irene Sanders had caused. He reluctantly, and against his better judgment, signed the document and turned it in the next day.

Schulz and the other artsy members of the department, who were often offended by Irene's theater work and pop singing, were utterly appalled by Morton's courting of Ralph Woods. Morton and Van Dale paid little attention to their protests. When Richard McArthur contacted Morton and Van Dale about an impending suit, they got busy trying to undo what they had so recently set up. They called Ralph in once more and told him the deal was off. They said things had changed and they "must have the contract back." It was his duty to the school and to his department. In turn for giving up the contract, they promised to make him full-time. They also said they would provide him with a handsome bonus that would raise his salary to considerably more than he would otherwise earn at the college.

The contracts came out the following March. We usually got them in the mail over spring break when the college was closed. We had ten days to discuss the terms of the contract. If a faculty member was not on campus during that time, the letter with the contract simply remained in his or her campus mailbox. Ralph searched his mailbox in vain: He received no contract. Several weeks earlier, he had received a letter from Van Dale suggesting his position might be eliminated and his services no longer needed. Ralph had kept all of the paper work, and had written a diary of all conversations.

He turned everything over to his lawyer and entered into a long and painful period of waiting, which ended the next fall just before classes were to begin. Ralph's last check under his old contract also ended at this time. He had to settle. He made so little that he could not survive the loss of his paycheck. The settlement was invariably the equivalent of one-year's salary. Ralph could have continued the suit and had it drag on for years. He might well have won it, but he could not afford to keep it going. This was Morton's way of getting rid of faculty and administrators whom he did not want or who stood up to him.

Irene's contract, on the other hand, was the same as before and even included a raise, which was not necessarily true for the rest of us. She taught another year and then agreed to retire, with the additional year's salary as a pay off. She was not necessarily ready to retire, but there was little reason for her to take the abuse any longer. After she left the college, Charles divorced his wife and he and Irene were married. Morton also forced him out, but allowed him the pretense that he was leaving to go to California to take care of his inheritance following the death of a wealthy family member. This was true, but it was also an excuse.

There was a presentation at the Catacombs honoring Charles and re-naming the theater in his honor. Supposedly, funds would be allocated to fix up the old basement and make it into a first-class theater. None of this was ever done, of course. It remained the same old, grungy basement theater. Charles shook the dust off his sandals as he left. His motivation was to get away from his wife and marry Irene.

Chapter 17

MANFRED SCHULZ

Manfred Schultz had been in the German Army during World War II. He came to the United States country after the War with the sponsorship of a Methodist church in the conference. He was employed there as organist and choir director for several years and then came to the college, where he remained for the rest of his career. He became nationally known as an interpreter of Bach and was a published composer. He was a brilliant interpreter of Protestant neo-orthodoxy and able to integrate his theology into his popular music appreciation class.

In many ways, Schulz was a typical German intellectual, knowing everything and critical of everyone who knew less than he. In other ways, however, he was unique. Schulz was independent and tough-minded. He had headed the Music Department at one time, and conducted the college choir, but now he kept out of the limelight as much as possible. He came to one faculty meeting a year, and then only if there was some matter of importance to be voted upon. He taught his classes, conducted private lessons on the excellent organ he had built in the chapel, and went his way.

It was hard to figure out why he stayed at Worthington.

He despised Morton, telling me that, "There is something human which is fundamentally lacking in him." It was known that Schulz had been one of "the six angry young men" who went to the trustees early in Morton's tenure as president. Their first aim was accomplished: The notoriously offensive and incompetent dean whom Morton originally brought in was fired. The second goal of the conspirators was to have Morton removed. They failed miserably in this regard. He turned their bravery against them and used his agents on the trustee board to root them out. Schulz was the only one who survived, and this was rumored to be because of the uproar among vocal alumni .

He would discuss with his classes in church music the dreadful musicality of the "good old hymns." He would dramatically read aloud examples of the musical legacy of nineteenth century romanticism. It was generally suffused with bad poetry, bad theology, and bad taste. Schulz would critically dissect the content of such hymns as, "I Come to the Garden Alone," which he labeled as an example of Jesus eroticism.

He had a favorite escapade in which he would march around the classroom singing vigorously, "Onward Christian soldiers, forward as to war, with the cross of Jesus hid behind the door." He found the political and patriotic emphases in some of the hymns to be dangerous. Because of his experience in Germany under Hitler, where Nazi flags were brought into the churches, Schulz found the placement of American flags in churches to be idolatrous.

Many students were liberated from their conservative musical backgrounds. Others went home and informed pastors and parishioners concerning the blasphemy involved in some of the traditions in which they had been raised in the church. This filtered upward to superintendents and bishops, who were quite unhappy with Schulz. On the other hand, he played every year at Annual Conference, which was held on our campus. He played Bach and Mozart for preludes and postludes. He also played the standard music for hymn singing during the week of meetings. No one could say they were not moved by the majesty, virtuosity, and mastery of his playing.

Morton invited the new dean of the Duke Divinity School, Greg Johnson, to come and speak at Worthington. I had not met him, but knew of him from the time he was a leader in the Methodist Student Movement in the '60s. While Greg was on campus during his lecture series, he got to know the faculty and students and was well received. He knew I was a Duke graduate, and up-dated me on the professors I had worked under for my doctorate. We had a nice conversation and then he asked if he could meet with me in private.

We set up an appointment in my office for the following day, the last day he was on campus. He began by swearing me to secrecy.

"Do not tell anyone that we have spoken about this matter," he said. He had come to Duke from the presidency of a Methodist seminary in the West. This was the seminary from which Morton had received his theological degree. Greg told me a search committee was looking for a new president of the seminary. He was on that committee. Morton's name was on the list they were considering.

From our conversation, I understood why we were hosting Greg for a series of theological lectures. These things did not happen without a reason.

Then he made a jaw-dropping request.

"I want you to write a recommendation for Dr. Morton to succeed me as president of the seminary. I must have it within a week. I want to know how you feel about him. Would he make a good president for the seminary? Your comments would mean a great deal to me. Will you do this for me?" I was uncertain about this, but I did agree to write a recommendation.

I could not keep my promise not to speak with anyone and still send a letter to him within the next seven days, however. I mentioned his request to three people: Julie, Phillip Maddox, and Schulz. I valued the judgment of these three people and knew they would keep my secret. Julie knew of my profound disgust with the man.

All she could counsel was, "Be honest."

Phil was a dear friend whose advice and council I valued. He had also survived on this campus under Morton for years as head of a department. He had the genuine God-given ability to see both sides of any issue. I was careful in mentioning the matter to him. We discussed it and he simply affirmed it was difficult task. He did not indicate what he thought either way.

When I told Schulz about it, he responded immediately and emphatically.

"Say something good! Say something g-o-o-d!" He stressed that we needed to be rid of this man. "We need to send him off. Give him a promotion. Let him be someone else's problem."

It was an amusing conversation, and one that helped me see the real possibilities of this opportunity. I wrote the letter the next day. I did not show it to anyone and did not keep a copy of it. In it, I combined the insights of the three persons in whom I had confided. For Julie, I did try to be as fair as possible. For Phil, I reflected on Morton's years at Worthington and how he had taken it through difficult times. For Manfred, I gave Morton the strongest possible recommendation I could write without throwing up. I never heard from my letter. The search committee at the seminary chose someone else. Greg Johnson passed away suddenly from a heart attack the next year. It was a great loss.

Chapter 18

SUSAN PETERSON

Susan Peterson was an attractive, middle-aged wife of an officer on the local Air Force base. She followed Sarah Robinson as our Registrar. It was the difference between night and day. Miss Robinson had graduated from the college years ago and began to work for the college immediately thereafter. She worked her way up to Registrar under the presidency of Dr. Stephen A. McTaggart and remained in office until she retired under Morton. Her office was just down the hall from Morton's, but they were worlds apart. She was one of the few people Morton did not mess with. She was an authority in her own right, so what she said was right, if for no other reason than the fact that she said it.

She was intensely loyal, and she knew when to look the other way. Much of the time she moved about her little world of records unchallenged and unchallenging to other fiefdoms. She could be pleasant enough, flashing occasionally a winning smile. When anyone questioned her judgment, however, they had a battle on their hands. She used her power skillfully and efficiently. She was not corrupt, but she refused to see what was happening around her.

Miss Robinson's other main function on campus was to be secretary to every important committee. She took the notes at every faculty meeting and edited copies of minutes, which we all received in campus mail. Even after she retired, Morton retained her as secretary to the Board of Trustees. Vast amounts of facts, figures, names, and dates could pass through her quick and accurate mind, be transcribed onto paper, and filed away in containers of records on dusty shelves. She had to understand the lies, deceptions, and follies represented in the material she handled. It never seemed to register with her, however. The quickness and accuracy of her judgment as Registrar did not seem to carry over into other areas, or she would not have remained as long as she did.

She was replaced with a bright, attractive, caring, and innovating woman half her age. Miss Robinson was at best inscrutable. Susan Peterson was forthcoming, approachable, and thoughtful. She went out of her way to help both students and faculty alike. She really wanted to be doing what she was doing, and it showed. Her husband was born and raised in Harrison, but Susan was from the north. She had met and married him when he was assigned to the Pentagon. She moved south with him when he was assigned to his hometown. They hoped to retire in Harrison, so, when her husband was transferred back north, she stayed at Worthington. Maintaining two households until he completed his latest tour of duty and could retire was not easy. She had worked in responsible positions elsewhere and knew things did not have to be the way they were. She was loyal to the administration and to all of us whom she served, but she also had a higher loyalty—namely to the truth.

Adam knew Susan well and respected her. They came to the college at the same time and shared many insights with each other. One day, when he and I were talking, I began to rave over how wonderful it was to have her as our new registrar.

Adam brought my soaring idealism back down to earth with the question, "You know why she was hired?" My response was an appreciation of her abilities, her work ethic, her efficiency, and other wonderful traits that would have recommended her to anyone who understood what a registrar should be.

Adam stroked his chin for about ten seconds and responded, "Naw, boobs, it was her boobs."

I was taken aback and asked, "What do you mean?"

"Haven't you noticed how stacked she is?" he asked.

"Of course I have. I am not blind, but that is irrelevant."

"Not to Morton," he said. "There were only two really serious candidates for the job: Susan and an old maid. Morton told his buddies he chose the boobs."

I sighed and commented, "Sounds like him."

Susan did her job extremely well the two years she worked as Registrar. She earned the admiration and respect of both the students and the faculty. The administrators took their cues, as usual, from Morton. Those who had been around a while knew it was only a matter of time until he made his move, so they stood back and waited. Morton was notorious for the attention he gave the women who worked for the college. Since, in effect, he did all of the hiring, except for the building and grounds crew, he had opportunity to inspect all of the women.

There were numerous tales of his suggestive comments, his groping, pinching, and cajoling the women in Stephens Hall. He did not limit himself to the administration building, however. He loved to sneak up behind a coed, the wife of one of the teachers or coaches, a secretary, almost any attractive woman on campus. He would tap the victim on the shoulder, and then kiss her on the lips when she turned around, and say, "Gotcha!" It was a source of constant irritation for the women and made the rest of us want to vomit.

Secretaries and other female employees had an agreement that they would not walk down the halls of the administration building by themselves. It was a terrible comment on the world of Morton, but a realistic understanding of the situation. There was a young woman who worked as cashier who caught Morton's fancy from the first day he hired her. Her name was Karen Boudreaux. She had married a Cajun from South Louisiana. She was tall and statuesque, with broad shoulders, large well-shaped breasts, and a wasp waist. With her phenomenal figure, Karen was nevertheless demure, almost shy, reserved, and pleasant to work with. She did her job well and went home to her husband and young family. When I had occasion to speak with her, we talked about the remarkable culture of South Louisiana.

One day Morton could stand it no longer. He had his secretary go out and buy a tape measure. Then he processed down the hall with several of his cronies to the Business Manager's office, where the only door to the cashier's windows was located. He went up behind Karen, who was counting out change to a student, and reached around her waist with the tape measure. When she jumped, he intentionally grabbed her with his greedy hands. He insisted on repeating his attempt to get an exact measurement of her waist while his cronies howled with laugher. Karen blushed hot and red. She took several sick days before returning. She was terrified from that day onward any time she thought Morton was on the end of the hall where she worked. This continued until she quit a year later to have her baby.

Susan Peterson was aware of Morton's reputation. Somehow she thought it would never happen to her. One day he came into her office ostensibly to discuss some academic matter. He began by asking about her husband, her two teenage children, and other personal matters. After answering his questions briefly, she turned to her desk to get the file with the information she expected to discuss with him. Morton moved quickly up behind her, grabbed her shoulders, and turned her to face him. He caught her with his arms and kissed her firmly. He held her so tightly she could not move, and indeed could scarcely breathe. He loosened his grip and moved both hands up to her breasts and began to massage them. This gave Susan her first opportunity to react. She shoved him back and brought up her right hand with the palm open. She struck him full in the face and knocked him over sideways to the floor. It was not that she had hit him that hard—he was off-balance from his amorous attempts.

Susan then shouted so loud the three other women who worked in the registrar's office all heard her shout. "If you ever try that again, my husband will kill you!"

Morton got up with a terrified look on his face, brushed off his rear end, and left the building as fast as he could. When we heard about it, there was secret rejoicing all over campus. Some said you could see the print of Susan's hand on his face for weeks. She was the only woman we ever heard about who put him in his place.

From that time on, things moved downhill for Susan. Morton left her strictly alone, but others let her know she was persona non grata. She was noticeably excluded from staff meetings. She was supposed to work closely with the academic dean, yet van Dale avoided her and made decisions without her. She was a devout Catholic, and as the Easter season neared, she began to get ridiculous questions about worshiping Mary and the saints, holy water, and how Catholic women used the rhythm method. She knew Morton was the source of this harassment, but could not prove it.

When she designed beautiful new programs for the approaching graduation ceremonies, Van Dale coldly asked, "Who gave you permission?"

She felt the eyes of Morton's cronies going up and down her body. They laughed at her behind her back and made suggestive gestures. She felt dirty and abused.

The last straw was an argument with the Business Manager. His main qualification for the job was the fact that he had ridden a small college in a neighboring state into the ground. He was pleased to have another chance and would do anything Morton asked him. Contracts were coming out in the spring. The major players in the administration had gotten theirs, the secretaries had gotten theirs, and the faculty had gotten theirs. Susan received nothing. She asked her secretary to go down to the business office and pick up her contract. The Business Manager's secretary told Susan's secretary to tell her to come and get it herself.

When she went to the Business Office, the Business Manager came out and asked her in the presence of his secretary, "What do you want?" She stated her business and he responded, "Why are you in such a hurry?"

After that, Susan went to Van Dale's office and asked what was happening. He feigned ignorance and said he had no control over the Business Manager. He told her to go to Morton. She then went across the hall reluctantly. She stood in the doorway repeating the facts and saying the Business Manager had been rude to her and Van Dale was less than helpful. Morton told her he was delighted she had come to him. He pretended to consider the situation as if he were hearing about it for the first time. He said he could do nothing about the rudeness of the Business Manager. Only the trustees could handle him, he said. After all, it was they who hired him. He seemed delighted with himself over this clever twist of logic.

Susan typed up a letter of resignation that day and had it on Morton's desk before closing time. She also typed up a letter that was in the campus mail to the entire faculty and staff the next day. Morton bragged about having been a boxer in college. For us she was the champ. She had actually knocked him down. For weeks we walked around campus humming the theme from the movie, "Rocky." At the same time, we were indignant about the way she had been treated. This was the South, and we were supposed to treat women like ladies, not trash.

After Susan left Harrison, she went to join her husband in Washington. At the end of his assignment at the Pentagon, he was transferred to San Antonio. This was to be his last stint before retiring and returning home. Sadly, he dropped dead one day on the job from a heart attack. Susan returned to Harrison and was hired at Worthington under the new regime after Morton was gone. She was the head of the Evening Division, and was effective in this new position, but never like she had been as Registrar.

Chapter 19

MAUD MITCHELL

My first chance to confirm what I had heard about Tommy Parnell resulted from his appointment as Dean of Recruitment. Maud Mitchell had worked in the Admissions Office for over a decade. She had already broken in two administrators and had served as their office manager. She would have made an infinitely better head of the office than Tommy, and knew more about it than he ever would. He considered her a threat and vowed he would sack her. Once he took over, Maud began to have insulting notes on her door. She was deposed as office manager and ostracized by others in the office, including some whom she had helped as students. Finally, Tommy fired her and she filed an age discrimination suit.

Even though she was over fifty, she was trying to finish her course work for her degree. I taught in the evening division and had her in a number of classes. She worked hard and did good work. She made A's, not because she was necessarily that smart, but because she was not content until she had done her best. This usually put her at the top of the class. I had also taught two of her daughters and one son. Maud was not a person Tommy could roll over easily without getting some attention. Almost everyone on our campus knew Maud or a member of her family. She was popular with the students because she was the parent of several of them and because she went out of her way to help them.

Maud filed a grievance on campus against Tommy for harassment. This was referred to a grievance committee, chaired by the Business Manager. On the committee, she asked me to represent her. Mark Springer represented the administration, and Kathleen Krantz was the third faculty member. The arrangement was odd, since Mark and Kathleen were both in the same department. Knowing how much contempt Kathleen had for Mark, both professionally and personally, I was not sure how they could work together productively on this committee. Our role was never clear to me. We were not to act as if we were attorneys, nor were we to perform as judges.

Daniel Callahan was the current Business Manager. He was the youngest of the dozen Business Managers we had in the period we were at the college. This was probably the most perilous position on the staff. Their tenure was usually short, and Daniel lasted only a year. Participation in our committee may have been one of the reasons. When any financial difficulties or irregularities were reported the Business Manager got the blame. Dan's predecessor got the axe after the school failed to pay the TIAA faculty retirement funds for an entire year. The following year it was reported we had to pay the funds plus the interest they would have earned, plus penalties for withholding the money. Blame, of course, was placed on the shoulders of the Business Manager, who disappeared over the summer. Faculty members thought someone should go to jail for this, but not the Business Manager.

Daniel was a young man with roots in the area and in the church. Both his father and his grandfather were pastors. His grandfather's first charge was Athens. He lived in the parsonage where we stayed our first summer. When he first came, he heard a black man was being held in the local jail, charged with killing a white man. He got word the prisoner was to be moved by the police into the larger jail in Harrison. Klansmen, including some members of the church, planned to follow the police car and, when it made a prearranged stop, abduct the prisoner and lynch him.

Pastor Callahan fell in behind the police car in his old Ford and refused to let the Klan car pass. This meant the police car did not stop and the prisoner arrived safely in Harrison. A cross burned brightly in the yard of the parsonage the next night. The bishop moved Callahan immediately for his safety. To me, this man was a real hero, and I respected his grandson for his heritage. I told him about my connection to the parish where his grandfather had served and we became friends.

When Julie and I first came to Worthington, the Business Manager was an older man who had a number of connections in the community. He had been the president of a local bank before he came to the college under McTaggart and was a real professional. He was an authority in his own right, and Morton could not push him around. Since he retired, younger, less qualified, less secure individuals had been hired and fired regularly. Daniel was well trained, but had no idea what he was getting into. He was required, during the proceedings of the committee, to review the allegations of both sides. He was not allowed to say anything or to vote at the conclusion of the proceedings. Morton's mandate was, of course, that he was supposed to keep a lid on things. Because of his integrity, he genuinely tried to make sense of the case and to come up with a fair verdict.

I relished my participation in the hearings as an opportunity to try and get at the truth of what was really happening at the college. Daniel never seemed to be entirely happy with me, but he was not able to say what he wanted me to do. He called me to complain about the way we were questioning the witnesses. He used the model of court procedure. He had legal training, but decided to go on to graduate school in business rather than to law school. Those of us on the committee knew this was no court of law. We had many complaints and knew this was a rare opportunity. It was clear Morton was putting pressure on Dan to shut us up.

Maud presented us with a list of twenty-two names—most of them character witnesses. Tommy's side offered only four names, all from within the recruitment office. The sessions of the grievance committee were farcical. We heard almost all of the persons Maud had asked to appear before us. We did not have subpoena power, nor were the witnesses sworn. From Maud's side of the case, that did not matter. Her witnesses spoke openly, freely, and confidently in praise of her character and her work. They characterized Tommy as rough, coarse, vulgar, and vituperative. They called him a liar. It was not necessarily easy for many of them to testify, because they worked for the college.

Tommy's witnesses, on the other hand, were tense and controlled. We got word they had all met with Tommy and the college's lawyer who coached them for hours. Tommy had put Byron Simmons in charge of presenting the charges. Byron was a former student of mine, in whom I found neither much promise nor anything to which I really objected. I always saw Byron as a rather shy person. Later I questioned whether he was shy or calculating. After finishing his degree, he remained at the college as one of the young recruiters who went out to entice high school students to come to Worthington. Two young women were hired at the same time he was. Tommy got rid of both of them: One went to the alumni office, and the other, Kelly Parsons, was forced out.

Kelly and I were good friends. When I taught her as a freshman she was gorgeous, but terribly naive. Later, when she was a junior, I was sitting with a group of students in the cafeteria one day at the beginning of the spring semester. Kelly came over and asked to talk with me. A young man with whom she had grown up had given her a ring over the Christmas holidays. I congratulated her. She told me what he had done was not appropriate.

When I asked her why, she blurted out tearfully, "Because I don't love him." I then asked her why she had taken the ring and become engaged. She continued, "You don't understand. It was my birthday and almost Christmas, and besides, his family and mine are best of friends. They think we are perfect for each other." We talked about another thirty minutes. I told her it was time for her to take charge of her life and quit being what others expected her to be. She agreed.

To my great surprise, the next time I saw her (some two weeks later), she told me matter-of-factly, "Well, I gave back the ring."

"Oh," I replied. "How do you feel?"

"Wonderful!" she said. And she looked it. I have never seen anyone grow up so quickly. In her senior year she was elected presiding officer of her sorority and Miss Worthington. She represented both the sorority and the college with dignity and maturity. Her head was not turned by so much attention. I was proud of her.

Tommy found in Byron someone whom he could shape and control. But the two young ladies, especially Kelly, would not put with his manipulation (which included his usual proposals for action), so he got rid of them. Kelly left Worthington and got a similar job in a private college in a neighboring state. She agreed to come back for the hearings. Her testimony about conditions working under Tommy was devastating. I have often wished for my son to marry a person as beautiful and as honest as Kelly.

She was never so gracious or so calm and collected as when she testified for Maud. It was truly amazing to hear and watch this poised and articulate young woman portray how the situation in the admissions office had changed when Tommy took over. She had begun working as a recruiter with Byron, and Mary Roundtree who had moved to the alumni office. Byron gradually moved into Tommy's orbit, while Kelly and Mary quietly and efficiently continued to do their work. When she and Mary refused Tommy advances, he worked to get them out, no matter that Kelly was the most effective recruiter the office had.

She talked about how Maud had been the human glue that held the office together. She undercut the accusations that would later be made by those working under Tommy. She vividly described the dehumanization of the office by Tommy and his pawn Byron. The major threat to this scheme was Maud. So Tommy set about to destroy her. Jokes were made about her, obscenities were written on the notepad on her door. Others in the office were told to disregard what she said. When Maud refused to quit, she was unceremoniously fired. Kelly was persuasive and convincing in her description of the situation in the office, which had cost both her and Maud their jobs. Going through the twenty-one other witnesses on Maud's list simply corroborated Kelly's testimony and added detail. Maud was by no means perfect, as her friends were readily want to say, but she was decent, diligent, and respected for the job she had done over the years.

Tommy's four witnesses included Byron, two young ladies who were former students, and one of Tommy's golfers, Bert Andrews, who had become a part-time assistant coach. Byron articulated the party line on which the college lawyer had drilled all four of Tommy's witnesses. He began to insinuate some of the themes and accusations against Maud, but was cautious not to overstate or to do more than begin the attack. There were points at which we felt he was lying, but we were not successful in catching him at it.

Another former student, Sandra Troudeau, joined the admissions staff shortly after Byron. She was from the Gulf coast, and obviously had some of the blood of the French and Spanish who had settled in that area. She was beautiful, and had served as Miss Worthington. A part of her appeal as a student was her sharp mind, modest demeanor, and ease with people. She had many friends, and seemed to seek out and befriend people who were not popular. I kidded her about being our "Cajun Queen."

I watched Byron and Sandra change as they allowed themselves to be shaped by Parnell's warped values I felt I hardly knew them anymore and was on my guard with them. Byron was rather asexual. I never saw him with a girl. Sandra, on the other hand, used her beauty to recruit athletes. She changed the way she dressed and adopted a flirty manner that did not become her. She had the reputation of sleeping around and having sex with Parnell. She was the next witness for the college's prosecution. I was ill prepared for the figure that walked suavely and coolly into the hearing room. She seemed to enjoy testifying before us. She led the charge, giving us accusations and gossipy details as if they were the truth. She was now, with icy precision, playing her part without that charm I regarded as essential to her personality. She seemed quite willing to engage in character assassination or any other hatchet-wielding task her controllers found for her to do.

The third and fourth witnesses were both disasters for the college's trumped-up charges against Maud. Ann Hanson was the stepdaughter of a former professor in Education. She could not have offered greater contrast to Sandra. Ann was of medium height, with long blond hair and blue eyes. In contrast to Sandra's dark, mysterious and duplicitous demeanor, Ann was vulnerable and nervous. She seemed on the verge of tears throughout her testimony. She tried to repeat some of the charges against Maud her coaches had given her. When she lied to us, however, the effect on her was far more profound than it was on us. I had taught her and was embarrassed for her. I am sure she was terribly relieved to get out of that room.

Bert Andrews came to us as a reluctant witness. He was about to leave the college and had no desire to take sides in this dispute. He gave those of us interested in giving Maud the benefit of the doubt some of our most useful information. When asked about the harassment, which allegedly went on in the office, he told us he had been out in the field and did not know much about the atmosphere of the office. He did give us an eyewitness account of Tommy and some of his golfers yelling catcalls and obscenities at Maud as she drove away from one of the campus parking lots.

When asked whether, in his opinion, Tommy ever lied or encouraged cheating by athletes, he would not give us a yes or no answer. He simply replied he could not say whether lying and cheating were part of athletics at Worthington since Tommy became AD. When pressed further, he told us he had no desire to criticize his coach or the college. He did say he had heard of things that had been said, and could not assert that Tommy always told the truth or advised his teams to play by rules. This statement was devastating for what it did not say.

The grand finale was Tommy's testimony. It was all we could have anticipated and far less. For all his bravado, Tommy was a little boy who never grew up. When children play a game, they like to make up the rules as they go to suit themselves and then to change them. After the game is over, a child cannot be depended upon to report what really happened. This is excusable for a child, but not for a man in his forties. Tommy lied to us on almost every issue. He lied when it was not necessary to lie. He made us suspicious on issues we might have taken for granted. There was something fundamentally annoying about him, but it was hard to determine exactly what it was.

I was familiar with Manowski's long list of rule violations by the various teams Tommy coached or supervised as AD. The most egregious, of course, were those of the golf team. He was able to get really talented players, because he wooed them, telling them all kinds of stories about our little campus. Most of us did not know him well because he palled around with Morton and his cronies most of the time. This was my chance to observe Tommy closely to see if what we had heard about him could possibly be true. It was also an opportunity to evaluate Morton's judgment in bringing his "boy wonder" to Worthington.

We got together on a Wednesday afternoon in a room we had gotten to know well that summer. Tommy was thirty minutes late for his appointment with us. We had a lot to discuss, so we were frustrated about his tardiness. It gave us an indication of how important he considered this enterprise to be and how much respect he had for us. When we sent for him, he strutted in, dressed in short sleeves and slacks.

He sat down in a chair opposite the four of us. The look on his face was a curious mixture of smugness, defiance, and boyish vulnerability. It was hard not to like him, but we knew we could not trust a thing he said.

Mark started off by greeting him and asking an innocuous question, "Tommy, how is the golf team doing this year?"

Tommy flashed his wicked smile and told us the team came off its championship year well. They had a lot of work ahead to rebuild the team after the graduation of some of the most important players. He affirmed that he was sure he could get them ready to defend their title. As witness to his claim, he gave us a list of his accomplishments before and after coming to Worthington.

We knew Mark was the administration's representative on the committee and watched him closely. He did pretty well throughout the questioning. What we heard not even he could defend. He did handle Tommy with kid gloves, however. We let the two of them exchange pleasantries for several minutes before getting into serious matters.

Then Kathleen broke in, "Mr. Parnell, why did you force Mrs. Mitchell to leave the Admissions Office?" Tommy did not seem to know that Kathleen was trying to trap him with a complex question.

He fired back at her with a scowl on his face. "Aw, Dr. Krantz, I didn't make her leave. She just didn't fit in anymore. She was too old." I glanced at Kathleen's inscrutable face. I was sure she had pitched him a hard ball, which he had popped up for an easy out. Maud's case was based on alleged violations of federal age discrimination statutes.

I broke in before Tommy had time to think of what he had said, and asked him if he knew anything about obscene notes being written on the pad on her door, the fire that was started by lighting a piece of paper on her door, and other acts of harassment and vandalism.

"Look Doc," he responded in mock earnestness, "I didn't do any of that stuff."

When I asked him who had done it, he professed innocence. He blamed the victim, trying to make it seem as if what had happened was Maud's fault. The many attempts to humiliate her and drive her away were natural responses to this inept old woman. With most of his answers and the information he supplied us, it was clear he knew too much to be innocent. Even if he had not actually been the perpetrator of some of the harassment, he clearly knew about it, and presumably condoned it. He seemed to feel it was all right to do this stuff and even found it humorous.

We then touched on the testimony we had heard from the other persons who worked in the office. Kathleen asked him if he had turned them against Maud. This he denied, but added her blunt, tactless manner was annoying to him. It was especially hard for him to take because she was a woman.

I would have loved to have been a fly on the wall in his office when he got back with his buddies. He must have cursed Kathleen up one side and down the other. She finally got him to admit he had discussed Maud with his staff and told them what they were to say about her. The more Kathleen got him riled up, the more he revealed to us.

I began a line of questioning about the alleged irregularities in the athletic program. Mark and Daniel were noticeably nervous. I tried to justify my line of questioning by saying that since Tommy was coach and AD in addition to being Dean of Admissions, we needed to explore how this concerned the office in which Maud had been employed. I then turned to questioning whether there might be a possible conflict of interest in Tommy's administration of scholarship money. Wasn't his primary interest trying to get funds for his athletes? That almost brought the house down. Mark, Tommy, and Daniel shouted simultaneously that it was irrelevant to the case at hand. Daniel stopped me after the session and got on my case about it. I knew I had touched a nerve.

When we came back with a unanimous verdict in favor of Maud Mitchell, it was the beginning of the end for Tommy. Manowski's revelations to the national accrediting agency got our entire athletic program put on probation. The faculty was able to overcome Mark Springer's objections to the establishment of a committee to investigate all aspects of the athletics at Worthington. Although Mark was put in charge of the investigation (a typical Morton touch), the result of the investigation threatened to wash the whole administration away. Morton had to have a scapegoat, even if that meant his spiritual son had to go.

We wondered what the price for Tommy's peaceful departure must have been. We found out Morton gave him the van bought by the boosters club for the athletic department. We did not know what other benefits he took with him. We suspected it must have included a large amount of cash as severance pay. We were glad to see the Tommy era over.

Chapter 20

DAVID FLOWERS

Worthington's parent school started in 1854 as a female college, a haven of culture and civility for the best of southern womanhood. It did not become co-educational until after the Second World War. This was a flourishing time for small church-related schools. Many formerly female colleges were transformed in order to accommodate thousands of young male soldiers who returned home from war and had matured beyond their years. These men were ready to rejoin a world not directly touched by the madness they had endured on the other sides of the ocean. The G. I. bill gave them the privilege of going to college as a partial repayment for putting their lives on the line.

The 1950s represented a high watermark for the college in terms of sheer numbers, but also in terms of the dedication and quality of students. This was especially significant because it represented the first generation of Worthington men, which was for many a contradiction in terms. It took tough former soldiers to endure the gibes of being called a "Darling," the old name of the cheering squad.

Elton McTaggart was president of the college for nearly twenty-five years—including these glory days. Many naively assumed this boom would continue forever. McTaggart was getting older, and had discarded a lot of his previous charm to reveal his real character. He had little use for the church. He emphasized the fact that Worthington was a private liberal arts college. It did not need the church. This attitude became disastrous in the '60s and '70s when government money no longer subsidized students in seemingly inexhaustible amounts. State colleges also rode the soldier boom and spread over the South like kudzu. The genesis of hundreds of redneck academies to avoid integration in primary schools paralleled the decrease of funding for public education in the state. Money taken out of primary education was transferred to higher education and state schools proliferated. No less than three state schools came to Harrison, one at a time, and began the rapid erosion of Worthington's domination of the college scene.

McTaggart loved to chew his cigars and became fond of emptying whiskey bottles. He also developed a keen eye for the young ladies whom he was supposed to be shepherding. He ran the school like a plantation, but he was genuinely concerned about his employees. He worked for what he considered to be the greater good for the college and its employees. His word was his bond, making contractual arrangements a formality. His era came to an end with growing impatience on the part of the trustees. The church was irritated at being snubbed by what was considered arrogant attitudes on campus. There were also rumors about McTaggart's lack of morality. The threat of state schools taking students away from the college was the last straw.

Rev. Jonah L. Nelson, the pastor of First Church, was the leader of the clergy appointees to the trustee board. His ability to wheel and deal would eventually make him the first bishop ever to come from the Harrison area. He had contacts all over the country and made extensive use of them. His idea was that the new president of Worthington should be as different from McTaggart as night was from day. If McTaggart were an old southern layman, the new president would be a young northern clergyman.

Nelson was on the board of a college in a neighboring state with a seminary professor who had taught Morton. He was enthusiastic about the possibility of his former student becoming president at Worthington. Nelson had the ability to sell Morton to the board and saw the appointment as an extension of his power. The new president would be beholden to him and could help him with his ambition to become a bishop in the church. He came to regret deeply his hasty action and was one of Morton's most profound critics. When he moved on to his episcopal appointment, however, he was out of the picture and had little, if any, lingering influence.

One of McTaggart's best appointments was a young coach who would have lasting influence on generations of students. David Flowers was the only men's basketball coach Worthington ever had. He had been the football coach at Harrison's largest high school. This was one of the leading coaching positions in the state. Many people were amazed when David responded affirmatively to McTaggart's invitation to move to Worthington. This was especially curious since the college had no football team. David had coached basketball previous to his job at Stonewall Jackson High School, and really wanted to get out of the high-pressure world of football. He was also highly flattered that he was invited to coach on the college level.

He was quite successful the first decade of his tenure at the college. The young men coming out of the military were good athletes. They were highly motivated and needed to work off some of their pent-up emotions on the basketball court. Coach Flowers was a man's man, and able to motivate his teams to play beyond their abilities. They beat teams from much larger schools and won a reputation all over the state and region. He also began an excellent baseball program.

The second and third generations of his coaching at Worthington were not as successful as the first. The end of the golden era for the college and the onset of the state school entry into the market both took their toll. There were not only fewer students, there were also fewer athletes available. The change from McTaggart to Morton underminded the sports program. Morton had the ability to play people against each other. David had never had any trouble with the other coaches. Suddenly there was jealousy, lack of cooperation, and persons wishing to leave to go to greener pastures.

David was easygoing, tolerant, and able to work with almost anyone. He resolved to keep his program going and to stay away from Van Dale, Morton, and Co. He did not realize Morton would not let anything alone for long on that campus, especially if he thought he could gain something by messing with it. The basketball program was popular and Morton could not stand anyone or anything that got more attention than he did. He became more and more jealous of David simply because he was so well thought of in the community.

In the 1970s the student population reached a perilous low. We were down to four hundred thirty students when Julie and I moved to Harrison. Morton was taking his lumps from the trustees. Even though he handpicked them, lied to them regularly, and padded the figures, he could not hide the grim reality completely. The trustees told him categorically that he had to cut spending. When his back was against the wall, Morton always looked for a scapegoat. This time it was David Flowers and the basketball team. In a stunning move, Morton eliminated the program entirely and promoted David to Athletic Director. It was questionable what this title might mean without the major athletic program, which for years had been basketball. The baseball coach generally controlled his own area quite well and did not need David's counsel or interference.

David did some teaching, continued to go out recruiting students, and oversaw the tiny program, but his heart was not in it. He seemed dazed and became morose and depressed. He seemed to lose the color in his face and the joy in his life. He became gray and drawn almost overnight. His life had been his basketball team and that was gone. If he had been made athletic director and a new coach appointed, or even if he had been fired outright, he could have perhaps understood it. The axing of his team and program was incomprehensible to him. He had been so successful in his work at the college that he had become an institution.

He was actually accused by Morton of wasting so much money that the college could not afford to continue the program. This was especially painful because David had so little money for scholarships.

He was proud of the fact that he made every dollar do the work of three. There was no rhyme nor reason for what happened, no matter how many times David went over it in his mind. There was no way he could grasp the bitter truth that Morton had sacrificed him and the basketball program to save his own hide.

David stayed around the college for several years, shuffling around like a man without a purpose before he finally hung it up. It was really more that he was pushed than he jumped, but he was ready for retirement and did not seem to mind having more time to reflect on his years of successful coaching and teaching. He then enlisted in the legions of the walking wounded from the college. David was a team player and possessed an athlete's ability to present a stoic face, not letting on that his heart was breaking. I did not realize how much pain Morton had caused him until I went through my own bout with him.

David always stood by me with his quiet resolve and strength. He was no rabble-rouser, and yet he was never afraid to tell anyone what he thought. He was a born encourager and a devoted friend. It always amazed me that this calm, plainspoken man with so much integrity could have been treated so shabbily. As one who seldom cussed anymore, he nevertheless referred to Morton in certain well-chosen terms. Like Adam, these titles became epic similes for our common enemy. He stayed in contact with me the whole time, both directly and indirectly. He urged me not to be bitter after everything was settled. He told me he still loved the college. The baseball field with its new stands and clubhouse were named for him after Morton left. He had the satisfaction of being honored many times for his long career in Harrison, both as a high school coach and as the basketball coach at Worthington.

This did not stop him from going through periods of sharp decline after he left the college. His doctors noted the onset of clinical depression. He was a pleasant, reassuring, and wise person; then he became dark, dejected, and morose almost overnight. We were afraid of what might happen to him during these periods.

The doctors tried many combinations of medications, which usually enabled him to make dramatic comebacks. Each time it seemed he lost some ground, however. He remarked to me one day that he was afraid he was wounded beyond healing by what Morton had done to him. I told him I understood.

He commented slowly and seriously, "Yes, I believe you do."

Chapter 21

DR. EDWARD FREEMAN

My office for eighteen years was in Freeman Hall, named after the college's most outstanding president. The school was founded as a girl's school in 1854 in an old aristocratic town as the Cochetta Methodist Female College. In 1872 it was taken over by the Methodist Church. Dr. Edward Freeman became president of the college four years later in 1876 when financial problems made the college's continued existence questionable. He remained president of the small college until 1909, when it was moved to Harrison. There were some half dozen chief executives in its new home, including two, Elton McTggart and Albert Morton, whose tenure was a quarter century each.

Although Dr. Freeman died in 1917, I felt close to him, especially during my struggle with Morton. I valued his opinion of our situation. He brought to the school a classical education, wisdom, and maturity in the administration of the college, and a deep and abiding piety. Although he was a layperson, he was theologically astute and devoutly Christian. He was a great teacher, who perhaps taught best by example. He could be a stern disciplinarian, but he was also a humble person who could readily admit his mistakes and forgive and forget. In short, he incarnated the spirit of the college so well it was impossible to think of it apart from him or him apart from the college. Almost every major higher educational institution in the state offered him its presidency at one time or another. Colleges and universities from far distances also sent their representatives to try to tempt him to leave. Dr. Freeman never seriously considered leaving.

Freeman had been dead almost as long as he lived when I first heard of him. I read his little-known autobiography with respect and almost reverence for this man, whose example should have been the North Star of our college. I was painfully aware of the fact that he stood ten feet taller than his successors. He is clearly one of the most amazing men the state has produced. His life traced the early history of the state and he knew most of the figures who guided and shaped its development.

He was born on the frontier near one of the rivers whose waters flowed toward the Gulf, providing a highway for travel and transport for both Native Americans and early European settlers. The forests were still in virgin condition, with pines and poplars, oaks and hickories, chestnuts and sweet gums. This was the habitat of flocks of wood pigeons, blackbirds, and wild ducks. Squirrels, raccoons, and opossums were the focus of the young hunter, who also tested his skills against wild turkeys and herds of deer too numerous to be counted. Bears and panthers still were in the big swamps. Frontier life was difficult, but built character for those born there.

His earliest teacher was his maternal grandmother, who used mainly as her text the King James Bible. Her insights and strict moral principles shaped his life. At each stage of his education, Freeman became close to his instructors, both personally and professionally. This was in part because his financial plight made him vulnerable and dependent upon the good will of those in charge. It was also true because of his precocity, and the teachers who recognized it and were willing to take him under their wing. This was nowhere truer than at the state university, which he entered during the school year 1859-60. In the fall of his second year, he was invited to become the private secretary of the president of the university, Dr. G. A. Landon. Landon was a native of Virginia, who was widely known for his great character and many talents.

During Landon's long career, he served as the president of some half dozen institutions of higher learning in the South. He was a universal scholar who mastered the full spectrum of knowledge.. He was also a deeply moral and spiritual person, whose life and teaching had a profound effect upon Freeman.

He said of his mentor, "There has never been a more excellent teacher."

The Landon family regarded Freeman almost as a family member. Landon's daughter, Rose, married Col. Augustus Johnson, who was later to succeed her father as president of the university. It was the strong wish of Col. Johnson that Freeman follow him in the presidency, but he refused.

Freeman was critical of the Southern Confederacy. He commented insightfully on the failure of leadership that allowed hotheads to rule the day. Talk of succession and the monopoly of King Cotton carried the day. He understood the modern world was moving toward freedom for the slaves. The rising tide of industrialization and nationalism strongly militated against the establishment of a small isolated feudal agrarian state in the American South. Yet as a young student, he was inevitably drawn into the war and fought in a celebrated battle. He showed himself to be a man of courage, incurring a minor wound, before taking leave of the war to go back to the university.

Eventually he joined the corps of students trained at the university to be civilian soldiers in a vain attempt to defend their school. Dr. Landon did not want to see the blood of more than a dozen of these brave young men poured out for nothing. They would be desperately needed in the post-war world. So he asked them to give up trying to be soldiers, disband and remain students. After surrendering, the young men watched sorrowfully as most of the buildings of their beloved campus were set afire by Union troops, burning brightly into the night. Because they offered only token resistance, the young students were not taken prisoner.

Freeman joined with other students who escaped and set out on a futile journey in search of General Lee's army to fight until the bitter end. They did not get far before they got word of Lee's surrender. This was followed by the tragic news of the assassination of President Lincoln, which brought no joy among educated southerners. After time to reflect and then looking to the future, the young Freeman was among the first men in his area to go to the headquarters of the Union army and take the oath of allegiance to the United States, "as if nothing had happened between January 1861 and November 1865."

He exhibited remarkable insight into the plight of blacks in the South. He was not born of a slave-owning family, nor did he ever own any himself. He respected, however, the way Dr. Landon managed a plantation with more than fifty slaves. Freeman showed concern for the well being of these persons and relief when they were freed. He deplored efforts during the Reconstruction period to alienate blacks and exploit differences and difficult situations. His advice was that whites and blacks "bear each other's burdens." He urged both sides to work to right a terrible situation, which was not entirely of their own making. He knew Dr. Booker T. Washington and heard him speak on a number of occasions. After noting his own innate prejudices, he fairly and correctly found Washington to be a person endowed not only with great talent, but also with tact and self-control, which were almost superhuman. He credited Washington with doing more than any other person to overcome the estrangement between the races, and said of him that he knew of no other man who went to his grave more honored and respected.

Following the war, Freeman finished his education. He had matured in a time of conflict, unbelievable destruction, and the arduous changing of a worldview. He was uniquely equipped to lead his area into a new order of things. His idea of going back to school to get a degree in law was permanently postponed, and he was definite about his decision to pursue his vocation as teacher. He dedicated himself "to endeavor to inspire young people with nobler ideals of life and to imbue them with the just fear of God and the love of their fellow human beings."

On the subject of his chosen vocation, he also said:

> After all, inspiration is the greatest quality in a teacher.
> Many teachers can instruct well, but not all can inspire
> great and noble purposes in the young. Without
> inspiration, education can never yield its best fruitage.

These brave and idealistic statements he more than proved himself capable of accomplishing.

After teaching for several years at the university, Freeman was invited to teach at and then to head several schools for young men in different parts of the state. He and his young family moved in 1866, 1874, and 1876 when they moved to Cochetta. There he began a thirty-three year period in which he worked in every aspect of the college's life, from teaching to recruiting, administration, and, even at times, taking care of some of the janitorial duties. Freeman was the third president, following two individuals of good character and a high level of learning, but lesser ability at financial management. The financial crunch of 1873 almost did in the little school.

Friends questioned Freeman's sanity for taking over an ailing girls' school.

"Why don't you stay at a 'real' [i.e. boys'] school," he was asked repeatedly. Many felt that southern girls didn't need an education, just training in the social graces. Freeman realized, however, that the new situation following the war would not allow the kind of smothering gentility that had prevailed before the war. Women would have to make their way in the world alongside the men. If ever the subject of women's education was vital, it was then. He was proud of the fact that the church had taken leadership in this area.

His initial contract was for five years. In that period, he was personally responsible for the management and discipline of the school, its financial stability, the employment of teachers, and the condition of the buildings and grounds. If there were deficits, it was his responsibility. Likewise, if there were profits, it was to his credit.

He was supported by a trustee board of seven men, three devout laypersons from the local community, and four Methodist clergy from all over the state. At the end of the five-year period, they saw fit to reward Freeman's success with a second contract. The school grew and succeeded, setting a pattern of excellence in education for women.

The changed conditions after the first half-century of the school made necessary the move to the state capitol. Plantation life was vastly changed by the war. Railroads built up new centers of population and concentrated business in new areas. Towns and cities like Cochetta were bypassed while others were favored and grew into major centers. Harrison was such a place. Its location on an important river made it a center of Native American settlements. It later became the site of a European settlers' village. It grew into a railway hub, being almost exactly in the center of the state. It was the third city in succession designated as the capital of the state. Hundreds of cotton bales were stored in warehouses, waiting to be shipped to the Northeast and Europe. They were burned to prevent Union troops from getting their hands on them. This self-inflicted wound may have prevented more widespread destruction at the hands of the invaders. In any case, Harrison recovered from the war and emerged still as the capital.

By the turn of the century it was a bustling little city with concerns about the educational needs of its young women. There was a search for someone interested in contributing a large gift around which the support of others could rally. The John T. Rivers family gave $50,000, which was matched by both the church and the city. The final gift was fifty acres of land donated by another prominent family at the edge of town.

The major difference between the half-century the school was in Cochetta and its first century in Harrison was leadership. Dr. Freeman carefully built up his faculty, surrounding himself with individuals of real character and ability. His standards were the highest, and the young women educated there went out to make their contribution to society, in spite of the limitations placed on women. Since school teaching was the area most immediately open to educated young women, many former students of Cochetta became educators. Thereby they passed on to future generations the qualities of their own training.

In the half-century they dominated the life of the college, McTaggert and Morton brought in an era of mediocrity and worse. They still bragged about the excellence of the college's tradition and its high standards. But this, like everything else about the life of the college, was based on distortion and deception. Memories of what the college had been were transplanted with the move and lived like ghosts on the campus.

Chapter 22

THE LESSONS OF A MASTER

One night while a production was underway in the Catacombs, I was working late in my office on the second floor of Freeman Hall. I went down the hall to the men's room and met a person in costume. He appeared to be an elderly gentleman dressed immaculately in a suit that reflected the style of the turn of the century, with a high collar and the soft tie of the period. I greeted him and asked if he was in the play being rehearsed in the basement. He told me he was not, and continued down the hall. I was puzzled, but did not inquire further.

I saw him again several weeks later. It was a similar situation: I was working late and went out into the hall. This time I made an attempt to engage him in conversation. I commented on the cooler weather that had come with the fall season and he agreed.

Then I asked him his name.

He responded, "Edward Freeman."

I asked him, "You must be kin to the former president of the college, after whom this building was named?"

He told me, "Yes, I am Dr. Freeman."

I said, "You mean that you are playing Dr. Freeman?"

"No, I am Edward Freeman."

"But he died in 1917."

"That is correct, but I have never abandoned the college for which I lived my life."

I was intrigued, if a bit bewildered. I wasn't sure if he was insane, or I was. I asked him to come into my office. We had the first of many conversations about the condition of the college. I was amazed with what he knew.

I asked Freeman why he was there. He did not give me a direct answer. I asked him if he were a ghost. He said he did not like that word, so I asked him how he would describe who he was. He said he understood my question, but could not answer me in any way that would be satisfactory—whatever that meant! I decided to let it go. Was he for real? I was not sure. With what I had learned about Dr. Freeman, this gentleman seemed convincing. I asked him again why he was on campus and why he was talking with me.

He told me, "Because you must do something about the situation here on campus. You must save this school."

That was both flattering and, at the same time, frightening. I asked him what he meant, and he told me it was time for Morton and his cronies to go.

I wondered if our encounter was real, or if this were some kind of dream. I dared not mention the encounter to anyone, lest I be thought crazy or dreaming while awake. I had read Freeman's autobiography and had a strong impression of what he stood for. I read it again. I felt I could not take my encounter with him or his words to me less than seriously.

Then, on another Wednesday night later that month, after my class, I came back to my office before driving home. Freeman met me in the hallway again. He looked exactly the same.

I tried to joke with him, asking, "Are you in another play downstairs?" He did not acknowledge my remark. He was, as usual, all business, but pleasantly so.

He said, "We need to talk." That began a series of discussions that radically reoriented my understanding of who I was and what we should be about in a church-related college. I found in Freeman a thoughtful, worthy, and challenging friend and mentor.

I repeated my original question to him: "Who are you?" His answer was as disturbing to me as the first time I heard it. I was still not ready to accept it at face value.

I reiterated my second question: "Why are you here?" His response was equally challenging.

He told me I had a mission. "You must save the school."

Finally, my third question was quite simply, "Why me?"

His answer was very important to my self-understanding and my future. "I chose you because you are ordained and you have the courage of your conviction. You know what a church-related college is supposed to be."

"I thought I knew what we were supposed to represent, but I am not sure after teaching here a number of years. How do you know that I could change things?"

"I understand that," he said, "but I trust you. "The dead know everything, at least, everything they choose to know. This applies to character as well. I believe that you can make a difference. Someone has to do something about this situation."

He told me Bishop G. Bromley Oxnam had framed the best definition of what it means to be a Methodist church-related college or university. He had been both a university president and a bishop. He presented the definitive statement of the identity of church-related colleges and universities to a meeting of school executives in 1942. Unfortunately, no one took him seriously. He said a few Bible courses and an occasional chapel were not enough. Being an excellent educational institution was also not enough. He said we must "stand deliberately for something in the field of religion and in practices that religion demands." Bishop Oxnam's words were clear and bold:

> There is a Christian world-view, a Christian way of life,
> a Christian commitment to the Christian leader. One is
> your leader, even Christ . . . Our schools must be Christian
> without apology, and Methodist with pride. Our faculties
> must be Christian. Our efforts should be to make the

student Christian just as truly as we teach him to think. We must seek to graduate Christians as certainly as we graduate doctors, lawyers, and musicians.

Freeman told me this statement was made years after his tenure and a quarter century after his death. Nevertheless, it expressed all he stood for as a college president.

He continued his first of many lessons with a comparison: "May I borrow your copy of your catalog?" I got it for him. "Look at the purpose statement which you helped write. As you know, it was presented to representatives of the University Senate, on one of their periodic visits to evaluate your campus and its program. It says that your college is a four-year coeducational college affiliated with the United Methodist Church that offers:

> A program anchored in the liberal arts tradition of western culture, inviting students to join the faculty in greater familiarity with and understanding of the cultural heritage of civilization. The college affirms the importance of such an education as a basis for responsible participation in society, with tolerance and appreciation for the beliefs and values of others.

Dr. Freeman commented critically, "Where is the scandal of the Christian Gospel?" Any good secular state school could ascribe to these words. What is "the cultural heritage of civilization"? Of course, "responsible participation in society, with tolerance and appreciate for the beliefs and values of others" is important. This supports a good American, pragmatic education for citizenship, fitting in, and doing one's civic duty. What does this have to do with our Christian, and more particularly, Wesleyan responsibility for evangelism and discipleship?

The college's purpose statement continued to deal more specifically with the college's church relationship. It said a church-related college:

> Affirms the value of an educational orientation grounded in both the classical and Judeo-Christian traditions. Students are encouraged to study both ancient and contemporary sources for the enduring values and standards of our society. Critical and objective perspectives are encouraged in the development of a mature personal philosophy.

Freeman highlighted some of the phrases from the statement: "Students are 'encouraged to study' the classics 'for enduring values and standards of our society.' They are also 'encouraged in the development of a mature personal philosophy.' What does all this 'encouragement' mean? Are these not alternatives to the discipline and development of the Christian faith?"

He contrasted this with Bishop Oxnam's statement that the church should be "convinced that we stand for something." What does the college stand for? What does the faculty stand for? What do the students stand for? These are nice sounding words, but what do they mean? How do you measure the success or failure of an education that deals with enduring values and personal philosophy? These phrases are so subjective and vague as to be meaningless! How does one stand up for such theoretical concepts? Is this really what we teach or seek to embody?

He went on to discuss how Methodist colleges were influenced by the needs of his century. He was a citizen of his time and place. His life was lived out in service to a calling to establish educational institutions in furthering the ministry and message of the church. He was especially concerned with the status and role of young women in the post-Civil War era in the South.

One of the primary aspects of the Methodist movement in the prior century was John Wesley's inspired educational work to enable the ignorant masses of England to become literate, at first to read the Bible, and then to read the numerous tracts and books the movement generated. This was transferred to this country, with the founding of

119

the Methodist Church in 1784 in Baltimore. Initially there was no great impetus to get involved in the task of founding colleges. The clergy were involved in an itinerate ministry to the frontier, where they were relatively few in number and dedicated to covering a vast territory.

The image of the circuit rider on horseback came to represent their service. These men covered large areas of ministry composed of churches they could only visit once a quarter, or at best, once a month. The men were predominantly not college graduates, nor was an extensive education required of them. They were pressed into the service of vital piety and conversion.

Freedman related the effect of the preaching of the circuit riders and the spirit of the camp meetings on his childhood and youth. He confessed:

> The ministry of preaching, administering the sacraments,
> teaching, and leading by courageous example inspired me
> and led me to the altar to confess my faith and become a
> member of the church.

Bishop Francis Asbury opposed the effort to start Methodist colleges, opting instead for the establishment of elementary schools. The other earliest bishop of Methodism in America, Thomas Coke, was an Oxford-educated leader. He was the only educated participant in the Christmas Conference in Baltimore in 1784. He disagreed with Asbury, and ten years after the church was begun in this country, in 1794, Coke's view predominated. Cokesbury College was built and incorporated. It burned to the ground a year later.

The second college burned a year after that. Out of this failed effort began a program to establish a network of Methodist colleges throughout the country. It was late and lagged behind most of the other major denominations. Nevertheless, like everything the early Methodists did, it was carried out with determination and diligence. In 1820 (after Asbury's death), the General Conference urged that each annual conference sponsor its own institution of higher education.

From 1829 to 1850, some four hundred schools and colleges were established. These numbers eventually grew to nearly one thousand two hundred such institutions. The Civil War marked the demise of many such schools. The Great Depression caused many more to fail. Fewer than 10 percent of Methodist institutions of higher education remain: Eighty-seven universities and four-year colleges, not counting two-year colleges and other schools. The Methodist Church has been responsible for the founding of more colleges than any other Protestant denomination, and for many years, more than the Catholics.

Freeman summarized his view of the essential elements in Christian higher education in the time in which he served a college president:

(1) Colleges were closely identified with their church or denominational sponsors. Administrators, faculty and staff members, and students understood themselves as responsible to the faith of the church.

(2) Most of the teachers were ministers, who had to be able to teach a number of subjects because they had mastered multiple disciplines.

(3) Students came primarily from the churches of the sponsoring denomination, although others were admitted.

(4) Funding came primarily from the churches of the denomination.

Church-related colleges and universities underwent vast changes in this century. They seem to have lost their purpose, their direction, and, ultimately, a coherent reason for their existence. From the side of the colleges, it seems to be better to be cut adrift from the bondage of the church relationship. The faculty and student body relish their diversity and see the church as antithetical to academic freedom. In a secular society, the churches have enough problems of their own and do not want to have to worry about how their colleges are doing. They surely do not want to be constantly dunned for money, or shamed that they have not sent more students to their college.

Freeman helped me evaluate the educational process in which I had participated and led others through. How had we come to the situation in which the profession I had chosen as my life's work had moved so far from its origins?

Departments of Religion and Philosophy are engaged in an objective study of the religious phenomenon. For the most part, professors do not think of themselves as ministers. Many, but not all, have graduated from seminaries and are ordained. They consider that churchiness, however, would make them look like less than scholars to their colleagues in other disciplines.

Pursuits of "the scientific study of religion" are much more respected than considerations of vital piety. The struggle between faith and reason, which Kant, Hegel, and other philosophers dealt with in earlier centuries, has apparently been won by the rational side. The original concern for evangelism and religious instruction has melted into the general culture and purposes of the American academy.

When church-related becomes more a liability than an advantage, where do guidance and governance come from? Are not our colleges like a compass in which the needle points in all directions simultaneously and therefore in none? In the faculty's struggle with Morton and his cohorts, to whom could we appeal for control—the faculty, the department chairs, the trustees, the bishop, the conference? Not apparently, but actually, power resided in the presidency and in that office alone. That was dangerous, and our campus paid a huge price for it.

The attempt to define a Methodist church-related college has failed. The only generally agreed upon definition has been that if a school considered itself to be Methodist college or university, it was indeed a Methodist college or university. This was agreed upon after more demanding understandings, like Bishop Oxnam's, were rejected.

Recently the term 'value-centered' has replaced religious language. The problem with this rather nebulous definition is, whose values? Obviously, the values (or lack thereof) of the president and the administration have dominated this college. There is a demoralized faculty with no real church orientation or loyalty to a religious tradition. There is a diverse student body, which is not bad, but students are not challenged to move in any direction or to hold onto to any tradition in a rather tumultuous age.

The trustees have been almost completely removed form the life of the campus. They are largely recruited from the world of business and politics and respected for their fortunes and prominence, not because of their moral and religious leadership in the community. True, there are bishops, other clergy, and church representatives on the board, but they are no longer a majority and usually go along with the machinations of the power brokers appointed by the president. Where are the values? What is the message? What do we stand for?

Freeman affirmed that: "In my day, I believed we could have successfully and clearly answered those questions."

Encouraging young people to become thinking persons, to make good moral decisions, and "to discover the implications of an ever-changing and complex culture for their lives and for their future" may sound worthy to contemporary ears. This can never replace the Wesleyan pledge to unite knowledge and vital piety. Morality, theology, and piety depend upon each other and are not sustainable without mutual support and reinforcement.

Finally, they depend upon the context and the community, the church, or, in this case, the college. Church-related colleges have fostered the self-deception that the essence of the Christian faith could be abstracted and applied apart from the Christian church. Defection from Christian sponsorship is contrary to the purpose of the founders of these institutions. Christian scholarship and rational discourse are not opposed to each other; indeed they are the soul of the church-related college or university, properly understood.

Chapter 23

THE GANG BANG ON THE GREEN

Paul Crane was the Dean of Students for most of the time I was at Worthington. He was generally personable, open, and honest with students. He also had to be careful with how he dealt with any issue that might involve the administration. He was in his late twenties when he came to Worthington. I watched him age. He had the virtue of always looking younger than he actually was. He was relatively short, with a good build, in good shape, and had a boyish appearance. He and his wife were divorced and there were no children. He had the depressed look of someone who was carrying the weight of the planet. He kept his own counsel, and tried to maintain some distance from Morton and Van Dale, but one could only guess the compromising situations in which he was involved. Some of them had the potential of exploding into scandals.

One Saturday morning in July, at 7:30 a.m., Paul called me and made a special request. He had a difficult job to do and wondered if I would go with him. A young man, Marvin Smith, one of our best baseball players, had been in an accident. He had a summer job working for a local furniture company, making deliveries of purchases to customers' homes. The truck had been in an accident with another vehicle and turned over. The driver of the truck was able to crawl out of the wreck. Marvin had been trapped inside the cab, which was struck on his side by the car. He had died at the scene.

His body was being held in the morgue at a local hospital. Paul had been called to come and identify the body. He did not know Marvin well and asked me to help him. He looked up the classes Marvin had taken and realized I had taught him in freshman Religion. I will never forget looking at the body of this athletic and personable young man. He lay on his back on a slab and looked as if he could get up and walk away. Then I looked into his still open eyes and realized his life really had ended. His arms awed me, with his muscles bulging from his short-sleeve shirt. How could anyone so young, strong, and virile be dead? I recognized Marvin immediately, and agreed to sign the form with Paul identifying the body

The second situation was much more complicated. Helen Cohen came to us as a freshman student. She was Jewish, which was not unusual in our student body. We had many non-Christian students and made every effort to accommodate them. My colleague, Phillip Maddox, taught Helen in Old and New Testament classes, so I did not know her except by sight. I learned about her from one of my students. Melody Gates was a likeable freshman coed in my Religion classes. She had grown up in one of our churches and had been involved in the youth fellowship group in the church. She worked for several summers at our denominational camp with young children. She brought with her a little wooden cross from the previous summer camping experience. The children in her cabin made it for her and proudly presented it to her at the end of the camp. She hung the cross on a wall in her college dorm room.

Helen and Melody had been assigned to be roommates. Initially this seamed like an interesting pairing of two talented and able young women from different backgrounds. Helen was not nearly as involved in her religion as Melody, but they were able to share valuable insights.

A problem arose, however, relating to the cross. It kept disappearing from its special place on the wall above Melody's desk and winding up on her bed, or on her bedside table, or somewhere else in the room. Her naiveté and childlike innocence were part of her charm. She came to me and asked what might be happening with her cross. She knew her roommate must be taking it down, but she had no idea why. I asked her if she had any idea what the Christian cross meant to Jews. She looked at me with a puzzled expression.

She told me, "It represents the cross on which my Savior died. It is also a precious gift from the children I worked with last summer. Why should this concern my roommate?"

I told her she needed to discuss this with Helen.

She came back to me the beginning of the next week. Her eyes were wide open. She said Helen told her the cross was "the most hated symbol for Jews." It was used by those who despised her people in the Middle Ages who killed Jews and drove them out of Europe. The Nazis' symbol was a twisted cross—that brought back memories of the Holocaust. The KKK, who hated Jews as well as Negroes, burned crosses. Melody said she had no idea Jews felt like that. She still did not think it was fair to see the cross that way, but she would take it down so she would not offend Helen.

I did not see Melody again until the spring semester when she was in my New Testament class. She was a good student and had done well in her first semester. I spoke to her about her paper in the previous semester, which I thought was excellent. I asked her about Helen. She said they had decided to switch rooms. She had a new roommate. She did not think Helen had a roommate.

We had a group of students on campus who were designated by their critics as "The God Squad." They generally came from mainline Protestant denominations (mostly Baptist and Methodist), but were going to charismatic or Pentecostal churches. They liked the "what's happening now" churches. They were excited about the music, the emotional and spiritual electricity, and the dynamic personalities of the pastors or youth leaders. I was concerned they were being led astray from their church backgrounds, but I could not say a great deal and still maintain the kind of objectivity necessary for me to teach them.

They prayed for other students, and preyed upon some of them, whom they considered to be especially at risk spiritually. They paid special attention to fraternity and sorority members, persons they considered to be agnostics or atheists, and persons who were members of other religions, especially Jews. Rabbi Eric Zimmerman was a special target. We were fortunate to have him as a member of our faculty. He taught courses in the History of Judaism and on the Prophets in alternate years. His synagogue honored him by paying him to teach for us, so he cost us nothing. He also invited us to bring our Bible classes for a night at the synagogue each semester.

We began with a question and answer session with the rabbi where students were allowed to pose any question they might want to ask. I deeply dreaded the question, "Why did the Jews kill Jesus?" which came up every time we were the guests of the synagogue. Eric handled it as well as anyone could.

Sometimes he was dead serious: "We had nothing to do with his death." Sometimes, he treated it ironically: "Why don't you ask me why I don't stop beating my wife?" Following the discussion period, we attended a regular Friday night worship service and joined the congregation for refreshments following the service. The students loved the refreshments and did not forget what for many of them was their first exposure to Jewish worship.

The "God Squad" was determined to convert the rabbi. That would have been a great prize for those religious enthusiasts. They asked me again and again why we had a rabbi teaching in a church-related college. I always had a retort and tried to brush them off as soon as possible. When they asked me about converting him, I had had enough and asked them why they would want to do that? What would they want to change about him? He was a dedicated man of faith, a spiritual leader of his congregation, and a valuable member of the community. He was intelligent, dedicated, and an incredible resource for the college.

Then I advised them to leave him alone. They did begin to back off, realizing they would get no help from the college. They did not have the moxie to move on the rabbi by themselves. Then I began to hear of their efforts to convert "that Jewish girl." With some apprehension, I asked who that might be, and found out they were after Helen Cohen. They befriended her for ulterior motives. She needed friends, because she was obviously lonely, but when she found out they wanted to convert her, she felt hurt and betrayed.

After I heard about the pressure they were putting on Helen, I talked with several of them. They admitted what they were doing, and pardoned themselves by saying, "it was for her own good." I told them if they cared about her as a person, they would become real friends with her, no strings attached or ulterior motives. I said I doubted they would be able to pressure her into becoming a Christian, and if they did, it would be perverse. If they wanted her to see the merits of the Christian faith, they should love her as she was and stop their attacks on her faith. There was a chance, I concluded, that she might convert, if she saw how real and warm their love was for her as a person of sacred value. If she understood this as an outpouring of their faith in Jesus Christ she might want to join with them in their faith. But this was not the point. I tried to get them to see what they were doing was destructive and hurtful and, ultimately, unchristian.

Late in the semester, I heard Helen deeply resented the way the super Christians had pressured her. She had withdrawn into herself and developed a serious drinking problem. She had begun to pal around with some of the basketball players. Then I heard rumors about "the gang bang on the green." I was concerned about this, so I asked Paul Crane what happened. He refused to go into detail, but he did tell me a group of jocks had gotten Helen drunk and forced her to have group sex with her on the green one night after midnight. This was within feet of the sacred grove of trees in the ravine and the amphitheater where graduation, homecoming, and other major campus events took place throughout the year. I could not help but think of how offensive this must be to the mystical spirits of that special place.

This was a desecration and further destruction of a troubled young woman. She came to us for an education and instead was discriminated against, pressured to abandon her faith and treated as a sex object. I could not get any other information on the event. I never knew exactly what took place, but Helen seemed to disappear from the campus, never to be heard from again. The only way this administration could deal with the issues involved was to get rid of her. The athletes got off scott-free, of course. I felt sorry for Paul, but this was the job he had signed on for. I did not understand how he could work in such circumstances, but if he quit, Morton would find someone who did not have the moral convictions or qualms of conscience that so troubled Paul.

A third event that touched all of us to the core was the suicide of a young freshman. One morning, I was listening to a local radio station as I shaved and prepared to go to school for my 8:00 a.m. Bible class. A breaking news report came from Worthington College. Students going to breakfast had cut across the green and discovered the body of a young man, who had evidently taken his own life. He had shot himself in the face, so it was a while before he could be identified.

I called the campus and got a name from the operator. She said they thought it was Andy Thompson. I knew Andrew Thompson and was shocked. He was a likeable young man everyone seemed to know. I got a call that classes were cancelled for the day, but I drove to the campus as quickly as I could anyway. I parked my car and walked across campus toward the cafeteria. The first person I saw was Andy Thmpson. I looked at him as if I were seeing a ghost.

He looked at me fearfully and stammered, "Oh no. It wasn't me! There are three of us on campus with the same name. I wasn't the one. Man, I have been totally creeped out by the way people look at me!"

He told me it did something to him when people thought he had died, and he planned to take life much more seriously.

The press was picking up details about the suicide and further reports were being issued on radio and television. Reporters were prowling all over campus.

The young man who died had been a student at the best private high school in the area: The Franklin Academy. It was an excellent school that had been organized thirty years earlier. It was nothing like the so-called redneck academies that sprang up like weeds after the public schools were integrated. The strong support of the Jewish community was vital to the academy. Most of its graduates went on to attend the best colleges, including Ivy League schools. The organist at one of the churches I pastored was a math teacher at the academy. When I asked her about Andy, she said he was an excellent student, but immature and impulsive.

Andy Thompson had gone through his adolescent rebellions and seemed to settle down. He did not get much support from his parents.. They were busy with their careers and did not have much time for him and his siblings or any real interest in their accomplishments. There were some serious blow-ups, but things seemed to be better between them. He did have some drug and alcohol problems, but he excelled in math and the sciences and was highly regarded among his teachers and his peers. When he read about the Worthington early admissions program, he contacted the college and was admitted. He skipped his senior year and began as a freshman in college straight from finishing his junior year of high school.

Although he still lived at home, he spent most of his time at the college. He pledged a fraternity and seemed to be doing well. His grades the first semester were outstanding. He began the second semester, but, according to his friends, became more and more depressed. He felt he did not belong and lost interest in his work. More and more of his time was spent in front of his computer playing games. His drug and alcohol use got out of hand. Still, no one understood why he decided to kill himself.

He wrote out a suicide message on his computer and sent it out to his friends as a delayed e-mail. They received it at dawn after he was already dead. The message was cryptic and ironic. It basically condemned the school, all adult authority over his life, and the political views of the leadership of Harrison. It was a rant, and much of it did not make sense. It showed numerous distortions and the pathology of drugs and alcohol in an adolescent mind.

Morton was predictably paranoid about the effect on the image of the college. He and Van Dale huddled with Chaplain Brunner, who was a good soldier. As a retired colonel and chaplain in the Air Force, he knew how to curry favor with those in charge. He was more of a chaplain to Morton than to the students. I called Van Dale's secretary and volunteered the services of our department to counsel students. I never got a call back. Classes were canceled the next day, and an assembly of all campus personnel was announced with no explanation of what would be discussed.

We all expected something like a memorial service. We could not have been more surprised when Morton, Van Dale, and Brunner stood before us. Brunner began with a rather cold prayer full of platitudes and general references which revealed he knew little about the young man or the situation and seemed to care less. Then Morton lectured us for thirty minutes on the details of the young man's death and why it was not the fault of the school. He had barred the press, but was well aware representatives were there, and carefully measured his comments knowing they would show up in print.

Toward the end of his boring and self-serving comments, Morton referred to the fact that Andy Thompson had pledged a fraternity. Without saying it, he inferred that this association might have something to do with the mental condition that caused him to kill himself. He also sought to blame associations the young man had outside the campus. This reached the tipping point. We were all feeling insulted and used. We desperately needed consolation, reassurance, and great words of faith from the Scriptures of the Jewish and Christian religions.

All we got was Morton's nonsense. Suddenly there was an explosion of emotion from a young man sitting near the front of the chapel. Ronald Pierson sprang to his feet. He was a senior and the chief officer of the fraternity that pledged Andy. The implication that the fraternity had been anything but a support to a troubled young man was too much. I had taught Ronnie. He was a serious young man. He had done good work for me. I did not see him as a future

131

campus leader, but was pleasantly surprised as I watched him grow in self-confidence and ability.

I helped establish the rival fraternity on campus, and was the advisor to the chapter. I was careful to be sure this did not stop me from being open to other groups. I listened to Ronnie shout at Morton, defending the fraternity, and then storm out of the chapel. There was applause, and I was pleased to join in, but I was concerned about Ronnie. I was sitting in the last third of the middle section of the chapel. I had no trouble getting to my feet and leaving the chapel. Once outside, I looked for Ronnie. I caught a glimpse of him walking fast on his way to the cafeteria. I ran after him and caught him before he reached his destination. I grabbed his shoulders and turned him around and held him in my arms. He cried on my shoulder like a baby. This was what the students needed, not Morton's cold, self-serving, and arrogant defense of the establishment.

The next day, the whole matter was relegated to page 6 in the local newspaper and generally forgotten. Soon life on campus was back to normal. The blood in the grass was soaked up and washed away. Andy was largely forgotten, except by those who loved him and considered him to be a friend. As Dean of Students, Paul Crane had to help divert attention from the campus. After that I watched him grow more depressed, and even unstable. I worried about his emotional health. I wish we could have joined together and combined our talents and human relation skills and dealt with the tragedy and the hurt our students bore.

Chapter 24

ELLEN PEOPLES

Ellen Peoples was one of the small number of black students on campus. She was an enjoyable person to be around, with an inviting smile, who never met a stranger. She took only one of my courses, but did not finish it. I was disappointed in her as a student. She missed class too often and seemed always to have some excuse. I gave her make-up exams and extra work to try to pull up her average in the course. She withdrew near the end of the semester with permission from the dean and registrar, ostensibly because of illness. There seemed to be too much going on in her life for her to go to class.

She also came to me for counseling regarding a personal problem: She was almost certain she was pregnant. I did not flatter myself that I was the first person she had come to about her problems (or would be the last). She told me she was going regularly to several other persons on campus for counseling as well as someone off campus. I warned her to be discrete and careful about sharing.

Frank Bertram was smart, but troubled. He and Ellen had unusual backgrounds. Frank came from a poor white family. His father was proud, but not educated. He wanted the best for his children and was usually decent with them when he was sober. His drinking and abusive treatment of his wife and family, however, became more frequent and more severe. Frank's mother was possessive of the children and resentful of her plight.

133

Frank dealt with his troubled home situation by plunging himself into his studies. He was a graduate of the same magnet school as my son. He had high scores on the SAT. He took stands on a number of controversial issues, espousing conservative social positions on theological issues. For example, Frank spoke out often and strongly against abortion. He went to pro-life rallies and attended a charismatic church. His family did not attend church, and his father was critical of his religious faith and his stand on a number of issues.

No one could have expected that Ellen and Frank would be attracted to each other. They were different types and of two different races. After all, this was still the Deep South. She was a bubbly extravert, and he was withdrawn and reserved. It surprised almost everyone, even their closest friends, when suddenly they were seen together everywhere. When Ellen's grandmother found out about it, she hit the roof. She was a devout Roman Catholic and raised Ellen in an oppressively conservatism home. Ellen was able to recite her catechism with what seemed to us a sincerity and depth of faith that were impressive.

When, however, it was time for her to sow her wild oats, Frank was there to help her throw off the traces. Perhaps what they had in common (beside their conservative religious backgrounds his Protestant, hers Catholic) was a profound need to rebel against confused and oppressive family situations.

In any case, Ellen was in my office crying. She had told Frank she was pregnant. She was concerned about his reaction to this news, but they had already talked about marriage. She asked me if I would perform the ceremony. I told her I would need to counsel both of them before giving a final answer. I liked both of them and was not dismayed as much by their racial differences as the virtual impossibility of their being able to establish any kind of stable home environment in which to raise a child.

I remembered years before when we had our first interracial couple on campus. They fell madly in love. They were seen everywhere together and seemed to be constantly expressing signs of their affection. Morton was afraid our racist trustees would find out about it. So he dispatched David Ellisor to handle it. David was a retired minister who served as a kind of vice president, but without the title. His career had been interrupted years earlier by his courageous stance against segregation. His family had been so harassed by the Klan that they were forced to leave the South. David knew it was time to move north when his son found a rifle in their home and ran into the front yard where a cross had been burned the previous night. The family moved to Massachusetts, where David served with distinction in a small church near the Harvard University campus. He came back home in retirement and was hired by the college.

This unique and dedicated pastor was dispatched to tell the couple they had to cool it or be booted off campus. I felt for David. He had been reduced to acting as a tool for Morton. He obediently carried out his task. He was long since worn out, and went to his grave too soon, an old and broken man.

"Morton either ran you off or used you up, leaving nothing but an empty shell," Adam reminded me. There was no David now, however, to warn Ellen and Frank. Nobody seemed to care anyway, and certainly not Morton. Things seemed to be falling apart all around him and he had no time to worry about an interracial couple.

Ellen had served the administration well over the two years she was a student at Worthington. She was strikingly beautiful and articulate. She wanted more than anything to please. When her grandmother kicked her out of her home, the school was ready to offer her room and board on campus. She found part-time jobs and seemed to be getting her life under control. She was a valuable asset for the administration. Any time attractive students were needed to put a good face on the college, she was there. She sang with the college choir. She performed in theater productions. As a black woman, she was especially effective in presenting the wonderful situation on campus for females and minorities. I only knew her in passing during this time, and resented her unblushing exaggerations.

135

The classic example of her being able to express what the administration wanted said was when representatives of the University Senate, the denomination's national college management council, came for their periodic evaluation. The team consisted of a retired college president, an administrator, and two professors from other colleges. The leader of the group was a retired black college president with a national reputation. The way Morton prepared for the various meetings involving the team was truly a work of art. We called these meetings "tea parties." Morton was a master of this kind of thing.

"Image is everything," he was fond of saying. Ellen was a member of a group of carefully chosen students who met with the delegation. She performed beautifully, telling the delegates how wonderful everything was. She was evidently coached, because she knew so many details.

I was on a panel of professors who met with the visitors. We were prepared, and tried to acquaint them with some of the problems on campus. We especially wanted them to understand the situation of the students: Run-down and rotting dorms, inferior food in the cafeteria, overemphasis on sports, scholarship manipulation, a 50 percent retention rate for freshmen. We had real issues and offered them valid statistics. The team did not listen to us. The black retired university president who headed the visiting group was especially resistant to our "faculty gripes." He finally told us they had heard directly from a student panel about the way things were. He cited Ellen by name and told her that her comments contradicted our concerns.

Now I faced a different person. She was a young woman "in trouble," as we used to say. No longer was she the manipulated darling of the campus public relations office. Her moods were as far down now as they had been elevated before. In both cases—the ups and the downs—I felt that she was purposely exaggerating, distorting, and amplifying her emotions. She would have been better off if her life had not had such extreme highs and lows, but then she would not have been Ellen.

I continued to meet with Ellen as she tried to convince the elusive Frank that he needed to fulfill his marriage promises. When he hesitated to tell his family about the pregnancy, she accused him of not wanting to support the child. In a moment of panic and revenge, Ellen saw to it they knew. His father exploded in episodes of red neck vituperation. His mother, as usual, tried to mediate and moderate her family's crisis. This was one for which she had, however, no real sympathy. This spurred on Frank's desire to run from the issue. It also reinforced Ellen's resolve to have the baby and to make him support his child.

Several months after our initial session, she came to my office to tell me about the latest episodes in her continuing struggle with Frank. She had tried to convince herself that Frank would come around after the initial shock and be the person she believed him to be. We rehearsed all of the realities of her situation. I told her it was hard to fight a shadow. She tearfully agreed. I never thought of providing any Kleenex tissues in my office until it was too late. A lot of tears had stained that old green carpet.

After we had gone over the basic issues involved, she changed the subject. She told me she had been fondled by one of her teachers. I was surprised, but on that campus anything was possible. I did not want to come out directly and ask who the guilty party might be, but I was quite curious. I did ask her how it happened.

"I was playing the piano," she said, "and he reached over my arms to correct my hands on the keyboard. His hands then moved up my arms to my breasts." I forced myself to continue gazing directly into her eyes, not letting my eyes stray to her chest. I begin to inventory the male teachers in the music department in my mind, unsure about the teacher to whom she was referring. My curiosity was getting rather morbid and conflicting with the purity of my motives as a counselor. I led her a bit more by asking how she felt about the man and what he had done. She told me he had tried to kiss and embrace her and she had resisted. I asked if he had known she was pregnant, and she affirmed that he did. I thought that in a curious way this might make her seem both more vulnerable and more available.

I continued my line of questioning concerning what happened after that and she told me he had apologized and asked her forgiveness. She had expressed moral indignation and complained about the violation of the trust she had placed in him. He then broke down and cried, begging her to forgive him. He said he was lonely and confused. My mind began to repeat her words and reach the unbelievable but inevitable conclusion. I put two and two together and asked if an older and respected member of the music department had fondled her.

She shifted her gaze down to the floor, paused to take a deep breath, and answered slowly, "Yes."

I covered my shock while asking her further if she had told anyone else about this. She said she had discussed it with Fran Simpson at the Counseling Center. I asked her about Fran's reaction. I had never found Fran to be anything but fair and intensely interested in the students' welfare. Ellen said that, at Fran's request, she had written it up as a report, which remained in the resource center files, with a copy going to Dean Van Dale's office. I asked her if she had met with Van Dale. She told me she had not yet done so. He never acknowledged receipt of her report.

I discussed the matter with Fran. I told her I had trouble believing the music teacher could have done what Ellen suggested. Fran came up with the name of a former student of mine who had filed a complaint years earlier. This former student had finished her PhD, was teaching in the history department of a state university and had just gotten married. She was contacted and asked her about the incident. She verified that something had happened, but did not want to discuss it at length. She only agreed to testify in any possible lawsuit if she were subpoenaed.

Ellen asked me about filing a suit against the college and/or the professor. On the one hand, I was deeply desirous of someone finally challenging the Morton administration.

On the other hand, how could I desire to bring shame on a person whom I genuinely respected? He was getting older now and would be retiring. Could I sacrifice him to get even with Morton?

What should I say to Ellen? How should I answer her question? I told her to contact my lawyer and spell it out for him, then she could make her own decision after evaluating all the issues involved. Ultimately she decided not to sue. Richard O. McArthur was my lawyer and my friend. He agonized over the issue and saw it as an important challenge to the college, but also knew that Ellen, as a young black woman, pregnant with a mixed-race baby, with no real family support, would be extremely vulnerable. Morton's legal hounds would run her to the ground like a wounded deer, and ruin any chance for happiness and normalcy she might ever have.

We learned later that there were other complaints filed about the same time. One involved an incident in which a student was threatened with a knife by a baseball player because she refused to have sex with him. There were also two complaints of sexual harassment filed by women who took business courses in the night school. The individual in question was a junior level professor. He was not only accused of harassment and suggestive language, but also of repeatedly making proposals that the women sleep with him. Van Dale handled these in typical fashion: Questioning the integrity and the motivation of the women involved. Rather than punishing anyone for misbehavior, the school was more likely to defend the offender. This was due in part to Morton's fascination with sex, and in part to the fact that information regarding misconduct could be stored and brought out any time Morton needed something against someone.

Chapter 25

REBECCA SMART

Rebecca Smart was a multi-talented student whom I taught, and for whom I had unqualified respect. She was involved in many areas of campus life, but not in flashy positions that would place her in the limelight. She would typically do the hard, invisible jobs, like editor of the yearbook. Whatever she did, she did well, but without expecting a lot to be made over her. She was a full-bodied young woman with a sensuous appeal, but, atypically for Southern girls, she did not flirt.

She dated and later married Kevin Hartwig, a serious, no-nonsense, pre-med student who was one of the officers in the social fraternity on campus I helped charter. It took some getting used to seeing them together and to realize they were serious about each other. I never was good at matchmaking, although a number of students met and fell in love in my classes. I realized later that I introduced Rebecca and Kevin to each other. It was an honor for me to perform their wedding ceremony. I kept up with them for years afterward, tracing their movements to grad school in Illinois and then to work in California.

Rebecca was highly motivated and intelligent. She got things done, even if she had to do them herself. In addition to being editor of the yearbook, she also did most of the candid photography. On a Friday in late October, she went to a reception in one of the private dining rooms in the cafeteria. The occasion was a reception for a popular dorm mother who was being forced out so a dorm residence program could be instituted. Rebecca took a picture of the dorm mother, the president, and the president's secretary. This picture later became a prime artifact in our attempt to prove Morton's affair. Rebecca later told me that about five minutes after she had taken the photograph, she was standing in the line for the punch bowl. She felt a tap on her shoulder and turned around. Morton kissed her squarely on the lips. He pressed himself against her body and maintained the kiss for fifteen seconds.

He then pushed her away and merrily proclaimed, "Gotcha!"

Rebecca told me she was so shocked and repulsed that she did not know what to do.

She was one of many victims in the president's bizarre game. With my own eyes, I saw him lay one on the wife of one of the young assistant coaches. We collected stories about his bestowing kisses on dorm mothers, students, faculty and staff members, and some innocent bystanders. How do you explain a middle-aged minister and college president going around campus playing Gotcha? Rebecca thought of bringing a harassment suit against him, but that was not a time when many such suits were filed. Chances of it succeeding were slim.

Morton had been doing such things for years, just not so publicly and frequently. It was could not be ignored, and yet most people pretended not to see what happened. I certainly looked the other way, until I could not stand it any longer. I was especially offended when he preyed upon students.

Adrian Anderson was a Business major, a gifted musician and president of her sorority. She was a valuable member of each class in which I taught her, from freshman Religion to upper-level Philosophy. She took enough hours to have a minor in Religion and Philosophy. She was quiet and thoughtful until she had a contribution to make. She was also my most creative critic. More than once she held my feet to the fire, and I enjoyed it. It was seldom as a professor that one had a worthy opponent in an undergraduate class. She was one. This was especially true in my Ethics class. I thought Adrian would make a good lawyer.

She and I talked about her situation. She had dated several boys on campus and had gotten in over her head each time. She had been sexually active, but did not necessarily enjoy it.

"Everything that it is possible to do had been done to me," she confided to me in one of our counseling sessions. I later performed her wedding service. The marriage went well for about a year, and then the young man wanted to leave her. Too much about her background (the abuse, her parents' divorce, her personal lack of decisiveness) worked against her. The young man too had a troubled background with an abusive alcoholic father.

The incident with the baseball player her senior year was truly frightening for her. She was walking across campus to the library one night. One of the athletes came up to her and tried to get her to go out with him. She insistently, but politely, refused. She was dating a young man at that time, and had no interest in this obnoxious jock anyway. He took out a large knife and threatened her with it. He even went so far as to grab her, turn her around, and place the dull edge of the knife against her throat. She broke away from him and ran away sobbing hysterically. She had serious flashbacks of the night when she was a teenager and a group of neighborhood boys gang-raped her. Her regular routine was interrupted for months while she was in counseling, trying to unpack what had happened.

She went to the office of the school counselor and talked for several hours with Ramona Stewart, who wrote it up and sent a report to Van Dale's office. She then went to the office of the Dean of Students and asked for the baseball player to be brought before the judicial board. In a few days, she received a letter from the office of the Dean of Students fixing a time and place for the hearing. She arrived there five minutes early and waited in the outer office. She watched as the baseball coach and his assistant went into the Dean of Students' office ahead of her.

The hearing consisted of adversarial questions addressed to her by Van Dale, the dean of students, and the coaches: "Do you know what a knife looks like?" "What is the difference between a pocket knife and a fixed-blade knife?" "Are you sure that he [the baseball player] really had a knife?" "What did you say to him that made him want to take you out?"

She felt exhausted following the session. She went back to her room, did not leave it, see anyone, or eat anything for several days. She considered suicide, even taking out the pills and putting them beside a glass of water on her nightstand.

She called her psychiatrist, the school counselor, and her boyfriend and was able to regain control of herself. She moved off campus and resigned her various offices and positions. She did not march across the stage at graduation, preferring to receive her degree in absentia rather than to be in the same place with the athlete who threatened her. When she and I talked what had happened, she said she would never set foot on campus again until women were taken seriously and protected from abuse. I told her I fully understood, but honestly did not think anything would be done unless and until there was a change in administration or a million dollar suit was filed against the college. I was not comfortable being that honest with her, but this was a time when the only weapon we had against repeated abuse, neglect, dishonesty, and evasion was absolute and consistent honesty.

Chapter 26

PEYTON PLACE

On campus we worked with a special group of people. College-age young adults have a lot of sexual energy that creates a certain amount of tension on campus. That is natural, but it needs to be channeled with maturity and sophistication by faculty members and administrators. This was not the case on our campus. The atmosphere was charged with the electricity of the president's affairs and the wanderings of many faculty members. I took it as a special mission to try to deal with this troubling situation. I knew how difficult it could be during the sexual revolution of the '60s and '70s.

I lived through three different phases of mini skirts, each one with less underwear. I have to admit it was difficult to teach Bible to a classroom with numerous coeds almost naked before me. Julie told me she did not like the way I looked at some of the young women. I told her she had two things to worry about: First, that I would ever stop looking, and second, that I would do more than look. I promised her neither would ever occur.

In our little world, which was dominated by a sexual predator, it became clear that almost anything was possible. We often spoke of our little Peyton Place. The chairs of the Music and Drama departments were involved in a soap opera affair for years until Charles Arnsdorf's wife divorced him and they were married. The chair of the Art department courted and then married a beautiful young graduate, who had been a Miss Worthington. She later divorced him, freeing him for other relationships with students. One of our English professors had an affair with another beauty queen; his wife divorced him and he married the student. One of the Biology professors had an affair with a student. The golf coach was constantly on the make and had an affair on campus with the Assistant Dean of Students. And these were just the situations I knew about. There were no limits, and the students knew it and acted and reacted accordingly.

Ironically, this degree of excess would not be tolerated on a state university campus. The professional and ethical standards and controls mandated by such institutions would not allow it. The separation of church and state is supposed to grant freedom to church-related institutions, not license for such behavior. What better cover could an amoral individual like Morton find than presiding over a church institution as an ordained leader who had complete control? No one would expect or even acknowledge that such a situation could exist.

Rather than sexual transgressions being discouraged or even punished, at Worthington they were tacitly encouraged. A faculty member involved in affairs had to be able to manage some control over his or her actions and not cause a public scandal. Otherwise, Morton and company did not care. On the contrary, they found faculty peccadilloes to be humorous. Making fun of us gave them a sense of power. When a challenge came from one of us, they would see what they had to use against the individual, in case they needed it.

Julie and I joked about it. How could anyone be monogamous at Worthington? What was wrong with us? The answer was we knew who we were and valued our relationship and our integrity too much to violate our vows to each other and to the church. Anyone who would take advantage of his or her position of authority as a pastor or as a professor clearly would betray everything they were supposed to stand for. My contempt for such a person was unlimited.

I was accused of being too close to my students, especially the girls, by jealous colleagues. I knew best how to work close in. I could and did accomplish things with students that were unique. I considered myself a midwife, one who was present and assisting at the birth of an individual. I counseled individuals, male and female, who were profoundly emotional. I helped them deal with their crises, but I never took advantage of them. My contact was not sexual. It was at best therapeutic. This was true even when I might have wished it to be otherwise.

In the conflict with Morton, some of his cronies said about me, "Look at him, freely and openly hugging girls in public!"

My response, and the response of my lawyer was, yes, I do hug in public, and even in private—young men as well as young women. I am deeply touched and profoundly grateful for the affection and respect of those whom I taught and counseled. All the more reason I would never violate that trust. My greatest allies in my struggle with Morton were the students who refused to believe any propaganda that suggested I had violated their trust.

One year within the annual conference, there were eleven cases of divorce, affairs, separations, etc., among clergy members. Three of the situations involved former students of mine. They were young married men who had finished seminary, been ordained, and been assigned to churches. They had affairs with a secretary, a choir director, and a church member.

I sought out all three, and asked them, "Didn't I teach you how to zip up your pants? How could you be disloyal to your people and violate your vows?" I was rather savage in my questions. They had betrayed the trust I placed in them. The bishop forced one to leave the ministry, moved the second into exile in a church on the edge of nowhere, and gave the third a lateral move so he lost nothing. These actions were not so much based on merit, degree of guilt, or moral and professional behavior. They were political, depending upon whom the young pastors knew and who was willing to stand up for them.

There was another bizarre situation involving sexuality during my tenure at Worthington, which never came out into the open. A young man was hired by admissions. He was a talented musician and interested in theater. We got to know him and were impressed with his ability. Julie worked for an Episcopal church as Director of Christian Education when we first came to Worthington. She asked the young recruiter to help her with a Christmas play for children. It was successful and a lot of fun.

Because of his artistic interests, the young man brought to the college a number of talented musicians. The majority were young men with vocal training. Without intending to go there, I began to wonder if a number of our new students might be gay. Others noticed too, including the administration. The answer seemed to be that some were indeed gay, but others seemed not to be sure of their sexual identity. The disturbing reality that soon came out, because of student complaints, was that our friend was pressuring these recruits to have sex with him. He was fired. We never heard from him again.

Roger Godsey was an outstanding student and an independent thinker. His mother was a second career pastor in the southern part of the conference. Roger was a student assistant for Phil Maddox in the department. His participation in class and his term papers indicated a critical ability that went beyond repeating what he had learned from textbooks or lectures.

Our Jan Term, "Church Hopping," involved touring a number of churches and synagogues in Harrison. The person in charge (pastor, priest, rabbi) talked with us about unique aspects of his or her ministry. During our tour of the Orthodox Church, we were engaged in a discussion with the priest concerning his belief in the Trinity. Roger Godsey interrupted his comments and challenged the whole idea of God being three-in-one. Implicit was also a challenge to the divinity of Christ. He was an excellent thinker and a typical intellectual in that he was rather passive and kept his own counsel. This assertiveness was refreshingly out of character, but not appropriate. I was glad he was showing his independence and working out his own faith in this way, but I was concerned about the pastor whom he verbally attacked. When we returned to campus,

I took Roger aside and told him he had not been respectful of the priest or of the tradition from which he came. I also called the priest the following day and thanked him for his hospitality. I told him I hoped he was not offended by the student's remarks. He assured me he understood.

At the honors convocation the year Roger graduated, he got top awards in his major, Religion and Philosophy. Additionally, he received awards as the top graduating senior in the departments of History and Psychology. None of us had ever seen one student get three awards. I have written many recommendations for students for graduate school and seminary, but never one so glowing as the one I wrote for Roger. He began his studies the next fall at our seminary in Atlanta.

I do not remember any accounts of Roger dating. He was shy and did not seem comfortable around women. That was not an issue, however, and I only noted this in retrospect. We were surprised, therefore, that during his senior year, he dated a young freshman. She was personable and attractive, but rather immature, and certainly no intellectual match for Roger. They were married during the summer and moved to Atlanta.

I looked forward to hearing great things from Roger's seminary work. I considered him to be more of a candidate for a doctoral program and a teaching career than a parish ministry. I certainly never expected what happened at the end of his first year in seminary. We got word he had come out of the closet, divorced his wife, and left the seminary.

He knew that if anyone guessed he were homosexual, a career in the church would not have been possible. His marriage was a way of hiding his sexual nature. When he got to seminary, he could not stand the hypocrisy of the way in which he was living. I grieved the loss of this talented young mind. The last I heard, Roger owned a computer business. I also heard he would have nothing to with the church.

Chapter 27

GREENCHEESE

The other side of my calling was my pastorate in a two-church charge in the country. The Methodist churches at Athens and Pinetucky were reluctantly joined together by a superintendent who recognized years before they were only several miles apart. Both were also twenty miles from Harrison. They were, however, very different in terms of the composition of the congregation. Pinetucky was more down home than Athens. The composition of the congregation was mainly good country people who had few pretensions.

Athens, on the other hand, represented a community's pride in education. Before the Civil War there was no concept of universal education. Only wealthy families who could afford boarding schools could aspire to seeing their sons receive an education. And, of course, only the sons of these aristocratic families were considered. The girls were trained in manners and the social graces. They needed to know household management, social graces, and manners.

The old town center of the village contained the Baptist Church, the schoolhouse, the teachers' residence, the village government, the sheriff's office, and the jail. Over the years, this changed with the opening of public schools and the centralized village administrative offices in Harrison. All that remained was the historic Baptist Church.

The school building was torn down. Around the turn of the century, the old house for teachers was moved about a mile down the road and became the home of the Matthews family. Teams of mules pulled the huge, old house along its route inch by inch on greased logs. They say it moved so slowly you could not see it move. If you had a fixed point, like a small tree or stake, you could check it after an hour or so and see some movement. The house was repaired and remodeled to suit the Mathews family and became a landmark in the community.

Olivia Peale Matthews was the matriarch of the small Methodist Church. Julie and I were often honored guests at Mrs. Matthews's large dining table. Her son, Anderson, led the Athens church in almost all areas of its congregational life, including the building of the new sanctuary. His wife, Mary Beth, was the organist and choir director. Their four children were raised in the church. The family possessed a lofty sense of dignity and class-consciousness. They had high standards and lived up to them.

On the other hand, on political and social matters, my ideas could not have been more different. My responsibility there, however, was to preach the Gospel, not to try to convince or convert anyone to my views. I realize this sounds dangerously like the hypocrisy that was most abhorrent to me. Over the years, because of our long-term relationships, they changed and I changed.

One Sunday after church, Anderson took me aside, and told me he had something important to share with me. Dr. Simon Burton Greencheese was coming home to Athens. Simon was the consummate Southern gentleman. His surname had all the folly and comedy of a family of immigrants who came to this country and translated their name literally. In southern Germany and northern Switzerland the name *Kräuterkäse* is unusual but possible. *Kraut* means herb, among other things, and *Käse* means cheese, so then, herb cheese, which is a popular food in southern Germany and northern Switzerland. The herbs gave the cheese a green color. So the usual translation was "Green Cheese."

Using the surname without the umlauts or shortening it into some English appropriation was possible. Translating it to Greencheese was unfortunate, but no German immigrant wanted to have a name that had *Kraut* in it. In any case, this was a good family with a noble tradition. In the colonial period, the first of the Greencheese family entered the Carolinas. Eventually they spread across the southern United States in much the same way as my ancestors and thousands of others who settled the region. Simon was proud of his family, and did the ancestor study to find them and to trace their European origins. It became a special part of Simon's charm and effectiveness that he had a name that, after you heard it one time, you could never forget.

His speech and his rhetoric were classic appropriations of the style of the nineteenth century preachers and very effective. This traditional exterior effectively masked one of the most liberal and progressive spirits ever to come out of the South. He graduated from Birmingham Southern College at the top of his class. He and David Ellisor were classmates and debating partners. He was accepted by Columbia University where he planned to attend law school. Things changed when his father passed away. His father had a long career in ministry and retired with his mother to a small cottage across the highway from the Athens church. Simon considered his father's death his call to ministry. He changed his plans and attended Candler School of Theology. He became one of the most famous ministers to come from this area.

He was the pastor of some of most outstanding churches in the conference, including Main Street, the second church in Harrison. He was also a district superintendent in the southern part of the state. He was deeply concerned about the clergy he represented. Some of "his boys," as he called the ministers under his charge, got into trouble because of their views on integration. They signed a petition asserting that public schools should not be closed to prevent them from being integrated.

Dr. Greencheese spoke out publicly in defense of the ministers he represented and became the target of segregationist all over the state. From being one of the most outstanding and influential ministers in the state, he suddenly was no longer appointable. No church wanted the primary advocate of integration. The bishop was concerned for his safety. Dr. Harry Emerson Fosdick sponsored his move to New York, where he was appointed in the New York Annual Conference. There he served churches in Brooklyn, Niagara Falls, Rochester, and other communities. He was famous for his old-school rhetoric, his brilliance, his ability in debate, and his classic Southern accent. He was nearly as popular in the North as he had been in his native South.

His return to the South was occasioned by a tragedy. He had been cut off from his roots and from the real possibility that he could have become one of the strongest and most effective bishops the South ever produced. He was treated as most Southerners have been who are courageous beyond their time and place and go against the prevailing authority. We have often alienated and rejected the best of our kind. Simon was among this vaunted tribe.

A second dimension of this sadness was the death of his daughter, Tina. She attended her father's alma mater, Birmingham Southern College, which was one of the best church-related colleges in the region. Because Tina and her roommate participated in a lunch-counter sit-in, Southern expelled her. She transferred to Hendrix College in Arkansas for a year, and then was readmitted to Southern. She received her theological degree from Duke and began a doctoral program.

In North Carolina on Labor Day weekend, 1972, Tina was in the family car with her husband, who had a doctorate in history, their infant daughter, and her brother. They were following an overloaded log truck when the bindings broke and the logs tumbled onto the car. Tina and the baby were killed. The two men survived. Tina was like a comet that flashed across the skies and suddenly was gone.

In many ways, Simon and his wife, Ruth, never completely recovered from Tina's death. He decided to leave his church in New York and return to the South. Tom Franks considered Simon his mentor in ministry and a strong influence on his life and work. He was a superintendent when Simon returned and convinced a local church to accept him. It was still not easy to find a pastorate for a minister who had expressed him or herself so strongly on the issue of integration. After several years of this appointment, Simon decided to retire and to move back to the cottage in Athens where his parents had lived in retirement.

What Anderson wanted to discuss with me were two letters he received as leader of the church congregation. The letters were sent anonymously to the Athens church warning about the return of this arch-integrationist. There were slanders, slurs, and threats, the usual tools of the Klan. Anderson said he had not agreed with Simon about his positions on politics and race relations. He did, however, respect him and considered him to be a friend of the family and of the community. Simon's sister had been a schoolteacher in Athens for many years, and had taught with Mrs. Matthews, Anderson's mother.

Anderson told me he was not in the habit of reading anonymous letters and would not read these. He brought them to me as his pastor to do with as I pleased. I looked them over without reading them and then threw them away. Then we set about welcoming Simon and Ruth back home—although they had never lived in Athens. It was a wonderful enrichment to the community to have them among us. If I had any feelings of inferiority at all, I would have been intimidated to have this powerful preacher in my congregation. I included him in sacramental services and welcomed his preaching, but allowed him and Ruth to attend services without singling them out. They seemed to appreciate this. I found their presence to be empowering and supportive.

Julie and I spent many hours visiting in their home with its souvenirs from a rich life in ministry. Since the death of my major professor in seminary, I never felt that I had a mentor. Simon came to fulfill this role for me. This was odd since I came to know him only after his retirement. He shared with me from the great treasury of his wisdom and experience, and I absorbed as much as I could. I have a Greencheese story for almost every circumstance and situation.

I knew it must get tiresome hearing me recite these stories in my sermons, in my lectures, and in my writings, but he was simply one of the wisest persons whom I have known.

Simon told us a tale about when he was pastor of a large, old church in a changing neighborhood in Brooklyn. He sponsored many cultural activities, including dance classes for Jewish girls, outreach to needy persons in the neighborhood, welcoming blacks into the congregation, and many social programs. He usually wore a clerical collar. One night after a long meeting, he went out to his car and got in. Suddenly, there was a man at the window of the car with a gun pointed at his head. Simon rolled down the window and told the man to put the gun away.

The robber replied, "Give me your money or I will kill you."

Simon responded, "Don't you know who I am?"

The man responded cynically, "I don't care who you are. Give me your money!"

"Look at me," Simon implored.

"Oh." The man paused and recognized him. "You're the preacher at that church over there." He put the gun down and added, "This is a dangerous neighborhood. You better be careful. Don't worry. I will watch out for you."

I cannot imagine anyone else standing up to a guy with a gun and getting a result like that. The man with the gun listened, of course, because Simon was known as a pastor who cared about the neighborhood. His reputation circulated to all levels of the community, even reaching those who lived by the gun.

Simon was an incredible historian. He wrote a multi-volume history of the annual conference in our area. In order not to hurt anyone, he mandated that it not be published until fifty years after his death.

After he had been back a year or so, I had an idea. I asked him if he had ever taught history to college students. He said he had. I asked him if he would like to teach the Church History course at Worthington. I checked with the dean and he approved it. Simon began the next fall. At first the students were afraid of him. He knew so much and demanded so much of them.

Some of them complained to me, "I have other courses to study for!"

Gradually, however, his charm and his intriguing presentation of the history of the church took over. Students who studied under him treated him with an almost worshipful attitude. They told me how much they had learned from him. Many of them who went to seminary later told me they felt they were prepared for graduate work because of his courses. I was pleased with his teaching for us. It was exactly what a church-related college should do. Just getting to know Dr. Cheese was a blessing for the students. Taking his course was a fantastic learning experience.

The pastor of the Baptist church in Athens was Rev. Dr. Marshal Priest King. Marshal was a chaplain in the Second World War. As an Air Force Colonel, he was chief of United States chaplains in Great Britain. He told me he had a distinct advantage, being a marshal, a chaplain, a captain, a priest, and a king! He met there a wonderful English woman named Ellen, whom he brought back home as a war bride. He had served for many years as a college president and a leader in the State Baptist Association. After he retired, he served as part-time pastor of the little Athens Baptist Church.

The three of us, Simon, Marshall, and I, along with our wives, met often in each others' homes. Both the Methodist and the Baptist churches had their annual big events: Homecoming and Revival. These were weeklong celebrations of the heritage and history of the churches, which included preaching and dinner on the grounds. This meant that Simon and I, with our wives, would be honored guests at the Baptist Church, and that Marshal and his wife would be our honored guests at the Methodist Church. Relationships between two churches of different denominations had never been closer. We did not try to take each other's members or cultivate the jealousy of the other church. Simon presided over the service of the rededication of our marriage on our twenty-fifth anniversary. I had the incredible honor of being asked to officiate at the funeral services of both Ruth Greencheese and Ellen King. They were two of the most amazing women I had ever known. Simon and Marshall were dear friends and mentors through the most difficult period of my life.

Chapter 28

PRISON CHAPLAIN

In addition to teaching classes in Religious Education part time, Julie worked for eight years as Director of Christian Education in a local Episcopal Church. Her seminary degree was in Religious Education, which prepared her for this diaconal ministry. Being an incredibly independent and creative person, she eventually grew tired of doing the same thing and looked for new outlets. Morton had an incredible ability to put together jobs so the same person would wear two or three hats. He offered Julie the position of Dean of Women, which she would hold in addition to her part-time teaching load. She would have made an excellent dean, but we were suspicious of Morton's deals. She wisely turned him down.

While she worked in a local church as a Christian Educator, she often went to the state women's prison as a volunteer, getting to know the chaplain and some of the inmates well. He informed her during one of her visits that he had decided to return to the pastoral ministry, and had been called by a local Baptist church. The chaplain was concerned about who would follow him. He explained to her that there were things he could not do that kept him from fulfilling his role as chaplain. During the blistering hot summer season, for example, he could not go into the open dorms and visit the women. They were packed into overcrowded areas, with the only cooling coming from large electric fans. The majority of women, therefore, wore the least clothing possible. He could not go there and still represent the church.

Another example was counseling. He did not dare be alone with a woman in his office during counseling sessions. Having another person present, most often a security guard, compromised the situation. It was hard enough to earn the trust of an inmate so she would reveal the intimate details of her life. With someone else in the room, this relationship was impossible, especially if that person represented the institution. A woman chaplain, on the other hand, could be involved in many areas of the inmates' lives that were off limits to him.

Then the chaplain posed the question, "Would you like to take my place?"

Julie brought this proposal home and thought and prayed about it. It was a challenge and an opportunity. She did not feel qualified since she did not have the seminary degree required for ordination to pastoral ministry, which was a requirement for chaplaincy. After inquiring, she found out—since the chaplains were hired by the state and only secondarily appointed by the church—she could serve for a year without church certification. She decided to apply and was accepted.

It was quite a different lifestyle from working in education in a local church or teaching in college. She continued to teach part-time, worked full-time at the prison, and was a full-time mother and wife. It was not easy, but she felt it was an important and vital ministry.

When I got marketing calls at home for "the lady of the house," I would answer with sardonic pleasure, "I'm sorry, she cannot come to the phone, because she is in jail." Interestingly, these characters did not call back and we seemed to appear on fewer and fewer to-call lists.

One of her first actions as chaplain made the Catholic priest, who came to counsel the women in the prison, a friend for life. Previously, under the administration of the Baptist chaplain, he had been forbidden to bring communion wine into the prison. All forms of alcohol were contraband, and the former chaplain strictly enforced this rule. Julie made the sacramental wine an exception.

She had to deal with all kinds of religious groups and unique individuals. Some of the Pentecostal and Charismatic groups presented problems. She resisted claims that the only true scripture was contained in the King James Version of the Bible. She also would not allow anyone to disavow baptism in the name of the Father and the Son and the Holy Spirit. They went against some two thousand years of church history to allege that the only valid form of baptism was solely in the name of Jesus. Otherwise she tried to be as open to diversity and difference of interpretation as possible. Two of the most valuable contributions to her ministry were made by the Mennonite We Care Foundation, which supplied her with volunteer chaplain's assistants. These women were incredibly dedicated and useful. The other group was called Kairos. Established and organized by the Episcopal Church, but ecumenical in its scope, it represented a three-day weekend retreat for the women.

As the probationary year came to an end, we had some real decisions to make. Julie wanted to continue in her role as chaplain, but she had to have additional seminary work toward the Masters of Divinity degree. She contacted a number of seminaries to ask if they would give her credit for her Masters of Religious Education degree, since she had taken many of the courses that were required for the M.Div. The answer was almost universally negative. They would require two years of seminary work in addition to her work at Drew. The only exception was Drew, which agreed to credit her with her work there, plus coursework elsewhere.

They accepted her life experience, working as a Christian Education Director and Instructor in Christian Education, her academic work in Christianity and the Arts at Berkley, and her semester as Minister in Residence at the Claremont School of Theology. They also gave her credit for her experience as a college teacher, an educator in a local church, and as a prison chaplain. Putting all of this together, they told her she could complete the requirements for the M.Div. in one semester. She and Catherine went north. They lived on campus and Catherine enrolled at Torey J. Sabatini Elementary School near the campus. It was not an easy time for our family, but a productive one. Catherine benefited greatly from her semester in New Jersey. Steve and I kept the home fires burning. We all met back together for Julie's graduation.

Julie had to give up her job when she left. The head of the state prison system would not agree to hold it for her. In her absence there was no chaplain for a number of months. Then word came that she would indeed be rehired. She had to work hard to catch-up. Then there was the considerable task of supervising the building of a new chapel. This was an exciting time for her because it utilized all her artistic talents as well as her ministerial duties. She was the first woman in the history of the state to serve as a prison chaplain.

The next step for her was to apply to the Board of Ordained Ministry for elders' orders and full membership in the conference.

The initial question from board members was quite telling: "Why do you want to be ordained?" She had served as Christian Educator and was well known throughout the conference as a consultant and teacher. It was not easy for a woman to be ordained in the Deep South. Furthermore, we would be in that strange and hard-to-place class: The clergy couple. The board politely told her to wait until the next year. Was she really serious? She was being tested and they had more serious business to conduct.

The next year she came back after carefully preparing her ordination sermon. It was, as is typical of all her work, creative and innovative: A videotape with musical accompaniment and Scripture readings. She appeared on the tape in costume and mime make up. The entire sermon was mimed and acted. When the Board met, only one member had seen the tape—the only woman on the board—who admitted she did not understand it. Julie got multiple questions about why she did not present the normal written text of a sermon she had preached in an actual service.

The instructions in The United Methodist *Book of Discipline* encouraged creativity and even suggested alternate forms of presentations. The Board was having none of it.

We waited while young men whom we had taught and sent off to seminary breezed trough the Board on the first try. Julie came back the third year. Her final appearance before the Board was carefully studied and traditionally prepared. She was the sixth generation Methodist clergy in her family. She had heard her father's sermons all of her childhood and youth. She knew how to do it. It was in her genes. She put up with none of the nonsense about women clergy and clergy couples. She was absolutely positive about her calling. She had prepared a killer sermon. She brought reviews from her prison congregation of her effectiveness as a pastor and preacher and critiques of her sermon. The committee did not challenge her again.

Chapter 29

CHRYSALIS

Following World War II, a movement began among peasants in Spain. It was called *Cursillo*, representing a "short course in Christianity." It restored color, vitality, and warmth to a faith that had become formalized and doctrinaire. It was developed in the Catholic Church, and then spread to the Anglican and Episcopal churches in this country. It consisted of three days of intense instruction in the faith by laypersons and clergy, unique worship experiences, and sharing in table fellowship with small groups.

The Catholic and Episcopal versions of the three-day weekend had Latin and Greek names for the different elements of the weekend. It inspired many variants, including Kairos prison ministry. The Methodist version of this movement is related to the biblical story related in Luke 24:13-35, and called Walk to Emmaus. The content of the talks is basic Wesleyan theology. As chaplain, before inviting Kairos into the prison, Julie was required to attend a Walk to Emmaus weekend. She found her weekend to be deeply meaningful.

After her experience, she invited me to participate in my Walk. It was a powerful experience. I participated in the leadership of other weekends and invited members of my congregations to get involved. I begin to hear about a variation called Chrysalis for high school youth. The name comes from the lifecycle of the butterfly. What begins as a clumsy caterpillar enters a dormant tomb-like cocoon, or chrysalis, and then emerges transformed as a beautiful butterfly. I saw numerous lives and relationships changed.

I expressed interest in the possibility of starting Chrysalis in our annual conference, but was told there was no organization in our area. I contacted the Nashville headquarters and found out there were two girls in our conference who had attended a Chrysalis weekend in Tennessee. I called one of them and asked if they were interested in organizing in our area.

The Nashville headquarters sent me information about up-coming weekends. I talked with our son, Stephen, to see if he would like to attend a boys' Chrysalis. We registered for a weekend in Nashville, but it was cancelled. They told us there was a group planning a weekend in Ocala, Florida. I registered Steve and myself and we made our plans. When we got there, I was told the clergy person who was to be the Spiritual Director of the weekend was not able to attend. The Lay Director asked me if I would serve in that capacity. I said I would, but since I had never been on a Chrysalis weekend I needed a copy of the manual. They said they had the Lay Director's manual, but they were told the clergy manual had not been published yet.

I winged my way through the weekend, using the clergy manual for Emmaus and my training. By the grace of God, it went well. Steve and I went home, got together with the two girls and the leaders of the Walk to Emmaus, and planned our first weekend. I was the first Spiritual Director of our new community. We continued for several years and were able to touch the lives of scores of young people, including my daughter, Catherine. She was a strong participant in the second generation of beautiful butterflies. Then I got an idea. Why wouldn't this same plan, perhaps with some changes, work for college-aged youth? I posed this question to members of the board. They liked the idea, but did not know how we might proceed.

I was asked to be a member of the National Chrysalis Board. We had periodic meetings in Nashville. After a year, the director left to take another position. Without a new director, the board assumed responsibility for leading the movement as it developed nationally.

It was several years before I pursued my idea. By this time, we had a new director of the national board. At a meeting, we discussed the idea. She told me there had been several groups that had sponsored a young-adult weekend, but without the official approval or sponsorship of the national board. Since I taught at a college and was on the board, she wondered if I would like to organize the first fully sanctioned college weekend. By this time, the two young women who helped organize the first high school weekends were college students. They were invaluable in getting our new venture off the ground. Our questions about changing the basic plan, the talks, or other aspects of the weekend for college students were answered. We found that everything should remain basically the same. The fact that an older group was involved gave new meaning to the entire retreat without changing the plan.

We had weekends for several years, beginning at the conference camp, then moving to the church-run youth center on the Gulf. At our first weekend at the beach, I was leading the worship service the second morning. The night before, we heard one of the most important talks by a young adult: The Prodigal Son talk. He spoke of how he had stumbled in his life and how God's forgiveness had brought him to a new understanding of his faith. This was followed by a service in which the participants wrote on pieces of paper things they wanted to purge from their lives. Then they took the pieces of paper and nailed them to a large wooden cross. Later that night, after the pilgrims had gone to bed, we took the pieces of paper, burnt them, and put the ashes in a large bowl.

The next morning we had a worship service on the beach. I had led this service many times, but never on a windy beach. I told the participants what we had done with the pieces of paper and assured them their sins were forgiven and washed away. Then I lifted the bowl and threw the ashes out on the beach. The wind caught them and blew them downward toward the sand. I looked on in momentary disbelief, fearing the ashes would be blown back into our faces. But then something truly amazing happened: The remnant of the confessions and dirty secrets written down on the papers, reduced to ashes, spread across the sand. A large wave surged on shore and covered the ashes and then retreated, taking everything with it. The strand was completely clean.

Some of our participants came from other schools, but most were from Worthington. I related to my students in Chrysalis in a deeper and profoundly meaningful way. Chrysalis made a lasting contribution to the religious life of our campus. By the time I left, there were more than forty students at Worthington who had been on a weekend. There was a closeness among us. We had reunions and continued to work on weekends, but determined not to become clannish.

We were so successful that word began to spread throughout the churches of the conference that something new was happening at Worthington. I was told that Morton and Brunner, as they went to churches and meetings, had started taking credit for something called "Chris-SAY-lis." This was ironic, since they had never spoken to me about this new movement, and did not know enough about it even to pronounce it correctly.

Julie took this one step forward. She developed Epiphany, a weekend retreat for incarcerated youth, which took elements from Kairos, Walk to Emmaus, and Chrysalis. She combined them with original aspects designed for youth with serious problems. The young offenders became Epiphany stars in a spiritual weekend like nothing they had experienced before. Many had seen, if anything, only the dark side of religion. Ministers and church members had been abusive. Parents beat them, often in the name of God.

Julie adapted the program to the needs of incarcerated young people (lots of refreshments, but no caffeine and restricted amounts of sugar). She wrote the instruction manuals and designed outlines of the weekends. By the time we left Worthington, Young Adult Chrysalis weekends were taking place all over the country and Epiphany was in twelve states.

Chapter 30

JANUARY TERM

An interesting divergence from our regular course schedule was the January Term. In the period between semesters we generally offered an array of special courses that took us away from our standard curriculum. Students received credit, but no grades. Some of my offerings were trips to Israel, preparation of a solar greenhouse, a course in Death and Dying, a study of Liberation Theology, an evaluation of commercial advertising called Subliminal Seduction, and a popular tour de force called Church Hopping.

In the latter, we got to know more about the local religious scene by visiting a number of local institutions and meeting with the person in charge (rabbi, priest, pastor). Before our tours, I would ask the clergy person who was to meet us to tell us about the theological perspective, the architecture, the atmosphere, the program—anything that would help us understand what was most significant about their brand of religion. It could be quite revealing.

For example, the pastor of the Presbyterian Church proudly showed us around a church building that was an excellent example of Scottish Calvinistic design and practice. The priest of Saint Peter's took us on a tour of the church that ended up in the sacristy for a snack of unconsecrated whole-wheat wafers. My colleague and former superintendent, Charles Stevens, who was pastor of First United Methodist, told us about the church budget. My rabbi friend showed us the Torah scrolls. The pastor of First Baptist took us on a tour of the curious round sanctuary modeled on the cathedral in Florence, Italy. One of the most interesting visits was with the priest of the Greek Orthodox Church. He showed us the beautiful icons and the fenced-off sanctuary where only the priests were allowed to go.

We lived in our own home, which we had bought after several years in an apartment when we first came to Harrison. We were happy in our home and proud of our children. I used my spare time to develop our yard and to plant a garden in the back. My pride and joy was my Solar Greenhouse, built during the Carter administration, with grants for the initial costs and for a seminar designed to teach others. Friends from the churches I pastored helped me build it as a retrofit on the back of our house.

I had a seminar in the Jan Term called Winter in the Solar Greenhouse. The title tempted fate because it turned out to be the coldest winter anyone could remember. It got down to ten above zero, which was supposed to be the coldest it ever got there. We needed to finish the greenhouse, and I had intended to have the students help me. It was too cold to get out there, however, so we sat in my den and reviewed the basic concepts of solar heating.

Our Winter Caravan, involved taking groups of students out to churches in three different states to lead specific events. We led worship services, youth groups, older adult meetings, children's classes, retreats—any ministry assignment presented to us. I saw some of our students rise to the occasion and show their leadership abilities. We helped others realize where they needed to develop their skills. The congregations were appreciative and supportive. Years after a group went to the Athens church, members of my congregation remembered one of the young people and asked that he come back and lead our revival. He had finished seminary and was an associate pastor in First Church in Harrison.

My Death and Dying seminar began in the Jan Term. One year, we were discussing sober serious issues Kübler Ross brought up in her book, *On Death and Dying.* Julie was teaching her course in Clowning and Miming. We were surprised when Julie's crew of clowns silently trooped into the classroom, surrounded my class members, joined hands, and began to sing, "Ring Around the Rosie," as they revolved around us. It was a teachable moment because neither class had ever thought of this little relic of medieval Europe and the black plague as more than a children's song. Somehow "ashes, ashes, we all fall down" came to have a new and rather macabre meaning.

I took two different groups to Israel, the first with Julie and the second without her. The first was rather touristy. The second, with Dr. Jim Franklin, was much more meaningful because of Jim's knowledge of the ancient archaeology and the contemporary crisis. I have a photo of my student assistant standing before a Roman statue of the emperor that had just been unearthed in Caesarea on the Sea. This statue would later become famous because of its unique features. It had not yet been made off limits to tourists, so I climbed up behind it and put my head in place of the emperor's missing head. My student assistant stood in front of the statue and pointed up to my head as another student took the picture.

The statue was carved out of purple Egyptian marble and had been brought by the Romans by boat down the Nile and out into the Mediterranean. Shipping trade in the area was made difficult because no previous port on the lower part of the Israel coast was able to survive the silting effect of the tons of sand brought up by the Nile. The genius of the corps of engineers under Herod the Great, however, solved the problem. They built the port of Caesarea with cement channels out into the sea—pointing north—that were protected and not prone to silt-up. The statue was carved without a head or hands, which were supplied from Rome, carved in white marble. They were changed periodically when there was a new emperor. So it was really the statue dedicated "to the emperor to whom it may concern." I styled myself "Emperor Latrinus I," and tried to look noble as my picture was taken.

I chose my student assistants when they were sophomores so I could train them and keep them until they graduated. Eva was one of the best. She had expressed interest in going on the trip with us, but her mother was unsure. The mother worked as a civilian at a large army base. She consulted some of her bosses, asking them about the advisability of her daughter traveling to Israel. They could not give her any particulars, but felt it was potentially a volatile period. I assured her Eva would be safe and that I personally would watch her carefully.

I kept my eye on her during our treks around the northern part of the Sea of Galilee, as we made our way around the Temple Mount, and as we sat inside the ancient wall of Megiddo. We listened carefully as Jim Franklin and his Golden Retriever walked along the wall as he taught us, giving some of us a case of vertigo. In the ruins of Beersheba, I stood with my arm around Eva's shoulders.

At the Catholic Retreat Center at Tantur, near Bethlehem, one of the chaperones, Barbara Allen Stephens, became upset with me and the students. It was our second night at Tantur, after we had been in bungalows along the western shore of the Sea of Galilee for a week.

There were no facilities for washing our clothes in the bungalows. Our first night in Tantur, there was no time for washing our things, so we all wanted to get a load done the second night. Barbara was uptight because her sister-in-law had come with her. Barbara's brother was the mayor of a city in central Florida. The sister-in-law considered herself something of a celebrity, and had little to do with the students or the rest of us. Barbara catered to her.

The first forays into the washroom in the basement, where the washing machines were placed, left the students confused. The machines were made in Germany and were typical German quality, designed to last at least a century. The instructions were in German and inscrutable to our students.

They knew I was fluent in German, so they came to ask me to go with them to show them how to use the machines. The cycles were long with boiling water, designed to get clothes "German clean." We began after dinner and it took hours for everyone to have their turn. I went down several times to be sure everythijng was going well.. The last group came back with their clean clothes after midnight. We were loud in the halls (which was verboten). One thing Barbara's sister-in-law insisted on was obedience to the priests' rules for absolute silence at night. She had gone to bed and was furious with us for waking her up. Barbara came charging down the hall.

We were in two different sleeping areas, one for men and one for women. We slept in bunk beds lined up along the walls. That night we were congregated in the men's area with the students sitting on the beds. Throughout the trip, the leather cap I wore was a prize for the students. Periodically it disappeared, and I would go on a treasure hunt to find it. While we were talking, Eva grabbed the cap from beside my bed and ran into a side room off the men's sleeping area. I chased her and came back with my prize. As we came out of the side room laughing and joking, Barbara was standing there glowering at us. Before the students she accused me of showing too much affection to Eva, and hinted at an affair. I admit, we looked guilty as sin, but there was nothing to it. There was no reasoning with Barbara. She was irrational and condemned me before the students.

That night, Kevin, one of the students, and I talked for a long time. We were lying down in ajoining bunk beds. I was quite honest with him that Eva and I were friends and I had promised to take care of her. We were playing like children, which was one of the best things about our fellowship and friendship. I told Kevin I never wanted to be thought of like many of my colleagues at Worthington. He knew what I was talking about and said that could not and would not happen. He said the students knew and would defend me, if necessary. Nevertheless, I barely slept that night. Strangely, my body tightened up and my legs became so stiff I doubted whether I could walk. I have never had that feeling before or since. I simply could not understand how so many of my colleagues could have affairs and act as if it was all right. I would have been a nervous wreck if I ever tried it.

Eva tested my faith in her a few nights before we returned home. She and another female student came to me and brought two new friends to meet me, two young Palestinian men. They were polite, intelligent, well-dressed, and Christian. They came to me as a father substitute to ask if they could take the co-eds on a date. It would be a foursome and they would attend a pop concert in the city. This was a perfectly reasonable request. The four young people could not imagine the turmoil that was going on in my mind: Dates—with Palestinians? Are you kidding? I promised Eva's mother I would look after her. What if something happened? Long story short: I trusted the two young women and they had an enjoyable evening with two young gentlemen.

Barbara was a powerful person, who worked in Church Relations on campus. She and I established a program called The Laity School, in which we offered courses in six areas of churchmanship. I organized the courses and taught most of them. Over one thousand people participated in the three years the program existed. Barbara was a member of the Pastor-Parish Committee at First Church that brought charges against Tom Franks. She was also a member of the episcopal committee and knew the bishop well. Morton offered her a position at the college and courted her favor. I respected her, but was careful about what I shared with her. She was powerful and emotionally unstable.

It concerned me deeply that she charged me with doing what so many of my colleagues were doing. In later conversations, I told her she was wrong. I explained that Eva's mother and I had an agreement that I would take care of her and that was what I was doing. She looked at me skeptically, but we managed to move on. When we got back to Worthington, I made an appointment with Morton and told him what had happened. If ever anything was made of the Israel trip, I wanted to be able to say I had told Morton all about it. I honestly think he was afraid of Barbara. Later I was surprised that Morton did not try to use this against me. I presume she would not let him, but never knew for sure.

Chapter 31

A BOLT OF LIGHTENING

Jack Taylor sponsored an annual Worthington Scholarship Banquet. He and Morton got together and developed a list of fat cats, rich old ladies, and politicians to invite. It featured high-level speakers who were acceptable to a conservative audience. One year it was Bob Hope, another it was Art Buchwald, and so on for more than a decade. One year, we were told Elizabeth Dole was to be the speaker. I was excited she was coming. She was attractive and known to be a person of conviction. She had served in leadership positions in the House of Representatives and as head of the American Red Cross. She was also the wife of a Republican candidate for the presidency. I wanted my Contemporary Issues class to hear her.

The problem was the great event was not for students, or faculty, or anyone else on campus except Morton, his cronies, and a few handpicked representatives of the school. It began with a cocktail party (at a Methodist college!) followed by a sumptuous banquet. Serving tables were college students. Members of the Student Government Association were invited. The college choir also sang, but otherwise there was no place for students or faculty to be served or to hear the speaker.

If this were a time for soliciting scholarship money for students, why would you not feature all the students you could pack into the house? What could be more appealing than a group of our best students? If the speaker had anything to contribute, why not share that with the entire campus? If this event was to make a contribution to the community, why not have the faculty there to soak up the intellectual nourishment and share it? An event like this could resonate for years. Imagine students telling their children or grandchildren they heard Bob Hope speak at Worthington? Instead, Morton and Taylor restricted it for themselves and the affluent people they courted. For me this was an abomination.

A further reason this event was dreaded by the faculty was that it had political implications. As a result of Ronald Reagan's Southern Strategy, there had been wholesale defection from the old Democratic solid South. The new Republicans were but old Democrats writ large. Their elite united the old segregationists, the old money, and the nouveau riche in a new and powerful coalition. Morton had made the transition from the old Democratic power structure (including Governor Walker's crowd) to the new Republicans, whom he now courted. This was especially impressive since he came from the West and had no political convictions. He did have, however, an incredible ability to smell the money. Furthermore, he could pass it off as working for the good of the college.

I made the unforgivable mistake of carrying my feelings about the Scholarship Banquet into the classroom. I told my Contemporary Issues class Elizabeth Dole was coming, but we could not hear her. I told them how much it would mean, but why it was impossible. I spoke of Morton's Republican friends and asked why they would bring important national figures to the campus and not invite the students and faculty?

The next day I got a call from Sam Sherman, one of Morton's cronies, who was an ordained Baptist preacher, but was employed by the college to carry out Morton's errands. He invited me to meet with Morton and himself that afternoon. They worked me over pretty well. Did I not realize that one of Jack Taylor's sons was in that class? (No, I really did not realize Jerome Taylor was the son of the big man.) Taylor was one of our most important contributors. How could I insult him and his family? He financed this wonderful annual event and I dared question his motives before my class. I ate crow and humble pie without the wine of compassion or consideration from these two erstwhile clergymen.

I got Taylor's home telephone number and called him that night. He was righteously indignant and treated me like he would one of his employees who had insulted his company. Did I not realize he had donated $50,000 to start the golf team, and more money for the soccer team? Did I not understand how much money and support his scholarship events had raised? How could I talk about all this in a class with his dear son present? The only weak answer I could come up with was that I was just trying to make the students think. After all, that was the purpose of the class. Taylor was not a thinking man and his strongest emotions had been raised. He let me know I was lucky he did not nail my hide to the wall. I also apologized to the class for getting carried away, and to Jerome for commenting on the event his father sponsored.

Several days after the scholarship event, I discussed this with Jennifer French. I knew her for several years before she came to Worthington. She was one of the two high school girls who, with our son, Steve, worked to start Chrysalis in our area. She was now a senior at Worthington and the Student Government president. She and I talked from time to time about the situation on campus. She was a person of powerful convictions, excellent leadership ability, and strong will. She was also one of the few students who attended the event and heard Mrs. Dole. She said she enjoyed hearing her and appreciated her openness and honesty. She told me that Mrs. Dole, is was a Methodist, had not participated in the cocktail party, and had turned her wine glass upside down at the meal. She said to some of the students that she drank socially at political and other events, but did not think it proper to drink alcohol at an event sponsored by a church-related college. It was interesting to hear there were still prominent people who understood what we were supposed to be about.

I told Jennifer what had happened in my class. She said she had heard something about it. She agreed with me about the tragedy of not including students and faculty. We talked at length about the situation on campus. I was amazed how perceptive she was and how much she understood about Morton's lack of leadership. She asked if I knew about the affair. I told her I had been aware of it for some time. Then Jennifer said someone had to do something about this deplorable situation. I strongly agreed, not anticipating what she would say next.

She raised her right hand and pointed her index figure directly at me, and said in a strong voice, "You have to do something about it!" She then looked me straight in the eyes and said emphatically, "You are the only one who can fight him. You are the only clergyman on campus who will stand up to him. You are a department chair and you teach Religion and Ethics to half the campus. You've got to do it!" The words were like a bolt of lightening, and there was the resulting clap of thunder. Her voice was like the voice of God. No one else could have drawn forth such a reaction from me, only one of my students, only an original member of the Chrysalis community. There was no doubt what I had to do after that.

Chapter 32

MIDNIGHT MADNESS

Col. Alexander B. Dunn, the head of Campus Security at Worthington, was a retired state trooper. He was aware of almost everything that happened on campus, but kept his own counsel. He was careful about what he said and what he did not say. At first, I was not sure about him. Over the years, however, I got to know him. I would see him at off times when I came on campus late at night or early in the morning. He had a small staff, but a good one, which included women and blacks. He did not have to resort to underhanded methods to survive. He was in charge of keeping order and maintaining some semblance of decorum on campus. He did this with fairness and a kind of casual demeanor that belied his inner strength and control.

In a world revolving around Morton and his intrigues, Col. Dunn was an exception. He was not involved in the politics of the campus and he was pleased to be out of it. I never knew how much he knew, but figured behind that confident smile and easy manner, he was well aware of what was happening. There were activities that went on at the highest level that were on the edge of the law, and perhaps fell into actual illegalities. They were not under the jurisdiction of Campus Security, however, and Col. Dunn knew it. He did not overplay his hand or flaunt his authority.

The first time he opened up to me was one evening when I met him on my way to a night class. We had been noticing a strange car parked in one of Morton's reserved spots. A local car dealership had an on-going relationship with the college to supply a vehicle on a corporate lease to the college.

Morton often traded cars when his fancy craved a more prestigious vehicle. He usually had a flashy new Buick, which he parked in one of the two parking places reserved for him. The oddest part of this whole car thing was the fact that Morton lived less than one hundred yards from the parking spaces. The president's residence had a large garage that could contain his two vehicles. Nevertheless, he would drive his new Buick from the garage to one of the parking spaces each morning. We regarded it as showing the flag. The flashy maroon and white beauty indicated he was in charge and he was present on campus.

It was, therefore, shocking periodically to see a dark Chevy parked in one of his two spaces with no ticket and no action to move it.

When I asked Col. Dunn about it, he laughed and said, "That's Junior's car."

I said, "You mean his son is parking there?"

He said, "No, Junior, you know, the golf coach."

I was shocked, "You mean that Tommy Parnell is parking in Morton's place?"

"Yep, we got word to leave it alone. He can park there any time he wants. After all, there are two spaces reserved and one is never used." He laughed about it as he walked away. It was clear he knew very well the gravity of what he was telling me.

Charles Smith was a student in four of my classes, namely two Bible classes and two Philosophy classes, including Ethics. His future wife was also one of my students. They asked me to perform their wedding ceremony. He was a Business and Accounting student and went on to get a master's degree in Accounting at the local branch of the state university. He was likeable and easy going. He did not have the buttoned-up look of most of our Business students. He was smart, however, and well respected by his teachers. He worked in the college Business Office before taking a position in a local accounting firm.

He casually asked me one day, "Do you know what happens to funds sent by the United Methodist Women to be used to educate young preachers in your department?" Knowing Charlie, I suspected this was some sort of joke. But he was serious. "It was transferred to the Athletics Department and administered by Coach Parnell."

Then I got serious. "How do you know?"

"I worked in the Business Office," he said.

"Do you have evidence to back that up?" I asked. The answer to that question led us on a wild version of Midnight Madness, which included a late night trip into Stephens Hall to the Business Office and the Academic Dean's Office. Charlie said that to get the complete picture, we needed access to the files in both offices. The Administration Building was not locked until after midnight. Because Charlie worked there, he had keys that would allow us access to the building and some of the offices.

It was like something out of a Grisham novel. The two of us, flashlights in hand, went through the files in the Business Office and made copies of some of them. Then we went down the hall to the Dean's Office. Charlie had borrowed keys to that office. We were about to start looking in the Dean's file cabinet when we heard someone at the door. There was a new security guard, a young black woman, who took her work seriously. I had met her in the hall one night after class. We spoke briefly. She had just started and was still learning the campus.

She found the door open. She entered the room and swept it briefly with her flashlight. Charlie and I were frozen behind the file cabinets, which were in a separate room off the main office. Then we heard another voice. Col. Dunn had joined her and asked what she was doing. She told him she had found the door open and was checking the office. He walked into the office and moved directly to the file cabinets. He held his light down, but it was enough to see us. He looked directly into my eyes and turned around.

He told the young officer, "Everything looks good. The secretary must have forgotten to lock the door. Let's check the Student Center." And they were gone.

We got copies of receipts for the money coming in on a regular basis from women's groups in several conferences. Faithful church members thought they were supporting the training of future clergy, church musicians, and Christian educators. We could directly trace where the money was going because of entries in the Athletic Department's ledgers. We lacked directives from the President's Office saying how these funds were to be distributed, however. Charlie said the Academic Dean had copies of these orders. We did not have time to find them. We left the Dean's Office and Stephen's Hall as quickly as we could.

I never dared mention that night to anyone, especially Col. Dunn. He knew me, and I like to think he guessed what we were up to. I appreciated his trust in me and tried to live up to it. That night gave me the first real evidence of how things were being managed on the campus. I already knew enough to see there was more than a moral or ethical problem. My eyes were now open to far deeper problems that dealt with financial irregularities and possible illegalities.

I was actually quite happy with my teaching at Worthington, but I knew none of us had any security with Morton as our president. There also was the danger that he would cause the college to fail economically and none of us would have a job. His policies were self-serving and dangerous. We could not run forever on his flattery of little old ladies and his lies to our contributors. If they ever knew his true character, we all would be finished.

I was a marked man. I was walking around with a target on my back. I had seen how Morton operated. When anyone stood up to him or questioned his leadership, that person would eventually disappear. It usually took two years from the beginning of a process to its conclusion. Morton had used this procedure many times and had become an expert in applying the necessary pressure to bring it to a conclusion.

No matter who you were, he could eventually ruin your reputation, either through some real offense, or with some trumped up charges. Almost every summer we witnessed the disappearance of someone from the faculty, administration, or staff. Often it involved a contest of lawyers and a settlement involving a year's salary for the offender. These funds came from the budget of the college, which was already starved. Meanwhile, life went on as usual on campus. This was the deceptive calm before the storm. Morton did not forget, nor did he forgive. One would assume the conflict was over, or at least subsiding, then Morton would set his trap. I knew these things, but I also knew my responsibilities, both with a full-time teaching position and a part-time pastorate. I knew not to let down my guard, and, above all, not to do something stupid again like challenging Taylor's scholarship event.

Chapter 33

METHUSALEH'S AGE

Phillip Maddox retired as Chairman of the Department of Religion and Philosophy and I became his successor. Phil had been good to Julie and me. I had profound respect and admiration for him and for his leadership. I had worked under him for a dozen years. He had been a good mentor and guide. I planned to continue the mission of the department as he had done when he took over. Basically, we had two primary tasks. The first concerned a major contribution to the core curriculum and the Religion and Philosophy requirements of the college. This involved our obligation to all of the students who graduated from our institution.

The other concerned our responsibility to our majors, minors, and especially those who felt called to ordained or consecrated ministry in the church. There was always the challenge that we should be supplying more candidates for ministry. I was never worried about the number of pre-seminary students we mentored. I was impressed with the students who came to us and dedicated their lives to the church.

An important aspect of our mission was the fact that the Methodist Church was largely over-extended. The focus of the 19th century was village life. My mother and father both came from villages like Whistle Stop in *Fried Green Tomatoes*. Churches were vital anchors to this society. Most villages in the 19th century in the South had at least a Baptist and a Methodist church, and perhaps a Presbyterian church. This was a time when these villages were usually ten miles apart, because this was the distance one could travel in a day using a wagon or buggy, or an early automobile. New technologies in transportation, communication, building, etc., resulted in much greater concentration of commercial and family life in urban areas.

These small churches were originally served by circuit riders, who rode from place to place, starting churches, taking in new members, baptizing, administering the sacraments of Baptism and the Lord's Supper, and counseling the people. Although the dynamics had changed drastically, these small towns and churches were still there. Many were struggling for their existence, but they still needed preachers. The bishop and cabinet were dependent on the college to supply student pastors to send to these churches. This was not always a good idea, but a necessary evil. Our curriculum, therefore, contained many courses in Bible and theology which supported our departmental majors. In a more urban setting, perhaps it could be alleged that students should wait until seminary for this education.

We knew from the seminaries where our majors attended that they were prepared and did well. We were also responsible for those who would go out to serve small parishes while they were still with us. We were expected to supply partially trained preachers, associate pastors, musicians, and Christian educators to churches. If we had not served this need, they would have had to have done without. We hoped to provide motivation for these student leaders to go on to graduate school and seminary to complete their training.

As the new chair of my department, I wanted to begin an ambitious effort to attract new candidates for ministry and encourage support of local churches. I requested a meeting with Bishop Langston and his cabinet. Around the table were the nine superintendents, the Bishop, and personnel from the Conference Office who served the local churches. The cabinet was polarized with different theologies, philosophies, and political views. I knew that would be the case, and was prepared to speak to the different views as best I could. I also wanted to let everyone know I was available and that we in the department sought to be of service to the churches.

The college was known in the conference as being liberal in a conservative area. I got some surprising and bizarre questions from the superintendents on one side of the table. One asked me if I had said Methuselah was nine-hundred-years-old. I dodged the question by saying I used "It Ain't Necessarily So," from *Porgy and Bess*, when we dealt with the age of this Old Testament figure. The rounded-off figure fit better with the lyrics of the rousing song. The fundamentalist superintendent told me a young woman from one of his churches was in my Bible class. She came home disappointed that I did not know Methuselah lived 969 years.

I told him I tried to get the students to discuss what it might mean to live to a prolonged old age. In ancient society, long life was a special honor given by God. In our society, where we shuffle old people off into nursing homes to live out their lives and die, old age is a curse. He did not seem impressed and was still concerned I did not know how long Methuselah lived. I assured him I knew the age attributed to this biblical figure in the text and simply used the rounded-off number for class discussion.

We went on from this kind of discussion to my ideas and plans for the department. We were developing within the department, and especially in my wife's work in Christian Education, teams of students that would go into the churches and lead services, youth meetings, workshops, and other events. The Jan Term groups had given us a valuable start. I suggested other ideas we had and asked them for theirs.

Toward the end of our discussion, one of the superintendents, who was conservative, but also supportive of the college, asked me a pointed question. He had served a church in Harrison before becoming a superintendent. I had taught his son, so I felt I knew him fairly well. His question was not hostile, but brought me crashing back to reality.

He asked me, "Are these your ideas, or those of President Morton? Have you cleared your remarks with him?"

I felt the air go out of my tires as I answered, "These are my ideas. I am chairman of the department. No, I have not cleared them with the president. It never occurred to me to do so."

Chapter 34

THE NEW MAN

An item of immediate concern was finding a new member of the department to take Phillip Maddox's place. I expected this to be my job and was gearing up to see who was available. Having gone through the process nearly two decades earlier, I had some idea of how difficult it was to find a job. It was even more a buyer's market than it was earlier. Morton invited me to a meeting with him and Van Dale. I expected him to authorize me to begin the search and report back to him. The opposite was true: He indicated that he and Van Dale would look at possible applicants and get back to me when they had results. I knew this was not the way it was supposed to be done, but there was little I could do. This appointment was, of course, extremely important. My plans and hopes for the department were dependent on working with an assistant professor whose ideas were as compatible with mine as mine had been with Phillip Maddox's.

Morton and Van Dale called me back to review their efforts after several weeks. They had two names: One from Drew, where Julie and I had done our seminary work, and one from Duke, where I had studied for my doctorate. This was all a bit too cozy. As important as these two schools were to me, I would not necessarily have picked candidates from their doctoral programs. This would have seemed rather prejudicial to me, and it would have involved persons whose training and influences were too much like mine. We needed new blood, new ideas, and new creative talents.

A further mystery was the fact that the Duke candidate, Mark Jennings, had the same advisor I did. I asked a friend, who was the pastor of a local Methodist church and a Duke graduate, why Morton would go back to the same well again and again. After all, if hired, Mark would be the third Religion professor at Worthington from the same graduate school and the same teachers. His response was rather chilling. He said Morton shared the general view that Duke was rather liberal for the South. For him, that would mean that drawing Religion faculty from there would mean a staff that was less concerned with moral questions and more open ethically. I appreciated the insight, but also deeply resented the inference.

We invited the two candidates to Worthington for interviews. I was not sure Morton and Van Dale had even studied their dossiers and resumes. The Drew graduate was not strongly prepared. Furthermore, he disclosed to Julie and me that he had just gone through a divorce from his wife. While we did not see ourselves as being in a position to judge his private life, we did not think his divorce would play well in the conservative area in which we lived. He had not mentioned it in his correspondence with us, which we found to be less than honest. Because we knew the school and the faculty well, we were not impressed with his course work or his dissertation (which was not yet complete!).

We felt we had much more in common with Mark Jennings. His grandfather had been a bishop in the Methodist Church and had episcopal oversight in China. He was a native North Carolinian. He knew the Southern way of life. He had a rather antagonistic attitude toward Southern fundamentalism, which might cause problems with his working in our area. I certainly did not agree with it, but knew how to live with attitudes and convictions different from mine. Mark seemed rather immature in his black and white judgments. He was a good family man, however. We liked his wife and fell in love with his two children.

His college major was Chinese. He saw no need for a college Religion major, or even minor. One would get all that in seminary. I tried to explain our situation at Worthington and the fact that students needed our major to work in the churches while they were in college or later while they were in seminary. We knew from following up with our students that our majors did well in seminary. This was true with those who drove back hours to little churches they pastored, as well as those who lived on campus full-time. I would have preferred they did not have this burden, but knew they would not have been able to afford a seminary education if they had not served as pastors while they studied.

I thought Mark could come to understand the nature and mission of our department over time as he worked with us. I overestimated his ability to learn and change. There were other areas in which we did not agree. I found him to be rather arrogant and difficult to reason with. I was chair of the department, and Mark's superior. He acted as if he were my equal, although he had only taught as a student assistant and I had twelve years of experience. I finally decided to recommend Mark as our new faculty member. He had finished his requirements for graduation. He had written a good dissertation. The Drew man, on the other hand, was not finished with his dissertation, was divorced, and seemed unsure of himself. I regretted that we did not have more candidates to choose from.

Mark was quite happy to get a teaching job and to join our faculty. When he got settled, I discussed with him the traditions of our department and of the school in general. Our first responsibility was the teaching of the Bible courses. Phil and I had both taught two sections each semester (Old Testament in the fall and New Testament in the spring). Then we divided the rest of the courses according to our preferences and training. Phil taught the Logic course, and I the Ethics. I taught the two-semester History of Western Philosophy, alternating with a two-semester Church History course (until Simon took these courses). Phil taught a course in Eastern Religions. He taught a Jesus course and I taught a Paul course. We team taught the two-semester Contemporary Issues courses. He generally taught one course less than I because of his responsibilities as chair. I recommended to Mark that we generally kept the old divisions, at least for the time being. It was a heavy load, but with two full-time professors, we knew it would be.

Mark was not necessarily satisfied with the school, the department, or life in Harrison. He was not a happy person. I tried to keep the pattern of departmental meetings Phil had established. I got tired, however, of Mark's know-it-all attitude, and his lack of respect for my leadership and for other members of the department. I did not want to give him a forum for his ideas. He had not been teaching long enough to know what he was talking about. Both Phil and I pastored small churches in the conference. We knew the pastors and bishops over the years we taught together. We knew the needs of the school and of the conference. Mark thought he knew better and wanted to do away with most of what we had accomplished.

He did some bizarre and risky things, especially in such a conservative part of the country. He was careless in stating his views around campus. He made friends with the skeptics and sycophants, rather than with the philosophical and religiously oriented side of the faculty. In his classes, he said some remarkable things. He did not like teaching Bible and let his students know that. His Jesus course must have been interesting. I heard about one of his remarks soon after he made it.

A conservative student with a Baptist background attended the Methodist Church and felt a call to ministry. Ray was older than most of the other students and had a wife and family. He was appointed pastor of a small church in the country, and he and his family lived in the parsonage there. As far as I could tell, he was pleased with his appointment and his church valued his ministry. It was hard for him to understand women in ministry. Nevertheless, he made a point of taking one of Julie's Christian Education courses. They had some interesting discussions and became good friends and sparing partners. He was majoring in our department. I had him in a number of classes and respected his honesty and his ability to grow. He became more tolerant and open to other views and theologies.

He was appalled, however, when Mark posed the following question for discussion at the beginning of the Jesus course in which he was enrolled: "Did Jesus ever have an erection?" That was easily one of the most ridiculous ideas I ever heard. There was, of course, no way to answer it, and even if there were, it would be irrelevant. Mark's point, of course, was to deal with the humanity of Jesus. I got that, but there were a thousand other ways to pose the issue, which were more respectful and less controversial. When Ray came to me, I told him honestly that I would not have asked that question and considered it to be offensive. Mark was absolutely wrong. I was careful in approaching him because I did not trust him. I did ask him about it and told him students were coming to me with complaints.

Ray was obviously not satisfied, because he went to the superintendent and then the bishop with the issue. Word about Mark also reached Jim Bob Matthews, who was pastor of a large Methodist church out east where white flight had rallied. I had to answer questions about our new faculty member from all sides. The amount of dust this controversy stirred up was not worth it. This discussion took us in directions that were not useful in building the department.

I was forced to take up for Mark and to equivocate when asked about his reckless behavior and speech. This reflected on me as well as on the college. Van Dale contacted me when he first heard of what Mark had done. Morton did not get involved in this discussion and sent all inquiries to me. I am sure he enjoyed the confusion immensely. I seriously questioned Mark's fitness to teach in our situation, but I did not want there to be tension between the two of us.

Meanwhile, I knew Morton was not happy with me and that he perhaps knew some of our feelings about him and about his administration of the college. I stayed away from him and watched what I did and said. Since he had a church background, with his father serving as a pastor and a district superintendent in a western state, it would have seemed that Morton would have been close to members of the Religion and Philosophy Department. Looking at the twenty-five years he served as president of the college, this was clearly not ever the case.

A small art film theater near the campus invited local clergy for a special free viewing of the film, "The Last Temptation of Christ." At the monthly meeting of the Clergy Association, we discussed who among us would attend. We had some fears because we knew of the reputation of the film and how the local press would present our participation. Julie and I planned to go. The theater was only partially filled when we arrived. We took our seats and were surprised to see Morton, his wife, and Mark Jennings sitting six or eight rows in front of us.

They seemed to be having a nice conversation before the theater darkened. My suspicious mind immediately questioned why Mark was there with the Mortons. It was apparent Morton was taking Mark under his wing. I already believed I could not trust him, and this contact with Morton made that conviction stronger.

When the film was over, Julie and I tried to leave the theater quickly and to work our way through the gaggle of the press. We were not successful in emerging without getting stopped. Several years earlier, I had been interviewed by a reporter from a local television station. He stopped me, asking for my opinions. I told him I was still gathering my impressions. We agreed that he would come to my office the next morning for my comments. I really did not want to get in the middle of some sort of argument between our educated community and the fundamentalist clergy..

I told the reporter my strongest feeling after viewing the film was one of relief. He asked what that meant. I told him I went to see the film because I was used to dealing with what was being said about Jesus. The central character in the film had nothing to do with the Jesus I knew and studied.

Chapter 35

THE COUNTESS

Mary Elizabeth Ashby was born in August 1707, in Northamptsonshire, England. Her father's family was one of England's oldest and most aristocratic. They suffered for their loyalty to the crown during the Cromwell period, and were rewarded for their support of King Charles II during the Restoration. Prior to the Reformation, they were Roman Catholic, but during the civil wars they became members of the established church. Her family was wealthy and titled, but also torn by conflict. Her father married and entered a military career, serving in Ireland. Mary spent most of her childhood there. She had a tutor, but lacked the educational opportunities she would have had in England. She was intelligent, independent, and extremely well organized.

Mary was determined to find stability and happiness in her adult life and marriage. This she found in and through the person of Harold Stewart, who, after the death of his brother, became the ninth Earl of Worthington. The young Harold entered Oxford at the age of fourteen. Later, when he was full of life and enjoying the Grand Tour of the continent at age twenty-eight, his mother, Lady Catherine, was concerned about finding a fit partner for her son. Mary and her sister had recently moved into an estate belonging to their father. It was only about five miles from the Stewart family estate. Lady Catherine found Mary to be a woman from the correct social echelon, of sufficient wealth, and having family connections worthy of her son. She worked her magic in matchmaking and the two began dating.

On June 3, 1728, Mary was married to Harold and became the Countess of Worthington. He was thirty-two and she was twenty-one. Although not as religious as Mary, the Earl was a devoted student of the Bible and tolerant of his wife's interests. He supported her and was interested in her considerable accomplishments. They were deeply in love with each other and their marriage was productive. In the eleven years following their wedding, a total of seven children where born to the Earl and Countess. She was active in the society of her day. Her poor health, however, was exacerbated by her frequent pregnancies. She consulted a number of doctors and took their advice to spend long months at Bath, "taking the waters," with various treatments and cures. She had many contacts there with other members of the nobility. Bath was a playground of the idle wealthy. Their style of life seemed trite to Mary and caused her to consider devoting her life to more serious pursuits.

The prevailing philosophical system of the day was Deism, with its concept of a God who was remote from the world. Rationalism also prevailed with an exaggerated confidence in human reason, and a rejection of transcendence, revelation, and any trace of the supernatural. Religion was carefully disciplined by the state, and was largely intellectual, cold, and controlled by a hierarchy dedicated to maintaining the status quo.

The changes of emphasis in religion since the Reformation resulted in widespread materialism and preoccupation with acquiring wealth. Primary concerns were commerce and trade. It was the Age of Gin, with plenty of cheap liquor to drown the anger and frustration of those who were poor and outcast. Poverty was not addressed by agencies of the state. Those on the peripheries were left to their own devices, which provided an incentive for widespread criminal activity.

Mary devoted herself to serving her family and reaching out in Christian charity to her neighbors. She also was aware that her good works were inadequate to satisfy either herself or the demands of God. During one of her pregnancies, she became seriously ill. She was aware death was a real possibility. She thought of her husband and her five young children, as well as her unborn child.

She was deeply concerned about her spiritual condition, affirming, "I would do anything to come to the true knowledge of my Saviour." She recorded the date of her conversion as July 29, 1739. This liberated her from years of self-doubt and thoughts of unworthiness. She devoted herself fully to Christ in appreciation for her life and her salvation. She dedicated the rest of her life to service to the Kingdom of God.

The Countess's spiritual uncertainty and search for meaning coincided with one of the most important revivals in English history. The brothers, John and Charles Wesley, were speaking to thousands and were soon joined by George Whitfield. Whitfield commented that it was ironic that, "religion, which had long been skulking in the corners, and was almost laughed out of the world, should now begin to appear abroad, and openly shew herself at noonday."

The Wesley brothers were denied placement in local churches by the bishops of the Church of England. So they went out into the streets, fields, and mines to preach to the lower classes, the poor, and illiterate masses. John Wesley decided to become a missionary to the Indians in America. On his shipboard journey across the ocean, he encountered the Moravians, German pietists, whose profound example and faith changed his life. When he returned to England, he learned from them and even went to Germany to their headquarters to meet their leader, Count Ludwig von Zinzendorf. Although there were many aspects of the Moravian spirituality Wesley rejected, he accepted the genius of the German pietists and their social concerns.

Wesley replicated in England the social revolution the Moravians had accomplished in Germany with his own modifications. Small groups for prayer and Bible study, schools for poor children, orphanages, literacy training for adults, homes for unwed mothers, and other social agencies were a result. This unprecedented activity by the churches was resented and rejected by the state churches in Germany, and later in England. The most characteristic aspect of the Wesleyan reforms centered on John Wesley's conversion. It occurred at a meeting of an Anglican society, on Aldersgate Street in London on May 25, 1738.

While listening to a reading of Luther's *Commentary on Romans,* he later recounted, "I felt my heart strangely warmed." This resulted in what exponents regarded as pietistic renewal and continuation of the Reformation. It took the form of a thermal current welling up in English society that stood in sharp contrast to the coldness, rationality, and formality of the Church of England.

The Countess was swept along in the warmth and flow of this current of religious faith and practice. Her friendship with the Wesley brothers began in 1740. She attended services regularly at the Foundry in London and generously supported the Methodist societies meeting in the area around her home.

She resisted the rising opposition to the Methodists, such as the statement of the vicar of Dewsbury, who called the movement "an impious spirit of enthusiasm and superstitions [which has] crept in among them," or the complaint in an anonymous pamphlet which labeled them as "crackpot enthusiasts and profane hypocrites." These insults and attacks seemed only to strengthen Mary's support and conviction that the new movement was truly Gospel inspired.

She had the greatest respect for John Wesley, but probably was, like him, too much of a leader and too independent to be his disciple. Eventually she turned to the more Calvinistic side of the movement, represented by Whitfield. She entertained both the Wesley brothers and Whitfield many times in her home. All three of them spoke often of her warm and supportive friendship.

Whitfield's insistence on election and perseverance appealed to Mary. It gave her confidence in God where she had been insecure previously. The Calvinist idea of the imputation of the righteousness of Christ involved the denial of any virtue or value in the individual worthy of God's grace. Everything depended on Christ and what he gave in the donation of grace to the believer.

Wesley's position followed the classic opposition to Calvinism's denial of free will represented in the theology of the 16th century theologian Dutch Jacobus Arminius. He rejected the choice between free will or bondage of the will, however. His theology represented a position somewhere in the middle: There was freedom of the will, but it was limited. He did not trust a radical view of conversion. The will of the believer to change and his or her efforts to live a new life were extremely important. Wesley's view was evolutionary, a process through which a person turns to God, who meets him or her midway, and then travels with them on their way to perfection. Good works and means of grace are a part of this process, but one did not earn salvation through them, but participated in them in response to God's grace.

In Calvinism, one should not receive the sacraments unless and until he or she was elected by God and deemed pure. For Wesley, one receives the means of grace available in the sacraments in order to respond to God's offer of salvation. Through them, a person is enabled to change their way of living and begin to do works of righteousness. Wesley increasingly stressed believers working for and attaining perfection in this life. For Whitfield, this sounded like working out one's salvation through good works. Wesley believed perfection was attainable for one who continued to strive to do the will of God. This life-long effort was the road to salvation.

Initially, Wesley's view appealed to Mary. She appreciated the challenge of striving for perfection, even if it was unattainable. As determined and decisive as she was, nevertheless, her old self-doubts told her this understanding came dangerously close to replacing the role of God in salvation with one's own ego. Eventually, she rejected Wesley's position, and was, "against sinless perfection, and the instantaneous gift of sanctification."

Mary tried to mediate between the Wesley and Whitfield. Their different views of the process of salvation ultimately lead to the same result but through different routes. When she was unable to find a way to reconcile the enormous egos of these leaders, she inevitably chose to side with Whitfield and became a leader in Calvinistic Methodism. Her genius, however, was not theological, but organizational. Following the example of both Wesley and Whitfield, she organized societies and created chapels for meetings and preaching. These were not churches and were not recognized by the established church, which resented the placement of chapels in the vicinity of established parishes and drawing away congregants and contributions.

The Countess used her position and influence to protect the evangelical revival and the preachers. She had cachet with the wealthy and privileged, and used it to gain respect and respectability for the new movement. She invited the leaders of Methodism to preach in her home to guests from the titled and prominent classes. She became the patron and director of more than one hundred places to hold services, ranging from hired halls, barns, and disused chapels, to large and elaborate places of worship. Her special genius provided preachers, leaders, and places for the education of clergy. She usually did not preach, lead Bible study, or fulfill the many functions of a pastor, but she did lead and direct many who did.

The established church frowned upon any of its clergy's participation in the ministry of the Methodist chapels or preaching areas, although they were intended as extensions of the ministry of the established church. The Methodists strictly and purposely stayed away from administering the sacraments until they were forced out of the established church. The leaders of the evangelical movements had difficulty finding preachers to fill the pulpits in their chapels. They often used students and others who were not ordained, although they made every effort to find the most qualified and dedicated persons.

The Countess was increasing involved in sponsoring theological education. She wanted to establish an educational facility capable of training men of evangelical persuasion who could be sent out to supply vacant pulpits. These were not persons assigned to established churches and parishes with state provided benefices and salaries. They were itinerant pastors supported by local congregations and available to be moved about as the Countess chose.

The Countess took out a twenty-five year lease on an estate in Wales, which she developed into an academy for training preachers. She sought out godly young men, who were zealous, able, and suitable candidates for the job of traveling preachers. She started with a class of seven young men. In the years of its existence, there were never more than twenty student preachers at a time. These men were sent out to churches even before they finished their course of study. Many of them were quite successful, but others failed at living the rigorous life of an evangelical preacher.

Wesley had wished to establish an academy for the education of young persons from his faith communities. He wanted to provide for the education of preachers and ministers for his chapels. He also wanted to to make education more available to those who did not have the wealth and position to attend Oxford and Cambridge. He resented, however, Lady Mary's accomplishment and questioned the use of the term college. He was not at all sure of the quality of the education one would receive there. In a letter written in 1770, he did not mention her efforts in education, but was critical of her character and her position in their discussions. The letter was offensive to the Countess and ended their long friendship.

At the Annual Conference of Wesley's ministers in 1770, he outlined the major aspects of his position, beginning with the statement: "We have leaned too much towards Calvinism." He stressed the goal of holiness and the role of good works. This caused a gulf to develop between the two branches of Methodism and alienated the Calvinistic side. The distinction between faith and works became a stumbling block.

Shortly before his death, the ill and weary Whitfield exclaimed in a fiery sermon, "Works! Works! A man get to heaven by works! I would as soon think of climbing to the moon on a rope of sand!"

In his will, Whitfield left his Orphan House in Georgia to the Countess. It was already being styled a college, and Whitfield suggested the Countess might wish to develop it on the model of her own institution in Wales. Her plans and efforts, however, were never fulfilled because of the failure of the leaders she sent to direct them. She was too advanced in years to travel to America to direct it herself. This did not diminish her dedication to education, and more specifically, education based upon and centered in the Christian faith.

She confessed regarding her school in Wales, "My heart is much united to my great charge there, and the college means more to me before the Lord than anything else in the whole world."

Although a layperson with no formal theological education, the Countess was a pioneer in the organization and independence of the new churches. She also established the first college and theological education institution growing out of the Methodist experience. In these areas, she preceded the Wesley brothers, who maintained their positions in the Church of England.

No doubt, the Methodist Church has been instrumental in providing educational opportunities to advance the position of women in America. This is especially important in the South, where traditionally, men were educated and women were trained in the social graces. Naming a college after this often overlooked woman in the history of Methodism was meant to provide a role model and inspiration for young woman.

Her dedication and witness to the reorganization of the church and to the spread of the Gospel is unique. Her choice of leadership, direction, discipline, and constant oversight of her college would present a challenge to any institution of higher learning, especially one named after her.

Chapter 36

"BLOODY MARY"

One evening, I returned to my office after a night class. I climbed the stairs to the second floor of Freeman Hall, and entered the hallway where my office was. I noticed a woman walking toward me from the other end of the hall. She was of average height, with long black hair, and a striking long dress. I greeted her, and she responded with perfect British accent, one that did not seem to have the stiff upper lip treatment. She was pleasant, and yet remarkably regal. I remarked that her dress was beautiful. It looked like a long dress a movie star would wear to the Academy Awards. She said she had it made for a birthday party in London on January 14, 1739. It was the twenty-third birthday of the Prince of Wales.

She was like a person from a distant era, but still charming and personable. Once again, I tried to remember what drama or musical the Arnsdorf-Sanders team might be rehearsing. My guess was some sort of fantastical baroque opera, but I was not sure.

"January 1739?" I replied, playing along. "You remember that year?"

"Oh yes," she replied, "Mr. Whitfield had returned from America and was ordained by the Bishop of Gloucester that month." I knew about Whitfield from my study of church history. He was both an associate of the young Wesley brothers, and, ultimately, an antagonist, due to his strict insistence on maintaining his strong attachment to Calvinism.

"Yes," she continued, "that was six weeks before a dozen of us ladies presented ourselves at the entrance to the House of Lords at 9 a.m. We demanded to be admitted to register our protest during the discussion of the treatment of our sailors by those barbaric Spaniards. The incident of Jenkins's ear, severed by those perverted papists, was the last straw! We demanded the continued right to sail the waters around their costs and conduct shipping to their ports."

"Oh, I commend your courage," I said.

"But you know that the Lord Chancellor refused to admit us. Can you imagine twelve gentlewomen locked outside the gallery door, knocking and screaming all that day? But you should know about this. Your ancestor, Lady Mary Wortley Montagu, recorded a colorful description of the event, in which she was a participant."

"I am aware that I am descended from Lady Montagu, but I did not know of this event." I was a bit startled by all of this, but things began to come together in my addled brain. "You must be Mary, the Ninth Countess of Worthington," I said rather majestically.

"Well of course, young man. It took you a while."

She did not fit my image of the Countess at all. I thought of her as a rather dour older woman dressed in a black dress. This, of course, was according to the familiar portrait of her that was painted after Whitfield's death. A copy of this portrait hung in our college library.

I diplomatically responded, "I must admit that I thought of you more in terms of your later years and the founding of churches and a college."

"Oh, when I was a young married woman and mother in my thirties, I was in society as due my station, and rather assertive, if I may say. I later gave up most of my privileged status and used the wealth from my husband's estate to further the goals of the spiritual reformation in which I was engaged, both in England and in this country."

Then I asked her if she was acquainted with Dr. Edward Freeman. She acknowledged that she was. The two of them had conferred about the situation at the college that bore her name.

"He is a remarkable gentleman, you know," she said. "He and I have had many discussions about the church's role in the development of higher education in this country. Both of us are deeply concerned about the situation on this campus. We have watched you and your work here for a number of years. We know about your teaching, your church work, and your development of the weekend retreats. What are they called?"

"Chrysalis," I said.

"Ah, yes, Chrysalis. It is wonderful! Naturally, I would prefer if it were based on a theology more like Mr. Whitfield's predestination, with less of Mr. Wesley's perfectionism. I do like the three stages of grace, however, you know: prevenient grace, justifying grace, and sanctifying grace. Since I was the one who was trying to bridge the great and painful gap between the two positions, however, I will not register my objection."

She had a large bag hung over her right arm. There were strands of what looked like a red wig hanging out of it. I asked her what the red wig was for.

"Oh, that," she said. "I was afraid you might ask. Perhaps you have heard stories about the famous 'Bloody Mary'? There is a legend on campus that a beautiful, young, redheaded coed died on campus. Her boyfriend reportedly left her for another. She was so upset that she committed suicide by cutting her own throat. Every fall her ghost walks about the campus dressed in white with blood streaming down her body. The freshman girls see her and are terrified. I heard the story years ago and began to represent her."

"So you're Bloody Mary."

"In my younger days I was quite interested in the theater and did some acting. I always enjoyed it. As I got older, I would not allow myself such indulgence. But, since I am not living any longer, I feel much younger and I like to have some fun. It is my school, after all, and I can play some games if I want to. The students make a lot out of it and seem to have fun getting scared."

The Countess changed the subject radically and became serious. "This is all beside the point. I am here to pledge my support to you, as Dr. Freeman has already done. He did this in his own modest and honest way. I am here for a very serious purpose. You are about to face the greatest challenge of your life. You must stand up to the gross pretender who controls this campus. For too long this college, named after me, for God's sake, has been under the control of this evil man.

"You have Dr. Freeman's view from the nineteenth century and now I will give you mine from the eighteenth. You can see what was intended for this college and others like it. Now, in your twentieth century, its purpose has been derailed and profaned. In many ways, it is more secular than the state schools. And the morality! No school should put up with what Morton is doing. He hides behind the separation of church and state in this country. What about the origins of this school and those who labored to establish it and insure its continuation? Can their efforts be so easily abandoned and, indeed, falsified?"

"I know all that, but what can I do by myself?" I replied.

"You can liberate my school. Nothing less, nothing more. I have confidence in you, otherwise I would not be here. You are uniquely prepared. You have a history of standing up to bullies."

"I have a different perspective," she affirmed. "It is different from yours. I know what needs to be done. Although you won't see or hear me, you will know that I am with you."

"What do I need to do?" I asked, feeling vulnerable.

"Don't worry. You will know, step by step, as you live through these next months. Listen to the voice of God within you. God will guide you. Most of all, never compromise your integrity, or your sense of what is right. This has been Morton's weapon all these years. He has forced good people to abandon their values and do his bidding. Face him head on with your faith and your convictions and he will fall."

She saw me gulp and look down. It then occurred to me that I should ask her if she knew about the rumors concerning a large grant given to the college that would be devoted to supporting religious life on campus.

She then responded, "Yes, I have heard about that, but you have to be aware that your president is doing everything in his power to misdirect the money and use it for other purposes. The mission statement written by the donor is wonderful! You must see it."

I told her I had not seen it, nor had anyone in the administration discussed it with members of my department or with me, so far as I was aware.

"I am not surprised," she said. "I will get a copy for you and slide it under your door. I am not really supposed to interfere, but this is very important. Enough! I am preaching to a preacher. I have had a bad habit of doing that over the years. Just this for now: You must preach about this. It is your calling, your talent, and your responsibility. Now, go home to your good wife. Pray to your God and stay close. Remember Mr. Wesley's final words, before his death: 'The best of all is, God is with us.' I must confess that John and I are very close now, since we have crossed over."

Chapter 37

THE VIRTUAL CHAIR

I was aware there was something else going on at the same time we were dealing with the changes in our department. That might have been one of the reasons Morton paid so little attention to finding a new professor for the department. He was busy dealing with a gracious lady who wanted to help the college. Margaret Jenkins Pitman was the widow of the wealthy owner of a grocery market chain in the southern part of the state. She had been a generous donor to the college for a number of years. She was getting older and wanted to make an outstanding and definitive gift that would perpetuate the memory of her family and be instrumental in supporting religious life on the campus.

Morton sat on this offer for some time so he could shape it for his own purposes. The proposed figure was $600,000. Although our department, the chaplain's office, and the office of church relations should have been directly involved in the discussion about this gift and how it should be used, none of us heard anything about it until Morton had taken charge of it.

The day after the Countess visited me and promised to send me a copy of the mission statement, I found it under my office door. Mrs. Pitman clearly declared her desire to support and develop religious life on campus:

My understanding and view of this college has always
been that one of its primary purposes as a church-related
college has been to advance the purposes of the Church
of Jesus Christ, among which the first and foremost of
purposes is His Gospel. In a college setting, it seems
to me, that advancement of the Gospel is accomplished
both academically through strong Christian curricula,
and relationally through fellowship and mutual nurture
in His name.

I was amazed how concise and perceptive this statement was. I
also understood why the Countess found it meaningful. It was an
amazing summary of what a church-related college could and should
be. In a few words, Mrs. Pitman was faithful to both the heritage of
Christian higher education and the contemporary challenge. I could
imagine that Morton and his cronies scoffed at the pious language
of this statement and would do anything to see that Mrs. Pitman's
vision was not carried out. It was months before I heard anything
else about it. Then I met with the dean, who told me we had a grant
for an endowed chair in the department.

I wondered if this was in addition to the grant for religious life
on campus or an altered form of it. Of course, this appealed to me.
It was clear that, as head of the department, I would be the primary
candidate. With a secure chair under me, I would get a raise in salary
and protection from the miserly handling of our pay. I would also
gain prestige, both on campus and professionally. I did not intend
to remain at Worthington for my entire career, so being the holder
of an endowed chair would be a real asset in seeking to move up
in teaching. I should have realized Morton would never let me be
promoted to the holder of the chair. I knew too much.

I discussed this whole matter with Adam. One of the main
reasons he left a state university position and came to Worthington
was the fact that there was an endowed chair in Business he would
occupy. He also wanted to get out of the politics of a state system

and the poor leadership of the university. Little did he know what he was getting into. He told me the donors for his chair were business people. They had insisted on how the donation would be set up and that the chair would, indeed, be established.

He told me there were other chairs that had been set up at Worthington but were never filled. The interest, which was to be used to pay the salary of the holder of the chair, was diverted year after year and used for other purposes.

I said to him, "That is illegal. You can't do it."

He replied, "Oh yes you can. Morton does it all the time. You say that the donation is for religious life on campus. Morton does not care about that, and really does not desire it."

He continued to say that just because Morton was an ordained minister, did not mean that he was religious. "He does not really believe in anything except himself. He wants that money. There are physical chairs and metaphysical or virtual chairs. I am willing to bet this chair will be far from substantial. Morton would not have changed it from a fund establishing religious life on campus to an endowed chair if he had not meant to rob the fund."

I felt like Adam had slugged me in the gut. I had a sneaking suspicion he was right. After years of being critical of Morton, we did not know the half of it. He had found out that my pearl of greatest price was the department and what it might become. He would destroy me by destroying the department. He did not want any department, or any other dimension of campus life to be strong. I thought being chairman would mean more responsibility as well as more opportunity. I now doubted that either one of those was true. I naively thought if someone opposed him others would follow, and the revolution would be on. We were too dispirited and demoralized for that ever to happen.

I found out Mrs. Pitman's address, and wrote to her on school stationary thanking her for her insight and her profound Christian faith. This seemed to be an innocent and gracious act. It was, however, dangerous. She was Morton's prize and his alone. Everyone needed to back off and let him have his way. When I knew how corrupt he was and what his intentions were, I decided to get involved.

I had written a Lenten study for a denominational publisher. My little book was used in Methodist churches all over the country. I decided to dedicate it to Mrs. Pitman and thank her for what she had done for the school. I admit that it was both sincere and political. She was flattered.

She told me, "Nobody ever dedicated a book to me."

I was sure Morton would learn of my contact with Mrs. Pitman. I got word from Van Dale to leave her alone. I maintained contact with her, however, and eventually told her what Morton was doing with her gift. She asked me what I thought she should do about it. I told her I would not be bold enough to try to tell her that.

She appreciated what I said, but finally told me, "President Morton has been very nice to me. He knows the college better than you or I. We must listen to his advice and let him use the money as he sees best." While this conclusion made me ill, I did not loose respect from Mrs. Pitman. Her appreciation for authority, respect for the clergy, and desire to avoid conflict were characteristic of her generation of Southern women.

I was honored when the bishop asked me to use my study as the basis for the Bible Study at Annual Conference. I took the Gospel of Luke as my main focus and divided the study into four sections for the four days of conference. Neither Morton, nor anyone else from the administration, ever congratulated me on this honor. Every year we had a breakfast for clergy alumni of the college during conference. Julie and I were always invited, along with other members of the department, the chaplain, and the director of church relations.

That year we were not invited. Moreover, the breakfast was intentionally scheduled at the same time as the first of my Bible studies. I thought it was a shame that so many of my former students and colleagues in ministry could not be present for my study. I expected the support of the college administration and their use of my study for publicity.

Chapter 38

THE LITTLE EWE LAMB

Every year, Chaplain Steve Brunner would ask me to preach in Chapel. I looked forward to these opportunities to speak to the small group that voluntarily attended the weekly services. This was a far cry from the mandatory services and colloquia when I was in college, where the whole student body and most of the faculty and staff assembled weekly for worship and learning. Nevertheless, we still went through the motions and there were some merits to our efforts.

Two of my sermons in the Worthington Chapel series concerned Morton's leadership and the lack of any kind of moral standard on campus. In the first, I cautiously approached the subject of his affair by referring to the Old Testament prophet Nathan's visit to King David after the Bathsheba affair. (2 Samuel 12:1-12) The prophet came to the king and told him a parabolic story about a rich man and a poor man. The rich man had many flocks, but the poor man had only one little ewe sheep that was his pet: "He brought it up, and it grew up with him and his children: It used to eat of his meager fare, and drink from his cup, and lie in his bosom, and it was like a daughter to him." A traveler came to visit the rich man. He prepared a feast for the visitor. Instead of choosing and preparing one of his own sheep or cows from his large herds, he took the poor man's lamb.

David's righteous anger against someone who would do such a thing burned hot.

In response to Nathan's tale, he blurted out, "As the Lord lives, the man who has done this deserves to die; he shall restore the lamb fourfold, because he did this thing and had no pity."

Nathan replied, pointing a bony index finger in the face of the king, "You are the man!" In the exploding silence following these words, David's sins came back to haunt him.

Nathan then related the sordid story of how the king had taken Bathsheba, the wife of Uriah the Hittite, and made her a part of his expanding harem. After she became pregnant with David's child, he called Uriah home on leave from his military position. His farcical plan of trying to get Uriah to sleep with his wife failed, and with it any possibility of attributing her pregnancy to her husband. Uriah abstained because of the vows he had taken as a warrior in service to the King. Then, as a final resort, David conspired to have Uriah killed on the field of battle. He was the poor man and David was the greedy, rich bully. Nathan pronounced a curse on the house of David and went home.

As I was reading this Scripture from the Chapel pulpit I noticed someone slip into a pew in the rear center of the auditorium. It was the president. He only came to the weekly services occasionally. I was well aware of his presence, but felt empowered rather than intimidated. It was finally time for someone to tell the truth. I found ways to apply the stealing of a ewe lamb to the lives to students. Cheating off the test paper of another person, copying a term paper and turning it in as your own, telling lies about another person (either verbally or in social media), taking someone's boyfriend or girlfriend, these were all stealing a ewe lamb. I invited the small group congregated to find other situations in their lives where this applied. Without compromising the point of the sermon, I was pointing a bony prophetic finger at the face of Morton.

Incredibly and inexplicably, Morton came to the front of the Chapel following the service and complimented my sermon. Why was he there in the first place? He seemed to have a sixth sense. Had he picked up something about my determination no longer to accept the status quo? I finally stood up for what I believed and preached about it—to Morton, no less.

My next idea was to contact my former District Superintendent, Charles Stevens, who was the pastor of First Church. He ascended to this high pulpit following the bizarre attempt by a conservative faction of pastors to topple the former pastor, Thomas Franks. Tom was the leader of the liberal faction, which traditionally meant proponents of integration. He was accused of having an affair with one of his parishioners. The church trial was a kind of kangaroo court conducted with pseudo legal measures, but without anyone who testified being sworn. The charges were extended to relationships with a total of seven women. None of the charges were proven, but Franks was suspended and removed as pastor of First Church for "undermining the ministry" of his associate minister, who was his primary accuser. Ironically, his associate freely admitted that he had an affair with the woman in question.

There was a traditional relationship between First Church and the college, so the trial had a direct effect on us, and on Methodism throughout the region. The newspapers were filled with stories about the trial. Tom Franks was a good friend, and I had taught his two children. His son, Wayne, was still a student and a member of the fraternity I served as sponsor. I tried to mentor him through this difficult time.

Stevens was one of the few church leaders who did not take sides in the debate over the alleged guilt or innocence of Franks and how the trial should be conducted. He was also seen as having benefited more than anyone else by the results of the trial. He replaced Franks as pastor of First Church and as the best prospect from the Conference for the episcopacy. Neither he nor Tom ever came close to becoming bishop, however.

Tom Franks was known for his intellect and his preaching. He was easily the best preacher in the Conference. He was friendly, approachable, and proud of his country origins. Charles was the opposite. He did not seem to have the greatest intellect in the world, nor was he the best speaker. He was a tall, thin, rather Lincolnesque figure. He had played basketball in college, and then graduated from a Baptist seminary. Tom was short of statue and leaned toward you and spoke right in your face. (This could have given the impression that he was too friendly with women.) Charles was reserved and seemed to lean away from you. His face was inscrutable. He had the appearance of a tall, thin water foul with a short beak and songless croak. One wondered what was going on behind those unfocused eyes.

I called Charles one night. We exchanged pleasantries and talked about our respective lives. I expressed appreciation to him for something that happened years before in one of my little country churches. As District Superintendent, he came annually to meet with the church officials and me at our Charge Conference. I also had him come periodically to preach at our annual homecomings and revivals.

One night, when our daughter was three years old, our family rode with Charles to one of these services. After we returned home, we discovered that our daughter's principal love object, a pink stuffed animal, did not make it home with us. I contacted Charles. He found Bear, in the back seat of his car. Without my requesting it, he drove over that night with her beloved toy. Catherine's fitful crying ceased, and she went peacefully to sleep. She held Bear tightly pressed against her chest with one hand, and sucked the thumb of her other hand.

In our conversation, I told Charles that, although she had grown up and was a high school student, Catherine still had Bear (with numerous repairs and replacements of body parts). We were still grateful to him for his gracious action in returning him that night.

He laughed and I changed the subject. I told him that we at the college were disturbed at the rumors we were hearing about Morton and his secretary. He responded that both the Morton and the Reich families were members of his church. He said there had been a lot of talk in the church, and the divorce of Tom and Audrey Reich had been connected to her relationship with Morton. I told him I had taught both Audrey and her daughter, and I was concerned about them. I said that both colleagues and students were asking me questions I could not answer.

Charles said he could not get involved because of the tensions between the families and his relationship to the college. He then asked if I would be willing to talk with Tom Reich. I thought at the time that this was an irregular and improper request. I should never have gotten involved in this toxic situation. After six years of working with Charles as my superintendent, I considered him to be my friend, however, and told him I would consider his request. He gave me Tom Reich's telephone number and told me Tom was distraught over the divorce. Although my motivations were not completely pure, I had never refused a request to counsel someone who needed me.

I called Tom and told him who I was. He said he appreciated my call and we talked for about an hour. This was followed by two other long calls. Prior to Morton's attack on me, I never met Tom face to face or shared any information with him outside of these three telephone conversations. I did not mention my relationship with Tom to anyone.

I learned a lot from our conversations. Tom and I became good friends and, eventually, comrades in arms in the struggle against Morton and his cronies. Tom told me his wife had taken the job as Morton's secretary because she wanted to finish her college degree. The job did not pay well, but it offered free tuition at the college. As a middle-aged woman, this worked well with her plans, and was seen by the family as a temporary position until she graduated. As a college employee, she also received reduced tuition costs for her daughter.

Tom told me Audrey was repulsed by Morton and found his treatment of college personnel to be disgusting. She worked for him for five years before he began to put pressure on her to sleep with him. When he became Rotary District Governor, he was required to visit every club and speak at one of their meetings. He received a stipend for his travel costs and an additional amount of $2,000 for secretarial work. He asked Audrey to go on speaking tours with him.

She refused him, saying that was not a part of her responsibilities to the college. He tempted her with the money, however, and she finally agreed. At first she insisted they sleep in separate rooms, but her resistance was soon overcome.

Audrey had discussed the Rotary trips with Tom before she accepted Morton's invitation. He was firmly against it. She told him they needed the money and she had no desire for this to be anything more that a job. The trips became more frequent and lasted longer. Tom noticed she had changed and seemed nervous and distant. He finally confronted her. She admitted she was having an affair with Morton, and Tom divorced her. Before this happened, however, she had told Tom what she had learned about Morton and the way he conducted the business of the college. Tom shared with me some of the things she had told him over the five years she had worked at the college. He answered my many questions and gave me information about Morton that filled in many of the blanks in my attempt to understand what was happening at the college.

Tom retired from his position as a vice president of a Savings and Loan the year before the divorce. This was just before the bank for which he worked became insolvent in the S&L crisis. He knew enough to get out before the bank failed. He thought his early departure would enable him to preserve his pension. Unfortunately, he was only able to save part of it. Before coming to his position in the bank, he had been a federal bank inspector. As such, he acted as a law enforcement officer and carried a weapon.

He expressed to me how much he hated Morton. Before the divorce, he hired a private investigator and paid him to get information and photographs. This proved to be indecisive. The PI offered numerous excuses, but Tom suspected he had sold out to the other side. This caused him to suspect that Morton knew he was on to him. After his divorce, he obtained a license, bought a gun, and began to practice at a local range. Then he began to stalk Morton, looking for an opportunity to kill him.

In our third conversation, I urged Tom not to throw away his life for the sake of killing someone as worthless as Morton. I told him we needed to end Morton's reign at Worthington. There was a way to stop him that was honorable, ethical, and for the good of all. I also tried to appeal to Tom's Christian conscience. We talked a lot about his grounding in the faith. We discussed his family and his childhood. This conversation was as healthy as others had been morbid and self-destructive. I urged him to listen to his pastor and to Bishop Peter Samuels, who was retired and in residence at the church.

I asked him to stop stalking Morton and obsessing over his wife's infidelity. Get away and get some fresh air. Read the Bible. Fight evil with good. To my amazement and profound joy, he listened to me and to others who were advising him. He became a homebody, abandoning his nefarious activities planning the demise of his rival.

Six months after I talked with him, he had a circulatory blockage that required heart surgery. While he was in the hospital, I visited him. He had grown up in a fundamentalist church and had returned to his childhood faith. He spent hours recuperating at home watching televangelists, reading his Bible and religious books. I tried to raise his theological understanding. His evangelical enthusiasm became rather frightening, but I decided, since he was in such a better place than he had been previously, that I should leave him alone.

Chapter 39

THE MYSTICAL STAIRCASE

The next episode was, if anything, bizarre. I had heard that Morton's attacks could be weird and contrived: Accusing Irene Sanders of mistreating other members of her department; Selling off Andrew McNeill's wilderness teaching lab, even though the document deeding it to the college strictly forbad it; Deciding the college could not pay taxes and retirement insurance for one year and then blaming the business manager at the time.

I wanted to build our department and to be in direct contact with the churches of the conference. I had met with the bishop and cabinet. We developed and sent out teams of students to lead events in churches. I preached in a number of pulpits, as many as I could, since I was pastor of a small charge in the country. I was also scheduled to be nominated to the Board of Ordained Ministry of the conference. I was asked by the bishop to lead the Bible Study at Annual Conference. I felt everything was going well. Like Icarus, I should have been aware that my wings were beginning to drip wax in the hot summer sun.

Another project was the printing of a brochure to be sent to all the churches, which stated the purpose of the department and introduced our faculty members. I was convinced that most churches, particularly those located over one hundred miles from the campus and those in the back woods, knew little about the college and the department. If they had heard about us, it was probably propaganda from the fundamentalists. About the only time they heard from us was when we were trying to raise money.

My idea was to ask, "How can we serve you?" and not, "What have you done for us lately?"

Each department received some funding for advancing and developing its program. It was part of the department chairperson's duty to find uses for the funding and initiate projects. I applied to the dean and the president to use the money allocated to our department to print brochures to be sent to the churches. They said that sounded good. They told me to talk with a person who worked with the admissions office on college publications and brochures. She was young and enthusiastic. She said the college worked with a local printer and set up an appointment for me to meet with a representative. I felt they were taking my recommendation seriously and we began working together. The cost for printing 10,000 of the brochure was nearly $2,000. This was more than we had in our budget for that year, so I waited for the next year and used the appropriation for two years to pay for the brochures. I confirmed with the dean that we could do this.

I had seen other work from this firm that they had done for the college and for other customers. Their photography was extraordinary. They approached their work artistically, not like usual commercial advertising. When I saw the proofs for the department's brochure, initially I was disappointed. On the cover was a photograph of the stairway going up from the first floor to the second floor of Stephens Hall. I taught Bible in a large classroom on the second floor for my total tenure at Worthington. I knew this image well. I asked the representative of the publisher about what I considered a curious choice for the cover.

She told me this shot had been chosen from a number of photographs. She said what she liked about it was an almost mystical quality. The steps ascended, which was inspiring. There was bright sunlight coming through the windows on the landing between the floors. The photographer had used a filter that muted the sunlight and gave it a soft blurred quality. It was a familiar place, but transformed by a different perspective. She felt it had a religious quality, which was subtle, and even subjective, but real. She thought of it as the entrance to the spiritual world of Worthington.

Gertrude was the black housekeeper for the Stephens Building. She was a kind of Aunt Jemima figure, always dressed in a white uniform, and mostly drifting about the building attempting to justify her existence by puttering with cleaning and dusting. My friend, John Donner, was the first black staff member, who ran the print room. He told me Gertrude was there for a purpose. He warned me to look out for her and to be careful around her. She belonged to Morton and acted as his spy for anything going on in the building.

He also told me there was a locked room in the basement. One day, on his way to the print room, which was also in the basement, he saw the door was open to the room. He looked briefly inside and saw a rather elaborate suite. Gertrude was coming out of the room after having cleaned it. He asked her what in the world that room was used for, and she told him it was where Morton took his girlfriends.

On a Monday morning in April, I mounted the stairs between the first and second floors of Stephens. This was the area in the picture on the cover of our departmental brochure. Gertrude was on the landing between the two floors, looking out the window toward the small building next door where admissions had their offices. After I had taught my 8 a.m. and 9 a.m. classes, I came back down the stairs and Gertrude was there again. I was still several stairs above the landing when she turned excitedly and rushed down the stairs. She walked quickly down the hallway toward the president's office. Morton came out of his office and stopped me. He announced that my brochures had arrived. I thanked him and told him I would go over to see them before my next class. He said to wait for him there, that he would be over in a few minutes. His manner was serious, if not angry.

When I went into the front door of the Admissions Building, a young man I had taught some years before, Byron Simmons, met me. He had worked in admissions since graduation. He functioned as the head of admissions without the title. In one of his more curious appointments, Morton had made Tommy Parnell Dean of Admissions, in addition to his positions as Athletic Director and Golf Coach. This, of course, was an impossible and unthinkable consolidation of power, designed to recruit more athletes. Parnell's judgment about desirable students for Worthington was a joke, especially with his reputation.

I went over to the Admissions Office and asked Byron to show me the brochures. I saw the panel truck parked out front, and walked past the delivery men who were bringing in heavy boxes. Byron opened one of the boxes, and I took a handful of brochures out and began looking at them. I told Byron to have the boxes moved to my office. He asked me to wait for Morton.

When he got there, Morton asked me, "What are these boxes?" As if he did not know.

I told him, "Dr. Morton, I am very excited about how well the brochures we have been working on for the department have turned out." He asked to see one.

He said, "Who gave you permission to have them printed?" That also was a strange question, because I had gone through all the channels to authorize the project, including discussing it with him and the dean. He took one of the brochures from the box, and turned it to the information about the faculty.

I considered this a rhetorical question, so I did not answer. He went on to his next question. "Is that your wife's picture in there?"

I found the question insulting, but managed to answer, "Yes, it is. She has taught Christian Education part-time almost since we arrived here eighteen years ago. She has done an excellent job and is very popular in the college and in the conference." He did not reply. Now I knew some of the cards he would play.

I told him I was going to move the brochures to my office so we could distribute them to the churches.

He said, "Hold up on that!" Then he instructed Byron to secure the boxes. The only copies of the brochure I ever saw were those I had taken out of the box. I shared them with department members and kept only two. They were beautiful, and exactly what I had hoped they would be. This was our opportunity to build the department and develop our service to the church. That would be great for us and for the college. I could not figure out why Morton had reacted so strongly to a departmental brochure. Then I realized he had played me. He always found what was most special to someone he attacked and then took it away. Mine was the department. Morton destroyed $2,000 worth of brochures to get at me. I now knew the stairway did not lead upward for me, but downward into the battle with Morton.

Chapter 40

SANDRA HIXON

Gladys Hixon was an elderly member of the small church I pastored in Athens. She was a grandmother in her eighties, almost blind, and hard of hearing. She was a lovely person, always concerned about others in spite of her own limitations. She had a wonderful smile, and a modest and self-effacing manner. Her two daughters were well known in the community. One of them, Sarah, was a schoolteacher at the private school. She was out-going, intelligent, and a good teacher. I knew her and her family, but they did not live in the community. Sarah had joined her husband's church. Her sister, Betty, was a widow with two grown daughters. She was as reserved as her sister was extroverted. I did not know her well, but I came to know both of her daughters well.

One of the daughters, Sandra, was a student at a branch of the state university in Corinth, forty miles south of Harrison. She had worked at a number of jobs before going back to school. She was older than most of the students. I had met her and gotten to know her through the family. One evening, she called me at our residence in Harrison. She asked if she could meet with me at the church in Athens the next morning, which was a Saturday. When she arrived, she had a bandage on her left arm. She told me she was recovering from a recent injury. She had suffered a deep cut when she walked through a plate glass door at the Episcopal student center just off the university campus.

She was brought up Methodist, but when she went off to college, she had been impressed with an Episcopal chaplain. He spent a lot of time with her, counseling her and recommending professional treatment for her emotional and mental problems. She was on medication, which had enabled her to remain stable and able to concentrate on her schoolwork. After being in counseling for a year, she got involved with a charismatic group in the village. The pastor told her faith was sufficient to cure her and, so she no longer needed the medication.

Without her meds, she became confused and anxious. She wanted to find the chaplain who had meant so much to her, so she walked to the Episcopal Center late one night. She was able to get into the building, but found no one present. She panicked and wanted to leave the dark building. She ran to the rear entrance and crashed through a plate glass door leading to a patio. She was cut by the broken glass. She lay in the doorway for some time and then managed to stand up. She wandered into the village. She lost a lot of blood. A policeman driving his route that night saw her staggering down the sidewalk. He stopped and carried her to his vehicle. He then rushed her to the emergency room at a local hospital. The chaplain and her counselor spoke in her defense when she had to answer the charges of breaking and entering at the center. She was put on probation and required to receive therapy for her illness.

She asked me if I thought she were crazy. I told her emphatically, "No! You are a very talented person who has some mental problems. You need treatment and time to recover." She planned to check into the psych ward of a local hospital in Harrison for treatment the next day. She asked me if I would come to visit her and I told her, "Of course."

Jefferson Hospital was the oldest medical facility in the city. Lining the walls of the main entrance were pictures of old Dr. Jefferson in his buggy and later in his Model T. He had built the hospital around him over the years, beginning in a Victorian three-story house. The modern hospital had replaced the old buildings one by one until it became a major medical facility. Of the three large hospitals in Harrison, it probably was my least favorite, especially its psychiatric ward. There was a lock-up with visitation reserved to specific persons and limited times. I had met the doctor who was in charge of the ward and found his ideas to be old-fashioned and oppressive. He was known to favor heavy doses of medication and isolation for patients. When I had visited persons in the ward previously, it felt like I was going into the prison where Julie worked.

Among her many talents, Sandra was an excellent artist. From time to time, we hung her paintings in the church foyer in Athens. Once she became a patient in the hospital, she made plans to get the other patients in the ward involved in art therapy. To say I was skeptical would be an understatement. I felt her manic side was showing. I tried to calm her down. I told her she had a noble idea, but she needed to concentrate on getting well. She told me she felt this was her mission. The other patients needed something creative to work on while hospitalized; this would help their healing and hers as well. She regretted that all these people were isolated in their rooms except during group therapy and meals. She had seen the effects of some of the medications used in the ward and did not want everyone to be doped up and vegetating alone.

I watched a miracle in the ward over the six weeks Sandra was there. After only a week, drawings began to appear on the walls of the hallway. Soon they spread all the way to the common room. The drab walls of the ward were soon brightened by colors and creative images. The artwork was surprisingly good. Sandra was insistent (even obsessive), but also persuasive. She made a difference in the lives of the patients, and also in the lives of the hospital staff. When it was time for her to leave the hospital, the staff and the patients regretted her departure. She was incredibly proud of how far her fellow patients had come in their artistic self-expressions.

After that, I only occasionally heard from Sandra over the next several years. She was working at a well-known restaurant in the country near the Athens community. They specialized in real Southern country cooking. I had not realized she was as good at cooking and restaurant management as she was in her artwork. Indeed, she cooked like an artist and painted like a good cook. Whenever we ate at the restaurant, I knew I was feasting on the best of regional food. It was also always a pleasure to see Sandra's smiling face.

A year later, I was surprised when one of the cafeteria staff at Worthington hailed me. She was dressed in white like the rest of the staff, so I had not really noticed her. When I looked in her eyes, I knew it was Sandra. She hugged my neck and greeted me warmly. We talked for several minutes. She gave me credit for her healing. I tried to pitch that back to say she had shown great strength and creativity and the credit was hers. She had also been instrumental in helping others come back to themselves through her art therapy. I looked forward to seeing her in the cafeteria every time I ate there. She quickly moved out of the kitchen into serving and was managing the cooking staff in record time. I realized I had consistently underestimated her ability and her persistence.

She got involved in campus activities. She and a new professor in the Art Department became friends. Ellen Maclean was a middle-aged woman who grew up in Scotland. She was a delightful person. I could listen to her accent all day. She was creative, but also wise and motivated by ethical issues. The few discussions I had with her were about a society based on racism and discrimination.

Sandra and Ellen shared their interest in art and art therapy and their strong Christian faith. They started a small prayer group. There were others who had met with them, but, sadly, not many of our faculty and staff were people who seemed to be interested in prayer. Sandra asked me if I would join them. I was preoccupied with my situation at the college, so I was not a faithful member of the group. It was, however, deeply meaningful to me. I was able to share my concerns in confidence and know there were people praying for me.

We were careful not to become a gossip session called a prayer group. We did talk about our personal needs and concerns. When

Sandra asked me if I knew about Morton's affair, I told her I had not discussed the matter with anyone who was not involved. She told me she had heard about it and that Morton was after me because I knew about it. I did not deny the veracity of what she said, but made it clear I could not be seen as a source of information. That would play into Morton's conspiracy against me.

She and Ellen offered prayers for me, for the campus, and for the Morton family. Sandra said she would not stand by and watch Morton destroy me. I told her I deeply appreciated her concern. I asked her not to do anything for me, however. She did not owe me anything. I also cautioned her against mentioning my name or doing or saying anything that could be traced back to me.

In my wildest dreams, I could not foresee what would take place during the following week. Morton did not eat in the cafeteria often, and almost never with the students. If he were in the cafeteria at all it was in the Private Dining Room. This was an elegant area that was restricted to special meetings of faculty or staff or outside groups of people Morton was trying to impress. The menu for these meetings was quite different from the usual fare in the cafeteria. It was served by wait staff in uniform and on their best manners.

On this occasion, for some reason, Morton was casually sitting at a table with students and engaging in conversation. It was something many of us faculty members did on an almost weekly basis, but he was almost never seen slumming with the students. Sandra saw him sitting there and went up and greeted him. He turned on his charm and asked her how her work was going. This was to show the students he cared about employees. Sandra was charming back and smiled as she asked Morton about his wife and family. He gave some vague answer, while his face tightened, indicating that he was thinking, "That's none of your business." Sandra knew where she was going and cut to the chase.

"Does your wife know about your affair with your secretary?" Students present could not wait to tell me about the encounter. Morton was gobsmacked! The blood drained from his face, they said, and the pseudo smile melted from his countenance.

He stammered, "I don't know what you're talking about." He excused himself and slipped out of the cafeteria.

Sandra lost her position in the cafeteria within two days of the event. She expected and even anticipated the result of her actions. She lived quite modestly and needed her paycheck. She did not want to work for such an immoral figure, however. She felt he was openly risking, not only his family's security, but also the reputation of the college. Many who knew her thought she must be crazy. She acted impulsively, it was true, but also upon the courage of her convictions. Finally, although I had asked her not to, she did it for me. I only hoped I could be half as courageous as she when my time came.

Betty Hixon's second daughter, and Sandra's younger sister, was Noel. She was married to a young man from the community and had two small children. They were an attractive and loving family. Noel's husband, Robert, was raised in the Church of Christ. Noel switched her church affiliation to bring her family together in one church. She had expressed to me her appreciation for what I had done for Sandra. I told her Sandra was a brave person and had a remarkable recovery from her mental instability.

We also spoke about the scene in the cafeteria. Noel was not as shocked as I expected her to be. Robert worked for the college. It was through him that Sandra got her job in food services. It was also through him that she knew about the affair. Robert had begun doing contract work for Worthington. When the long-time head of Buildings and Grounds retired, Robert was offered the job. It was several years before I realized this aggressive young man was charged with the upkeep of our creaking old buildings, including Freeman Hall, where my office was located. I had moved my office after Phil retired. I was down the hall in what had originally been a dormitory room. Most of these rooms were now empty. By moving down the hall, I had more space and more privacy.

I visited Noel and Robert's home in Athens to see her grandmother Gladys, who was living with them. I mentioned to Robert that, when it rained, water leaked into my office. I had several containers to catch it, including one on the desk I had bought from Harold Manowski when Morton forced him out of his position as chair of the Business Department. He told me he was aware of my situation. The report I had sent in had reached him. He said there were three rooms in a girls' dorm that had leaking problems worse than mine. He said he would get to us as quickly as he could, but right now he had another priority. I asked him what that might be. I had no idea what I was bringing up. He looked at me seriously, and told me he had to ask me not to speak to anyone about what he was going to tell me.

He continued, "I am not like Sandra. I have a family and I need my job." I responded that I understood him, and that, as a minister, I knew what confidentiality meant. He then related to me one of the strangest and most bizarre aspects of the Morton story.

Dean Edgar Stone and his wife, Dr. Patricia Stone, were important members of the faculty for more than four decades. He was the Academic Dean and she was the chair of the Religion Department. After Dean Stone passed away, Dr. Stone continued to chair the department and teach for a number of years before she retired. Phillip Maddox replaced her as chair. The Stones lived in a modest home on a small street that paralleled Fairfield, the main street in front of the college. This meant that it was hidden on a cul-de-sac, but still within easy walking distance of the administration building.

Following her death, Dr. Stone's will specified that the house and lot be donated to the college. Knowing the Stones, this was not surprising. They had no children or close relatives and were deeply devoted to the college. I remembered meeting Dr. Stone when we first moved to Harrison, and I knew when she passed away.

Robert told me his crew was occupied putting a new roof on the Stone house (instead of repairing roofs on campus buildings). They were also remodeling the old house and moving in new furniture. One room was prepared especially for Morton and his girlfriend. It was a love nest, with fancy bedroom furniture. Expensive sound equipment, television sets, and other entertainment features had been bought for the house and were being installed.

Robert expressed his disgust at the trash his crew had to clean up, including beer and liquor bottles, cigarette butts, syringes, and condoms. The smell of marijuana drifted throughout the house. He made no accusations, but said I could draw my own conclusions. I asked him how much the college was spending on Morton's love shack. He said he carefully kept copies of all the receipts, in case he ever needed them to protect himself against the college. He had not tried to total them up; his best guess was a figure in excess of $100,000. He was not finished and not ready yet to attempt a definite tally.

Chapter 41

THE CONTRACT

Our contracts for the new school year starting in the fall were late that year, but the timing was usually erratic. It often depended on what game Morton was playing. They came from the dean's office, but they were signed by Morton.

I went by the campus post office in the Student Center mid-morning before my Contemporary Issues class and found a letter from the college. I put the envelope in my pocket and opened it in my office after class. It was the standard contract. I looked at the salary and it was about right, with the slight increase we expected. Then I did a second take and found that something was missing. I was continued as a full professor, but nowhere did it say I was chairman of the Department of Religion and Philosophy.

I went to Van Dale's office and asked his secretary if I could see him. He ushered me into his office. I took out my contract and said there was a mistake: Nowhere did it mention that I was chairman of the department.

He said, "Yes, I know." There was an earnest, even desperate look on his face. His voice was gentle and imploring. I had never seen him like this. He begged me not to make a big thing of this. "Just sign it," he said. "You can teach and have time to write and advance yourself professionally."

I looked at him in disbelief.

"Are you kidding me? Why do you let that man push you around? You know better than this. No, I will not accept this contract."

He looked at me with hopeless, dead eyes and did not say a word. I stormed out of his office. It was clear now how Morton would play the game—from the bottom of the deck. This may have been one of the worst decisions of his life. I would not roll over and play dead, as many of my colleagues had done. I could never anticipate Morton's moves. He was too clever for that. I did know how to react, however. It was like a card game in which Morton was the dealer and controlled the deck.

It was time to lawyer-up. I knew to visit Richard McArthur, Esquire, who was a Princeton graduate. He was one of the most liberal lawyers in the state and a previous candidate for state Attorney General. I considered him my friend. He had invited Julie and me to his home a number of times. He was the son of an Episcopal priest and had been an active layperson in the church where Julie had worked for eight years as Director of Christian Education when we first came to Harrison.

The traditional worship at Church of the Resurrection was far too tame for Richard and his wife. They preferred to consider themselves charismatic Episcopals. I had previously thought that was a contradiction in terms, but he showed me it was not. He invited me to come to a worship service held by a charismatic group. He moved his membership and served on the board of this new congregation. It was not necessarily my cup of tea, but I attended out of respect for Richard.

When one had to fight Morton, McArthur was the first choice of most faculty or staff members at Worthington. He knew the situation as well as anyone. He had the reputation of being a fighter for the rights of others. It was apparent he did not win many of these cases, however. He was good at negotiating settlements, which was exactly what I did not want. For many reasons, personal and professional, however, he was my lawyer.

The college's lawyer was Jeffrey Steinhauser, a young Jewish professional who was well known in the community. I had met him through Richard. They were good friends, and often faced each other over Worthington controversies. In his autobiographical book, Richard styled himself "the people's lawyer." To his credit, he handled many civil rights cases and cases for the poor of the state. He had a passion for justice and partiality for the poor. He also knew the limitations he faced in dealing with Morton and a church-related college.

Morton knew the game he was playing well. He usually trapped his victim in a web of intrigue and worked to oust anyone who disagreed with him. He consulted Steinhauser to deal with the legalities. Suits were filed and settlements worked out. No faculty or staff member had the resources to fight these legal battles for an extended period. We could not find any case in the twenty-five years Morton was at Worthington that was won by the person wronged.

The suits were almost all destined to end with settlements. We even knew the customary amount was $20,000. Both parties were sworn to secrecy, but rumors circulated about the negotiations. These suits were almost an annual event, usually playing out over the summer. The payments to the person forced out were hidden, listed as "operating expenses" and never questioned. It was hard to imagine what this did to the finances of the institution, since these payouts were a terrible drain on the budget. This amount did not cover the personal and professional damage Morton had done to the faculty or staff member.

We had two weeks to return the contracts. I told Richard I did not and could not accept the demotion. It was hard to imagine Mark Jennings as chair of the department and my superior. I also knew I would never have any peace with the administration, no matter what I did. Morton intended to get rid of me. Van Dale gave me no support, although he recognized that the demotion was not deserved. He would not help me with a decision and simply wanted me to go away. This was the dean with whom I had worked for eighteen years. He knew of my accomplishments and of the good work of the department under Phillip's leadership and mine.

I talked with Julie and our children, and I discussed the situation with Phil Maddox. My family did not and could not understand all that was going on. I knew that whatever happened, it would have a profound effect on our lives. Phil was a great friend. He was receptive to my plight. He shared my pain. He was also primarily a diplomat and a reconciler. He could not imagine himself in my situation, nor could he fully comprehend the depth of depravity at Worthington—although he had been there a lot longer than I. He was a dear friend, but I understood that he was not a fighter. He simply told me he would pray for me.

I went to see Bishop Peter Samuels. He was retired and in residence at First Church. According to Charles Stevens, he had joined him in counseling the Tom and Audrey Reich. He had served churches in the conference for a number of years before he was elected to the episcopacy. He had two terms as bishop in other conferences and then he retired. He also was a friend of Julie's father. They had served in neighboring parishes when they first began their ministries in the Tennessee Conference. He and his wife had been supportive of our work at Worthington.

I spoke to him in his office at First Church for about thirty minutes. He seemed to be well aware of the situation. Charles Stevens had told me that the two of them had counseled Tom and Audrey Reich about the affair. He made no comment about that, however. I assumed he knew who Morton really was. His moral and ethical failings were no secret in the conference. The conservative pastors objected to Morton because he was "too liberal." The liberals tried to take up for him, but felt rebuffed by him any time they tried to have any involvement with the college.

I would have appreciated more from the bishop. He was cordial, but noncommittal. I could see why he had been a bishop for two terms. He was a diplomat and did not take sides. He advised me concerning the contract not to sign anything. I did not tell him, but I had already signed and returned my contract, adding the sentence: "I do not accept my removal as chairman of the Department of Religion and Philosophy."

Richard McArthur told me my words compromised the contract and Morton could sue me for breaking the contract. In some ways, I regretted not having spoken to the bishop before I signed the document. I had made my decision, however, and our meeting would not have changed my mind.

I was tired of playing defense with Morton, always reacting to his latest outrage. After I returned the contract to the dean's office, I determined not to wait for Morton to sue me. I was convinced the most effective strategy for dealing with him was to respond aggressively. He was not used to that and was much better at playing offense than defense. In my eighteen years at Worthington, I do not remember anyone who successfuilly fought back. It was my intention to keep him off balance and, therefore, vulnerable.

I spoke with Reich again for the first time in several months. I told him briefly what was going on. We agreed that we needed to work on strategy. He invited me to come over to his apartment. There had been a time when I would have been afraid to be seen with him. Now, I figured the dye was cast and it did not make a great deal of difference. We made a fundamental decision not to deal with the issue of the affair, at least not initially. That issue was fraught with danger. Morton would expect us to attack him on it. We would have to get pictures or film and other documentation of him and his mistress together. Tom Reich had already tried that and failed. I considered that to be dirty pool, and I did not want to play that game. We decided we would go after the misuse of the Jenkins-Pitman money.

We discussed delivering a copy of Reich's affidavit and a copy of one I would write to the bishop. These were the only documents we ever wrote mentioning the affair. We also discussed writing letters to the faculty, the trustees of the college, and the clergy members of the annual conference. I said that from my experience in mailing newsletters from the churches that this was labor-intensive and expensive. Reich said he would work on the letters and pay for mailing them. I asked him how much he was willing to pay for this endeavor and he said $10,000. I was amazed. I also knew that when Reich looked into your eyes and committed himself to something, he meant it, especially when it involved money.

I also discussed our ideas with Adam. He told me he had friends on the faculty at the state university where he used to work. He asked that we give him copies of anything we wanted to mail along with names and addresses. I said I had something in mind for the response to Morton's attack on me. If Morton played his next card, and sued for my contract, we would start writing letters. We all agreed on the plan.

Chapter 42

INTO THE LION'S DEN

I received a call at my office from Van Dale's secretary, Barbara. She asked that I stop by the office and make an appointment to meet with the dean and the president. After my mid-morning class, I went by and asked her what this was about.

She simply said softly, "You know." She was a good person and had been there for a number of years. I was still amazed that the office staff seemed to know a lot about the controversy and looked up to me as a kind of hero.

Barbara Myers was a middle-aged woman who had raised a family from her first marriage. Now she was enjoying some freedom and security from a second marriage that enabled her to go back and finish her college degree. It was interesting to compare the women whom Morton hired to work in his office and those chosen by Van Dale. I had Barbara in several classes in the evening division. I made it a policy never to ask Barbara or any of the others what they thought of the situation at Worthington. It would not have been fair. When Morton began to attack me, however, I spoke more plainly with them.

I asked Barbara how much Van Dale knew about the affair. She replied that the only thing she had ever heard him say about it was to deny any knowledge of it. She said this had all changed a few days before our conversation when Van Dale returned from Morton's office down the hall, wide-eyed and pale. He said he had gone over to see Morton. Usually, he told Audrey he was there and she would call Morton on the intercom. This time, however, her chair was empty. So, Van Dale, in one motion, knocked on the door with one hand and opened it with the other. He discovered Morton sitting behind his huge desk with Audrey on his lap and the two of them engaged in a passionate kiss. He closed the door as quickly as possibly and returned to his office. He was not sure whether they had known he was there.

He told Barbara what had happened and commented, "I thought it was over! The trustees warned him to replace Audrey and then stay away from her. It has to stop." She said he was deeply concerned about what would happen if the trustees found out.

I asked Barbara about the meeting we were supposed to have. She said Morton was impatient to get it over with. I told her to help me stall. I was not going to do anything without consulting my lawyer. She said she would do her best. She added, "I don't know how much more the dean can take."

When I told Adam about this, he laughed at the special Worthington double-talk involved here, especially significant in the mouth of Van Dale: "An affair, which did not exist, was supposed to be over, but obviously was not."

I went back to my office and called Richard McArthur. He said he would talk with Jeff Steinhauser and get back to me. When he called back, he said Jeff had told him that Morton was trying to build a case against me, including the charge that I had not fulfilled the role of department chair as outlined in the Faculty Manual. I got out my copy of it and read through the various articles. There was nothing there I could reasonably think I was not doing and doing well. On the contrary, this was the best year we had had in the department in a number of years.

I insisted McArthur and Julie accompany me to the meeting. Richard agreed, but then called me back. Steinhauser told him that if my lawyer were there, then Morton insisted his counsel would have to be there too. This would get everybody lawyered up and not allow much possibility for communication between Morton and me. Richard suggested it be the four of us: Morton and Van Dale, Julie and me. I did not like anything about this, but I did not have a better idea.

Richard then brought up something I had already been told. He urged me to be careful of what I said. Morton taped every conversation that went on in his office. He said to give simple answers. Do not let Morton back me into a corner or get me irritated. Be aggressive without being disrespectful. Stand up for my side. Do not mention the affair.

As Julie and I walked through the main entrance to Stephens Hall, we waved at Mrs. Smith at the switchboard. She was a dear lady who had worked there since before we arrived.

She obviously knew what was up because she motioned me over and whispered, "Is your lawyer coming?" I told her no, that Morton would not allow it. Her face reflected her disappointment. Then her saintly smile broke out and she wished us well. She said the secretarial staff was supporting me, and added, "I am praying for you." These were the last words I would ever hear from her.

It was not until the next morning, after she did not come in to take over the switchboard, that word began to spread. Mrs. Smith had passed away that night with an aneurysm. The irony was that she had taken care of her invalid husband for years. He had Lou Gehrig's disease and no one ever thought he would outlive her.

I was nervous and up-tight. This was not my cup of tea. Julie was cool, calm, and collected. Her natural smoothing, reconciling, bridging abilities checked in at crucial points.

When we entered the room, Van Dale was seated and looked guilty and withdrawn. Apparently he was supposed to welcome us and begin the conversation—instead he just sat there. During the entire meeting, he never spoke more than one sentence at a time. Mostly he denied knowing or having information about any aspect of our discussion. He could have been of great help to us, but he chose to sit back and let Morton bully us.

There was an awkward silence as we came in and sat down. Morton did not look up or acknowledge our presence. He sat behind his desk, fumbling with his lapel mike, trying to get it to work. He took out his recording device and reconnected it. It still did not work. Then he took out another one and set it up, leaving both of them plugged in. He commented that one of them had to work. This was already more than comical, so I took out my brand new Radio Shack mini recorder and placed it on the desk pointed at Morton.

His launch words were, "Let's talk about the—"

I interrupted and asked that we begin with prayer. This was said out of real conviction. It was also a delaying tactic to keep Morton waiting another several minutes. I prayed the following words:

> Gracious God and Father, we thank you for the significance
> of this day for what it means to us. We thank you for
> Worthington College, for its young people, and for our
> part in their lives. We pray that you guide us to do those
> things which are pleasing in your sight, which help build
> your church, and which contribute to the education and
> the spiritual advancement of our students. In the name of
> our Lord and Savior, Jesus Christ, we pray. Amen.

I looked over at Morton. The expression on his face indicated he already had his verdict: guilty as charged! All that was necessary now was to establish the charges. This kind of meeting was standard in the process of demeaning and tearing down staff and faculty members who opposed him. He worked himself up and attacked with all the bluster he could muster. It was frightening and overwhelming. Others had told me that one must maintain his or her cool and try to contradict Morton as the argument developed. Letting him get away with too much could put one in an impossible position. I knew one did not win against Morton. But I was not willing to back down and let him run over me.

I knew he was determined to tear me down, and probably would succeed, but I firmly believed he could not destroy me without destroying himself. I had no idea how he would attack me. He prided himself on shock and surprise. He would attack, and either incapacitate you emotionally so you could not respond, or make you so angry you would strike out at him and overstep your boundaries, and thus play directly into his hands. He had been quite successful with this strategy over the years.

So, I tried to cut him off by jumping in and pretending this was a meeting to share with the president and the dean the many accomplishments of our department in the past academic year. We had been able to get Mark Jennings to develop his courses and begin teaching without falling apart. I reluctantly decided to use Steve Brunner to teach one section of Bible each semester. As a military chaplain, he did not have the academic background to teach college-level Religion courses. He also was lazy and did not challenge the students. It was worth mentioning him, however, since he was securely in Morton's camp.

Julie continued to do an amazing job with her Christian Education courses. We had a number of Christian Education majors and a number of Religion majors who took her courses in preparation for their ministries in local churches. The SACS evaluation had questioned our ability to offer a Christian Education major without a person with a PhD in the area. Julie had a master's degree and years of experience teaching. There were relatively few people with a doctorate in the area. We were prepared to make the degree a minor in CE if necessary. The Religion major could carry it. These were areas in which I thought he might question us, so I tried to preempt his attack.

I also stressed our accomplishments outside the classroom. We had pioneered Chrysalis and touched the lives of literally hundreds of high school and college students. Our outreach to local churches had increased and gotten us a lot of attention. We were involved in training future leaders, and offering leadership groups to go out to local churches and lead youth events, programs, worship services, and other activities. We had developed brochures to be placed in the local churches advertising who we were and ways in which could serve the local church.

I had also undertaken a study for curriculum revision within the department. The Contemporary Issues course, for example, was developed in an era when there was violence in the streets and attacks on almost every institution in our society. Civil Rights, women's issues, the Vietnam War, liberation theology, etc., were all a part of our reading and discussions. Since that time, emphases had changed and there were new concerns that should be addressed. We had sought new texts, which would help us to relate traditional philosophical issues to contemporary concerns. My efforts were designed to update our curriculum rather than to replace it. I had recently brought the results of my efforts to a faculty meeting and gotten revisions passed by the faculty. Their responses were generally favorable and enthusiastic.

I said we needed help in the department. A few of us were carrying a heavy load. I had taught as many as twenty hours in a semester, counting night school and continuing education courses. I asked Von Dale how much we spent in the department in comparison with other departments.

He responded, "Well, it's the most efficient monetarily in terms of cost per credit hour generated." Rather than congratulating us for reaching the largest number of students and the widest public on the smallest budget, Van Dale made a telling comment. He told me, "You just don't know how to say no. These kids want a seminar, so you offer one." This of course, was not true. I was careful in developing seminars and other courses outside the basic curriculum. I consulted the students and tried to offer courses that would be interesting and useful for them.

We were on a roll, but soon Morton began to turn on us. He centered on the issue of the SACS study. I told him Phillip Maddox had responded to these concerns in the past, and Julie and I had continued to respond. We understood they were questioning our ability to offer the major, and were working on how we could protect our efforts and satisfy them. Morton then replied:

> I think this is the first time we've had an explicit recommendation from the committee saying that you must have a full-time person with a terminal degree if you're going to offer a major in Christian Education. That was a part of the report. Dean Van Dale spoke to you immediately after the team visit and wrote you a memo saying that we could not offer the major in Christian education with—

I interrupted him to say that the dean's memo asked us to deal with the recommendation, but was not as black and white as he portrayed it.

Then Julie spoke clearly and decisively to the unique nature of the Christian Education major and our department's handling of it:

> Dean Van Dale, it might be helpful for you to have the most updated version of the SACS report that I have been asked to respond to. And, you know, I would presume there is some place here for conversation that the Christian Education degree is not—and I address this in the next to the bottom paragraph, criteria four and five of the outline—a degree based on just my teaching or anybody who teaches Christian education. It is a complex degree. How can I instruct students in techniques for teaching the Bible and without saying that Bible is taught by doctoral professors? So I don't know whether SACS understands this degree. They may or may not, but it seems to me that there's some confusion on that.

Morton responded, "I agree. There certainly should be this discussion, but this discussion should have taken place before this brochure was printed because we had the clear information from the visiting team, and this is a little late to start talking about—"

Now I knew where he was going. He was about to say we could not use the brochures because the Christian Education major was mentioned.

The other grievous fault was that the chaplain was not listed in the brochure. In all the time I was at the college, we never considered the chaplain to be part of our department. He was part of the administration.

I said that, but Morton was ready, "He teaches three hours a semester in your department? Then he is a member of the department." My memory was that a person had to teach six hours a semester to be considered a department member.

Then Morton took the argument another step further. "With whom in the department did you talk about the brochure? In your Department of Religion and Philosophy, have you reviewed this with your department members?"

"No," I answered. "I considered it my responsibility to develop the publicity we would use to develop the department. No one else had the experience and expertise to do it."

He pressed his argument. "Do you recognize that's a duty of yours as department head?"

I told him I would be glad to share information with department members and had already done so.

He told me, "It's a little late, having put into print and never having had a conversation with Mark Jennings or the chaplain about a document which is to represent the institution, the department . . ."

I responded that I had worked with the people with whom I had been told to work on designing a brochure for the department.

It was clear he was using Mark Jennings and Steve Brunner against me. He asked me how many times I had met with them in the present semester (since the beginning of the year). I told him none. I had no intention of inviting Brunner into our meetings, nor had he ever expressed any desire to participate in department meetings.

That would be a real Trojan horse. Jennings was spoiling for a fight. He disrespected me and the traditions of the department. He wanted for us to meet so he could begin dismantling the department and gutting the major. He was like a spoiled little boy, wanting his own way about everything. I had no doubt he had gone to Morton. We could have dealt with the duties of a junior member of a department, but there seemed to be little desire to do that.

Morton also held against me that Mark had voted against my recommendations for core requirements in the department when it came up in the faculty meeting. He said he had never seen it or had an opportunity to discuss it with me. In any logical world, his loyalty would have been placed in doubt. It was his responsibility to come to me if he had questions, not to go to the president.

"Look," I said to him, "I am chair of the department. I have been here eighteen years. I am a senior member of the faculty. Both Brunner and Jennings are relatively new here. Neither of them has much experience in teaching or running a department. If they have questions, they should come to me. Is that clear? It is ludicrous to imply that I need their approval in running the department."

Morton changed the subject, and forbad me to distribute the brochures and ordered me to return them to the office to which they were delivered. I told him I never received them. They were still at the office. He had ordered them to remain there. Julie again expressed what the brochures meant and how unique our program was:

> You know, something does need to be done that makes what we are doing here visible to a lot of people. I think our uniqueness in the state and in the region is a factor that could be a very positive recruiting tool. Not only that, but it is our responsibility to the church, what the church has asked us to do. We are unique.
>
> Our uniqueness should be a selling point. The fact that a person can come here, get a degree in Christian Education or Church Music and be certified as an

associate in Christian Education or in Church Music, they only have to take two more courses. That's usually done in one a year. So this saves somebody—I mean, you can't say this, you know, hard and fast—but somewhere around two years of work to be certified as an associate. That's no small thing when you're working to have certification.

There needs to be an effort to try to say that we're doing some things at Worthington that we can be proud of. We are unique. We offer some special things here. Let's get our people in so we can do that job. You know, in terms of the number of people we've reaching, I think there's the potential there, and will continue to be.

We can offer a special emphasis in church vocations. We need to let people know about this. The brochure is one way of doing this. I acknowledged my shortcomings, but appealed to you, President Morton, to let us proceed to build our department. The brochures were simply to inform the church about who we are and what we were trying to do. There are no policy statements. In a few years, we can have a second edition in which we explain more clearly what our efforts in Christian vocations are about and how our offerings in Christian Education are unique.

Morton was untouched and Van Dale looked like he was asleep. I told them I wanted to see a lot more done in terms of church relations and outreach. I told them I found Steve Brunner uninterested in reaching out to the churches. We went on back and forth talking past each other with no real resolution. Morton's machine ran out of tape. He was badgering me over and over about consultation. I finally got tired of ignoring the elephant in the room, so I broached the subject:

Well, let me say this, and I think this needs to be considered, and I have talked with the dean about it, there are matters that some of us are very concerned about on this campus. As a Christian minister, as a member of this conference of the United Methodist Church, I'm seriously concerned about the moral tone of the college.

Morton asked me, "What does that got to do with doing your duty as a departmental—"

I replied, "Everything, simply everything!"

It was clear I had touched a nerve.

Morton continued, "If you have something specific to say, go ahead and say it."

He tried to get me to say something he could use against me, but I told him I had no more to say, "Not at this time."

He persisted. "That does not give you any excuse for failing to consult with the dean and with the president regarding significant events having to do with the department such as core requirements."

I was tired of playing games and being accused of something I had not done. "Okay. But I did consult with the dean about core requirements. I gave you copies. I consulted with the registrar. I consulted with Mark Jennings. I consulted with everybody."

He asked me why I did not come to his office and engage in conversations with him when I had ideas. He accused me of not coming in because I might hear alternative perceptions. That was enough. The faculty knew he was not interested in discussing anything with us.

I thought I should break the news to him. "I guess we generally have come to have an idea that with you, Dr. Morton, conversation doesn't always go anywhere and we don't always feel heard."

To which he replied,

"Well, you know, it would help if you at least started the conversation and if you would engage. If you had some problem, but you've not had a discussion to bring it forward. But if you really are not, you know, satisfied working with the chief executive officer in the institution, one obvious option is to resign as chairman.

"Well, I have—"

"If you cannot work with—"

"—You know, the contract thing is—and I—you know, I'm posing serious questions."

"Yeah. I think it's time we talked about that."

"Okay."

"Let's review what's happened regarding your contract. You were offered a contract on March 30 as—"

"Correct."

"Dean Van Dale and I received a copy of a letter or a memo advising of conditions that you were setting forward for you to consider a contract—"

"Correct."

"—And, in fact, returning the original contract offer."

"Uh-huh."

"The Dean then checked with you on that Friday, and you proposed a meeting the following Friday, and then you called, I believe, the day before and changed it to—"

"That is correct."

"Now, let me ask the question. Is this your position statement now?"

"I'm prepared to amend that." I told Dean Van Dale—he asked me if I were willing to compromise, and I said I certainly would be.

Morton went on and on trying to convince me that all this was my fault because I was not timely in turning in my contract. It was clear any further discussion of these issues was pointless. The die was cast and Morton would never relent. I thought the meeting was to discuss my contract and why I had been removed as the chairman of the Department of Religion and Philosophy. True, we had discussed the trumped up and spurious reasons he was giving, but we had not discussed the contract. Even then, at the end of the meeting, he did not deal directly with the supposed reasons I was removed. Instead, he wanted to talk about why I did not have a contract, since I was late in getting the document back to the dean.

If we had had a meeting a month before contracts came out and he had expressed legitimate concerns about my leadership, then there might have been some merit to his position. Facing Morton was one of the most difficult things I have ever had to do in my life. It was not as bloody as I had thought it might have been, however. I stood up to him. I had also tried to hear his criticism and be conciliatory, without abandoning my position. But there was clearly nothing to be accomplished in talking with him.

My comment about the dismal moral condition of the campus seemed to change things. Morton finally stopped punching at me and became a bit more conciliatory. Van Dale got more involved, probably to keep the subject of Morton's affair from coming up. We reached a point where everyone was a lot more straightforward in our conversation. Morton kept saying I should come to him and discuss my ideas. I said I would be willing to do that.

I did benefit from this opportunity to see his cards, so I could guess how he was going to play them. I understood, for the first time, how morally bankrupt he was and how corrupt and misleading his perverse logic was. I understood I had lost my former position. I could not go back, as much as I would want to. I could stand up and defend myself, however, and represent what a church-related college should and could be. Morton had put me in the position of having nothing to lose. He, on the other hand, was risking his little empire.

Coming out of the meeting, I could identify two different positions. I knew Morton's criticism of me was a charade. He understood from my conversations with Tom Reich that I knew enough to bring him down. He almost dared me to come out with it. In our meeting, when I mentioned the moral climate on campus, he became attentive. It was the one card I did not intend to play. It was worth more unused.

It would have been better for all concerned if we could have reached a compromise and withdrawn to our respective corners after the meeting. I would have liked to renegotiate my contract. I could have pledged to have more departmental meetings, and to have Jennings and Brunner become more a part of the department without sacrificing principle. I would not have agreed to stay in the department with Jennings as chair, however. He was rather sophomoric, a know-it-all, a person who had no understanding of the academy-church relationship in our area.

He intended to do away with the majors we sponsored, and ultimately to do away with the department. When later he had his chance, he did all these things. He saw himself as an academic and wanted as little to do with the church as possible. This position was not unusual in his generation. We only talked briefly about my stand. One day he asked me if I wanted "to commit academic suicide." I told him if it were a matter of doing what was right versus teaching, I would choose the former. He just walked away shaking his head.

It was said that Morton had been a boxer in high school and college. I believe that was true. I certainly took a lot of blows on the chin and to the gut. He only knew how to punch, however. There are times when the most powerful punch is the one not thrown. He was becoming more and more reckless, and more and more careless. He was flailing at me and few of his blows hit the target. Now was the time for the war to begin in earnest.

Chapter 43

THE CHURCH'S ONE FOUNDATION

I sent a letter to the bishop about Morton and what I had learned. I was careful about what I said. I did use the word "affair," however. I indicated that he and his secretary were involved in violations of his ordination vows and in a way that threatened the school and all it represented. This was the only time I ever used that word in anything I wrote. It was also one of the few times I ever discussed it in any form with anyone not involved in my challenge to Morton and the legal ramifications of my charges. The bishop never acknowledged receiving my letter.

Later, after discussing the letter with Reich, I took a copy of his affidavit and one I composed with the help of my lawyer, and tried to give them to the bishop. He refused to accept them and said it was proper to give them to the superintendent. He could not and would not receive any documentation from me. A few years later, the law of the church changed to mandate that bishops were required to receive such documents and to act upon them.

The first day of Holy Week, I received a letter from Neal James, who was head of the Faculty Affairs Committee. (This was a curious and ironic title for a committee at Worthington!) Neal indicated that the committee was about to meet, and asked whether I wanted to file a grievance against Morton. I wrote back to him immediately and said I would like to do so.

Things were evidently moving forward on several fronts. I had a visit on Maundy Thursday in my office from the DS. His office was down the hall from mine, but there was no way he would ever come to see me. But there he was. He was an older man whose name we always enjoyed: Marion Looser. He asked if he could speak with me. He said he would honor my challenge to the credentials of President Morton. He had asked for the Conference Committee on Investigations to meet as soon as possible following Easter. He asked me if I still wanted to go forward. I told him I did.

The next morning, on Good Friday, Neal James came to my office. He said the Faculty Affairs Committee had refused to accept my petition to file charges against the president. He apologized, saying he understood what I was doing. He could not convince the committee, however. It was stacked with Morton sympathizers. He said he was on my side, but his position was compromised and he could not help me. I told him I knew what he meant. He was living with a co-ed, a major in his department and a beauty queen, while his wife was divorcing him. There was no way he could afford to criticize Morton's affair, or anything else about the college.

That afternoon Bishop Phillip H. Langston himself knocked at my office door. This was too much! For the bishop to come across town unannounced, hat in hand, on Good Friday, and ask to speak with me, was curious. He asked me how I was doing and inquired about my family. He told me he was on a pastoral visit. I asked him what he meant. He said he was concerned about me, and asked whether I wanted a full-time appointment to a parish for the coming year. I was appalled by the question. I told him I was appointed beyond the local church as the chair of the Department of Religion and Philosophy at Worthington College, and part-time to the Athens parish.

He said that yes, he knew, but there would be changes and he wanted to be sure I was taken care of. I told him I considered this to be a prejudicial question. I had written him about the situation at the college. He knew about Morton and the affair. It was time for him to do something about it. I did not consider his actions to be pastoral at all, but partial to a man who had violated his vows.

I said to him, "The church's one foundation is Jesus Christ her Lord. You have compromised your witness because of the petty politics of this conference. May God forgive you!"

He got up silently, looked at me sadly, and left my office. I had never spoken to a bishop of the church like that and never expected to do so. I always looked up to bishops, like a little boy looking up to God. Now I found myself looking down at this pitiful man, although he was taller than I, and he was my bishop.

I came to understand that virtually everything I had learned in the South, both directly and indirectly as a child and adolescent, was not only deceptive, but false. The results of slavery and racism tainted every aspect of our society. The liberation of my mind and spirit was the result of attending a church-related liberal arts college. Now, teaching in the same kind of college caused me to take a stand based on what I had learned from my teachers and mentors throughout my education. I could have become disgusted and disillusioned. How could I deal with such a monstrous distortion of all that I valued and to which I had dedicated my life? The corruption of the college, and of the church system, was because of individuals like Morton and the weak and ineffectual bishops who were so afraid of him that they refused to stand up to him.

I met with the Conference Credentials Committee after Easter. They wanted to know the nature of my charges. I told them the president had misappropriated money given for religious life on campus. They responded that the donor had agreed to change the gift to endow a chair in Religion. I said she had been deceived, and the money would be held and the interest drained from it each year and used for other purposes. They responded that the chair had already been offered to someone.

I told them I knew Dr. James Franklin had been asked if he wanted to hold an endowed chair in the college. I knew Jim well. We had taken a group of students to Israel during January Term several years earlier. Jim had a PhD in Education, and had studied Archeology in Israel. When he was not working or conducting tours in the Holy Land, he delivered lectures in this country. Morton invited Jim to come to Worthington and give several lectures. It was excellent. The students were impressed. While he was on campus, he took me aside and asked if we could talk. He said Morton had offered him the chair if he would come several times a year and lecture. He would be paid for the lectures and his travel. Jim could not understand how this could be considered an endowed chair in Religion. I told him what Morton was doing and told him not to fall for it. He thanked me and said he would not touch it with a stick.

I told the Credentials Committee members I had spoken with Mrs. Pitman and warned her about what Morton was doing. The DS asked me if it were proper for me to get involved. I told him that this money could be life's blood for not only our department, but for religious life on campus, and for the school in general. I said we could become again what the founders of this college had intended for it to be. Mrs. Pitman had proposed advancement of the Gospel accomplished both "academically through strong Christian curricula, and relationally through fellowship and mutual nurture in His name."

Committee members did not seem to be impressed. They told me I must have evidence. All I had given them was hearsay. They pressed me as to what charge I would file against Morton. I was far from ready to file specific charges. All I could come up with was the verdict in the Thomas Franks case. After being charged with having had affairs with seven different women in the parish, all he was convicted of was hindering the ministry of his associate. The associate admitted to having an affair with one of the women, and alleging that Tom had also slept with her. There were also allegations that Tom Franks, his associate, and Morton had been involved in Saturday night parties in which they played poker, drank whiskey, smoked cigars, and had attractive women entertain them. None of this was ever proved, however, and the only thing the jury of ministers could hold onto was interference with the ministry of a fellow pastor. This was later overturned by the Judicial Council of the Methodist Church.

This was a charge that was slippery and ambiguous enough to latch onto. I knew nobody wanted to deal with such a charge again. The conservative pastors hated Morton and would side with me if given a chance. This kind of charge was meaningless enough to be confusing and threatening enough to incite fear in Morton's crowd. The committee wanted to fish in deeper waters. They kept asking me questions about Morton's private life. I did not want to give them any ammunition to use against me. I indicated that I was concerned about the poor moral and ethical example of the president, especially since he was an ordained minister.

They asked me if I had counseled the husband of Morton's secretary. I was shocked by the question. I answered them honestly that I had not counseled him, but that I had spoken to him three times on the telephone. I told them I had discussed the situation with Charles Stevens, who was their pastor. He said he and Bishop Samuels were concerned about the relationships of the two families in the church. Charles told me it was difficult for him to deal with the situation, and had asked me to talk with Tom Reich, who was depressed and in real pain over the divorce. I told them I did talk with him, but I did not counsel Tom.

They replied that Charles Stevens had said I had counseled Tom Reich. The room reeked of the rancid odor of betrayal. Charles had set me up to get rid of Morton. I thought he was my friend. I never imagined he would use me to get rid of this monster. The mere act of contacting Reich sealed my fate. Charles thought he was on his way to the episcopacy. He, no doubt, had helped get rid of Tom Franks, and now had a lofty perch from which he aspired for higher glory. In the process, he needed to get Morton out of the college and get control of that institution in addition to First Church.

I wanted to be sure I was not misjudging Charles, so I called and asked him why he had said that I counseled Reich. I recalled our telephone conversation and then said that I had spoken to Reich on the phone three times.

"You asked me to talk with him," I said. "I did talk with him, but I did not counsel him."

Charles's answer was chilling, "Counsel or talk, I guess it's just a matter of semantics."

Our friendship, my career, and my future—all of this could be trashed based on the distinction of whatever the word semantics might mean.

Chapter 44

THE WORDS OF THE PROPHETS

Chaplain Brunner had asked me if I would preach in Chapel on April 15. I already had my tax day jokes in mind. He called me back later, however, and asked if I would be willing to trade dates and be in chapel one week earlier—April 8. That date was special to me: The anniversary of the battle during the Civil War in 1864 in my little hometown. Jokes about income tax day changed to Civil War stories, except it was the civil war at Wortington. My answer to Morton would be once again to preach about his apostasy, but this time, in much plainer language:

Williams Chapel
Worthington College
April 8, 1991

This may be the last time I speak in Chapel, after eighteen years of teaching here. Today, I am honor bound to speak my mind and duty bound to speak my heart. My calling as a minister of the church of Jesus Christ causes me to do so. The administration of this college has challenged my leadership here. I will not remain until and unless that challenge is removed. My plans and goals for the college, and especially for the Department of Religion and Philosophy, are a part of my calling as a minister of the Gospel. Ironically, the reason for this challenge is my stand against the immoral behavior of the leaders of this institution, including other ordained ministers.

The Simon and Garfunkel song, "Sounds of Silence," says that the words of contemporary prophets may be found plainly written on the subway walls. This signifies to me that the meaning of our situation is clear to those who have eyes to see. To this I can only say, "Amen." It does seem, however, that many have failed to see the truth. It is high time, however, that the scales fall from our eyes.

The words of the prophets are with us, whether we want to see them or not. In the past two years, I have come to value more highly the ministry and message of the prophets. They have spoken to me in new and challenging ways. While under attack by the administration, I have come to understand my own situation in terms of the utterances of those courageous individuals who spoke out thousands of years ago.

Two figures in the history of Judaism come to mind. One is the prophet Jeremiah, who railed against idolatry, forgetfulness of tradition, and ingratitude to the God who had brought the people of Israel out of Egypt. He blamed the leaders of his country as the offenders and enemies of God. He counseled the armies of his country to lay down their arms and not to fight against the forces of Nebuchadnezzar of Babylon. They could not and would not win. For his troubles, he was put in prison by the rulers of his country. Later he was liberated as an enemy of the state when the Babylonians conquered the country. In his "Lamentations," he shed bitter tears over his country and its apostasy. He was a true prophet.

Titus Flavius Josephus was the chief northern commander of the Jewish revolt against the Romans in the first century. He counseled his fellow Zealots to abandon the struggle against overwhelming power. He escaped and surrendered to the Romans, and became a key figure in the war against the Jews. He aided the enemy in destroying Jerusalem by giving them key information about the Jewish forces and the defenses of the city. He was rewarded by the Romans with a title and a residence in Rome. He betrayed his people and saw them killed and enslaved. He was a craven coward and traitor.

Jeremiah spoke truth to power and was willing to risk everything because of his calling and his faith in God. Josephus saw his relation to power differently. Both read the balance of power and the turning of the gears of history correctly. Both knew their small fourth-rate country could not prevail against the might of a major world power. Both counseled capitulation and surrender to their people. Both wrote the history of their times, with the destruction of Jerusalem and the demoralization of the country. Jeremiah stands as a great moral witness to the power of God, and the future of his country beyond idolatry, destruction, and exile.

Josephus is disqualified by the court of human history as a moral witness. He reported from a safe distance the agony of his people and their loss of all they held to be holy and priceless. He was objective and passionless while they bled. He projected no hope or future beyond the triumph of those whose ruthlessness and idolatry stood against all the teachings about the God of his people. He represented cowardice, betrayal, and alienation.

If I am to play a role in recording the history and destiny of this college, I will choose the role of prophet, as painful as that is. The great prophet Jeremiah is my ideal and my role model. I, too, feel God calling me to stand up for the truth as it is revealed to me. I cannot submit to the immoral situation I know to exist here in the leadership of this institution. Those in authority seem to have no idea of the great tradition of church-related liberal arts education, which has meant so much to this nation, and especially the South. Knowing what I know, I cannot be a Josephus and write the history of my time and this institution from a safe objective viewpoint.

In a Chapel service several years ago, I related how the prophet Nathan stood before King David and told him the story of a rich landowner who stole a little ewe lamb from a poor man and had it slaughtered to feed his guests.

When David responded indignantly, Nathan pointed a bony finger in his face and said, "You are the man!" In effect, I was relating this to the moral life of our leader, who was present that day. He did not seem to get it, however.

Today, I have read the account of the prophet Elijah who stood before King Ahab and his pagan Queen Jezebel. He stood for the traditions of his faith, and he alone spoke against the enemies of the faith. I see an obvious parallel to my role today in standing against our leader and his female friend.

The line of the prophets is a long and valiant one: Samuel, Nathan, Elijah, Elisha, Amos, Hosea, Micah, Isaiah, Jeremiah, Ezekiel, Second Isaiah, Daniel, to mention a short list. We may also add Jesus, Peter, Stephen, Paul, Augustine, Thomas Aquinas, Martin Luther, Jean Calvin, John Wesley, Martin Luther King, Jr., and John XXIII. I also find prophetic dimensions in the courageous actions of contemporaries. For example, a noble woman has given this college $600,000 for Religious Life on campus. She has stated her purpose in doing this in words we all should know:

My understanding and view of this college has always been that one of its primary purposes as a church-related college has been to advance the purposes of the Church of Jesus Christ, among

257

which the first and foremost of purposes is His Gospel. In a college setting, it seems to me, that advancement of the Gospel is accomplished both academically through strong Christian curricula, and relationally through fellowship and mutual nurture in His name.

This is so profound and prophetic that I thought that we would soon see a rebirth of the values and convictions upon which our founders established this college. What I saw instead was the miserable misappropriation of this precious money to purposes far from those for which it was intended. I could not stand by and let this continue, so I contacted the donor and asked her to insist that the academic "chair" to which her money had been assigned be filled. In doing this, I gave up my rightful claim to be considered for this chair. After seeing the process carried to its conclusion, the president informed me that I would no longer be Chairman of the Department of Religion and Philosophy. He blamed me because of my demands that the money be used for its intended purposes. This matter is ludicrous and will not stand the light of day.

During the past two years, it has become clear to me that the Lord has called me to fulfill a prophet role on this campus. Frankly, I did not realize that when I accepted the call to be a minister in the Church of Jesus Christ that God would call me to play such a role. I understand a prophet to be someone who has a unique and distinct message; One who sees into a situation with startling clarity; One who suddenly and unmistakably knows the truth and its implications; One who must speak out in a way that will forever change the reality of the situation.

This kind of insight shakes a person up and removes him or her from the everyday world of complacency, compliance, and composure. It clearly places one against the standards and practices of his or her contemporaries. This means telling the king what he least wants to hear, speaking out against the injustices of the kingdom, and bearing the consequences of speaking out. Also required is challenging the domesticated divines who are on the payroll and tell the king sweet nothings. A prophet is called to be a name-caller, a whistle-blower, one who is set apart as "that individual," in Kierkegaard's words. It is the prophet's sad lot to not only have to tell the truth, but to live it also in a time that does not want to hear or see the truth in any form.

It has become clear to me that teaching biblical and philosophical truths in the classroom was not enough. I had to do more and to speak out prophetically against what was happening on this campus. I could no longer continue to live a lie or be a witness to falsehood by my inactivity.

I became directly involved in this matter because a colleague in ministry asked me to counsel one of his parishioners. This man told me how his marriage and his life had been disrupted and then destroyed. His ewe lamb had been stolen by a cruel usurper. I worked with others to help him and saw him change for the better. He renounced his efforts to strike out against the person who had hurt him, and sought God's will for his life. The role I played in this matter was positive and resulted in good for all concerned.

The adversary of this man found out that I had talked with him and has chosen to attack me because of what I know but never intended to use against him. He has determined to destroy me, although what I have done directly benefited him, and may have saved his life. Since he is my superior, as well as my colleague in the ordained ministry, his anger has not allowed me a moment of peace since that time. The man whom I counseled has given me his support and allowed me to use his affidavit to defend myself. In all of this, I have known the satisfaction only a prophet of God can know. In the midst of the furnace, I have breathed the cool and gentle wind of the Holy Spirit. I have also seen the mouths of the ravening lions stopped so that they could not devoir me.

I commend to you the words of the prophets. First of all, they are sad words. Isaiah of Jerusalem, for example, offered a sign to King Ahaz, the sign of one who is to be born and called, "Immanuel," which means, "God is with us." He then knew the sadness of being turned down flat. The king wanted no sign. For Christians, Isaiah was way ahead of his time. We see the fulfillment of the sign as being deferred until the time of Jesus. If the king had only listened, his country, its capital, and its Temple could have been saved.

We have signs here, the latest of which is the generous gift of a noble woman designed to implement and to strengthen religious life on campus. Unfortunately, the administration has perverted this gift and chosen to destroy the Department of Religion and Philosophy, and religious life on campus. This college has thereby said no to the sign. A sign deferred, however, by God's grace, will come again. The good news of the prophets is that "God is still with us," even in the belly of the whale. God will not be mocked. The Messiah will come in God's time. It may not be in my time, or in yours, because of the blind refusal to accept God's will, but it will come. I firmly believe this; otherwise, I would not be here this morning.

The Jesus who wept over Jerusalem will soon die for the redemption of the beloved City. Surely he weeps over the situation here. It grieves his heart. I am only his most humble servant, but I am willing to die to my calling here and my love of this campus in order to see it reborn. It must be liberated from the scourge of this administration and all the evil it represents in order to fulfill its destiny. The good news is that God is not finished with us. The voice of the prophet says, in proleptic proclamation, "The time of bondage is over, the time of freedom is at hand!" Spring is coming, although our eyes and our hearts tell us it is still winter. The future will not be as the past. The oppressive atmosphere will not last. The tyranny of this administration and the profligacy of the president are over, although it seems that their power is still strong enough to crush anyone who stands up to them.

Prophetic words are accompanied by prophetic deeds. The two go together. It must be so now. The prophetic messengers of the Bible often performed strange and bizarre acts. So shall it be here also. In just a moment, I will leave this Chapel and walk over to the office of the Harrison District Superintendent. My daughter will walk with me. I will leave documents with the Superintendent that make charges against the president of this college under ¶2621 of the 1992 *Discipline of the United Methodist Church*. He is accused of, "immorality," and "practices . . . incompatible with Christian teachings," and "relationships and/or behavior which undermines the ministry of another pastor."

You are invited to go with us to the Superintendent's Office, if you choose to do so. I should warn you that the administration will not look kindly on your actions, and may attempt reprisals against you, and certainly against me. I also assure you that God's love, mercy, and grace will surround us and ultimately keep us safe. We will in no way try to disrupt the normal operations of the supperintendent's office.

Let us stand and sing a song with prophetic meaning and power, "The Battle Hymn of the Republic," as we march the short distance to the office of the superintendent.

Chapter 45

THE SOUNDS OF SILENCE

I have prided myself in being able to get through all kinds of services, including weddings and funerals, without becoming emotional. I was not able to get through preaching in chapel that day without my voice becoming weak and strained. Julie was not able to be there. My high school-aged daughter, Catherine, insisted on being a witness. I did not think it was a good idea, but I knew she would blame herself the rest of her life if she were not there. She was crying before the service ended. As I walked out, I held my hand out to her, and she joined me. I put my arm around her as we marched across the campus to the superintendent's office.

Morton was not in chapel that day, but Van Dale was. News must have spread fast, because by the time we got to the superintendent's office, he had been called and warned we were coming. I knocked at the door and his secretary met us. She said he was not in. I had gotten to know her well over the years and knew she was covering up. Later, she told me the superintendent had run down the hall and was hiding in the bathroom. It was fun to imagine him cowering in his stall afraid we would burst in on him.

There were twenty-five of us—students and faculty—outside his office. We had a brief prayer meeting and sang hymns. We waited, and then gradually our crowd melted away. Finally, I dismissed the rest and gave my charges against Morgan to the secretary. There was a reporter from the local paper who had identified herself when we were marching over. I was not sure who had contacted her, but I was glad she was there. She stayed and asked me additional questions. She told me the article would be in the next day's paper.

I could not wait to see what she had written. The next morning, I was disappointed. The article was essentially a coldly neutral report, which wound up making me look rather absurd. The words used to describe me, "popular but disgruntled," became a kind of epic simile they used to refer to me any time there was a report about the situation on campus. Mid-morning the reporter called and apologized. She said her editors would not print her article as written.

She checked the files, and there was a large collection of articles about Morton and the campus that had never been printed. She said there were individuals in the community who would not let anything critical be reported. She said, as a Methodist, she was quite concerned about the college, but there was nothing she could do. She suggested I submit an article to *The National Methodist Reporter.* I was not sure they would print it.

I began to hear rumors from the Morton camp. I was a religious fanatic, with delusions of grandeur, styling myself "the prophet." I must have had a breakdown and become a fundamentalist, or crazy, which for them was the same thing. What were "the words of the prophets?" There were all kinds of speculations about that. They were obviously trying to read into everything I said and find hidden meanings. I must say, I was flattered that a group of Morton's men poured over reports of my sermon. They did not even have a copy of the text.

Mitch Barnett, the chair of the English Department, was telling people I must be some sort religious fanatic or pervert. Look at the way I hugged girl students on the campus. I reported this to my lawyer, Richard McArthur, who had a talk with Jeff Steinhauser, the college's legal counsel. He told Jeff that if this talk about me did not stop at once, we would file charges against Morton and we had volumes of material to use. This issue never came up again.

Several weeks later, I was teaching my Paul class mid-morning in the large second floor classroom where I had most of my classes. We were dealing with Paul's three major journeys and his struggles in spreading the Gospel. There was a knock at the door, and one of the secretaries from downstairs asked me to come into the hallway. She said there was someone there to see me. It was Rich McArthur. He said the school had filed suit against me saying I had invalidated my contract. The result was that I would be fired. I asked Rich what we should do. He said he considered the plans we had made involved our only course of action. So we counter-sued the school for damages.

The counter suit was hard-hitting and specific. It was filed against the institution, but also against Morton as a third-party plaintiff. One of the eleven provisions of the document read as follows:

> Dr. Morton has used his position as President of Worthington College to engage in a personal vendetta against the defendant in an attempt to silence a vocal critic of his administration. He has tried to cover up the allegations made by the defendant against him. Dr. Morton has caused Worthington College to file a law suit against the plaintiff challenging his professional status as a professor of religion and philosophy and also his livelihood and position as a tenured professor at Worthington College.

It was frightening and breathtaking to read these words in a legal document. They were powerful and accurate. I was a little person, and not worthy to challenge the great and wonderful Wizard of Oz. And yet, we were fighting back in a reasonable and rational way.

The exchange of charges in our suits produced a temporary standoff, which maintained the status quo. This would go on through the summer and into the fall. As long as we kept the suit in effect, there was no action. Morton was still president and I was still teaching and chair of the department. We were boxers in the last round of a bruising fight, both too tired to land another blow.

Motion was scheduled to visit the Rotary club in which I was a member. The president of our club called me and said Morton had contacted him. He said it would be better that I not attend that meeting because of the disagreement between us. Was he afraid I might stand up and challenge him in the meeting? This annoyed me, but I trusted my fellow club members, who knew me well enough not to buy Morton's allegations. I did not go to the meeting.

I contacted the minister who was the head of the Board of Ordained Ministry for the conference. He was a graduate of the college. He told me he knew more than I might imagine. He said he had a large folder of complaints about Morton and about the college.

I asked him about launching some sort of investigation. He laughed. He told me the conference has no power to do that.

"There are no real charges against him, unless you want to file some." I told him I had filed charges based on the handling of the Jenkins-Pitman money. He asked me what evidence I had. I told him, in effect, that I had none.

He continued, "We all know what he is and what he has done, but no one is willing to sacrifice themselves for this piece of crap. Do you want to do that?"

I was not sure how to answer him.

I told him I needed help. I asked him if he, or the bishop, or BOOM was ready to save the college? He laughed again.

"Look, if you have some sort of misguided Messiah complex, you go ahead. But be assured that not one of your brothers or sisters in ministry will join you. You will be left hanging by yourself from a big tree way out in the woods."

Well, that was that! In his crude manner and language, he had told me about the difficulties I would face, and that I was all alone. I wondered if he realized what he had described was about to happen to me was a lynching!

Several years later, he turned in his credentials after he had been caught in an affair with his church secretary. His wife divorced him. I wondered whose situation was more lonely, his or mine. He was cut off for doing what was wrong. I was alienated and exiled, but maintained my credentials and my self-respect, for doing what I knew was right.

Chapter 46

DEAR FACULTY MEMBERS

I contacted Reich and we began to work on Plan B: Letter writing to faculty, administration, and trustees. The first letter was addressed to the faculty. The plan was rather audacious, but neither of us had anything to lose. I was still convinced that if people really knew what was going on, they would rise up and do something about it. Reich thought the letters should be anonymous. I immediately reacted against that. There were already unsigned letters circulating on campus that were hilarious and crude. I wanted nothing to do with that. The Klan did things in the dark with their heads covered. It was imperative we be accountable for whatever it was we wanted to communicate. We then spoke of a letter we both would sign. That idea did not appeal to me either. I saw no need for Reich to get involved in this. He had a weak heart and an excitable temper. Putting the two of us together would immediately signify an alliance and, to the Morton crowd, a conspiracy.

There would be no mention of the affair or any other aspect of Morton's personal moral failures. The letters would focus on professional, legal, religious, and personal matters. Morton would deny everything, but I would be able to inform the faculty of what had taken place. I wrote a draft of the letter and brought it to Reich to read. We changed a few things, but basically it went as written. I kept remembering all that Freeman and the Countess had taught me.

There was so much that needed to be addressed, but I knew I had to keep it brief and focused on the misdeeds of the administration. I used plain paper with my home address. We ran off the letters at Kinkos, and then took them to Reich's apartment and stuffed the letters in the hand-addressed envelopes. We went to the post office and mailed them. The letter read in part:

> To my fellow faculty members at Worthington College, I am sure that you have heard of my situation at the college with respect to the suit brought against me by the administration. The local newspaper has said that my fate is in the hands of the local courts. I disagree. My fate is in the hands of Almighty God. I do look forward to the judge's decision, however.
>
> I am writing to you to clear up three misrepresentations, which have been spread on campus by the administration:
>
> (1) That I did not file a grievance against the president;
> (2) That I had no right to preach in Chapel as I did;
> (3) That I sued the college.
>
> I would like to report to you in detail regarding these matters. I cannot enclose all of the relevant documents, but I will leave packets with the chairpersons of the departments.
>
> Regarding the first point, i.e., that I did not file a grievance. You will find in the packet a number of documents, which trace the development of my grievance from March 24 (before the contracts came out) to April 21, when President Dr. Albert L. Morton told me that my time was up and I could no longer file anything.
>
> I first gave notice that I desired to file my grievance under the new ¶13 of the Faculty Manual under grievance

procedures. I received word from Dean William Van Dale, however, that I could not file under this paragraph because it had never been added to the Manual. I asked why and he told me that President Morton had never taken it to the Trustees for approval. I remind you that the Faculty overwhelmingly approved the motion from the Faculty Affairs Committee to add this new paragraph on April 12, 1991. By refusing to submit this to the Trustees, the President has defied the faculty and shown bad faith in his dealings with us. There is no excuse for holding this matter for a whole year.

I contacted Dr. Neal James, chairman of the Faculty Affairs Committee, to see that this issue was placed before the Trustees and to ask that it be made retroactive to cover my complaint. I wrote to him on April 6 and got an answer back on April 17, Good Friday. When I learned that my request had been denied, I wrote to President Morton to ask that my grievance be changed to employ the usual channels, since the new procedure for grievance against the president was not available.

My letter was dated April 18. President Morton responded to me in a letter dated April 21. He lectured me on procedure for filing a grievance and told me that my time was up on April 16, one day before the Faculty Grievance Committee met and rendered its decision. I contend that this represented bad faith on the part of the President and denied me due procedure. This is especially true since the President was charged by the Faculty with the responsibility of submitting the motion to the Trustees. This would have empowered the new procedure, but the President failed to do so. He has, therefore, heaped scorn upon the entire structure of relationships between the Faculty, the Administration, and the Trustees in the way this has been handled. He has also misrepresented the facts when he has told you that I did not file a grievance. He has repeated this untruth to the school newspaper, the local community newspaper, and the Student Government Association.

Regarding the second point, my preaching in Chapel, I joined a copy of my sermon with a copy of my contract in the materials I have left with department chairpersons. After I received my new contract on April 1, and was denied the college's grievance procedure, this was the only course that was open to me.

The president is in charge of contracts, so I could not appeal this matter to him. The appeal procedure for contracts goes to a member of the Trustee Board. My appeal to him would necessarily include a copy of my sermon since it relates exactly what has happened. I feel even stronger about what I said after certain administrators reported that I called myself a "prophet." I did say that the classical prophets do speak to our situation. I never called myself a prophet, however. I did not go crazy in chapel, nor have I become a wild-eyed fundamentalist. I feel strongly about my call to preach and to remain faithful to my vocation as a minister. The administration has chosen to attack me rather than to deal with the issues I have raised.

How would you feel if you had taught at Worthington College for eighteen years, were head of your department, and then received a letter on March 16 (just eleven days before the contracts came out during spring break) to the effect that you were being removed as department chair? This letter clearly violates ¶2, page 20, of the Faculty Manual, and the dismissal procedure of the AAUP. My letter included with my contract on April 1, 1992, and my sermon in Chapel on April 8, 1992, are direct responses to this travesty. I was denied any recourse within the normal channels of the college, as guaranteed by the Faculty

Manual and the AAUP documents. I have used, therefore, means outside of these normal channels (which have been denied to me), not because I arbitrarily chose to do so, but because they were the only ones available to me.

Regarding the third point, that I have filed suite against the college, I respond that the college filed suit against me on May 1, 1992, alleging that I had invalidated my contract by my grievance statement included with my contract. I was acting in accord with the Faculty Manual and the AAUP documents when I responded as I did. The President and the Dean breached my present contract, which runs to September 1, 1992, by preventing me from teaching two classes during the second summer semester (which I had done for eighteen years). They have also violated my tenure by their actions.

I have included copies of the college's suit against me, dated May 1, 1992, and my response on May 29, 1992. Notice that I am listed as "defendant" and the college as "plaintiff." My response was a counter suit, adding President Dr. Albert L. Morton personally as a third-party defendant and making him responsible for compensatory and punitive damages. This matter is still before the court, but it is incorrect to say that I have not responded to the frivolous suit against me in the name of the college.

Abbott Lawrence Lovell was the controversial president of Harvard College from 1909 to 1933. He expanded the size and influence of Harvard, with remarkable increases in its student body, its endowment, and its buildings on campus. He was a great reformer of undergraduate education.

More than a century ago, Lovell is quoted as warning colleges and universities in this country that, "institutions are rarely murdered. They meet their end by suicide. They die because they have outlived their usefulness, or failed to do the work that the world wants done." They also meet their demise, in one way or another, by forgetting who they are. They fail to acknowledge their mission, as established by those who founded them and worked for generations of students to realize their ideals and purposes.

My colleagues, I solicit your help, your concern, and your prayers. I have done nothing to justify the vicious attacks on me launched by the administration. I am willing to answer any questions you may have and to make available to you all of the significant documents from this case. I would appreciate your help in correcting the misrepresentations the administration continues to spread about me. I hope you realize that these kinds of attacks have been leveled at faculty, administrators, and staff members throughout President Morton's twenty-five year career. I must warn you that no one is safe, and that unfortunately you might be next.

No one said a word to me about the letter, except Adam. He called me after receiving it, and said, "What in the world are you doing?" I told him this was the only way I could get information out. He said, "I understand that, but why send the letters personally and printed at Kinkos?" I asked him what he meant. He said, "Look, I have friends at the state university where I used to teach. I can get your letters printed (as many as you want), prepared, and mailed. I need someone to pay for all this, however.

You cannot stop with this pitiful faculty. They will not do anything. Morton owns them. If the letters go through the university, nobody can trace them to me, or to you, or to anyone on this campus. We will have Morton's fools looking under every bush and around every tree for clues. All I need is the money. Can you handle it?"

I asked Reich about it, and he said, "Let's do it. I'll pay for it." So the second letter went out with information about Morton's misuse of the money. It went to faculty, trustees, and conference ministers.

I chose not to know to how many individuals the letters were sent—it had to have been between seven hundred fifty and one thousand. I did not know how the letters traveled to the university, or who carried them, or to whom they were given to be processed, or how they were paid for. The less I knew about all that, the less I had to do with it. I simply wrote the letters and gave the hard copy to Adam. I am not even sure how many letters there were—I think there were between seven and nine. There were various other letters that went out in copycat fashion. They were unsigned. Morton tried to tie them to me, but I always signed mine. My style and my arguments were out there.

Chapter 47

THE GREEK CHORUS

Thank goodness the semester was about over. It was hard going on with any degree of normalcy. I conducted my classes as I had done for eighteen years. The lecture classes were not so hard. I knew my material and I had my notes. The discussion classes were more difficult. It was hard not to bring examples from present reality into our discussions. I decided to offer a second Ethics course that semester due to student demand. Teaching Ethics on that campus was difficult and problematic, but necessary.

There were reasons, of course, that Morton and Van Dale did not desire these discussions of ethical and moral behavior, especially if I were conducting them. Students asked me probing questions about the meaning of the ethical theories we were exploring. There were times when their perceptive and accurate use of the tools I was giving them was frightening. How much could or should I say? I did not want to be a hypocrite in simply teaching about ethical theories and not applying them. The students were my most important critics, the only ones who mattered.

The students fed me with leads on every issue, and were my silent partners in every aspect of this sad debacle. They reached out to me when I was depressed and despondent. They gave me a cause beyond my own personal desire to defend myself and to get even with Morton and the administration bullies. I tried to stop them when they wanted to do anything overt to help me. I did not want them to get hurt. I took the abuse, but they gave me the means to counter Morton's plots. Ultimately, they helped trap him in his lies by carefully chronicling them and passing their findings on to us.

They were like a Greek chorus, constantly observing, conferring, collecting information, and drawing conclusions. I felt especially sorry for my majors. They knew things were tense. They looked at me as their mentor, and I realized I could not guide them through this. They were like sheep without a shepherd. They began to look around for someone to guide them. Naturally, they gravitated to Mark Jennings, and I did not try to stop them. Some of them also realized his different set of priorities and refused to switch. I knew at some point I would have to cut them loose.

The support of the fraternity chapter I helped establish and for which I served for years as advisor and sponsor was especially touching. They gave me a plaque honoring me and thanking me for my service. After things really became tense, they contacted me and asked for me to attend a meeting. They were hearing things and wanted to know how they could support me. I told them how much I appreciated that. They were clearly ready to put themselves on the line for me, and they wanted my guidance about how they could best register their protest to the administration and the trustees. It was tempting, I will have to admit, but any encouragement I might have given them would have been self-serving.

I told them the most important thing they could do for me was to remember this situation. When their time of trial came, I asked them to remember me and to honor me by standing up for what they knew was good, right, and just. Any kind of protest action they might make would be interpreted as my using them. It would give the fraternity and its members a bad name. Morton would twist it and use it against them and me. This was one occasion when I felt I needed to be absolutely honest with students and ask them to consider the effect of their actions on them, on the school, and on me.

The student newspaper had been most accurate in reporting the on-going crisis. There was much they could not write because the administration censored them. In the interview immediately after my sermon in Chapel in April, I talked more about the attack on me because of "a counseling situation" involving Morton's "supposed enemy." The students knew about the affair and filled in the details. In their interview with Morton, they asked him to comment on the Reich divorce and what his relationship with his secretary had to do with the dispute between him and me. They also made him discuss the chair in Religion and Philosophy and the $600,000.

Morton told the newspaper he consulted with Chaplain Brunner, Mark Jennings, and Byron Simmons, whom he now referred to as "Dean of Admissions," about the brochures. They decided "they were not the type of brochure we wanted to send out." He also alleged that the project cost $3,000, which was "well over budget." That, of course, was not true. I worked with the advertising agency hired by the college to keep costs down. I was adamant we stay within the $2,000 available, which we paid out of our annual budget of $1,000 for two years. It was interesting that Jennings was among those with whom Morton was conspiring. His answers to the student reporter were incredible, and the students knew it. By drawing him out, the students were able to get answers to questions we could not obtain. He could not resist lying to them.

Van Dale's attitude toward students was appalling. He referred to them as, "these kids." He and Morton regarded them as children, whom they ignored and lied to. In my estimation, this was their most strategic error. Under these circumstances, I found our students to be amazing. They were the unsung heroes of this whole sad story. They were perceptive, intelligent, and keenly observant. They were aware of the affair before those of us on the faculty had any idea. They watched Morton and found him still courting his secretary, even after being warned by the trustees. After the semester ended, they called Morton to a command performance, asking him a whole range of questions, which no administrator ought to ever have to answer.

Chapter 48

LOADED DICE

I got a memo from Morton asking me to be on the committee to evaluate candidates for the chair in Religion. This was relatively meaningless since I was never notified about a meeting of this committee, and doubted it ever met. It was also a signal that I would not be considered for the position. One name that surfaced was a young man named Ralph Thompson. His nickname was Butch. He was finishing his dissertation for the doctorate at Emory University. He grew up in the conference, and served for a year as chaplain at Worthington before taking a full-time appointment in a church. He and his wife were attractive and were well received on campus. He had had no teaching experience and no reputation as a scholar, however. He was known in the conference and had a number of friends among the younger ministers. This was clearly a farce. Endowed chairs were not for beginners who had not even finished their dissertations.

Thompson's doctoral studies were in Religion and Literature, a hybrid discipline that was not as strong as a degree in New or Old Testament, Church History, Philosophical Theology, or Systematic Theology. Most of us were systematic theologians, which was a good degree for an institution like ours, because we were required to teach the whole spectrum of theological disciplines. Hurried selection of Thompson was a quick fix by Morton, designed to get me out of the picture as soon as possible, and to have someone to present at Annual Conference who would be easily recognizable.

A chair is considered a senior faculty appointment of someone who has distinguished him or herself in the field, and would raise the level of teaching and scholarship in the institution. Promotion to the chair would often reward years of accomplishment by faculty, so chairs are often filled from within. Butch Thompson was green, unpolished, and immature. I was not even sure it would be a permanent appointment.

Thank goodness the spring semester was finally over. I graded the last of my final exams, read all of the essays, and got all my grades in. Everything remained in an uneasy truce. Graduation ceremonies were held annually out on the green, except when it rained. One of the highlights of the ceremony was the presentation of the Myra Bradford Lee Faculty Award. The senior class voted annually for the faculty member whom they considered to be the most outstanding and the most positive influence on their lives. In the eighteen years I was at Worthington, I received the award twice. It was unusual that a faculty member would receive the award more than once, and unheard of that he or she would receive it three times. The name of the recipient was a carefully guarded secret. Because of the tension between Morton and me, however, I was told by the students that I would receive the award again that year.

Graduation Day was bright and sunny. The faculty procession advanced in order with all the usual pomp and circumstance. For a number of years, Morton had worn around his neck a heavy bronze seal of the college. Brian Washington and several other faculty members had found their own bling to wear around their necks to mock him. We marched in and took our places, with the faculty seated front and center in an amphitheater arrangement, with the graduates on our right.

As the ceremony progressed, before the awarding of the degrees, time came for the presentation of the Myra Bradford Lee Faculty Award. Morton informed the crowd that no faculty award would be made that year. He said that instead, he was going to make a special presentation to the Chairman of the Trustees, Jack Taylor.

Taylor was also the speaker for the ceremonies. I looked across at the faces of the graduates. They were sitting with their mouths open and expressions of disbelief on their faces. I thought they might undertake some form of protest. I believe they would have done so, if they had not been taken by surprise.

The trustees had told Morton, in no uncertain terms, that he had to let Audrey Reich go and not be seen with her any more. Jack Taylor found a new job for her. There was a large whites-only country club across from the college campus. There had been many complaints about Morton's membership there when no black or Jew could join the club or play golf there. Morton enjoyed his privileged position and refused to resign; his membership fees were paid by the college. The college also covered the tab for an extravagant leaving party at the club for Audrey. No one could remember when the college ever honored an employee in such fashion upon the occasion of their departure. This was all the more remarkable since nearly every summer, faculty, staff, and administration members disappeared with no notice made of their years of service.

A young woman in her senior year, majoring in Business, was hired by Morton as an intern secretary. She was attractive, intelligent, effective, efficient, and tough. We worried about her being anywhere near Morton, but she seemed to be able to take care of herself. She told us she could not say much about it, but no one could believe what went on in that office. She said there was a secure telephone in the office that Morton used to talk with Jack Taylor and others privately. She said she had no idea what was going on, but she knew the undercover dealings were not legal. She said she felt like she was working for the mafia.

I still heard from Charlie Smith from time to time. He was the former student who worked part-time in the Business Manager's office. He had helped me get information on the college's use of the money donated by the United Methodist Women for scholarships for pre-ministerial students. I performed the wedding service for Charlie and Suzie. They were among the scores of students who asked me to marry them. This, and an equal number of students who went into full-time professional ministry, I regarded as my major accomplishments during my time at Worthington. Charlie had recently secured a good position in a major accounting firm in Harrison. He and his wife were the proud parents of two young boys.

To celebrate their anniversary, Charlie and Susan got a babysitter and went out to a fancy restaurant in town. He called me in the midst of their dinner and asked me how I was. I told him it was tough, but that we were surviving. He wished me well and told me he had a pretty good idea of what I was dealing with.

We were about finished with the conversation when he paused, cleared his throat, and said, "Look, there is something you need to know. Morton and Audrey Reich are supposed to stay away from each other, right?" He got my attention with the question and I answered affirmatively. Charlie continued, "Well, Susie and I are having dinner tonight at Antonio's to celebrate the day you married us. We are sitting here enjoying our meal and looking across the room at Morton and his girlfriend who are having dinner together. They are laughing, drinking wine, holding hands, and looking lovingly at each other." I thanked him for the tip, and sat on my living room couch with my mind racing.

I had become a lightening rod, drawing reports of Morton's misdeeds and their implications. A lot of information came to me without my asking for it. I could not include a lot of it in my letters, so I routinely passed it on to the underground for distribution. I knew the Morton-Reich sighting indicated a direct violation of the trustees' instructions. I wrote up a report anonymously and put it into the hopper for someone to handle. It did not take it long before it appeared as a memo in the trustees' mailboxes.

Chapter 49

THE PRESIDENT AND THE STUDENTS

At the end of the semester, the Student Government Association requested that Morton meet with them to answer questions regarding the many rumors sweeping the campus. The possibility that I would get a copy of a tape with the entire discussion was remote. Due to the diligence of one of the students, however, I did receive an envelope containing a cassette in the mail, with no return address.

I never knew who sent the tape to me. In no way, however, did I underestimate the persistence and the desire for truth that motivated the students. I considered it important for the trustees to hear Morton's lies in his own words before the students. I had copies of the tape made and turned them over to the underground mailing team, who sent them to all the members of the trustees.

Morton brought with him a gentleman, Marvin Simonton, who was unknown to the students. He was introduced as "the Director of Public Relations, who is the new Business Manager." Morton was good at combining offices, but this was a new one. The students knew the old Business Manager, Steve Dorner was gone. (He was number twelve in the eighteen years I was at the college). No one had been told of the appointment of a new one, however. Is not managing the campus (which included the treasurer's job) enough without having to do public relations? Morton introduced him as a CPA for the past seven years at the local firm that served as auditors for the college. We often wondered how this firm could make legal sense out of the financial machinations. Having credentials with this firm was not necessarily a strong recommendation. It all sounded a little incestuous.

Morton began with statistical information on the college's finances and enrollment. He had the new business manager as back up. Here he was in his element. He was a necromancer and an alchemist with figures. It was as if he salted his audience with whiffle dust and pixie piffle. Since students had no way of checking his figures or his assumptions about our situation and the future, they were the perfect audience. It was a mistake to take them for granted, however. They were not easily fooled. He began with reassurance:

> The first rumor or question, which I want to look at with you, is that the college is in poor financial condition and will close within the next few years. Have you heard that? Let's take a look at that. The fact is that the college is in very sound financial condition, and it is growing in all of those assets that provide, in the long-term, real financial stability.
>
> Now in evidence of that, let's look at some of the science of financial stability and vitality. First, enrollment: Enrollment over the past decade has increased 15 percent, over the decade, at a time when many private colleges and independent colleges have experienced either a decline or simply been stable.

He brought with him a chart with multicolor lines showing growth and prosperity:

> Now, secondly, let's take a look at the investment of funds in the physical plant: The green line shows the amount of money that the college has invested in the physical plant beginning in 1981, from a little over

$4,000,000 over the period of a decade, to something over $12,000,000. That is, we have actually tripled the money invested in the student plant in a ten-year period from $4,000,000 to over $12,000,000. In the last seven years, we have built three academic buildings that cost approximately $6,000,000, most of which is paid for.

Retention was a sensitive issue, since we all knew students were hard to come by. When they left after a semester or year, it meant a double threat to our future. When asked about retention, Morton said the obvious. It was down, but only apparently. Through a dandy piece of equivocation, he tried to throw enough sand in the air to get on to the next subject:

We must look at it over a period of time. Over the last ten years retention has increased. But you have to keep in mind that to look at retention, you don't necessarily look at total enrollment. You are really looking at retention of each class, so if you have a large freshman class that comes in, you will have a lot leaving. You have to look at each class and put it all together for the total. That will reflect retention.

Students are not normally interested in what happened over the past ten years, especially when they see their classmates leaving after a year or two. This kind of reasoning purposely obscured the real situation and blunted the point of the original question. Listening to Morton's reasoning was like begin charmed by a used car salesman when you don't know anything about automobiles. After flooding the students with a deluge of figures and rationalizations, Morton then asked his new Business Manager, Mr. Simonton, to speak on one of the rumors circulating on the campus. He said:

One of the rumors that we would like to address, which is part of the first one which Dr. Morton has been discussing, is that funds have been misappropriated within the college relating to personnel in the college. The only way I can address that is to say that I have heard other rumors that stated that my former employer was part of the problem and that we played a part in a cover up at Worthington.

This college is a relatively small account. There is no way that my firm would jeopardize its status and its reputation. There is no way that I would jeopardize my CPA certificate, because that is my livelihood. The firm has certain levels of reviews that are required by the federal government, and it would take collusion by no less than ten people for me to have covered up anything. And I will also say that I think I would know everybody well enough that, had there been something going on, I would know. That pretty much addresses the two financial issues that the rumors have been concerning. The floor is open for questions. Anything you'd like to ask me?

Mr. New Business Manager used circular logic that was both confused and confusing. He said, "This is true because I say it is true, and I would not misrepresent facts." This is not the greatest proof of honesty. It simply argues that he must be honest because if he were not, he would lose his job, and others would know he was not honest. After the numerous financial crises we have undergone at the college, few would find such an argument credible without support from accurate and verifiable figures. He also said more about the firm from which he came than the finances of the college.

Prompted by a student question, Morton went on to comment on the money from the Jenkins-Pitman Trust:

With regard to the possible misuse of the funds to establish an endowed chair in Religion, valued at $600,000. There was an agreement made in December that those funds would be invested in a permanent endowment and only the income and interest would be spent in support of the purposes of the Chair.

This was agreed to in the first year, that the income from that endowment would provide subsidy for the salaries. The trustees allowed a maximum of 6 percent to be paid in interest from any endowment. So there was no misappropriation.

He did not deal with the original purpose of the endowment, to fund religious life on campus. His statement was also carefully evasive concerning exactly how the money from the endowment would be spent, "in support of the purposes of the Chair," and as a "subsidy for the salaries."

Then a student asked about Butch Thompson and the chair. How much would his salary be? Morton gave an answer about how the salary structure was determined by discipline and region. He then got into a dissertation on salary structure, but failed to comment on how much a person fresh from graduate school with no experience should be paid as the holder of an endowed chair. He told them how Butch would be around for Annual Conference as occupant of the chair.

He finished by saying that, in the summer, "Dr Thompson's primary responsibility is that he has worked among the churches. He has to spend those three months getting acquainted with those churches, speaking to the families, looking at Bible studies, and generally moving around."

One of the students asked Morton a perceptive question:

In your role as president, do you see yourself in ministry, and if so, how do you find yourself fulfilling the disciplinary guidelines for Word, Sacrament, and Order?

Morton evaded and equivocated, turning and twisting, pretending to answer this important question:

My primary function in ministry is to do the very best job I can as president of the institution. I'm not engaged in performing the usual ministerial functions. My function is to be the most effective president that I can be at this institution. While I have an interest in teaching in a church school, and I enjoy preaching, it is more of an avocation that I try to do, for sort of self-fulfillment to keep myself fresh.

I try to provide an explanation to the ministers about the nature of the environment of the campus, but probably not in any different way than would be true if I were layman. I do not know, in fact, whether any of the previous presidents of Worthington were ministers. I am certain that my predecessor was not for thirty-one years. There is no expectation that the president of the college will be a minister, but I think that I must hold fast to the idea that my ministry is to be the very best chief executive officer of this institution, of this purpose and this commitment, that I can be.

He seemed to say it does not matter that he was an ordained minister in the United Methodist Church, and, as such, has taken vows to serve the church in whatever capacity he is engaged.

He shifted the discussion to his job as university president, and tried to blur the distinction between how a clergyperson and a layperson would function in this position.

He was asked a question about me. "Has the chairman of the Department of Religion and Philosophy been removed from his position?"

Morton's answer was a masterpiece of pushing responsibility onto his passive dean:

The reason is a decision made by Dean Van Dale, who, as the Academic Dean, is responsible for all academic departments. He made that decision as we reviewed the duties of the department and came to the conclusion that the present chairman is not adequately meeting those duties as listed in the handbook.

Now, what recourse does he have?

He may request a jury by his peers to review the reasons given by the Dean. The jury of his peers will be five people in number. There is a grievance chairman selected by the faculty every year as a way of maintaining the grievance process and allowing fairness.

Any personnel decisions may be requested for a formal hearing if they cannot be resolved at an informal level. If he were to elect that process, he would first write me a letter outlining and stating the reasons for his grievance, the kind of relief that he wants, and then he will either accept or reject the faculty chairman or nominate someone. He would name two faculty persons who would agree to represent him.

The Dean would name two faculty persons that would presumably be objective and have no specific interest in the matter. That group of five faculty members would hear the grievance and bring any witnesses before them that they chose in order to evaluate it, and then they would make their recommendation to me. If I accept the recommendation, that would be an end to it. If I do not accept their recommendation, then I can say that I, as president, have decided what must be done.

Then we would review his decision with three trustees that are appointed by the chairman of the board. He has not elected to file a grievance, he has not written me a letter, and he has not taken steps to pass before a jury of his peers. That is where we are in that situation.

He tried to lose and confuse his audience in a thicket of procedural language. He never dealt with the dean's supposed reasons for his conclusion that I was "not adequately meeting" my duties. A student perceptively asked what the duties of a chairperson were. Morton referred her to the fifteen duties outlined in the Faculty Manual. He then, rather incredibly, ended the discussion with a bow to academic freedom:

> And if he wants to contest that judgment by the Dean, then he would bring his own evidence to that hearing. And I think until that time limit has run out, it would not be right to give great detail other than to tell you that this is the way it has happened, because I value academic freedom very, very much, and this is the process by which that freedom is guaranteed.
>
> You would understand that the Dean would not arrive at that judgment cavalierly, but most carefully, with documentation that he would be willing to lay before this jury of peers should the department chairman request it. Until that time, that may be kept confidential.

The irony and hypocrisy of this statement was based on the fact that I dared to question how the president of the college, as an ordained person (whose ordination did not seem to matter), could function in that position while having an on-going affair with his secretary. He avoided dealing with my reasons for not signing the document as presented to me and not choosing to engage in a grievance procedure I could not possibly win.

Perhaps Morton's largest and most obvious lie was with regard to his secretary and their affair. There was no equivocation or evasion here. He simply and categorically denied it. Morton then took up the third question:

> The President has had an affair with his administrative assistant. That is false. There is not any evidence to that, and it is simply not true.

Why did she—–that is Mrs. Reich—leave the college after the last Board of Trustees meeting? She received an excellent opportunity for advancement for herself, both in terms of the immediate financial reward and benefits. There was no relation to the time of her leaving and the fact that we happen to have the Board of Trustees meeting in January. There is no discussion, public or private, of her decision, which was her own, to make a change in her job.

"Why has the position not been filled?" he asked. In his response, Morton spoke of himself in the third person:

The president has been very fortunate to have an intern. She was an assistant last summer and knows all of the operations very well. She will graduate in the spring. She volunteered and I convinced her to work for me through the spring. She will graduate formally in March and cross the stage in May, and will do a very fine job. I am very fortunate to have her. We have begun the interview process, and we have identified some candidates. So that position will be filled.

The lie and cover-up were perhaps more heinous than the affair. The interesting thing was that in this answer and in the rest of his answers, Morton provided more information than any of us had by the way he framed the questions in order to deny them

The next question dealt with the hurried departure of Chaplain Brunner at the end of the semester. Morton read the question, and then wove his web of confusion and deception:

Why weren't the students informed that Chaplain Brunner was leaving before Dr. Jennings was named as his replacement? Early in the year, in January, he came to me and said, "I have been at Worthington nine years." And he said, "Do you know how old I am?"

I said that I really don't know, but knew that he was past the normal retirement age. He said, "I am seventy-three years of age." And he said, "I think it is time for me to retire, and if it is my choice, I don't want any recognition. I don't want these parties. I do not want any lunches. I just want to quietly make my exit from this institution. I have had a marvelous time, and that is my choice."

I said, "All right. If that is your choice, that is the way it is."

Of course, the conversations began about what we were going to do. Who were we going to appoint? Bishop Phillip Langston knew that several of the ministers in the conference had indicated interest in the chaplaincy. He called me, I guess about the end of February, and acquainted me with the appointment schedule.

I said, "Bishop, I'm sorry, but your schedule of appointment is different than ours. We are not prepared to make that decision." So in fact, we did find a minister to go ahead, but the choice about the decision, not to talk about it, was Steve Brunner's own choice. Anyone who asked, I think got a straight answer, but there was no announcement, and that was by his choice.

Anyone who has ever dealt with Morton would know this was a total fabrication. He was never so generous in his negotiations. I have no idea why the departures of the Business Manager and the Chaplain were necessary, but it was perhaps because both knew too much. It may also have been because both could not stomach any longer what they were seeing. A third possibility might be that Morton was becoming so paranoid that he could not trust anyone. We must have rattled him. What he was doing to the department, the chaplaincy, and to church relations was insane.

The final major issue the students brought up was the fact that the old Business Manager had recently left to make way for a new Business Manager, whom Morton had brought to support him in his bizarre allegations before the SGA. There were all kinds of rumors about the sudden departure of the former Business Manager, including a severance package that included the company automobile he was driving and a number of other benefits. We all knew that the only other person in our memories who got such privileged treatment were Morton's former secretary and mistress, and the golf coach, Tommy Parnell. Morton's answer was a classic of twisted logic and prevarication. It also sounded redundant, since he had just said the same thing about the chaplain's retirement:

> Why did the previous Business Manager leave the college? He reached retirement age and elected by mutual consent to retire. Was he given a new car or a large sum of money as a gift when he departed? No. He was a retired Army Officer when he came to us. He was not interested in income, because he was already receiving an income from his retirement.
>
> As a part of his compensation package, instead of giving him the level of income that he could have qualified for as Business Manager, he elected a lower income, and as part of that compensation package, we agreed that he would have the privilege of driving a college car. We purchased a vehicle, a used vehicle, for about $9,000, and each year instead of receiving a raise, one third of the value of that car was credited as part of the compensation package. At the end of three years, that car became his personal possession, and when he retired, he got the vehicle, now four years older. Since it was purchased a few years ago, it was purchased by the college, and of course not having nearly its original value.

Was there a large sum of money given as a gift on his departure? Again, part of his retirement package was to provide some funds, not to exceed $3,000, for relocation. That is part of the retirement package he elected, and we were pleased that he was willing to do so. So, his retirement period, which would normally be May 31, was negotiated simply as a means to bring the new Business Manager to the board at the time when he would be most useful. This was by mutual consent of the Business Manager and the college.

No one remembered the college negotiating anything like this for anyone. We did not have compensation packages or retirement packages. We did not know where Dorner came from, or why he was hired by the college. What was special about him? What could he do for Morton that no one else could or would do? Morton came to like retired military because they became good soldiers in his little cadre; they had their military retirement and did not need large salaries or benefits, and they were easily disposed of when the time came.

Finally, Morton added one more question, which he himself asked. Clearly, the letters to faculty, clergy, and trustees had hit home. He said:

This is the last one I have, and then you can raise some more. Have anonymous letters been sent out to trustees, faculty, conference ministers, and so on? Yes. Perhaps beginning last summer and part of the fall. There may have been maybe seven or nine letters, which I must say from my perspective, are not only anonymous, but are scurrilous, completely indefensible.

The faculty developed a resolution condemning the anonymous letters, and requesting that the administration identify and fire anyone who had anything to do with them. Trustees appointed a committee to investigate any and all allegations put out in an early letter in the fall, which spoke to the allegations one by one, and then in the January meeting they condemned the anonymous letters and gave a united vote of confidence to me as president and to the administrative officers. The very concept of anonymous letters, and anonymous charges, is anathema in an academic community.

I wrote a number of letters that carried my address, the date, and my signature. There were others sent through the underground, which were both scurrilous and, in some cases, obscene. They were more satires and comical farces than letters, however, with little if any serious content. Refusing to acknowledge my letters and conflating them with the anonymous letters was a way of writing them off, rather than answering the serious charges I had made. It was also, perhaps, an underhanded way of accusing me of writing the anonymous letters as well. Obviously, Morton did not choose to accuse me before the students, who were inclined to believe me.

It is hard to think that this meeting with the students did anything to strengthen Morton's case. They had been hearing and processing rumors longer than most of the rest of us. Students had never been close to Morton, nor he to them. He spoke in incredible and mystifying detail while explaining each of his points. Students were not impressed with all the verbiage, and scarcely satisfied. If anything, they were more critical after they had heard the president try to defend his character.

His attempt to affirm the stability of the college and to explain major changes in personnel in the faculty and the staff was less than convincing. What had been merely rumors and innuendos now became a living drama, which they had heard and seen for themselves. Morton clearly underestimated them and their ability to process the information he had given them. This was the categorical opposite of all we were supposed to stand for in higher education.

Chapter 50

ANNUAL CONFERENCE

As the semester ended, the campus staff prepared for the meeting of the Annual Conference: The business, spiritual, administrative, and social event of the year for the United Methodist Church. It was a lot for our small campus to host a thousand clergy and laity from throughout the area served by the bishop. This required changing our gymnasium into a large assembly area. Dorm rooms were transformed from student residencies to hotel rooms for annual conference delegates. Lawns and trees were trimmed. The cafeteria was cleaned and polished, and new menus were prepared with meals designed for older palates.

We hoped the church would find some way to deal with the scandal of the Morton administration. A rather amazing event seemed to indicate a new playing field. In the spring, Bishop Phillip H. Langston was attending a bishops' meeting in another section of the country when he had a heart attack. He had heart bypass surgery and was hospitalized for weeks before he was allowed to return home. He was not able to participate in any of the functions of his office for months.

Bishop Peter Samuels was a retired bishop living in Harrison. He had spent most of his career serving churches in the conference before being elected to the episcopacy and moving to another area to serve. He was, therefore, the ideal interim until Langston recovered. We were elated! Not only did Samuels know the situation on the campus well, he was in residence at First Church, and knew the relationship between the Morton and Reich families. I had spoken with him about the situation, and he listened to me and counseled me. He was diplomatic, but I was keenly aware of how much he knew. We felt he was a friend of the family. Surely, he would know how to deal with this situation and keep Morton from destroying our department and ending our careers at Worthington.

Methodist bishops are notoriously powerful in their areas. Whereas Catholic and Episcopal bishops serve spiritual functions, Methodist bishops are political. Our bishops have virtually absolute control over the lives of ministers in their areas. We generally agree to their decisions as God's will, but are not always sure God had been consulted. We saw Bishop Samuels as good and wise, whereas Bishop Langston was opinionated and remote.

Sadly, we did not know that two of the many unwritten rules among bishops were:

(1)   Never interfere with the leadership of a Methodist college;
(2)   Never interfere with the administration of another bishop in that bishop's episcopal area.

This also applied to an interim situation when a bishop was temporarily replacing a fellow bishop who was unable to exercise his or her duties. Bishops grant courtesy and respect to each other and stay out of each other's business. We heard nothing from Bishop Samuels, and watched in disbelief as a strange drama unfolded at Annual Conference.

The previous year, I was chair of the Department of Religion and Philosophy at Worthington and asked to lead the conference Bible Study. I was the Spiritual Director, and founder of the Chrysalis and College Chrysalis communities, and pastor of a part-time charge. I had been asked by the bishop to serve on the Board of Ordained Ministry.

In a year's time, I was reduced to only my part-time pastorate in the Athens Church. The suit had not come to trial or been settled. My contract was in effect until September of the current year. My appointments to the college and to the church were still in effect. Yet the college presumed I was fired and gone. This was tacitly ratified by the church.

The final night of Annual Conference, Julie and I sat through the most disagreeable and disgraceful spectacle imaginable. The report of the Higher Education Committee to the Conference usually included a brief recitation of numbers and half-truths about what the college had accomplished. This year, however, Morton and his staff were present and did the reporting. We could not remember anything like this happening previously.

Rather than ignoring my accusations about his mishandling, corruption, and immoral behavior, Morton attempted to refute them with a celebration of the new order of things in the department and in religious life on campus. He introduced the faculty: Mark Jennings as professor and chaplain, and Butch Thompson as the Jenkins-Pitman endowed chair in Religion and director of Church Relations. There was applause as they walked down to the stage together, arm in arm, smiling, two young men wearing bow ties. Their little speeches to the conference were sophomoric and superficial.

Julie and I watched in disbelief. We were both members of the conference. We had served eighteen years in the college, educating the youth of the area, and sending approximately one hundred students on to seminary or graduate school. I did not even get the equivalent of the French Foreign Legion's ceremonial stripping of all the marks of rank and service. We were simply passed over and ignored. It was as if we had never existed.

A group of former students and pastors who were graduates of the college told us they were working on a letter to be circulated at the conference. I did not encourage it, nor did I know the contents until they passed out copies. It was quite touching as well as informative about what Morton was doing. They covered the replacement of the

Business Manager and the Chaplain. They listed the appointments of Jennings and Thompson. They also mentioned the brochures that were being circulated touting the new arrangement. Morton had apparently thrown away our brochures and prepared his own. The open letter read, in part:

> We come to you today as persons concerned about the future of Worthington College. According to the brochure presented in yesterday's Proceedings, Worthington College is "committed to providing academic leadership and spiritual nurture to its students and conference members." This is a worthy endeavor, but we wonder how it can be accomplished given the information presented in the brochure. How can Dr. Ralph Thompson, the first recipient of the Jenkins-Pitman Chair, be available to preach and present seminars and workshops in local churches, and yet prepare for and teach a full-time course load at the college?
>
> Why has Worthington gone from employing a full-time chaplain to hiring a part-time chaplain who also serves as a full-time professor? Why is there no mention of the instructor in the area of Christian Education or the chair of the Religion and Philosophy Department? How can Worthington College faithfully seek to prepare persons for Christian vocations and encourage persons to enter the ordained ministry of the United Methodist Church, when they seemingly only have two persons teaching in the Department of Religion and Philosophy?

The letter goes on to say that the signers are disturbed about my dismissal as head of the department and as a professor in the college. The writers continue:

> Quite frankly, this news is heartbreaking to us who have been so deeply touched by his life and ministry.

297

Why would Worthington College want to terminate the employment of a man who is so well-loved by his students and has been instrumental in promoting spiritual formation and growth within those students? Throughout his lengthy career at Worthington, he has lived before us as an "incarnational Christian." He illustrates the love of God as he conducts his ministry as a professor, a spiritual leader, and a friend. He has touched many lives representing the United Methodist Church to a wide variety of students and individuals.

He is one who teaches people to believe in themselves and remain faithful to the Gospel of Jesus Christ. For many of us, he is a mentor, colleague, and friend, who embodies what the Christian faith is all about. He has witnessed and ministered to each of us in a very special and powerful way. We, therefore, felt it would be unforgivable for us to stand by and allow this session of the Annual Conference to continue without expressing our deep concern for the future of Worthington College.

The letter ends by urging persons who agree with the position presented to contact the hierarchy of the conference, the leadership of the college, and the leaders of local churches to protest what had happened. It was followed by a second page filled with signatures.

This letter served as an affirming and inspiring summary of my teaching ministry. It was a touching and enduring tribute to what Julie and I tried to accomplish during our tenure at Worthington. It also offered comment on the character and dedication of the people who wrote and signed it. By doing so, they put themselves at risk in this deeply politicized arena. Unfortunately, the letter was stillborn. After it was distributed, we never heard any more from it. The oppressive fear of the prevailing authority prevailed.

I had forced Morton to fill the chair, but he had his own cruel revenge. When Julie and I were forced out, there were fewer persons teaching in the department. Furthermore, the quality of instruction and the courses offered decreased markedly with two junior and inexperienced instructors. The department, as it existed under Phillip and me, essentially was destroyed.

Adding chaplaincy to one teacher's duties and church relations to the other's was a farce. In reality, there would be no chaplaincy and no church relations. We had seen for years how little these two categories mattered to the administration. They were filled from time to time with persons who had other purposes than counseling students or reaching out to churches. This proposed combination and confusion of duties and titles was merely for show to hide what was really happening.

Morton had found a way of using the money from the endowment to cover the entire cost of the department by eliminating administrative and faculty positions. Instead of augmenting religious life on campus and the teaching of religion at Worthington, the money from the Jenkins-Pittman endowment was used to diminish them. Morton was saving money and leaving the department hopelessly understaffed and ineffective. Morton played with loaded dice!

Chapter 51

MERIT OR POLITICS?

During conference, I arranged a meeting in my office with Judge Samuel Demerest. Sam was a district judge in Monroe County, one of the poorest counties with the largest minority population in the state. Sam had a reputation for struggling with the issues he dealt with in his courtroom. He was also known to be heavy-handed in his judgments against black miscreants. He was a graduate of Worthington, and thought of himself as an intellectual and an original thinker. He worked on a book that traced the philosophical and theological foundations of our legal systems. He asked me to read some of his chapters. I found that he did a lot of name-dropping and made superficial references to a number of influential philosophers and thinkers. His discussion of legal tradition seemed to be much more solid to me and the conclusions he reached sound. We were supposed to be friends and I felt I enjoyed his support.

As a pastor of a two-point charge in the country, it was necessary for me to depend on lay speakers. I alternated Sundays between the two churches. Trained laypersons preached in both of my small churches on the Sundays I was at the other church. This was not the best system in the world, but it worked satisfactorily. I thought for years I would change the system and lead services in both of my churches every Sunday. This would have involved an early service in one church and the other church would have the coveted 11 a.m.

hour. The problem was that neither church would give in and take the early hour. This kind of rivalry was not unusual between small county churches that had been yoked together, often arbitrarily, by the Methodist hierarchy.

Two of the lay speakers involved in the rotation in my district were Sam Demerest and his brother, Ed. Some of the speakers were rather far-out in their theology; Others were popular in my congregations. The two Demerest brothers were solid and well respected by both congregations. Sam also served as Conference Lay Leader, the top lay position in the conference, and was often styled "Mr. Methodist." He also served the college in many ways. Morton asked that the conference appoint him as one of the required Methodist lay representatives on the Board of Trustees.

Sam and Ed and their wives sang in a group called The Demerest Family Singers. Their Gospel music was not popular at the Athens church. It fit perfectly the taste of the Pinetuckcy congregation, however, and they were invited at least once a year to sing there for a special evening concert.

I had wanted to have a conversation with Sam for some time. I knew it would be necessary to have another person in the room when we talked. I asked Sara Beth Matthews if she would be willing to do this for me. She was the wife of Anderson Peale Matthews, who was chair of the Administrative Board of the Athens church. She was the organist and the choir director. The Matthews family knew Sam and his wife well.

There was an obvious risk in involving the leading family in the Athens Church in my situation at the college. I knew, however, I could count on Sara Beth to keep confidential what was said in the meeting. I felt that I could be honest with Sam, I also realized he was on Morton's trustee board. The more I could get him to open up and discuss the situation, the better.

We sat down, exchanged pleasantries, and I asked Sam if he were aware of what was going on. I knew quite well that he was on the list of trustees to whom I had mailed copies of the letters. He acknowledged that he knew of the tensions between Morton and me. I wanted to appeal to the ethical and moral concerns his manuscript revealed to me. I asked him if he knew anything about accusations concerning Morton's affairs and immoral behavior. He said, yes, he knew about it.

He changed the subject and went into a long recitation of how much money Morton had raised for the college. He credited him with saving the college from failing financially. We had all heard that mythology. I wanted to challenge Sam, but I thought it better to let him go on. I asked him if he were aware of how much the annual conflict with those who disagreed with Morton cost in legal fees and settlements. He did not answer.

Did he know of the toxic environment at the college for faculty and staff? He did not dispute it. I told him I could not understand why the trustees allowed Morton to continue to be president of the college. He looked deeply troubled by my questions and sat silently. Then he said in a soft voice that the trustees had told Morton that he had to fire that woman and not be seen with her anymore.

I turned to my situation. I told him I had filed charges against Morton in both the church and the court. He had violated his vows as a Methodist minister. He had also misused his position as president to pressure women to have sex with him and to bully and harass those who worked for the college. He had misappropriated funds given to the college. Sam remained silent.

Finally, I asked him if he believed I could succeed in a church trial or in the courts.

He paused, and then replied quietly, "No."

Then I asked him my final question, "Is this based on the merits of the case, or is it political?" We sat in silence while he took several minutes to answer my question. I realized he was weeping.

"Political," he whispered.

By the time we finished all three of us were crying. I never spoke with Sam again. Within a year, he became chairman of the Board of Trustees at the college. I wondered how he was able to square with his conscience what Morton had done to me and to so many others before me. I like to think that what took place the next fall was, at lest in part, his doing, but I do not know.

I saw Bishop Kenneth J. Scott briefly at the closing service of Annual Conference. He had been our bishop before the two conferences in the state split into two different episcopal areas. He wisely chose to stay in his headquarters of the northern conference. He remained on the trustee board at Worthington by virtue of his office as bishop of the northern conference. He clearly knew the result of the quarrel between Morton and me.

He took me aside, and looked almost angry when he said, "You know you did not break him."

I responded humbly and honestly, "Bishop Scott, I did not intend to break him."

Then he said something I will never forget, "He broke himself over you!"

This statement took my breath away. I was not entirely sure what he meant, but I knew he understood everything.

This powerful epigram could have been uttered by an oracle or prophet instead of by a bishop. It provided both a summation of the past and a way into the future. It offered both wisdom and challenge. I said to him that Morton might be broken, but I was broken too.

He brushed my statement aside: "You may be wounded, but you are alive. You will heal and go on to do important things in your career. He is finished. He is dead. He will never work in the church or in an institution of higher education again."

Chapter 52

LET'S SETTLE

The summer began quietly, which was merciful after the traumatic spring. Nothing had changed. The suit was still in effect, although Morton had moved on, dismissing me and going ahead with his plans for the college and the department. It was hard for me to give up on overturning the whole mess, but I also knew deep down that it was impossible. Sam's word, "political," kept echoing in my mind. I knew it heralded the end of a way of life. We were not just defeated by Morton, we were defeated by a conference hierarchy and a trustee board that placed politics above principal.

Most people expected us to move as far away as soon as we could. That was normally what happened after Morton forced a faculty or staff member out of the college. I had determined that I did not want to let him destroy me and then disappear into that dark night. I would hold my head up high and continue to work in the church. These were noble, but completely unrealistic thoughts. I opposed the leader of the college and defied the authority of the bishop. In the South, no one is more dangerous than someone who does not respect and blindly obey authority. This applies even if the authority is not legitimate or credible.

I continued to pastor the Athens church. We had separated the two churches on the charge, and Pinetuckey had its own pastor. This was something I had wanted for a number of years.

The children were asking questions, Catherine especially.

"What are you going to do, Daddy, if you have no job?"

I could only assure her that we would be all right. We could not exist for long only with my small salary for pasturing a church part-time. The college had to continue to pay me through the end of my old contract in September, but that would come soon.

As soon as we entered the fall, I knew I had to take action. I sat down with Rich McArthur, and we faced the inevitable. The longer we kept the suit in limbo, the more we potentially hurt the college. If we persisted, we would need to take the case to the State Supreme Court. This process might take years. I felt we had a good case, but I also realized that Sam's insight into the legal system was telling. The fact that I was tenured and that my tenure was violated, I considered to be the strongest aspect of my case. Then Rich told me the state had no tenure law.

There was strict contract law, however, and I had violated my contract by writing on it that I would not accept it without being designated chair of the department. I could bring up the affair and the offensive way Morton had treated women on campus, but this was hard to prove and could get messy. I could charge Morton with misappropriation, and even theft of funds, but this also was hard to prove, especially with someone as amoral and slippery as Morton.

I finally told McArthur, "Let's settle." This was a relief, and took tremendous pressure off me. True, I would never see Morton brought to court before a judge and jury, as I had dreamed for months. I would also not have to have every aspect of my life and career analyzed by those who were intent on destroying me. Yes, it was time to settle.

It was interesting later to speculate about how many faculty, staff, and administration figures had disappeared over the years. We were naïve, and could not understand that Morton was able systematically to get rid of anyone with whom he disagreed. We also tried to guess how much money had been taken from college funds to pay them off. This involved paying legal fees and some sort of settlement. This usually amounted to one year's salary. A part of the deal was cutting out the tongue of the victim. The latter part of the settlement always contained a clause that the parties involved were not to discuss the terms of the agreement. I would be forced into such a deal, after I had already told the intimate world about my situation and predicted what the settlement would be.

Chapter 53

SHOTS FIRED

Nothing prepared us for the article in the local newspaper in late October with the title, "Worthington President Retires." After the article appeared, faculty and staff got the following memo from Morton, dated October 28:

> Today, I indicated to the trustees my intention to retire at the end of this academic year, May 23. In summing up a quarter of a century, let me say that the work has been and is a labor of love. I'm grateful for the cooperation, dedication, and multiple talents of so many who joined together for the good of the College and its mission. To have been a participant in realizing the distinctive character of education at Worthington has been a high privilege.

He went on to write about making it a good year, and to the appointment of a search committee. Obviously, he did not attempt to resolve any of the many questions that reverberated around the campus concerning him and his conduct as the chief administrative officer.

He had been warned "to stay away from that woman." The trustees could not ignore the underground letter sent to them about the restaurant sighting. This was the beginning of the end of the reign of Morton. The tape that was sent to the trustees with his remarks to the students also played a role. The trustees were furious. They called Morton on the carpet and began to work on his exit.

Nothing could happen, however, as long as my suit was in place. I was the one holding Morton up and giving him the space to keep on with his plots and schemes. We did not know it at the time, but, ironically, the most punishing thing I could do was to settle the suit.

As soon as we agreed to settle, the trustees fired Morton. They let him claim he was retiring to ease him out. There was no way he would relinquish his absolute power at age sixty when he was in good health. He had many more scores to settle and many more funds to milk. He was generously given until the end of the semester by the trustees. Allowing him to continue another seven months as a lame duck was a way of allowing him to save face and provide time for the controversy to die down. It also provided time to begin the search for a new president.

I had not been in touch with Reich in some time. We had not made any plans after the end of the semester and graduation. There was a lot going on for my family and me. I called him and we talked briefly. He was disappointed that we had been blocked by Morton, both in any action by the church and also in the courts. I did not tell him what Sam Demerest had said, because it was confidential. Any leaking of that conversation could hurt all three of us who were present.

I could tell Tom was upset with me. For him, Morton's retirement was no answer at all. He felt that Morton got away with his crimes. I had settled, and he felt that I had sold out. We discussed how Morton had wronged both of us, and how much money and effort we had expended. I left him with apologies and statements of appreciation for all he had done. I knew he was deeply disappointed.

I had a lot of questions about what the trustees would do about Morton. Why did they give him a semester before vacating his office? What unfinished business would he want to take care of? What would he do in the seven months that remained in his tenure?

All of this speculation was transformed, if not resolved, by a bizarre event only weeks after the announcement of the settlement and Morton's retirement. We did not think anything else could happen, but we were wrong. Early in the morning, on a crisp November day, Morton came out of the President's House into the front yard dressed in his pajamas and a bathrobe. The home faced one of the major roads that twisted through the campus. It was across from an open green area that served as a soccer practice field.

Morton bent over and picked up his newspaper, unfolded it, and looked at the front page. The figure of a man in an overcoat and hat moved quickly from behind Freeman Hall (the old building that housed a number of academic offices and conference rooms, including the Religion Department). The man was standing across the roadway from Morton before he was noticed. Thomas Reich carefully and nervously took a revolver out of his coat pocket and pointed it at Morton.

Two men in uniform sprinted from behind either side of the president's residence and positioned themselves beside Morton. They raised their guns, and two shots rang out almost simultaneously. Two men went down. Reich lay on his back with a bullet wound in his chest. Morton was on his knees, bent over, holding his face with his hands, shaking uncontrollably and whimpering. One of the security guards lifted him up slowly while the other inspected the body across the road.

News of Reich's attempt to kill Morton and his own resulting death hit the campus like a hurricane. The administration tried to explain what happened in an attempt to vindicate Morton. The trustees seemed to go into hiding. I am sure there were attempts to implicate me in what Reich had done, but the settlement contained clauses that protected me from the school and the school from me. They literally could not mention my name. Information about Morton's affair with Tom's wife and the resulting divorce circulated widely. The newspapers gave this as the reason for the attempt on Morton's life.

The files that had been protected by the media for so many years were opened and provided information for many stories. The students and many of the townspeople viewed this as a further indication of Morton's guilt in all that had happened. They made jokes that the wrong man had been killed. The wish was often expressed that the date for Morton's departure should be moved up. The trustees were obligated, however, to keep their agreement with him. They were also not ready to admit how misguided they had been.

Reich's daughter asked me to preside at his funeral service. We chose to have it at the funeral home rather than at the church. Both Tom and I felt that Charles Stephens had betrayed us and used us to get rid of Morton, so First Church was out of the question. Audrey Reich attended the funeral with her daughter, and both were in tears. I shook Audrey's hand at the end of the service. She did not look me in the eyes, but told me she was sorry as she continued to weep. I did not seek her out at the graveside. Frankly, she still smelled too much like Morton for my taste. I was not sure whether she was sorry for the affair, sorry she had gotten caught, sorry she had caused the death of her former husband, or sorry she had hurt me. Honestly, it did not matter to me.

I mourned my friend Tom Reich. I did not approve of his actions. I had told him that getting rid of Morton was not worth the sacrifice of his life. He obviously did not feel that my settlement and the trustees permitting Morton to retire were enough. He wanted Morton to be disgraced and to pay with his life for seducing his wife and destroying his marriage. I thought he had found enough security in his Christian faith to abandon his plans to kill Morton. I was wrong. He had deferred, but not denied his worst intentions.

I also mourned for Worthington. Could this little church-related liberal arts college have wandered any further from the intentions and convictions of its founders and of those of us who had worked so hard to establish and develop it? I wanted to speak with Dr. Freeman and the Countess of Worthington, but I did not hear from them.

I wondered what might have happened if I had remained quiet and not talked with Reich in the first place. How much pain and anguish would I have saved? On the other hand, I would have had to falsify all that I knew as true and right. I would have insured that Morton would control Worthington for a number of years to come, with all that would have meant to those who worked, taught, and studied there. I was not sure I could justify that.

Morton seemed to be visibly shaken by the attempt on his life. He kept the security guards for most of the remainder of his time at Worthington. He seemed to be more and more paranoid, glancing around nervously to be sure no one was about to attack him. The Buick rented by the college for him disappeared from his parking place in front of Freeman Hall and went back to the dealership. He was seen driving his own, more modest, automobile, which he parked inside the garage beside the President's House. He was out of town often during the semester, more often than anyone could remember happening in the past. In effect, Van Dale ran the college. Morton still pulled the strings, although he was not involved in the day-to-day administration of the college. His intentions for his last semesters at the college were changed by Reich's attack. He only wanted to get out of the presidency alive.

Chapter 54

A RETURN VISIT FROM MY FRIENDS

I continued to teach at the predominantly black state university in an adjunct capacity and to pastor the church in Athens part-time. The money from the settlement would not last forever without a full-time position. I developed a letter of application, including a resume, and sent copies to colleges and universities in the United Methodist system. I knew that without the recommendation of the president and the academic dean of Worthington, the chances were slim to none that I would be able to teach again. I had years of experience in teaching and administration. I had made contributions to my community and served pastorates. I had been published. All of these things were nice, but did not seem to be of any value in the job market.

Julie and I also applied with the Harrison District Superintendent for church appointments. We knew he was deceitful and resentful of my actions, but we had to deal with him. We met with him and the new bishop. Bishop Randolph P. Jackson was the first black bishop to serve in the area. We anticipated from him the warmth and compassion we had come to expect and respect from black leaders. What we found was a cold and busy individual, who had little time for us or interest in our situation.

Our preference was the large, old church on Main Street just down from the state capitol. It was across the street from a predominantly black church, which played a leadership role in the Civil Rights struggle. Main Street United Methodist Church was a historic church. A number of its pastors had been leaders in the conference, including Dr. Greencheese, who wanted us to go there. Before the Civil Rights struggle, it had been one of the premier appointments in the conference. By the time we were appointed it was greatly diminished. We wanted to see if we could keep it from failing. We were both committed to serving there. The Bishop agreed to appoint us to Main Street Church in a joint pastorate.

We asked for the designation "co-pastors," but, because Julie had only recently completed her requirements for ordination, we were told that I would be senior pastor and Julie associate pastor. We did not anticipate that a joint appointment would mean sharing one salary. This meant that with our educations and experience, we were supposed to serve on half salaries. This was the rather cruel twist the bishop and cabinet put on our appointments.

We soon realized we would never be treated decently as long as we remained in that conference. We found that the only churches available to us were ones that had been fractured during the civil rights struggles. Since we were a clergy couple and wanted to be co-pastors, we would be appointed to churches too small to accept two salaries. We could not survive long in such appointments. Most of our talents would be wasted in churches that were reduced to mere shadows of their former glory by the exodus of hundreds of parishioners.

We moved out of our home into the parsonage of the Main Street Church. I had to remove all my things from my office at Worthington. I had purposely left my office in tact, with hundreds of books along the walls on wooden boards mounted on large ornamental bricks. We called them "student bookcases." They were easily moved and held many books. Combined with my desk and other furniture, this was a lot to move. I did not want to do anything until things were settled. I contacted the head of housekeeping on campus—who was my friend. She said she would look after my things.

Six months later, when I went back to check on things in my office at the college, I found that the boards and cement blocks of my student bookcases had been removed. I asked what had happened to them and found out from Housekeeping that Butch Thompson had removed my books and put them on the floor. He then took my shelves and blocks and moved them to his office for his own use. I asked Campus Security to inform him that he must return them immediately.

Butch was fired a year later because of his drinking and womanizing. His wife divorced him. He had been negligent in his performance as professor and department chair. Students and other faculty members were annoyed and frustrated by his lack of attention to his duties and responsibilities. Taking my shelving without consulting me was just another evidence of how irresponsible he was.

Mark Jennings was designated holder of the Jenkins-Pittman Chair, head of the department, and sole full-time member of the department until a new professor could be hired. With Morton and Butch gone, Jennings came into his own. I wondered if he had undermined Butch Thompson in the same way he had done to me. In any case, he seemed to be the winner. Butch was incompetent, and Mark used his failures to his own advantage.

One night, several months after we had gotten settled into the Main Street parsonage, I was tired from unpacking and doing church work. Julie was attending a meeting on Prison Ministry in Nashville. I was alone and went to bed early. My dreams were especially vivid that night.

I was back in the classroom. It was my second period New Testament class near the end of the spring semester. I was lecturing on the Book Revelation. The images of hope and life beyond suffering and death came alive for me. I finished the class, discussed the upcoming finals with the students, and walked out the back entrance of Stephens Hall. I moved slowly on my way to my office along the sidewalk over the land bridge. Preparations had begun for graduation ceremonies.

It was warm, but not yet the stifling heat of summer. The campus was beautiful with the trees all decked out in their spring glory. I detoured from the path to my office in the Freeman Building and walked down onto the green. It was cooler down there and the air was dry. The mists of morning were gone. I once again sensed the history and importance of this area.

The Green Corn ceremony was over. The Grandfather Fire had been fanned with the wings of white doves until it burned to live coals, glowing in the morning brightness. This grove beside the living stream of water in the ravine still contained powerful medicine. The gods of these woods were alive and abroad on the campus. The spirits of the dead ancestors hovered near. The magic of this place waxed beneficial and was no longer capricious. Human lives were touched and changed. Prayers were answered. Wishes granted. Curses overcome. Visitors from beyond transcended the limitations set on human existence and made life better. There was a redeeming quality about this place that helped lift the miasma and restore the balance of good and evil.

I could hear the drums and the spirituals rising in the distance from the slave quarters. The words and music of "My Lord What a Morning" echoed through the ravine and woods. The sufferings and confusion of the past were over. The reign of evil was ended.

I saw a tree in the midst of the campus. It was broken, bent, and twisted. I went up to it and saw an old spike encysted in its tortured wood. I found a hammer and chisel and cut away the wood from around it and pulled out the rusted offender. The tree shuddered and then the wood healed over. It grew to its intended size: Immense, touching the heavens and supporting the clouds. It was Igdrasil, the tree of life honored by the Druids priests. It was also the tree in the Garden of Eden. It was the center of the earth and the focus of God's blessings.

At the base of the tree was a canvas. I reached down and picked it up. It was an apocalyptic painting Julie had done in seminary. There were eight earth-colored figures silhouetted against a fiery landscape. One of the figures was prone on the ground, with out-stretched arms, embracing the earth. Two others reached out to each other. Two others reached upward. Of the other two, one was bent over in anguish, and the other was bowed in prayer. This, of course signified their values.

They were enacting divine judgment upon themselves. The one reaching down valued material things; those reaching out affirmed personal values; those reaching up placed spiritual values highest. In the background, I saw a huge bird-like figure in the flames—a phoenix. The painting was symbolic of hope even in the midst fiery judgment.

The fiery background of the painting grew beyond the canvass and was projected on the sky like an IMAX movie. Julie was beside me. I took her hand and we walked into the picture. The flaming sky spread above us onto the horizon. The fiery phoenix was outlined against the clouds. The life-sized earth-colored figures stood around us.

The figures reaching downward were the earthy, coarse, and materialistic ground-grabbing greedy Morton crowd. Those reaching out to each other in embrace for the personal, social, emotional, and loving dimensions of life were corrupted by narcissism, self-interest, and lust. Julie and I joined the upward-reaching figures, seeking spiritual, intellectual, eternal, and self-sacrificial extension for our lives. We found ourselves with a small neglected minority. Simply living under such circumstances was difficult; education was nearly impossible. The guidance and leadership of two purely spiritual beings, the Countess and Dr. Freeman, had begun to restore balance and set us on a course that led upward once again.

Early in the morning, while it was still dark, I woke with a start because of repeated knocking on the front door of the parsonage. I got up and sat on the side of the bed. I put on a bathrobe over my pajamas and went down the stairs. I slowly opened the front door. Someone was standing there, silhouetted by a bright light.

It was the Countess, wearing the same incredible dress she had worn the first time we met.

I asked her, "Is that your dress you first wore in 1739?"

She responded, "Yes, it is."

"Fantastic," I said. She came across the room and put her hand on my shoulder.

"How are you?"

I told her that I was all right. "It has been a long time since I last saw you."

"Yes, too long," she replied as she turned and walked out the door. "There is someone who wants to see you." She led me outdoors. Dawn was breaking on the horizon. The stars were still unusually bright. It was good to breathe the night air.

There was an elderly gentleman waiting for us. As we approached, he turned around. It was Dr. Freeman. I smiled and took his hand.

"Dr. Freeman, how are you?"

"Oh, about the same," he said.

The Countess, in charge as ever, motioned to me to come with them. The three of us sat down on a bench in a neighborhood park and talked as we watched the sun come up for a new day.

"Look, I want to apologize to both of you. I tried so hard to change things at Worthington, but I failed miserably. I wanted so badly to restore sanity and sanctity, as you both taught me, but I could not," I said.

"No," the Countess said. "It is we who should apologize. We used you to get rid of Morton. You were wonderful! No one could have done it better."

"Yes," Dr. Freeman added. "We made a beginning. Albert Morton represented everything we deplored. He was destroying our college. You know the college belongs to us—you, the Countess, and me—we are the real owners. Our blood, sweat, and tears made it what it is. This man stole it from us. You did what we could not do, and no else was willing to do. You reclaimed it." I considered it a great honor to be included with the two of them.

"Do you know," the Countess asked, "who the new president is?" I told her that I was not sure. "A woman," she said. "Can you imagine? A woman! Is that not ironic? She has changed things. It is a beginning, just a beginning, but a beginning. Without you our college had no future. Now it is free to begin again."

The comments of these friends made me feel much better, spiritually as well as physically. Morton's control over my life had ended. I felt as if I had been made whole.

Printed in the United States
By Bookmasters